IT WAS A NIGHTMARE WORLD!

John Thomas Rourke could not move, could not wake up. But he could see the creatures through the window, creatures with bulbous heads and translucent wings flying through the water. Lights streamed from their heads and hands. In the distance was a great, black shape. Rourke had seen something that big in the water before—but why was an aircraft carrier deep in the water here? And just as suddenly he knew the carrier-sized thing was a submarine of monstrous proportions.

A bright yellow light flooded the water from the submarine and the winged creatures drew their wings about them, folding them back, slipping up toward the light and vanishing inside.

And suddenly Rourke felt himself being drawn upward toward the light. And he realized he was waking up and that soon the dream would be over . . . *if it was a dream!*

THE SURVIVALIST

MID-WAKE
BY JERRY AHERN

ZEBRA BOOKS
KENSINGTON PUBLISHING CORP.

ZEBRA BOOKS

are published by

Kensington Publishing Corp.
475 Park Avenue South
New York, NY 10016

First printing: February 1988

Printed in the United States of America

For Walter, Roberta, and Leslie; for Wally; and especially for all those who have become friends of the Rourke Family and the Ahern Family—all the best . . .

Any resemblance, etc. . . .

Acknowledgments

Jim Foley of Dacor Corporation possesses a knowledge of man living, working, and surviving in the undersea environment that is second to none. A long-time follower of the exploits of the Rourkes and no stranger to aiding this author in the acquisition and use of precise detail for underwater sequences in various Ahern novels, Jim peered slightly beyond the leading edge of technology for the diving equipment and techniques already in the think-and-plan stage which will, tomorrow, make man nearly as at home beneath the ocean surface as he is today on the surface of the land. As always, my friend, thanks.

Jack Crain—Weatherford, Texas, knifemaker—explores the leading edge of technology in his own way, fabricating by hand some of the finest fighting/survival knives ever conceived. When it was realized John Rourke would need the absolute best in an edged weapon of epic proportions and abilities, there was no one better to turn to. Many thanks, my friend.

Jerry Ahern
Commerce, Georgia
March 1987

Chapter One

His right forefinger moved along the ribbed surface from outer lip to suture, dwelling for a moment in the recurve of the spire, then moving to the apex and stopping there. The interior surface of his right thumb settled at the inner lip. He raised the object gently and studied it minutely. A simple univalve, not yet polished smooth by the cocoa-colored wet sand which still clung to it. John Rourke looked to the south and west. The sun washed the Yellow Sea with orange light. He remembered once, a very long time ago, picking up a large shell his father had brought back from "somewhere in the Carribean, John" and placing it beside his ear. He had heard then the same sound which he heard now, but now it seemed all around him.

John Rourke crouched nearer the advancing white froth, his right knee almost touching the surf, his right hand still holding the seashell. It had recently been placed here, and the organism which had lived inside it was not some relic from another age. The sea was alive.

She was almost a quarter mile down along the beach. Rourke watched her, the water seeming hesitant as it raced toward her, then slowed, then retreated. He let the shell fall from his fingers, washing his hand of sand in the cold water. The surf reached out to her, he realized, as he had always reached out to her. Uncertainly. Reaching, drawing back, afraid of her touch.

Rourke rose to his full height, his shoulders shifting under the weight of the double shoulder holsters and the

7

pistols which they carried. The wind was rising, a fine mist on the air, and he turned up the collar of his leather jacket against it. He found the battered Zippo in a thigh pocket of his Levis and drew a thin, dark cigar from his shirt pocket. The tip was already excised and he bit down on it, and cupped the lighter in his hands. He rolled the striking wheel under his thumb, his eyes squinted behind his dark-lensed sunglasses, watching Natalia across the blue-yellow flame.

John Rourke chewed down on the cigar, rolling it into the left corner of his mouth, cupping the cigar beneath his right hand. He watched her. His left thumb hooked between the haft of his knife and the black leather sheath's belt loop.

He watched her. . . .

He watched her. She was dressed in some sort of battle gear, Kerenin surmised. The jacket she wore was black, like the rest of her clothing. The jacket was wide open, a holster on each hip holding it back. The wind caught her hair as he studied her, her hair almost black as well. The helmet rangefighter's LCD readout put her at 125 meters. He touched his chest pack. Her face came toward him on zoom. She was exquisite. And she was not Chinese.

A white female who was some sort of warrior? The high, black boots—they looked to be made of some smooth substance. What was called leather perhaps. The hairless skin of a dead animal. Though unlike these, which shone with the ebbing sunlight, the footgear of the Chinese soldiers were of this substance. This woman was long-legged. Her stride was purposeful, like a man's stride. Kerenin felt a smile come to his lips.

He tucked fully beneath the waves, feeling his wings fanning outward. He drew his gloved fingers together, the fingers linked and drew himself downward, kicking, the wings responding as he rolled and settled to the shallow bottom of the shelf. His men waited, their transparent hydrogen-powered wings gently pulsating, keeping them

8

erect. He glided toward them on the blades of his flippers, his wings compensating for his buoyancy. The six leaders moved closer to him and they all placed their helmets near one another, huddling. It was the only way to be heard.

Olav Kerenin spoke. "Select six men. There is a woman walking alone on the beach and I wish her apprehended so I may interrogate her. Alexandre—you will lead this detail."

"Yes, comrade major." His youngest lieutenant nodded, carbon dioxide bubbling from the escape valve in the crown of his helmet as he spoke. "But Comrade Major Kerenin—six men plus myself for only one Chinese woman?"

"She is not Chinese, Alexandre." There were murmurs from the other men huddled with him, a sea of bubbles surrounding him. "And she is armed. Use extreme caution that she is not injured." Kerenin dismissed the woman from his thoughts, and Alexandre's question as well. The man at his right had spoken not at all. Kerenin addressed him. "Boris—you will lead the raid against the Chinese power installation. No prisoners unless an officer or a recognizably important civilian."

"Yes, comrade major."

"Comrades, you have your orders. See to them." Kerenin's wings opened wider as he pushed off toward the surface, the two Spetznas who always accompanied him rising from the ranks below and flanking him. Beneath him the others were dispersing, Captain Boris Feyedorovitch marshaling the other four officers to him, Alexandre selecting six men for his mission on the beach. Alexandre looked up and signaled the men of his unit to follow as he started for the surface. Kerenin let the young officer and six Spetznas pass, hovering instead over the staging area, his own two men still flanking him.

The hydrogen extractors on the "Iron Dolphins" were revving up, men making last-minute equipment checks of the cargo bays, then positioning themselves behind them, others straddling their machines and jump-starting them. Boris Feyedorovitch was hovering some ten meters below

9

Kerenin, at his unit's right flank. Feyedorovitch made hand and arm signals, the Iron Dolphins fanning outward as they started along the shelf toward the land-point a kilometer away. Kerenin checked his wrist chronometer. On schedule, perfectly so. Thanks to the Iron Dolphins they would be at the land point in just under five minutes.

Kerenin started for the surface, not quite Breaking Atmosphere, his two men flanking him, holding his breath and drawing himself into the shallows of the surf so he could remove his helmet without flooding its interior. This made for some considerable discomfort, the dampness always unnerving to him. He had voluntarily undergone hypnotherapy and no longer—at least consciously—feared Leak.

He could see the woman more closely now, perhaps a quarter kilometer away. He raised to his knees in the surf, separating helmet from suit. It was necessary to dip his face into the water again to breathe. As he raised his head, he at last had the seal and opened it, removing the helmet, exhaling, then inhaling deeply, feeling the slight burning sensation in his throat and nasal passages that was the usual thing when one shifted from derived oxygen to atmosphere. He signaled the two flanking men to spread out to either side.

He looked further out into the surf. Alexandre and his men were Breaking Atmosphere, some already with their helmets removed, others with their pistols drawn, but Alexandre signaled them to put the weapons away.

The woman seemed not to have yet noticed Alexandre and his six Spetznas. She was still walking, more slowly now. Kerenin thought he could detect her sweeping her hands back through her hair. The wind here chilled the exposed skin of his face, but his body was warm in the Environment Suit. He started trudging up through the surf, to get a closer look.

The woman saw them now.

They charged toward her, bright steel flashing in the woman's hands from the holsters at her hips. There was an earsplitting roar as a tongue of fire licked from one of

10

the objects, and Kerenin realized it was a handgun. One of his Spetznas pitched backward into the sand as Alexandre and the other five men swarmed toward her. There was another shot, and one of the Spetznas stumbled and fell forward, his right leg twisting beneath him. Kerenin, his helmet going to his left hand, broke into a run along the boundary of the surf, his other hand going to the holster at his right thigh but not yet freeing his weapon. His two men drew closer to him now.

The woman's pistols discharged again, Kerenin seeing the flashes in the twilight grayness as two of the Spetznas threw themselves against her.

As he neared them, he could see the woman, her guns gone but back on her feet, her body moving fast, her hands moving, one of the Spetznas who had brought her down cartwheeling head over heels into the sand.

And then in her right hand, as she edged away from Alexandre and the three men still standing, he saw a flash of steel. It was a—it was a knife, but unlike any he had ever seen, opening and closing as it sang through the air before her, like a shield rather than a weapon, separating her from the three Spetznas and their unit leader, but unlike shield or weapon somehow a living thing in her hand.

Kerenin moved in from the water, knowing he was indulging in morbid fascination. The woman was a fighting machine. Already, one of his Spetznas had sustained injuries from her knife. The man had fallen to his knees, crawling away along the beach as Alexandre and the remaining two men backed away from her, drew their sidearms, and then slowly closed around her. She wheeled, vaulted, feigned a thrust, keeping Alexandre and the two remaining men off balance. The third Spetznas was on his feet again, his right arm limp at his side, a piece of driftwood in his upraised left hand like a club.

Kerenin was about to signal his two flankers to join the fight, and had already started to push away from the rocks beside which he stood. But now there was another man, tall, lean, long-legged, and looking well-muscled, streak-

11

ing along the beach toward Kerenin's four men and the woman. The man wore a jacket of brown leather and faded blue pants and military boots. His eyes were shielded by dark-lensed goggles of a type Kerenin had never seen. The injured Spetznas swung his improvised club downward. The newcomer broke his stride, throwing something from the left corner of his mouth—smoke or steam issued from the man's lips, eddied, and dissipated in the air as in that split second pistols in both the man's hands discharged.

The driftwood club shattered, the already wounded Spetznas pitched into the sand. The woman fought like a cornered shark—her right hand lashed out, the knife opening and closing, opening, a scream from one of the two Spetznas still standing, his body tumbling back.

Kerenin heard the soft phutting sound of Alexandre's pistol, the woman wheeling toward him, slashing toward Alexandre with her knife. If one of the darts had hit her, the adrenalin rush she experienced must have delayed any reaction to it. But then the woman stumbled, fell forward, tried pushing herself up, the knife still in her right fist, then fell again.

The running man who had fired his handguns charged toward Alexandre and the two Spetznas, his pistols discharging twice more, one of the Spetznas going down. He wheeled toward Alexandre. Kerenin began to draw his sidearm, signaled his two flanking men into the fray. As the running man fired again, the already wounded, twice-fallen Spetznas rolled his body against the newcomer's legs from behind, the running man's pistol shots going wild as he stumbled, fell back.

Alexandre vaulted toward the newcomer, then suddenly Alexandre's body was sailing over the newcomer and into the sand. Kerenin's two men charged the newcomer, the man already to his feet, his pistols gone, sidestepping one of Kerenin's men, wheeling half right, his left foot catching the second man in the groin. The newcomer wheeled again and as he turned toward the second of Kerenin's men, there was a knife in his right hand, of huge proportions. The knife hand moved upward. Kerenin's man drew his sidearm. The man moved so quickly Kerenin's could not be certain what he was doing—but Kerenin's man screamed, blood spurting from his throat and vomiting from his mouth, his body flopping face forward into the sand.

Kerenin ran from the rocks now, his sidearm in his right hand. He steadied his pistol. The newcomer ducked, Kerenin firing, missing, the newcomer rising to his full height now, his pistols retrieved from the sand, held tight at his sides. The pistols discharged, one of the Spetznas who had accompanied Alexandre dropping his knife, clasping both hands to his abdomen, his legs torn out from under him, falling.

The man turned toward Alexandre, who was leveling his pistol to fire. Kerenin fired, then again. The newcomer fired. Alexandre's body lurched back into the sand. Kerenin fired again, the newcomer stumbling forward, both pistols discharging into the sand. Kerenin's man was up, his helmet in his right hand, crashing it down across the head and neck of the newcomer. The newcomer rolled into the sand, firing his pistols, Kerenin's man falling back. Kerenin was up, running. The newcomer was struggling to his knees, the right side of his face streaming blood from a wound near his temple, one of the darts protruding from the back of his neck. Then the newcomer's pistols fell from his hands and he dropped into the sand on his face. Kerenin slowed, and those Spetznas who still could closed in, some holding wounded limbs against the pain.

The newcomer rolled on his left side, his right hand groping for the dart in his neck, tearing it from his flesh. He lurched forward into the sand, his right hand groping. His fist closed over the haft of his massive knife and he tried to raise it. Kerenin's right foot snapped out, impacting the newcomer near the still-bleeding wound at his temple.

The man collapsed, his body inches from the now-unconscious woman.

13

Kerenin holstered his sidearm. "One of you—radio, along the coast. Have Captain Feyedorovitch send back a detail. Bags for the dead. A medtech." He dropped to one knee in the sand between the unconscious man and woman.

He could see their guns, partially obscured by sand kicked over them during the fighting. The handguns looked to be antiques. Kerenin picked up the two knives, the one the size and heft of something vastly more than a knife. He had seen history tapes which told of huge knives called swords being used by rich landowners to hack to death unarmed medieval farmers who protested for agrarian reform. This seemed to be such a knife. The knife the woman had used was little larger than a medical implement. As he inspected the edge, he deduced it would be just as sharp.

He could hear one of the wounded men using the radio and calling for assistance.

Olav Kerenin stood. The man and the woman. Their appearances seemed—he could not give words to his thoughts. They were not Chinese.

But somehow, he could not bring himself to think they were from Mid-Wake either. . . .

The communication came through his helmet radio on the inter-unit band, the helmet radio passively activated. He whispered into the chin piece. "Detach six men, one of them Nicolai Konstantin." He dismissed the communique now, the comrade major's passion for beautiful women something Feyedorovitch had learned to tolerate over the years since his promotion to second in command of the Expeditionary Spetznas, something which this time at least had gotten Kerenin into some difficulty.

It was hard to imagine a solitary woman inflicting such casualties on Alexandre and his six men. He amused himself with the thought that Kerenin's two personal guards might have joined the battle against her. Perhaps Kerenin himself.

14

Feyedorovitch spoke into the microphone, which was set into his helmet chin guard, again. 'First Unit—move out along the perimeter wall. Now!"

He watched the lieutenant move his men forward, crouched, in single file, their AKM-96s close to their chests. Feyedorovitch looked to his own weapon, tugging at the forty-round magazine to make certain it was properly seated. He eyed First Unit's progress along the power-station wall, speaking into his helmet radio again. "Second Unit. Begin penetration—now!"

The second element moved off toward his left, racing to the wall, Feyedorovitch watching. The three squad leaders fired their pneumatic L-18 launchers from hip level with a soft whooshing sound, the grappling hooks flying upward to the top of the wall, the ropes uncoiling behind them. As the hooks connected, two men ran forward, deadweighting the ropes, then starting the climb along the wall surface.

"Third Unit—advance on the wall. Penetrate—now!" Feyedorovitch was up, his corporal beside him as he ran, the three squad leaders of Third Unit firing their L-18s, Feyedorovitch starting up the nearest of the three ropes. He could still make a wall faster than any of his men, even the younger ones who were half his age.

Feyedorovitch attained the height of the wall. From this greater elevation, the setting sun could still be seen. He flipped the safety tumbler, his right thumb in the AKM-96's thumb hole as he started along the wall, Second-Unit personnel already moving along the perimeter. He watched as soundlessly they penetrated the guard tower. Second-Unit personnel were everywhere on the wall now, coiling their garrotes, sheathing their knives, dead Chinese bodies littering the catwalk.

Feyedorovitch stopped beside the guard tower. Two Second-Unit men exited and poled down the skeleton ladder, Feyedorovitch tapping one of them on the shoulder, gesturing toward the open flap of his holster. The Spetznas secured it shut and ran on, unlimbering his AKM-96.

Feyedorovitch checked his chronometer. First Unit would launch the decoy frontal assault on the entrance to

15

the power-station complex in exactly forty-three seconds. He continued on along the wall and, finding suitable cover, dropped behind it. He took another reading on the time. Then he spoke into his helmet radio over the inter-unit band.

"We open fire on my signal. I fire the first shot."

He raised the weapon to his shoulder, fixing the integral carrying-handle-mounted optical sight on three white-coveralled Chinese standing in the courtyard of the administration building. He was mentally ticking off the seconds.

Feyedorovitch fired a burst, then another and another, gunfire from his men along the wall general now, explosive charges detonating by the double gates leading into the power-station grounds, First Unit coming over the downed gates as the smoke cleared. Chinese defense force personnel were filling the courtyard, and Feyedorovitch ordered, "Second-Unit and Third-Unit demolition teams—move out!"

Three men from each side of the wall hurled ropes over the wall, then rappelled at high speed into the courtyard, First-Unit personnel drawing back toward the main gates, sucking the majority of the Chinese defenders after them. Feyedorovitch magazined another forty rounds up the well of his AKM-96. Light machine guns had opened up on both sides of the wall, firing into the courtyard now, Feyedorovitch moving along the perimeter to better observe the demolitions teams. As two men from each team put down suppressive fire, the third laid out long gray ropes of Synthex along the ten-meter-high walls of the domed powerhouse, setting detonators.

But Feyedorovitch's eyes were drawn away from the demolition teams—three men near the gates, one dressed in the effeminate style of Chinese leisure attire, and two others in faded, light-blue, close-fitting trousers, military-looking boots, and ordinary shirts. The Chinese was wielding what looked to be a captured AKM-96, one of the other two men, his forehead high and his hair obviously thinning, firing some sort of antique firearm that looked like a hybrid of an assault rifle and a pistol. But he

16

fired it with devastating effect. The third man was the tallest of the three and the other two men flanked him, black pistols in either hand, firing as the three cut their way toward the powerhouse. The man with the two pistols—his thick hair blowing in the heat wind from the fires which burned near the gates—looked extraordinarily fit, lean yet powerfully muscled.

The pistols in the third man's hand had apparently been expended of ammunition. He stuffed them into the wide belt at his waist and drew another handgun, this unlike anything Feyedorovitch had ever seen, yet its nature unmistakable. It gleamed in the light from the fires and when it fired, a tongue of flame perhaps fifteen centimeters in length licked from the barrel, the muzzle of the pistol rising as if from the concussion of the shot. Feyedorovitch realized the pistol had to be of immense power because, even with his AKM-96 on full-auto mode, its muzzle rise was minimal. And neither of the two men with the Chinese were Chinese.

The taller of the two non-Chinese men, the one with the fantastically powerful handgun, was nearing the demolition teams now.

Feyedorovitch spoke into his helmet radio. "Demolition teams—what is apparently some special defensive unit is closing with you." Feyedorovitch raised his AKM-96 to his right shoulder, finding the tall man with the spectacular handgun in the rifle's optical sight. As Feyedorovitch squeezed the trigger, the tall man vanished from his scope and a member of one of the demolition teams took the burst.

Feyedorovitch cursed under his breath, finding the tall man again. He could see him, staring up at the wall. As Feyedorovitch readied to fire, he recoiled, a tongue of flame leaping toward him as if through the scope itself. A chunk of the wall beside him ripped upward as he fell back.

Feyedorovitch, on his knees now, hands shaking as they grasped his rifle, saw the tall man, a knife in his right hand, the gleaming pistol inverted in his left hand like

17

some sort of mighty hammer as he attacked the demolition team nearest him. His knife hacked into one man's throat, the butt of his pistol lacerating another man beneath the lip of his battle helmet. The Chinese and the man with the thinning hair joined him now, closing with the second demolition team.

Feyedorovitch shouted into his helmet radio. "Unit Two and Unit Three—concentrate all fire on the three men attacking the demolition teams by the walls of the powerhouse!" But as he said it, Feyedorovitch realized it was too late, Chinese defense forces seeming to rally from their impending defeat, pushing Unit One forces back through the gates, other Chinese defenders taking up positions of cover and concentrating heavy automatic weapons fire on the walls.

Feyedorovitch looked once more to the Chinese man and his two unorthodox companions. They had AKM-96s now, firing at isolated groups of Spetznas still inside the compound, the effect of their fire devastating. With a dozen men like these, Feyedorovitch realized, he could do anything.

He spoke into his helmet radio. "First Unit. Withdraw to the assembly point and control the main entrance into the compound to cover withdrawal of Second Unit and Third Unit from the wall. First Unit—break off now!"

Feyedorovitch began moving toward the outer edge of the wall. Three men had turned another easy victory in the long history of lightning raids against the Chinese coastal deployments into the first defeat suffered at Chinese hands since the raids had begun.

He looked back once, saying into his helmet radio, "Second Unit. Disengage now! Third Unit—support Second Unit's withdrawal with suppressive fire into the compound. Move out, Second Unit!"

Feyedorovitch hurled his rappelling rope over the wall, planting the Scatter Frequency Detonator, flipping the lock, setting the timer for three minutes, activating the detonator switch, then flipping back the lock into the closed position.

18

"Third Unit—disengage now! Move out!" He locked the carabiner on his utility belt into the modified figure-eight descender and started over the wall, slinging his rifle onto his shoulder to free both hands. He was over the side, his left gloved hand feeding rope, his right controlling the rate of descent. As he reached the ground at the outside base of the wall, he unsheathed his knife and cut himself free of the line.

A glance at his chronometer told him two minutes and eighteen seconds remained until the Scatter Frequency Detonator activated.

"First Unit—cover withdrawal of Second Unit and Third Unit until you receive my signal. Second Unit. Third Unit. Withdraw to beach. Move out now!" Feyedorovitch broke into a dead run, gunfire from the walls raining down on him now, the Chinese defenders having retaken positions along the wall, he realized.

He kept running.

Each Spetznas wore an explosives pack on his equipment belt, hard-armored against any known projectile. Within the pack was a micro-receiver tuned to receive a specific three-band combination signal. Feyedorovitch had activated a Scatter Frequency Detonator only once before, years ago during his first cycle of Surface Training when he had been recently commissioned as an officer of Spetznas. But during training, no one had died as the result.

When the Scatter Frequency Detonator activated, anyone of the Spetznas living or dead within a two-hundred-meter radius would be vaporized.

He kept running, a minute left. "First Unit—remove belt packs—I say again—remove explosives packs. I have activated a Scatter Frequency Detonator which will initiate demolition in fifty-seven seconds."

He kept running. But he had at least given First Unit a chance. The ground rose sharply and Feyedorovitch and his Spetznas followed the rise, the smell of the sea beyond powerful, seductive, his eyes darting back to his wrist and the diode count on his chronometer.

19

As they cleared the rise, he knew they had more than the required safety margin. And he heard the first of the explosions, coming then with machine-gun rapidity. He kept running, seeing the ocean now, beckoning to him. . . .

Translucent wings. Bulbous heads. It was a dream. The creatures flew through the water. He saw them through his window. He had not dreamed since the Sleep, really. But this was a nightmare. He could not move. He could not wake up. Natalia was somewhere in the nightmare and he couldn't remember where. He watched the creatures, their movement through the water which seemed to surround him—but he wasn't wet—like birds through the air. There had been birds. But these birds were at once monstrous and graceful. His mouth was dry. His head ached so badly that he wondered if, when he awoke, it would still ache. The light in the water was not natural light, but lights emanating from the winged creatures' heads and hands and—There were things like huge sausages that bubbled through the water. These too had lights. He decided to try to move his head and perhaps the dream would go away. He moved his head and could see more through the little window, and in the distance there was a great, black shape, substance out of shadow. He had seen something that big in the water before. But why was an aircraft carrier deep in the water here?

The creatures with the translucent wings seemed to be lining up, like some sort of bizarre military formation, and he tried moving his head again to see better through the window. He laughed at himself—this was one hell of a dream, he thought. Perhaps his perceptions of such surreality were so realistic because he hadn't dreamed since the Sleep, not consciously anyway. His mind making up for lost time, he told himself. The creatures with the translucent wings and bulbous heads were definitely slowing now. The aircraft-carrier-sized thing was in fact a submarine, but of such monstrous proportions that in itself it was a more fantastic element of the dream than the winged creatures. It seemed so long as he floated closer to it that he could see neither stem nor stern. An Ohio Class Trident nuclear submarine—he searched for details—was 550 feet. He shook his head and it hurt, badly. No, 560 feet. That was it. This was easily twice that length and— The beam of the vessel. They were starting under it, the winged creatures extinguishing their lights as a yellow light flooded the water now, Rourke squinting his eyes against its brightness.

The winged creatures were hovering near the light—and they did look like giant insects, more than birds, he thought, flying around the light for its warmth and brightness. He doubted he would remember the dream, had never really made a conscious effort to remember a dream. Dreams had nothing to do with reality, he had long ago convinced himself, and because of that, they were of little concern except that they sometimes ruined a valuable sleep cycle.

Some of the winged creatures were drawing their wings around them, folding them back, then slipping upward toward the light and vanishing inside the monstrous submarine.

He could barely keep his eyes open now, the light making his headache worse, making him want to stop the dream so he could sleep properly. The quarrel with Natalia had been part of the dream, he realized now. When she had told him she could no longer remain with him because of Sarah and the baby, when she had told him that this war would go on forever and their lives couldn't go on this way forever. When he had told her that he needed her and she had started to cry and simply walked away along the beach and he had watched her instead of going after her.

Nightmare—losing Natalia would be the ultimate nightmare.

More of the winged creatures were vanishing into the light and now, his eyes hurting him, like an explosion going on inside his head when he looked at something intently, he could see something that looked at once cylindrical yet coffin-like. It was being manipulated into the light. A claw—huge, gleaming in the yellow light, came out of the light and took hold of the cylinder and then raised it up into the brightest part of the light and the cylinder was gone.

Rourke kept watching, knowing somehow that the dream would end and he wouldn't see what was beyond the light. Some of the bubbling, sausage-shaped things that the creatures had clung to were being raised into the light by the gigantic gleaming claw. He felt a change in motion around him and realized that he was being drawn closer to the light.

It hurt his eyes and he squinted them tight against it, the light getting brighter as he heard a clanging sound. The claw, he told himself. But as the motion around him stopped and then suddenly changed and he felt himself being drawn up into the light, John Rourke closed his eyes completely. He realized he was waking up and the dream would be over. . . .

John Rourke opened his eyes when he'd felt the pain in his arm, recognized it as some sort of injection device, not unlike—what was it not unlike? He couldn't remember and as the sensation subsided he closed his eyes.

Chapter Two

John Rourke opened his eyes. The pain in his head told him that he had made the wrong choice and he closed his eyes tight. There had been a huge claw hanging over his head. "That's stupid."

He opened his eyes.

A talon-like crane was suspended some dozen feet over his head, bright polished, of stainless steel or some similar substance, he decided clinically. The pain at the back of his eyes and in his neck was less intense than it had been. He moved his right arm. His right arm didn't respond.

He shook his head, the pain intensifying, but clearing his thinking. His wrists were bound behind him. He tested his ankles. They were bound as well. "Damnit," he whispered under his breath.

"John?"

Rourke turned his head to the right—the pain seized him and he shut his eyes against it momentarily.

"John!"

It was Natalia's voice. He shook his head again, at once intensifying the pain and clearing his head of it. She lay some ten feet or so from him, bound hands behind her back, ankles together, but lying on her stomach. He lay on his back. A puddle of water was around her on the steel floor, and for the first time he realized that his clothes were wet and he too was in water. Beside her was a dull, gleaming-wet, black, cylindrically shaped coffin, the lid open, a small window visible in the lid.

Rourke shook his head.

It hadn't been a nightmare at all. "Where—ahh—are you all right?"

"My head is throbbing—they gave you some kind of injection—I think they gave one to me too."

"Ahh—let me—let me—where the—let me think," he told her.

"I think they shot us with some sort of sleep-inducing darts. I remember feeling something hit my chest while I was fighting. But I don't feel any sort of wound there and I can see my jumpsuit—there's no hole there. And I started getting—like I was drunk. John—what's happening?"

She was frightened. He could tell it from her voice. He'd heard it in her only a very few times before. "Hang in there," Rourke told her, shivering now with the dampness and the air temperature. He twisted his head to the left. There was a massive, watertight door, closed. Rourke tried to move his body, pain spasming along his back and through his legs. But he shifted position. He could see a hatch opening, a large wheel at its center. "Were you awake at all when we were—ahh—"

"It was like a nightmare—those creatures with the wings and the big heads—did you see them?"

Rourke licked his lips, his tongue as dry as his lips. "Yeah—did you, ahh . . . Did you see something that looked like it was a submarine but, ahh—the size of an aircraft carrier?" Natalia nodded her head, turned her eyes toward the floor.

Rourke twisted his body, rolling onto his right side, flexing his fingers and wrists to restore feeling. "John—they took it. The little Russell knife. They took everything. Some kind of metals detector. They swept both our bodies with it."

"They—the guys from the beach?"

"They were wearing some kind of protective clothing—remember? I think it's a wet suit."

"Dry suit, more likely," Rourke told her. "Those transparent wings—some kind of propulsion system. They could have a way of extracting hydrogen from the water and the hydrogen—"

Rourke heard the sound of clanging metal—he twisted his head left. The watertight door was swinging open, slammed against the bulkhead, bounced back, and a long, black-sleeved arm caught it. A man, tall, athletically built, stepped over the flange and framed himself just inside the doorway. His face was high-cheekboned, lean, almost deathly pale, his pallor a striking contrast to the dark one-piece dry suit he wore and the overall good health his physique suggested. Heavy, bushy, dark-brown eyebrows were knitted together in apparent thought. Above these a high forehead and close-cropped, thinning, dark-brown hair. Below these eyes that seemed so darkly brown they appeared black. His nose was large, slightly hooked, almost classically American Indian in appearance. His mouth was overly large and as he smiled—his eyes didn't smile—his parted lips revealed such perfect white teeth that for an instant Rourke thought they were capped.

His voice was emotionless and very low. His Russian was curiously accentless and yet somehow strange. "Who are you?"

Rourke's mind raced. Natalia spoke, in German. "Who are you?"

The man stepped completely through the doorway now and three other men followed him, all similarly black-clad. For the first time, Rourke detected subdued gold braid on the cuffs of the first man's dry suit. Apparently a rank insignia. The man spoke again. "What language is this in which you speak?"

Rourke, in German, told him, "We speak German, of course. Are you speaking English?"

If they had been listening from the other side of the watertight door—Rourke was uncertain that it had been fully closed—or had the compartment bugged for sound . . . But then again, Rourke thought, if the man did only speak Russian, he might not be able to differentiate between English and German. "What do you want of us?" Rourke asked, in German again.

The first man turned to the other three and shrugged his shoulders, gestured them toward the compartment door. He passed through it over the flange, the other three following him, slamming the door shut again.

Rourke looked at Natalia. He gestured toward the doorway and she nodded that she understood, then said to him in German, "Who was that man?"

"Some sort of commander. I think I recognized him from the beach. Maybe they will realize," he said loudly, "that this is some sort of insane mistake. Are you all right, my darling?"

Natalia looked at him and smiled.

The sound of the door again. Rourke twisted around to see. The first man appeared in the doorway again, and this time a man in what looked to be a Naval officer's uniform was beside him. There was no way to tell specific rank, but judging from the lesser complexity of gold braid on the sleeves of the new man's blue uniform tunic—without lapels, buttoned high to the neck with no shirt showing below it—he was of lesser rank. Nearly bald, slightly shorter, and considerably less fit-looking, the new man spoke in awkwardly accented German, as though he had never really heard German properly spoken. "You are both German nationals? How can that be?"

Rourke made himself smile. "Sir, this is some sort of mistake. Please release us. My wife and I meant your men no harm."

The new man spoke in Russian, the same, curiously accentless voice. This new man was definitely outranked. He told the first man that indeed this man and woman appeared to be Germans. And that the man claimed the woman was his wife. The first man nodded his head thoughtfully, then walked over toward Rourke, rolling Rourke onto his stomach. John Rourke could feel the first man's hands touch at the third finger of his left hand. The first man rattled off a question to the new man.

The balding man repeated it in German. "Why is it that you wear what it known as a marriage ring and the woman you claim is your wife does not?"

Natalia answered before Rourke had finished composing the lie. "It was several months ago—perhaps a year ago. We were exploring some old ruins much further inland and my hand became caught, and the only way to free it was to cut the ring from my finger. But in my heart, I will always wear his ring." Rourke looked at her, the surreal blueness of her eyes, the love there.

He liked her lie better than his. He rolled onto his left side and told the newer man, "I demand that you release my wife and me. We have done nothing wrong. We were merely walking along the beach and your men set upon my wife, and I attempted to aid her and was also viciously attacked!"

The balding newcomer spoke in hushed tones at some length to the tall, athletic-looking man. The first man crossed the compartment again and stepped half over Natalia, one leg on either side of her. Rourke shouted at him, "Leave my wife alone, sir!"

The other man translated.

The taller man knotted his fingers in Natalia's almost black hair and drew her head up, her back arching. She let out a little scream, Rourke uncertain if it were contrived or genuine. Rourke started to speak. The first man, still holding Natalia by her hair, said in Russian, "Tell this man that I think he and this woman are liars. And that I wish the real truth from them or I will cause them a great deal of pain."

Rourke tried to place a suitably puzzled look on his face as the balding man laboriously and less than one-hundred-dred-per-cent accurately translated his superior's threat. Rourke intentionally made his breathing shallow so his voice would reflect fear. "Please—do not hurt my wife so! I will tell you anything you wish. But I can only speak the truth. We were walking along the beach." The balding man began a running simultaneous semi-translation. "We are survivors from a community in the Western Hemisphere which lived for many centuries underground after the great war between the United States of America and the Union of Soviet Socialist Republics. Many of us—many of us—we left our homeland in these last centuries and began exploring the world in order to seek out any others like ourselves who might have survived." His mind raced. "We were elated when we discovered that some Chinese apparently survived there along the coast." He tried to think if there could have been anything he or Natalia might have had which could have linked them to the Chinese. He licked his lips. He kept talking, keeping his breathing intentionally shallow, his words intentionally fast. "We were about to approach the Chinese. We had lost most of our belongings during the recent blizzards. We had eaten the last of our food and were nearly out of ammunition. We had no choice. Are the Chinese your enemies?" It was time to stop giving information, however spurious, and start getting some.

As the running translation wound down, Natalia spoke. "My husband is telling you the truth. We are pleased that you have found us. We wish to be your friends, to tell our people that other people still survive on the face of the earth."

The balding man was catching up on the translation again and Rourke caught the first man's eyes as "face of the earth" was translated for him. And the first man began to howl with laughter.

After several seconds—Rourke's palms were sweating—his laughter subsided. Still smiling—but his face, not his eyes—he said to the balding man, "Tell them that they are either very innocent of who we are, in which case their interrogation will be long and painful and useless, or they are very good liars. In which case they will have the opportunity to tell the truth as convincingly perhaps." And the tall man stalked from the room laughing again.

The balding man began translating into his sterile, fumbling German. John Rourke's and Natalia Anastasia Tiemerovna's eyes met. He saw real fear in her eyes and imagined she saw the same in his eyes. Bound, weapon-

28

less, beneath the sea, and prisoners of a Russian-speaking enemy force that by all rights could not exist and was possessed of technology that, on the surface at least, appeared vastly superior to anything ever experienced.

The balding man completed his translation and left, the watertight door swinging to behind him.

"We won't escape this—will we? We won't," Natalia whispered.

Rourke didn't answer her because if he told her what he felt, she wouldn't like the answer at all. . . .

The wind whipped the skirts of Han's black dragon robe. Maria Leuden thought of her own skirt and realized that subconsciously her left hand already had her skirt under control. The wind that noisily buffeted Han's garment was cold and there was a heavy mist on the air, the mist visible as long streaks of gray against the whites and yellows of the flashlights Han, the Chinese security personnel, and both Paul and Michael held in their hands.

She had given up on holding her flashlight. It was in the wide, deep slash pocket of her arctic parka, her right hand buried in the pocket beside it, her left hand freezing like her legs.

She dogged after Michael, feeling more like his puppy at times like these than his woman. She had become acquainted with the concept of dog following master from Bjorn Rolvaag, the Icelandic. Rolvaag and his dog were inseparable, Hrothgar his master's shadow. Rolvaag and Hrothgar now explored further along the beach on their own, the perenenially green-clad Icelandic policeman always solitary except for the dog, which sniffed at him, nuzzled against him, while he himself was almost invariably silent. Bjorn Rolvaag gave the impression of considerable intelligence, but since she spoke no Icelandic and he spoke neither German nor English, it was impossible to converse with him beyond a smile or nod.

Michael was examining the sand near her feet and, suddenly aware of him, she took a halting step back.

"What is it, Michael?"

"Heel mark from a Vietnam-era combat boot. See?" And he gestured with his right index finger to some ridges in the sand that seemed barely distinguishable in the beam of his flashlight from ordinary patterns in the sand. But she assumed Michael Rourke was right, as he invariably proved to be, as his father always was.

Paul Rubenstein and Han, the Chinese intelligence agent, each dropped into a crouch, flanking Michael. As she looked down at them she had the silly thought that some uninformed observer might think that three men were proposing to her at once. As a little girl she had read forbidden books that her mother had stored in a trunk in the hall closet, the books so old and musty-smelling that their memory was almost physical to her. And in these books men would sometimes drop to one knee to profess their love and sue for the hand of their lady.

Michael Rourke stood to his full height and suddenly she was looking up at him, into his eyes, his face intermittently in shadow and in light from the flashlight beams which played over the beach. The surf was loud, the wind louder, but as Michael spoke again she had no difficulty discerning his voice. "It appears he was alone. Now why would Natalia have left him?"

She wanted to tell Michael that she thought she knew why—Natalia loved Michael's father and Michael's father was married to Michael's mother, Sarah, and they expected a baby, and Natalia felt useless and afraid inside. It was the way she herself had felt after the death of Michael's wife had made him "available" and she had found herself insanely in love with Michael and he had refused all affection in his all-consuming sadness and lust for revenge. But then Michael had come to her in the night and made love to her and she had known that it would somehow . . . She didn't know what. "I don't know, Michael," she told him, because she really didn't know why Natalia would have walked away from John Rourke here on the beach. She would not have walked away from Michael.

Han's radio was making static sounds and she heard a voice that would have been one of the defense force people speaking through it to him. He answered in Chinese and then announced in English; "Your friend, Mr. Rolvaag—he has found something."

Michael, Paul in step with him, took off down the beach. Maria Leuden, hugging her coat around her, both hands in her pockets now, ran after him, her modesty be damned. Han was shouting orders to his men as she ran past him. The wind felt good in her hair, despite the cold and damp. She had felt more alive since she had left New Germany than she had ever felt there, and the only way she would return to it would be if Michael took her there, because she would always be with him. She kept running, breathless by the time she stopped. Rolvaag was stooped over, peering into the sand, his huge dog sniffing, whining, sniffing, moving between Rolvaag and some spot in the sand further along the beach, running, skidding in the sand on his hind feet, running again.

Michael was crouched beside the red-haired, red-bearded man. Maria heard occasional snatches of what Michael called "pigeon" English and Icelandic being exchanged over the heightening wind and the encroaching surf. About a battle or something.

Michael clapped Rolvaag on the shoulder, grabbed a handful of Hrothgar at the scruff of the neck and petted the animal vigorously. He looked up at Maria. "Bjorn seems to think there was a fight here. Several men with strange-looking footgear—I think they must have been wearing scuba gear."

"Scuba?"

"Self-contained underwater breathing apparatus. For diving."

"Ohh, yes." She nodded, recalling the term now. "But what would these scuba swimmers be doing here?"

Michael stood. "Logic supported by the physical evidence dictates that for some reason Natalia and my father split up further down the beach—back where I found that heel print. And then they got involved in some sort of

31

fight here with these persons in flippers."

"Flippers—ohh, flippers!"

At some time in the interim, Natalia and my father must have gotten together again. But then, there are these deeper ridges in the sand as if something was dragged into the water."

"Your father and Natalia?" she asked, frightened for them.

Paul Rubenstein answered her. "No—not heel prints or anything like that. Heavy objects, almost appearing cylindrical in shape. Most of the impressions are gone now, wiped away with the tide coming in, Maria. Looks like big tanks or something."

Michael hugged her to him and she rested her head against his right shoulder, his parka feeling rough against her cheek. She liked the feeling and she felt warmed now. "Must be Karamatsov," Michael whispered.

She stared up into his face, visible only partly in the light of Paul's flashlight. When Paul spoke, she still watched Michael. "If Karamatsov's been behind these raids Han's been telling us about—"

Maria Leuden shivered.

"Your Soviet nemesis." Han said slowly. "Perhaps he was preparing for some time to penetrate China in search of his nuclear weapons. And if he has seapower. . ." The Chinese let the thought hang.

Maria Leuden could see Michael's eyes now, narrowed almost to slits. "If he has seapower," Michael said slowly, "then he'll be using his divers to go after those missiles, to recover them from the train wreck."

"Either a submarine or—shit," Paul Rubenstein snarled, slamming his open left palm against his submachine gun, making the metal parts rattle like something cheap. "An island, maybe—ahh—"

Han spoke. "Surely Doctor Leuden's friends in New Germany would have detected such an island. Or, for that matter, could they not have detected a submarine? Hmm? This is most baffling."

Michael said, "You've been experiencing these raids for

32

some time now. And never an inkling of the source, Han?"

She nuzzled closer to Michael, burying her nose in the front of her coat. "This is the first defeat—the first true defeat that these seaborne invaders have encountered at our hands. They strike with uncanny quickness and withdraw into the sea, below the surface where we cannot follow them. And then at sunset!" And he threw up his hands in disgust.

Maria spoke. "They just exploded bombs attached to their own people—that is barbaric. Would even this Karamatsov. . ." And then she fell silent, because Maria Leuden knew Karamatsov seemed capable of any evil.

"We have encountered these personal explosive devices before. They prevent the taking and interrogation of prisoners, the inspection of equipment to determine origin. I believe the English word is 'insidious.' "

"Could be," Michael Rourke whispered. When he talked she could feel the vibration in his chest. "Maria?" And Michael looked down at her, touching the tips of his fingers to her chin, raising her face. "Do you have any idea what your country might have in terms of underocean capabilities?"

"Our commandoes have no training in undersea operations, as far as I know. But they don't tell archaeologists everything." She smiled.

Michael nodded. "All right—open to suggestions."

Paul Rubenstein spoke, his gloved right hand brushing at his nose. "We have to find Karamatsov's headquarters, Michael. And then get inside." Paul's wife, Annie, had told Maria that Paul had once worn glasses and sometimes, when he was tired or "uptight" as Annie put it, he would still brush against his nose as though pushing his glasses in place. When Michael had kissed Maria when she had joined him in the courtyard of the power station after the attack was repelled, he had made her glasses fog.

"If these men who attacked the power station took my father and Natalia and took them alive, then once these guys realized who they had, they'd get them to Karamatsov as quickly as possible. Promotion time. So, if they survived the fight and were somehow immobilized or so outnumbered that they had no choice, Natalia and my father'd still be alive. If one of Karamatsov's men captured a Rourke and didn't bring his prize to Karamatsov for disposition, he'd be in such deep trouble that he'd wish he had never been born. No—if whoever these troops were took them alive, they're still alive. And if they were killed—if they were killed, there would have been no sense in taking off the bodies. Their presence was already detected if this took place after the raid, or soon would have been if it took place before the raid." Michael looked up and down the beach, then out to sea. "It seems likely they were using this as some sort of staging area and spotted my dad and Natalia by accident. Shit."

"I'll get Lieutenant Keefler and his people airborne. Maybe—aw, hell." Paul Rubenstein stomped off across the sand into the night, the beam of his flashlight bouncing up and down as he cut over a dune and toward the rocks beyond. Then even his backlit silhouette disppeared.

Han said, "I regret that harm may have befallen such a fine man as your father and such a noble woman as Major Tiemerovna, Michael. I speak on behalf of the Chairman, I am sure, and certainly on my own behalf. Whatever can be done—er—I am truly sorry," and he walked away along the surf. Rolvaag, perhaps because he was unable to understand English, had drifted off already, Maria seeing him now for an instant along the beach, then losing him as he passed behind some rocks.

She was alone with Michael. He just held her, didn't speak.

It was hard to consider the possibility of John Rourke's death, and when she tried, it frightened her more than anything she had ever known. Because to consider the mortality of the father was to consider the mortality of the son, and without him she would wither and die.

"Michael?"

He turned toward her and she felt his arms encircle her, and she took her hands from her pockets and inched them

34

under his coat and around his waist. His left hand reached to her face and plucked away her glasses. She touched her lips to his fingers. He brought his mouth down over hers and she sank against him.

In the short time since they had become lovers, she had found that sometimes there was a desperation in him, and she felt it in him tonight.

Chapter Three

He had crawled toward Natalia, and Natalia toward him. At first they sat back to back to work at loosening each other's bonds. Then finally, in desperation, Rourke dropped to his chest behind her and tried to work at the restraints with his teeth. After a few moments, he realized that perhaps a rat could have gnawed through them, but no human could.

Then the door opened.

And it began again.

The tall man carried Rourke's knives and Natalia's knife in his hands, holding them as if his palms were somehow the baskets of scales as he spoke. "Translate."

The balding man responded to the direct order. And John Rourke learned that their inquisitor was named Kerenin, was a major. And non-Naval rank here aboard this undersea vessel only compounded the mystery.

"Strip her and search her," the tall man ordered.

John Rourke could not react to the words because they had been spoken in Russian. He felt his neck and shoulders tense, saw the muscles around Natalia's eyes tighten.

The translator began his work.

At the appropriate word, Rourke started to shout at Kerenin, "You bastard—you cannot do that!"

Apparently there was no need for translation, intonation and facial expression sufficient to convey meaning. Kerenin set down the edged weapons, then stepped toward him and slapped him backhanded across the mouth, Rourke letting his head sag away an instant before impact to diminish the effect of the blow.

When Kerenin had reentered the compartment, aside from the men who had originally accompanied him and the conventionally uniformed translator, there were three others, two of them women, all three of them wearing white coveralls with something that could have been medical insignia emblazoned over the heart—a similar insignia worn like a shoulder brassard—all three of them dark-haired, nearly Kerenin's own height, the women included. And all three of them looked simultaneously unpleasant and bored. The boredom in the eyes of one of the women seemed to wane now as she approached Natalia.

Natalia shrieked, "You cannot do this to me! You searched us with your machine. We have no weapons! Please!"

The translator, his balding head glistening sweat, paraphrased Natalia in Russian, but emotionlessly.

"First the woman, then the man," Kerenin said evenly, the translator not bothering to do his job this time.

"Who are you? I demand to see your superior!" John Rourke shouted.

This time, the translator translated.

Kerenin approached Rourke, hands easily on his hips, his mouth smiling but his eyes deadly. "I am Major of Spetznas Olav Kerenin. Since our last visit, a force of commandoes under my best officer has returned to this vessel through another airlock and I have learned they have suffered significant losses largely due to two other men dressed as you are and armed, as you were, with antique cartridge firearms. More Germans? More explorers searching for signs of life on the barren earth? We shall see. And during the attempt to subdue yourself and this woman you claim is your wife, several of my own men, including a member of my personal staff, were killed or seriously injured. Is this, perhaps, part of what they teach at the academy for German explorers? Hmm? Translate, Vznovski! Every word of it, man!"

"Yes, comrade major!" And the balding man began the translation, Rourke ignoring him, trying to think of something to say or do to gain some time. The bonds at his wrists and ankles were of some type of nearly translucent plastic, tubular and approximately a quarter inch in diameter, and, so it seemed, as impossible to snap as they had been to work loose or bite through.

Kerenin walked to the center of the compartment. From an equipment rack, he picked up the three knives he had just put down. One was Natalia's Bali-Song, another the little A.G. Russell knife, the third Rourke's Crain Life Support System X.

As the balding translator concluded, Kerenin began to muse aloud. "I find the firearms hopelessly primitive, regardless of what aesthetic appeal they might once have had. But these knives I find quite interesting indeed. Each unique in its own way. One is marked 'Bali-Song' with 'U.S.A.' appearing beneath it. And another—a picture of a stick-legged bird and what is apparently a name and then words which use the Roman alphabet. And this little black knife—a very strange-sounding name for German, I think—Russell? Translate this, Vznovski, as they begin to examine the woman for explosives and hidden devices."

The balding man began to translate, the woman who looked as though she was going to enjoy it grabbing Natalia by the hair and snapping Natalia's head back. Rourke said in German, "I must tell the commander something. Please?" And he looked beseechingly toward the translator, Vznovski.

Vznovski smiled for the first time, his shoulder drawing back as he began to translate.

A look of amusement entered Kerenin's face. "Wait with the woman—for a moment only. The man's tongue has perhaps loosened."

Rourke could see Natalia's eyes as Vznovski translated.

Rourke cleared his throat. Kerenin leaned closer toward him. Rourke eyed the knives, but neither the Crain nor the Russell was unsheathed, and if Kerenin had never seen a knife like Natalia's Bali-Song, he wouldn't be able to get it into action fast enough.

Rourke's voice low, almost a whisper, he began to

speak. "Ahh—I suppose that you have us at your mercy." With each word, he lowered his voice, Kerenin, despite Vznovski's running translation, leaning closer. "And, ahh—well—I don't know exactly how to say this, but you smell like shit—"

Kerenin's head was very close now and John Rourke threw his weight forward, his head snapping toward Kerenin's face, Rourke's head missing the nose as Kerenin dodged. But Kerenin didn't pull back quite quickly enough, the crown of Rourke's head impacting Kerenin over the right eye. The Russian screamed and fell back, blood oozing between his fingers the instant after his hands dropped the knives and went to his face.

Rourke saw Vznovski reaching for him from the left edge of his peripheral vision, hurtled his weight back against the two men who supported him, their hands banded at his biceps, hammering the one on his left side into Vznovski, the balding translator impacting the bulkhead near the watertight door.

Rourke's balance was going, Natalia a blur of motion as she launched her bound body against the woman who had grabbed her by the hair, their bodies impacting the other two medical personnel.

Rourke toppled forward, trying to drop to his knees, his knees taking most of the impact but his body continuing to move, slamming against the steel plates of the compartment floor. He rolled onto his back, one of the two who had held him coming for him, Rourke snapping both legs up, his feet hitting the man in the chest. He rolled across the floor, his left fist finding the little A.G. Russell Sting IA, closing over it.

He saw Kerenin's foot and tried rolling away from it, but now an explosion in his already aching head, and, Rourke slid across the floor from the impact. He still had the knife, snapping it free of the sheath, the sheath sliding over the plates, Rourke twisting the knife to work it against the bonds at his wrists.

Kerenin moved across the compartment in two swift strides, the big Crain survival knife in his right fist, hacking downward. Rourke tried to roll clear, but Kerenin moved faster, the primary edge of the Life Support System X flashing past John Rourke's face, Rourke feeling it against his throat, sucking in his breath.

Kerenin didn't speak. Kerenin didn't shift the knife. John Rourke didn't breathe. . . .

Michael Rourke slipped off his parka as he entered the security bunker of the power house. Han, already there, had changed from his traditional Chinese attire to the black battle-dress utilities of the Chinese Army. Paul Rubenstein stood beside him. Michael threw down his coat and joined them by the illuminated map table.

Paul looked up. "I got Lieutenant Keefler airborne and then I contacted Captain Hartman with German field headquarters. Hoffman puts Karamatsov's position as about four hundred kilometers from us at what used to be Tientsin."

"Yes—Tienjin, across Bo Hai. Before the Dragon Wind," Han added somberly.

"It's almost twice that distance by land, though," Paul said.

Michael looked at him, then back to the illuminated map table. "Could he have had a seabase here all along that we just didn't know about?" He looked at Han.

The Chinese smiled, then seemed to shrug his shoulders. "Possible, but highly dubious, Michael."

"Before the Night of the War," Paul began, "there was a gigantic Soviet Naval base at Cam Ranh Bay. What if part of it survived, somehow? And what if Karamatsov was looking to get those nuclear warheads and somehow get them to Cam Ranh Bay and be able to use them from there. I mean, there might still be hardware there that might be able to be restored. Hell—I . . ."

Paul Rubenstein fell silent.

Michael Rourke stared at the map, trying to think.

They were at Lushun. At one time it had been called Port Arthur. Almost at the same latitude across a bay almost large enough to accommodate a nation the size of Greece before the Night of the War, the Hero Marshal, Vladmir Karamatsov, and a Soviet force numbering into the thousands, waited.

With an expeditionary force of Karamatsov's personnel KGB Elite Corps, there had been a bold attempt to expropriate a vast portion of the pre-War nuclear arsenal of the People's Republic of China, the Soviet Union and China engaging in a devastating land war following the Night of the War—the all-out thermonuclear exchange between the United States and the Soviet Union. Then came what the Chinese called the "Dragon Wind", or Great Conflagration, when the ionized atmosphere had caught fire and extinguished the majority of life on earth, and forced those who could survive underground to wait until the planet had sufficiently restored itself to the point where life could be supported on the surface.

And Karamatsov seemed intent on the acquisition of more nuclear weapons with which to obliterate all life on earth forever. But his greatest passion, his ultimate motivation, was simpler and very clear. Karamatsov wanted the death of Major Natalia Anastasia Tiemerovna, who, in name only now, was his wife. And Karamatsov wanted the death of John Thomas Rourke, whom Karamatsov blamed for taking Natalia from him and whom, in this latter case rightly, Karamatsov blamed for once before destroying his plans to be master of the earth.

Why had Karamatsov taken his armies to Tientsin? From what base of operations did those who had kidnapped Natalia and Michael's father, John Rourke, originate?

Had the five centuries while earth restored itself to sufficiently sustain life merely been an interlude between the first battle and the last in a war that would forever end war by forever ending life?

"I'm going to Tientsin. If Karamatsov's got them, they'll wind up there," Michael declared, not taking his eyes from the illuminated map table.

"I'll go with you, Michael," Paul Rubenstein, his

41

friend, his sister's husband told him.

"I think the government of China needs to be represented as well." Han smiled. "Perhaps my meager skills may be of some service, Michael."

Michael Rourke reached across the table to both men, a hand to each man's shoulder. There was nothing to say.

Chapter Four

They had forced him to his knees, the LS-X knife to his throat, his head pulled back with a fist knotted into his hair. They had made him watch as Natalia had been made to undress, ordered to do so if she did not wish to see her "husband" with his throat slit.

Natalia, naked, in the center of the compartment beneath the massive grappling hook, had assumed the pose of the classic, startled nude. Her open right hand covered her vaginal area, her left forearm covered her breasts. But her head was raised and there was determination in her eyes, not resignation.

Instruments had been passed over her body, for detecting explosives or electronic monitoring devices, Rourke deduced. But there had been no actual physical search. As he had bitterly suspected, Kerenin had ordered her to disrobe as a means of demoralizing her, showing his power. And from the look on Kerenin's face, because he liked looking at her naked.

After some time, Kerenin standing very close to her, assaying her, not touching her, she was allowed to dress and was then rebound. New restraints were used. The plastic was apparently only removeable by cutting. Then she was forced to her knees and a knife placed at her throat, her knife this time. And John Rourke was released, his bonds cut. It was as if Kerenin, whose right eye was blackened and who was blood-encrusted over the eyebrow, were challenging him. Kerenin, despite his obvious fascination with Natalia, would kill her, Rourke had decided. And because of that, John Rourke had no choice but to cooperate.

He stood at the center of the room and undressed, handing over the battered brown-leather bomber jacket, the empty double Alessi shoulder rig, the light-blue snap-front cowboy shirt, his combat boots, the faded blue Levis—the belt already taken when his knives and the Sparks Six-Pak and a half-dozen spare magazines for his pistols had been confiscated, sometime before he had awakened.

As he tugged off his socks, threw them to Kerenin's men for examination, he said in German, "I hope they smell." He took off his underpants. He stood with his hands at his sides. One of the two women—the one who hadn't looked sexually aroused when Natalia had undressed—was staring at him. Natalia closed her eyes.

John Rourke stared at Kerenin. While there was life, as the expression went, there was hope. But the possibilities were rapidly diminishing. Which, of course, created a situation in which there was nothing to lose at all. Rourke continued to stare at Kerenin. And as the instruments which were to determine if his bodily cavities concealed explosives or electronic monitoring devices passed close to his body, he saw Kerenin's eyes flicker. Recognition in his eyes, John Rourke knew, recognition that if there was a way, Major Kerenin would be a dead man. . . .

The ship's brig lay a hundred feet or so forward of the compartment where they had initially been held and interrogated. It was facing the starboard torpedo room. There were no bars, but rather a bank of shimmering blue lights at the top of the entryway and at the bottom. As Kerenin's men had left, one of them had thrown one of the cut-off plastic restraints into the opening between the bands of light. The air in the opening had crackled with electricity, the plastic cord smoldering, then bursting into flame, the ashes which accumulated in the lower bar of blue light crackling.

44

The man had walked away.

John Rourke turned to Natalia Tiemerovna. She smiled strangely, then came into his arms, in German, whispering, "You should say, 'Look at the fine—'"

He hugged her tightly against him, knowing the rest, Oliver Hardy's famous line to Stan Laurel—and a fine mess it was this time.

Rourke glanced at his shoulder, saying to her, "I think we can safely discount trying to walk through the doorway." The ashes of the plastic cord were nearly gone.

"Do you have any idea where we're going?"

Rourke simply shook his head, drawing her close to him again, his lips against her left ear, barely whispering. The brig would be bugged for sound and, though she had detected no evidence of cameras, he guessed some type of visual coverage was also working, perhaps advanced fiber optics. "We need names, a solid cover story. Thank God I left my wallet with the rest of my gear. I still carry my Georgia driver's license and concealed weapons permit."

Her lips touched at his right cheek, then brushed against his left ear. "Anna—I used that name once."

"All right," he whispered, elaborately kissing her neck. "Michael used to always joke that we should have named him Wolfgang—he won't mind if I borrow it for a while."

"Will—we won't, will we?" And she buried her face against his neck. "I dream at nights sometimes that somehow I am your wife—that you would call me your wife—but—like this, it's—"

She was crying. He held her tightly.

"We'll get out of here. This is a tough one, but we'll make it out of here," he whispered, he lied.

Chapter Five

Otto Hammerschmidt had taken the train. The "Special" as it was called. He had no true frame of reference for the concept of a train, and especially something which moved so rapidly over land. When there were short distances to cover, he had always walked. Slightly longer distances and he had used a synth-fuel-powered internal-combustion-engine vehicle. Greater distances still and a helicopter or fixed-wing aircraft. Aside from a few forays on horseback over the years, some elementary training in the higher elevations of New Germany with cross-country skiing, and, as a youth, a bicycle, his concepts of transportation had been well-defined.

But a vehicle which moved on rails at enormously high speeds, faster than some small aircraft, and was powered by what seemed a ridiculously small reactor—fusion reactor, no less—stretched his powers of credulity.

There was a healing salve which he still had to apply to portions of his arms and legs and back—that was the difficult part—where the burns had been the worst, but other than that and the almost incessant itching of new skin, he was as fit as ever and better rested than he had been in years. The Chinese ran fine hospitals.

He had, upon release, asked to rejoin Michael Rourke and Paul Rubenstein, and of course Herr Doctor John Rourke and Fraulein Major Natalia Tiemerovna, at what he deemed was the potential "new front," Lushun, like a stubby Chinese thumb thrust into the Yellow Sea.

He had been told that the only way to get there, the

Chinese being without air transportation, was to take the train.

So, he had taken it.

When he had left the train at the conglomeration of prefabricated huts, military tents, and a massive and apparently explosion-damaged fusion-power station, he was met by a slightly built Chinese. The man spoke no German but excellent if odd-sounding English. His name was Wing Tse Chau and he was a captain of the Army, attached to Herr Han and Michael Rourke and their expedition to Tientsin. He handed a letter to Hammerschmidt.

Hammerschmidt unfolded it, struggling a bit as he read it, his reading knowledge of English once vastly better than his spoken knowledge of the language, until the advent of the Rourke family; now the spoken aspect was much better practised.

"This will take me a moment, Captain Wing."

"Certainly, Captain Hammerschmidt."

Hammerschmidt nodded, lighting a cigarette. A stiff wind blew, nearly extinguishing his lighter. And it was cold and damp here. He supposed he noticed it more after the sterile, temperature-controlled environment of the hospital. He realized that he was moving his lips as he read.

Otto,
My father and Natalia are missing. We have strong reason to believe that they were taken after encountering a superior force of Soviet commandoes who were part of an attack force on the power station at Lushun. Our only hope of effecting their rescue is to go to where they are likely being held now or will soon be brought: Karamatsov's Headquarters at Tientsin. If you are well enough, we could use your help and experience.

It was signed simply, "Michael." Hammerschmidt folded the letter and placed it in an outside pocket of his parka. "Aside from a few things that I do have, Captain

47

Wing, I will require your assistance to re-equip."

"This has been provided for, Captain Hammerschmidt. Welcome, sir." And Wing extended his right hand. Hammerschmidt took it, released it, then followed him off the platform toward a waiting electric car. . . .

Michael Rourke had learned of Otto Hammerschmidt's release from the hospital from Han after the Chinese intelligence agent had contacted the First City to notify his superiors in the government, and the Chairman in particular, of the decision to set out for Tientsin. He had learned also that Hammerschmidt would be arriving on the next Special from the First City. For that reason he had decided to wait. It meant a delay of lift-off time amounting to approximately eighteen minutes if Wing Tse Chau made good time from the train depot. Considering Hammerschmidt's abilities, he had considered the delay justified.

But the delay was getting to him now, just waiting.

He felt the pressure of Maria Leuden's hand on his hand, and he turned his eyes from the dirt track which led from Lushun to her face. "How are you going to tell your mother and sister?"

"I was going to do it, but Paul said he'd contact Annie by radio, tell her, let Annie decide if we should tell my mom. Maybe I let Paul talk me into it too easily. I don't know."

She leaned up and kissed him on the cheek.

In the distance he saw one of the Chinese electric cars coming. And he saw a German field cap waving through the open window. Hammerschmidt was coming. . . .

Paul Rubenstein sat at the copilot's controls, the helicopter pilot having left the cockpit to give him privacy. There was a lot of static and Annie's voice sounded distorted. But still it was Annie's voice and the sound of her voice warmed him inside.

"Say again, Paul. Over."

"Annie—your dad and Natalia are missing. But we think they are all right. I repeat—we think they are all right. Over."

"Paul. I'm coming. Over."

"No you aren't. Your mother needs you—hell, if you decide to tell Sarah. This situation could deteriorate instantly if Karamatsov moves his forces. I can't say anything more about it en clair. Over."

"I'll my mother. But I'm coming. Don't forbid me to. Please. Please, Paul. Over."

Paul Rubenstein's right fist balled over the microphone. "I'll arrange for you to be brought to the First City. I love you. Yeah—tell her about your dad. I'll keep you informed. Michael sends his love. I love you—Paul out."

He threw the microphone down on the seat as he stood, almost striking his head on the cockpit overhead, despite the fact that he had never considered himself nor been considered tall.

There was no other way than to let her come, he told himself. No other way. She was Annie Rubenstein now, but she would always be a Rourke. . . .

Natalia had fallen asleep in his arms. For some reason, they had not taken his watch and, periodically, he had glanced at the Rolex. The time so far spent in the submarine's brig was slightly over two hours. There was a toilet in the far corner by the bulkhead, and he had shielded Natalia from the open doorway with his back turned to her while she had used it. He had used it then, and debated the possibility of cannibalizing it to somehow short-circuit the electrical barrier which kept them prisoner. But there seemed to be no metal parts, all polymers instead.

He had advised that she rest, the exhaustion she felt evident in her expression, in her voice. But he had not slept. Since the fight aboard the Special—the high-speed Chinese train much like the Japanese Tokaido Bullet

Trains from before the Night of the War—there had been little to do except monitor intelligence data coming in from Captain Hartman's forces which pursued and harrassed the Soviet armies of Vladmir Karamatsov. That and ponder the mystery of the increasingly more frequent raids the Chinese reported on their coastal outpost, occasionally reaching as far inland as the First City.

And the mystery concerning the origin of these raids now seemed resolved. Some powerful Soviet force with extensive undersea maneuverability, their base perhaps the pre-War submarine pens at Cam Ranh Bay in Vietnam, or perhaps some island. And it seemed evident that Karamatsov had no knowledge of this Soviet force, and likely they had no knowledge of his land forces. If the two should link and form some sort of alliance, they would be irresistible.

More than the immediate concern of escape for himself and Natalia, there was the greater concern of notifying the High Command of New Germany and their Icelandic and Eden Project allies—and the Chinese for that matter—of the potential for disaster and that the timetable for a final confrontation with Karamatsov's forces had to be advanced. With the addition of Chinese forces to what he had come to mentally label as the "Alliance of Happenstance," the weight of numbers in Karamatsov's favor was greatly diminished.

But if this new Soviet force should unite with Karamatsov . . .

He had thought fleetingly that they likely possessed nuclear capabilities. He had left the thought unresolved because if they did, the situation was vastly worse. Scientists of New Germany had been conducting atmospheric sampling tests for decades, and the conclusions derived from these tests seemed incontrovertible. Several average-sized nuclear detonations in the megaton range, perhaps as few as one, could trigger a second ionization effect similar to that which all but consumed the world five centuries ago shortly after the Night of the War. But this time, because of the already tenuous environmental situation and the severely depleted atmosphere, all the gases associated with carbon-based life would be consumed. The planet would be forever dead and, eventually, for those who did survive in the underground redoubts like that of the Germans in Argentina, the Russians in the Ural Mountains, his own retreat in the mountains of northeast Georgia—there would be no world to return to, even to contemplate. And eventually, even if it were centuries from now, the last human life would end. Because of a bizarre interaction of the ionization effect with the Van Allen Radiation Belts, the Icelandics had survived at the Hekla community and elsewhere in their tiny country. But not even they would be saved.

John Rourke glanced again at the Rolex Submariner on his left wrist, Natalia's head resting against his chest, the weight of her body against his left arm. His arm had some time ago begun to stiffen, to tingle, but he had not moved her, flexing his fingers instead to restore circulation.

But now she stirred.

He spoke to her quickly, in German, lest she forget and use English or, worse still, Russian. "Anna," he said, calling her by the assumed name to which they had agreed. "Go back to sleep, Anna. Nothing has changed."

She looked at him, her blue eyes sleepy still, squeezing her eyes tight shut, then opening them. She smiled at him. "Your arm must be asleep, Wolfgang."

She remembered, he knew.

"My arm is fine, Anna."

He heard footsteps along the companionway, saw a fleeting shadow against one of the torpedo racks beyond their confinement on the other side of the companionway.

Kerenin appeared at the doorway, with him the balding man, Vznovski, who was the intepretor. Vsznovski spoke. "I am instructed to tell you by the comrade major that the submarine will soon be docking. You will accompany the comrade major into the city for further interrogation. Your wrists only will be bound. Should you attempt to escape—and there is no place to go—or cause any disturbance, you will be shot with the Sty-20s again."

51

Rourke looked quizzically at Vznovski. Kerenin, a massive bandage partially covering his right eye, told Vznovski to explain what the Sty-20 was. "These are our sidearms. Carbon-dioxide-powered, they can be used in atmosphere or in water. They fire darts such as those with which you were both subdued. Additional injection with the sedative contained in the darts while a portion of the substance still remains in your blood streams would prove most unpleasant and could result in permanent neuromuscular damage."

"My wife and I—we are both very interested in seeing your city. It will be pleasant to get into the night air. May my wife have her coat returned to her?" Natalia's coat had caused him a moment's worry, that some label or mark showing Soviet origin might have been present, until he had recalled that no garment she possessed, she had told him once, had any labels or manufacturer's markings. It was simpler that way, she had said.

Vznovski was laughing, translating to Kerenin, Kerenin laughing too then.

The two men walked away, still laughing.

"Perhaps their island or whatever is in the midst of a heat wave," Natalia suggested.

"Perhaps, perhaps not," he whispered. . . .

A man of Kerenin's height, but more powerfully built and with the look of a jungle cat who watched, listened, and waited to act, joined them in the companionway near the elevator bank. John Rourke had been gauging measurements for the undersea craft since their confinement in the brig had begun, and he was not at all surprised to find elevators here. If the length of the vessel was in excess of a thousand feet, as he had surmised during the dreamlike state in which he had been brought to it, then the height from the torpedo deck to the sail had to be—

The new officer spoke to Kerenin, Rourke listening, attempting not to appear to be. "She is a beautiful woman, comrade major. She should be Russian." Despite

52

the circumstances Rourke almost laughed. Natalia, her wrists bound behind her as were his, stood beside him and she simply looked away. "The man did that to you?" And the new officer gestured toward Kerenin's right eye. "With his hands and feet bound? Very interesting."

"Yes, Boris Feyedorovitch. Perhaps we can arrange that this self-proclaimed German explorer do the same to you."

Boris Feyedorovitch—first and middle or first and last name. Rourke logged it away. Boris Feyedorovitch spoke again. "This would bear out the opinions voiced so often, I have heard, in the Presidium—that surface civilizations beyond that of our enemies, the Chinese, do exist. You have not tried drugs?"

Kerenin glanced at Rourke, Rourke trying to make his face reflect puzzlement rather than interest. Kerenin looked back toward Boris Feyedorovitch and told him, "Their weapons reveal much about the state of their technology, if indeed they are who they claim. Their firearms do not utilize caseless ammunition, but rather brass or some other metallic substance is used as cartridge-case material, as with our deck guns until the last decade. The knives these two had—most curious. They appear to be very personalized, as though designed for their use and theirs alone. And there is something else, Boris. The sidearms carried by the man and woman. I believe them to be of United States of America origin, and yet as we both learned in Academy, many of the pre-War United States of America protectorate nations of Western Europe produced their own weapons. I should imagine that individual small arms were among these. So, why are their firearms not German? And her handguns." And he gestured toward Natalia. Rourke felt what was coming and felt as if his heart had skipped a beat. "The stylized winged surface creature—the bird. There is something vaguely familiar about it. It is emblazoned on the barrel of each of her handguns. It may be a manufacturer's mark, but it might well be something else. Something—something about it is—how should I put it?" He fell silent as the elevator doors opened.

The guards, two on either side of Rourke and Natalia, apparently Naval personnel from their uniforms, ushered them forward with shoves.

As he shouldered one of the guards away to allow Natalia the lady's prerogative of entering the elevator first, he began assembling facts. Kerenin was a major and, just guessing from a comparison of uniforms, Boris Feyedorovitch was a captain. Army? But, more likely, a modern-day Soviet equivalent of Marines. Rourke stepped inside the elevator and stood beside Natalia, watching as Kerenin and the second officer entered last so as to be able to stand at the front of the elevator. He gathered they had not entered first because of him and Natalia, prisoners.

Kerenin's uniform was a deep-blue close-fitting jumpsuit with epaulets of a complicated braid design. The second officer's epaulets were less complicated in design. Each wore the same insignia—apparently a unit insignia— on the right collar tab, but Kerenin's left collar-tab insignia, silver-colored, was more complicated in design, a series of interlocking circles. Four of them, Boris Feyedorovitch possessing only three. Rourke thought almost absently that the three interlocking circles actually seemed more aesthetically appealing from a design standpoint than the four circles.

The doors slapped shut, the interior of the elevator illuminated, it appeared, by rather than through lighted panels in the elevator roof. The interior was bright, polished metal, but he doubted by now it was stainless steel.

There was a slight lurch.

The elevator was moving rapidly now, Rourke's ears popping slightly from it. He opened his mouth and swallowed against the pressure. He noticed Natalia looking at him and he said to her in German, "Anna—everything will be all right."

"Wofgang—" she began, but one of the guards gestured with his Sty-20 and they both fell silent.

The elevator stopped and the doors opened.

He had read the elevator panel and judged they had stopped just below the sail.

Kerenin and the second officer exited, and Rourke and Natalia were shoved along after them into a wide corridor. There were instrument sounds forward, electronic beeping, printers. But the corridor ended abruptly about a hundred feet aft. Rourke felt the corners of his mouth turning down. The corridor—it was too open to think of it as a companionway—ending so abruptly only further confirmed his suspicions that the vessel had nuclear capabilities. Slightly ahead of the rough balance point between forward and aft sections was the logical point to position the missile tubes. Ohio Class submarines from prior to the Night of the War carried twenty-four Trident-II missiles in their tubes. Considering the vastly greater proportions of this vessel it might well carry more than double that number. Greater nuclear firepower than many of the smaller nations of the pre-War "nuclear club" ever possessed, concentrated in one floating missile base.

Kerenin started across the corridor toward an open watertight door, Rourke shrugging his shoulders, nodding to Natalia that it was all right, then starting after him.

There were stairs here and Rourke took them first after the second officer, who had followed Kerenin. Rourke glanced back once to see that Natalia was behind him.

He saw light overhead through an open hatchway, but—oddly—smelled no sea breezes, no smell of night.

Kerenin and the second officer, Boris Feyedorovitch, disappeared through the hatchway. John Rourke hesitated a moment, taking a deep breath, then stepped up after them.

He blinked his eyes in disbelief.

Chapter Six

The hatch opened onto the gap between the submarine's sail—it rose perhaps thirty feet into the air—and the missile hatches. He counted the hatches quickly. Four rows port to starboard, fifteen hatches per row. John Rourke's stomach churned. But neither the height of the submarine's sail nor the sixty missile tubes had caused him to blink. It was where the submarine was.

There was no island, at least not in any conventional sense. In five centuries, these Russians had been busy indeed.

As he looked over his left shoulder to starboard there was a vast expanse of water, a large lagoon the size of a small lake, fog banked at its outer edges and low clouds hanging overhead, but the light was bright as day. His watch and his internal time clock said otherwise. He raised his eyes toward the sky, squinting against the light. But there was no sun. There was no sky. Above him, perhaps a hundred feet distant from the water's surface, was the sea. Above him. Between the "sky" and the sea there was . . . There was a dome.

He looked aft. More submarines were alongside a metal dock, the dock itself as wide as a football field and many times the length of a football field. He was able to count five more submarines.

Natalia stood beside him. She gasped.

Kerenin and the second officer stood a few feet from them, Kerenin laughing. Rourke stepped closer to the two Russian officers so he could see around the sail and

56

forward. This craft was the first "in line" at the docks, but where the dock ended, perhaps a hundred feet ahead of the bow of the vessel on the deck of which Rourke and Natalia stood, there was an opening leading beyond the dock. As he watched, through it came what he assumed to be a mini-sub, perhaps half the length of the old Skipjack Class subs of the late 1950s, a massive transparent dome replacing the sail, giving the craft the appearance of a marine life-form with a solitary eye rather than a machine made by men. Twin fins cut the water's surface, the vessel riding low in the water.

The opening out of which it had come drew his attention. A vast hollow hemisphere, an opening cut into a vastly large hemisphere or dome, a concavity within a convexity. John Rourke's eyes followed the surface of the dome upward. The dome immediately over his head—the artificial sky—joined it, the actual height of the larger dome lost where the smaller dome and then the sea obscured it.

Natalia's voice sounded frail beside him. "Wolfgang?"

"There's nothing we can do now except see the tourist sights. I am here with you."

Kerenin started walking, the second officer beside him, the guards falling in and flanking Rourke and Natalia, a solitary guard walking behind them as they followed Kerenin and the second officer across the deck toward a long gangplank. On each side of the gangplank were three rows of chain, the chain rows there for safety, one perhaps a foot above the level of the gangplank, another two feet higher, the third at almost chest level. Kerenin and Boris Feyedorovitch started down the gangplank, Rourke falling in behind them, Natalia beside him. Because of the width of the gangplank, the flanking guards fell in behind Rourke and Natalia. For a moment, Rourke considered hurtling Natalia over the gangplank side, then jumping after her. But there was only the dock, unless something lurked behind the mists at the far side of the lagoon. Where could they go? And their hands were bound with the plastic cords which seemed escape-proof without a knife.

John Rourke exhaled loudly, realizing he had hesitated for a moment, then continued walking, his eyes and Natalia's eyes meeting briefly.

At the base of the gangplank, Kerenin and the second officer stood, waiting. A third officer, a junior grade by the lack of complexity of his braid and his apparent youth, joined them. Rourke heard the younger officer address Kerenin, then Boris Feyedorovitch as "Comrade Captain Feyedorovitch!"

That settled that. Rourke shrugged.

Rourke thumped his right foot against the dock surface. Although it appeared to be metal, it was not, unless it were some combination of metal and plastic. And he studied the composition of the hull of the submarine. Prior to the Night of the War, the Soviets had utilized a type of rubberized coating on the hulls of their underwater vessels. He wondered if this craft, like old Soviet submarines, was double-hulled.

As he mused over these concerns, on another level of his consciousness he listened to the seemingly unguarded conversation of the Russian officers. "The woman," Feyedorovitch said, "is very beautiful. But do you think, if they really are married, that she—"

Kerenin's voice sounded like the snap of an animal. "They must be more fully interrogated. In that process, many things may happen. To change the subject," and his tone moderated as he evidently addressed the younger officer, "you have acted upon our transmission that was sent as soon as we surfaced?"

Rourke logged away that detail. They had not yet developed some means of long-range transmission from ship to base. Perhaps only ship to ship, while still underwater. "All is in readiness, comrade major," the younger officer answered.

Rourke looked at Natalia, smiling with his mouth, feeling the tightness around his eyes.

Kerenin started ahead again, along the dock, Rourke and Natalia following in behind Kerenin and the two other

58

officers, the guards again flanking Rourke and Natalia, one behind them.

Kerenin turned off from the docks and into what appeared to be a large tube. It was, Rourke realized, a tunnel. Everything here seemed to be prefabricated, modular. The tube was of some transparent material and, as they walked, Rourke could observe on both sides of the tube what appeared to be a similar lagoon, missing only the mists which enshrouded the outer limits of the larger one. The lagoon seemed alive with dome-eyed mini-subs like the one he had seen from the deck of the Soviet submarine in which he and Natalia had been brought here. The lagoons, he knew, would be kept at their level by air pressure exerted downward, the air trapped beneath the domes. Early types of diving bells had utilized such a system. But in the early diving bells, as the air was consumed the water level rose. To maintain an all-but-constant level for these lagoons here, air pressure would have to be kept constant. The need for the fleet became suddenly obvious—the mini-subs, the larger vessels. There was some other enemy. The Chinese had no ability to pursue the Russians who attacked them into the sea. No power on earth existed of which John Rourke knew that possessed the ability to threaten these Russians in their underwater complex. But the fleet . . . There was indeed some other enemy. Regardless of the material used for the construction of the protective dome or domes, the material would be vulnerable to destruction. And the pressure of the sea against the material would be almost incalculably great. The slightest crack could start it, a hole would seal the fate of all who resided here.

The Soviet fleet—and perhaps what he saw here was only some small portion of it—would guard the perimeter of the complex against attackers.

And, granted that assumptions were dangerous, it was likely that whoever these enemies of the Soviets were, they would be potential allies.

They left the tube, into a still-larger tube, walkways on either side and vehicles—official, no doubt—parked along either curbside. Some type of electric cars, he thought idly, with gullwing doors.

Rourke followed the younger officer beneath the door opening and inside, sitting in the rear seat, Natalia beside him, a guard on either side of them, the other guards on a rear facing jumpseat, Kerenin and the other two officers in the forward facing seat in the center, a single-seat cockpit at the left front. The gullwing on the curbside whooshed closed, the driver consulting what appeared to be a very interesting electronic instrument panel from Rourke's limited sight position, then pulling away from the curb and into the "street."

The dream-like experience after being shot with the Sty-20 had occurred within the coffin-like capsule, and although the capsule could easily be utilized for transporting injured personnel away from a land-based battlefield to a vessel beneath the sea, it was more likely that the capsules were utilized for prisoner transfer. He had heard the Chinese agent Han telling of the disappearance of some Chinese after the mysterious attacks. If the Soviet fleet were a defense against some other underwater power, the capsules might well be used for prisoner transport in this context as well.

But did prisoners survive here? Were there potential allies here he could somehow make use of?

The vehicle was definitely electric or something utilizing a system other than internal combustion. The ride was so smooth, he barely noticed that the vehicle had turned. To their right now was the sea, a portion of the dome perhaps fifty yards from the road surface, a greenway there with trees and shrubs growing in abundance. Flower beds. He noticed older women kneeling beside them, tending them. But the women all were dressed the same. Medium-blue tunics and medium-blue slacks, scarves of the same color tied over their hair. To the left, he noticed several younger persons, men and women, dressed almost identically, all in the blue, collarless tunics and slacks, the men wearing long-billed baseball caps, the women scarves. Beyond that walkway, another dome rose, and beyond its surface

Rourke saw water. More vessels of the Soviet underwater fleet? Or something else?

The vehicle turned again, three vast domes suddenly visible as the vehicle moved away from them—one central and two the same size or slightly smaller, clouds visible near the height of the central dome, which he could better observe.

And now they were no longer inside a dome, but rather in a wide structure with a gently curved overhead and gently curved bulkheads, like the belly of a massive ship. The guard across which Rourke leaned to stare through the left-side Gullwing's window section elbowed Rourke in the ribcage, and Rourke leaned back.

He stared ahead now.

Vehicles of all descriptions were parked beyond an energy barrier similar to that at the opening of the submarine's brig, the vehicle slowing, Kerenin passing papers through a window beside him to the shorter of two blue-uniformed guards, these uniforms like his, only fitting less well and with different rank. Something else caught Rourke's eye. Each of the guards was only armed with what appeared to be one of the Sty-20 pistols.

He logged away this detail as well. Were conventional firearms not allowed inside the domes?

The papers were returned, Kerenin casually but with style returning a salute. The vehicle started ahead, the energy barrier turned off, crackling slightly as it reactivated behind them, Rourke watching through the vehicle's rear window.

The vehicles he had seen parked were more easily identifiable now as the Gullwing glided past them. Armored personnel carriers, massive, flat, their wheels enormous, their color gray.

More personnel in uniform moved about here, attending the vehicles or merely standing beside them engaged in conversation. At the end of this tunnel through which they now moved was another dome, Rourke squinting his eyes against the light as the Gullwing moved out beneath it.

It was landscaped beautifully here, structures rising out

of tree-lined squares, rising several stories toward the height of the dome. There were smaller domes on either side, quadrants of their hemispheres just visible toward the edge of the tunnel which they had just left.

The gullwinged vehicle stopped beside a rounded curb abutting a horseshoe-shaped driveway. The doors opened on both sides this time and as Kerenin and the other two officers got out, Rourke was tugged toward the driver's side door, Natalia toward the opposite door.

Rourke stood in the light. It wasn't sunshine, but felt warm to the skin. His eyes squinting against it now even more tightly, he looked "skyward," the building before which the vehicle had parked a full ten stories high. There were a half-dozen other buildings beneath the dome, none so tall as this, all of them prefabricated in appearance, their color a neutral tan, but pleasing, perhaps because of the landscaping which set them off.

The guard gestured toward the building, Rourke nodding toward him. It would have been easy enough to kill the man, but Natalia was on the other side of the vehicle. And where would they go, even if they could escape? Before escape could be considered, he had to know more.

Rourke stepped onto the curb, Kerenin waiting there. Rourke wondered, suddenly, why the balding interpreter had not been brought along. He licked his lips. Kerenin started toward the large glass-looking double doors which fronted the building. Over the doors, Rourke read the cyrillic letters which formed the words "Command and General Staff Headquarters Pacific Soviet Socialist Republic."

Chapter Seven

If the marble were a synthetic, it not only had the appearance of the real thing, but also the coldness of it. Rourke's fingers moved away from the gray and black pillar.

Kerenin alone conferred with the three men at the long, table-like desk at the far end of the vaulted room. Behind their seats there was mounted on the wall a familiar device—the hammer and sickle flag of the Union of Soviet Socialist Republics with the initials CCCP in gold or some similar metal beneath it.

Captain Feyedorovitch approached Rourke, his hands on his hips. He spoke in Russian, Rourke pretending to be uncomprehending. "I know that you understand me, and that you will not acknowledge that you do. I have seen a man just like you. He had your height, your coloring, your hair, even dressed similarly to you. A brother perhaps? He fought like no man I have ever seen. He was brave in the extreme. And because of that I will tell you this. Comrade Major Kerenin will have your woman, wife or not. That means that whatever befalls you, you will die in the last. Use this information for whatever value it may hold to you." He turned and walked away.

"Michael," Rourke almost said aloud. His son. He closed his eyes for an instant. Despite Michael's abilities, and Paul's as well—despite anything, there would be no help coming. He opened his eyes.

The guards were moving toward him and Natalia and Rourke waited. They gestured for them to move ahead,

63

toward Kerenin and the three seated men. Rourke moved ahead, his eyes focusing on each of the faces in turn. They all seemed piteously alike, dour-faced, balding, paunchy. All that was missing was for one of them to hold his hands over his eyes, the other his ears, the third his mouth. The heels of Rourke's combat boots clicked on the marble or marble-like floor, Natalia's boot heels clicking more loudly.

Both of them stopped a yard or so before the triumvirate.

A woman entered from the right, an officer dressed identically to her male counterparts, her hair nearly as short as theirs. She stood at attention. She was told to stand down and to translate both the remarks of the triumvirate and the remarks of the prisoners.

Kerenin began to speak, the woman looking to Kerenin for the assent to translate. He nodded and she began the unnecessary exercise. "You are both charged with multiple counts of murder, espionage, and crimes of intent against the Soviet people. Since the evidence against you is so overwhelming, there is no purpose in entering a plea. Have you anything to say in your behalf?"

Rourke stepped a pace forward. In German, the woman picking up the translation, he began, "My wife and I were walking along the beach. She went on ahead. She was set upon by soldiers under the command of this man. I came to her rescue when I heard sounds of battle. We were subdued, then kidnapped and taken aboard one of your vessels, where my wife and I were both subjected to threats of violence and forced to disrobe for unnecessary and demeaning searches of our persons. We are German citizens on a peaceful mission of exploration in search of remaining pockets of civilization following the great war between the Russian people and the people of America. We come in peace, seeking only knowledge. We were armed only for our own protection against whatever unknown dangers lay before us in our quest."

He stopped in order that the female officer serving as translator could catch up. He continued then. "We were both given intensive training in the means of self-defense and in various other skills needed for long-term survival. We encountered the Chinese, whom I presume to be your enemies. They had spoken of warriors raiding their cities, and I presume your people are of whom they spoke. We have no taste for warfare, my wife and I. We have come in peace. You are evidently possessed of great knowledge here. You are fortunate indeed. If you wish to make formal contact with the German people, we would be honored and the contact could serve to the mutual advantage of our peoples. If you do not, we ask only to be allowed to return to the surface, reunite with our few comrades, and continue our explorations in peace, someday returning to our loved ones in Germany, to our colleagues. You need have no fear that by some means any slight knowledge we may have obtained of your civilization here would eventually work to your undoing. No power on the surface of the earth could reach your homeland, nor certainly pose any threat to your homeland whatsoever. Please let us return to the surface in peace."

John Rourke fell silent.

The man at the center of the triumvirate looked to Kerenin as the female officer completed her translation. The man spoke, "Comrade major—is it possible they are indeed whom they claim to be? Or are you convinced otherwise?"

Kerenin cleared his throat. The female officer translated the triumvirate member's remarks into German. Kerenin spoke now. "I am convinced, Comrade Chairman, that this man and woman lie. Based upon field intelligence reports of Captain Feyedorovitch, it would appear that several persons of the white race have allied themselves with our enemies, the Chinese. Their origin can be only one place. They can only be cleverly placed agents of our enemies at Mid-Wake, Comrade Chairman."

Rourke's mind raced—Mid-wake? Mid-Wake?

Kerenin, staring at Natalia, then at Rourke, declared, "They must be fully interrogated, Comrade Chairman. With your permission, I would personally wish to undertake the task."

"Then take them away, major." The three men of the triumvirate, as one, cast down their eyes to study the paperwork on their massive desk. There was no sound for a moment except that of Natalia sucking in her breath.

Chapter Eight

Rourke had attempted to resist as they were taken from the great marble hall, but a knife—his knife—had been placed at Natalia's throat and he had submitted.

They did not return to the artificial sunlight, but were taken down a long flight of stairs, the smell at the base of the stairs a mingling of dampness, sweat, and human fear. Rourke imagined the smell was maintained conscientiously.

With a knife to Natalia's throat, Rourke, still bound, was placed on an examining table, his wrists still bound. His legs were spread apart and his ankles were shackled to each side of the table, then the bindings at his wrists were cut and his arms shackled over his head, spread wide to the upper corners of the table, the table of immense proportions and of stainless steel or some similar substance. The female officer who had served as translator before the triumvirate had accompanied them, and her face seemed to be growing paler by the second. Kerenin spoke and she translated his words, expressionlessly. But Rourke watched Kerenin's eyes.

"Perhaps you believe that it will be possible to defeat the techniques we shall utilize. You will soon find that you are mistaken. In the interests of being humane, I shall warn you that resistance is futile. You will spare yourself considerable misery if you speak now."

Rourke focused his attention on remembering the way to say "Fuck you" in German. He heard Natalia's voice. Her voice was higher-pitched than normally, but otherwise firm. "We know nothing that would interest you. We will be happy to answer any questions, major. It is just that you choose arbitrarily to believe that our answers are lies. They are not."

They were, of course. And the lies they told were an integral part of the one faint hope Rourke clung to. That the torture session would be unrewarding to Kerenin and that he would think them incapable of further resistance and for one split second be sloppy enough that he—John Rourke—or Natalia could get to a weapon. And that meant surviving what would come next and clinging to the lies.

Kerenin had apparently ignored Natalia's remarks. He ordered her shackled to the second table. Rourke knew that Natalia's pain would be the hardest pain he would have to endure—and for her, his pain.

Rourke spoke once more. "We can make up lies, major. But you will see through them. We have only one truth to tell. And we have told it to you."

Kerenin spoke, the female officer's complection slightly green-tinged now. "I somehow feel that both of you have endured such as I offer now before. You believe. But you have never known pain or suffering such as the devices in this room are capable of inducing." No drugs then, Rourke thought. That was a plus for being able to maintain the lie. To have revealed that he was American and that she was once a major in the KGB but had come over to the cause of freedom would have invited no less torture and possibly instant execution. To have revealed the war which raged on the surface between the democratic allies—New Germany in Argentina, the Icelandics, Eden Base in what had been the United States, and the Chinese, the current enemies of these Russians—and the Soviet forces under the command of Marshal Vladmir Karamotsov, Natalia's husband, would only have precipitated the total destruction of the allies, the final suppression of freedom.

Kerenin spoke once more. "We shall now begin. When you feel compelled by your own suffering or the suffering

68

of your comrade to have the procedures brought to conclusion, all that is necessary is that you tell the truth."

Blocks of what appeared to be metal were brought to the table by one of the technicians who had been present in the sublevel chamber. The technician placed the blocks on either side of Rourke's head, two of the guards holding Rourke's head rigidly in their hands. At the far edge of his peripheral vision, he saw similar blocks being placed beside Natalia's head. Switches were activated on the blocks, bands of steel or some similar substance rising out of each block, Rourke feeling their coldness against the skin of his temples and forehead. The blocks were moved, then another set of switches worked.

The technician told the two guards they could release Rourke's head now, the other technician making slight adjustments to the bands which now almost touched at the center of Natalia's forehead, then giving similar instructions to the guards who held her. Rourke could not move his head, the blocks apparently locked magnetically to the table. Kerenin's voice sounded almost casual. "You are perhaps not familiar with the use of ultrasonics. Research began centuries ago into the processes by which high-frequency sound waves could be utilized to control the human mind and body. Simply by adjusting frequency and target area in the brain, we can make you do anything we wish. For example. You will now lose complete control of your kidneys."

Kerenin nodded. Rourke remembered how to say "Fuck you" in German and shouted it as the pain in his head started, then fiercer pain still in his back on either side of his spine, Rourke feeling the wash of moisture between his legs, the female translator turning her face away in disgust.

Rourke's body was shaking. "The woman you call your wife—why don't we see how responsive she is to direct sexual stimuli, hmm? Translate, lieutenant!"

The female officer haltingly tried to translate as Rourke, at the edge of his peripheral vision, saw Natalia's body begin slowly to move. Her eyelids fluttered. Her lower torso began moving rapidly now, her back arching. Kerenin laughed. He gave a gesture with his hand.

"Humiliation is even more effective than pain. But we can cause pain." The female officer translated, the sound of Natalia's breathing still heavy. Kerenin pointed to both Rourke and Natalia, Rourke barely able to see him. "Hopefully, you both have strong hearts." Kerenin nodded. This was a well-practiced routine, Rourke realized.

And suddenly, he felt it, a terrible headache behind his eyes and then something like a vise beginning to clamp ever more tightly around his chest. They were giving him a coronary occlusion. He tried to control his breathing, to tell his mind that this was all—"Aagh!" Rourke's body lurched as the vise tightened and his lungs could no longer suck air, his left arm numb with pain. Natalia screamed, her body going rigid, Rourke wanting to shout to them that he was a doctor and that in seconds, he knew, Natalia would die. Her normally pale skin was ashen, her mouth wide, gasping for breath. Rourke's body shook. He was telling himself these men who were doing this knew their jobs and would know just how far to go before death became inevitable. He was losing consciousness, the numbness in his left arm replaced with pain almost more intense than the pain in his chest. Natalia was screaming. Rourke started to speak—he could only gasp for breath.

And suddenly, the pain was gone. His body sagged downward. He sucked air, feeling himself start to hyperventillate, a green wash replacing his vision. Was this natural or something induced by their machinery? he wondered fleetingly.

Kerenin's voice, the no-longer-under-control voice of the female officer translating. "I could have let both of you die, or just one of you. Now—let us see what fears can be dredged out of your minds. I wish to see both of you consumed with fear."

The translation ended.

Rourke felt a sudden relaxing of his body, almost a calmness in his brain . . . He wondered if he were dead. He had read of out-of-body experiences of persons who had technically died on the operating table. And this was—He was over the chamber where he and Natalia were being tortured. He could see himself, see Natalia, see Kerenin standing almost directly under him, see the frightened and nauseated female translator, see Feyedorovitch in the far corner. Rourke could see the dark stains which covered the thighs of his faded Levis. There was a look of calm on his face, a look that somehow seemed very strange to him. Natalia was screaming, her body twisting, writhing, her face contorted in agony. John Rourke tried to move, to reach down to touch her. He could not move.

Whatever they were doing to him had stopped. Kerenin suddenly had a blowtorch in his hand. How did he get it? He was walking toward Natalia there on the table. He started moving the blowtorch toward her face. Rourke tried to shout. He couldn't shout, couldn't make a sound. He tried to close his eyes for an instant, to think. His eyes would not close, he could not think.

Kerenin moved the torch closer. Natalia screamed and the blowtorch touched at her eyes, and their incredible blueness was gone, flames licking upward, tongues of yellow and orange but tinged still with the blue of her eyes. And suddenly her face was consumed with flames, with flames, and Rourke felt tears welling up in his eyes. And now there were tables beyond the one on which Natalia had—had—had died. He could smell her flesh still burning as Kerenin moved on to the next table. Rourke's wife, Sarah, was there, her abdomen swollen with the baby he had given her. Kerenin brought the blowtorch toward her and then her clothes were gone and she was lying there on the cold table naked and he could feel her coldness and Sarah screamed as Kerenin touched the blowtorch to her abdomen. Rourke was trying to scream. He could not. Sarah's body was aflame and he could see the baby, on fire, the fire spreading over her body now, consuming her, consuming her screams. On the next table he saw his daughter, Annie, and her husband, Rourke's best friend, Paul Rubenstein, this table wider,

71

their bodies lashed to it together but their bodies not touching. Paul cursed at them, fought at his bonds. Annie was crying that her mommie and daddy were dead. Rourke's son, Michael, writhed on the next table, blood pouring from his wrists and ankles as he fought the shackles which held him to the table.

Rourke was paralyzed. He commanded his legs and arms to respond but they would not. He realized that if he spoke the truth, at least Annie and Paul and Michael would be saved. But he couldn't speak. A single phrase in English would do it and Kerenin, who was bringing the torch nearer and nearer to Annie's long, dark, honey-blonde hair, would stop the slaughter. Annie. She was shouting at Kerenin now, her eyes focusing on his face, a hardness in her eyes that he had never seen and Rourke could feel his daughter's mind, feel her cursing Kerenin with her dying breath, feel her mind assaulting Kerenin's mind. Kerenin's torch drew nearer and nearer, the sound of the gas jet as loud as a drum beating now—and as incessant.

Rourke tried to shout.

Annie's voice filled his head. "My body might die, you bastard, but you'll never kill my mind and my mind will destroy your mind, eat away at it until all you can do is whimper!"

Kerenin dropped the torch. The floor caught fire.

Kerenin's body was suddenly a living torch and Kerenin had three hands, Rourke's two knives and Natalia's Bali-Song hammering down toward Annie's face.

But she wasn't afraid.

Rourke could finally speak. He shouted, "Annie!"

Everything stopped, frozen, and the flames became the mists which enshrouded the edges of the lagoon where the submarine had surfaced and John Rourke's body was drenched in sweat.

Natalia's screaming had stopped.

John Rourke opened his eyes.

Kerenin was saying to Feyedorovitch, "At least we know that Anna is really the woman's name. He called to her in his fear."

"Should—should I—"

"Do not translate, lieutenant. Sit down over there."

"Yes, Comrade Major Kerenin."

"Comrade major," Feyedorovitch began. "You have gotten nothing except provoking this man to call out his wife's name. You do not even know she is his wife. Utilize the drugs, I suggest."

"I do not wish to utilize the drugs, captain. You are dismissed."

"As you wish, comrade major."

And over the sounds of his own breathing, John Rourke could hear Feyedorovitch's boot heels on the floor, hear the door shut closed.

Kerenin spoke up. "The ultrasonics are having little effect. They are both very strong, very much alike. We will weaken then, however. Clean up the man. He smells."

There were murmured answers. Rourke found Natalia at the edge of his peripheral vision. Her eyes were closed and her body was still. But her breasts rose and fell as she breathed and John Rourke closed his own eyes now as he felt them removing the blocks from the sides of his head. . . .

Kerenin spoke to her and the physically ill-looking woman translated. "I admire your stamina, your courage. But this will be used to bring about the ends I desire. The man—you see him clearly?"

John Rourke, stripped of his clothing, wrists bound, was suspended from a large hook at the center of a two-meter-diameter capsule, the capsule of something like plexiglas. Natalia's own hands were bound behind her and she felt them trembling. She nodded that she saw him. Three quarters of the capsule's circumference were bounded by the sea. Distorted by the plexiglas-like substance, she could view sea creatures, bizarre in shape, some almost transparent, some almost luminous. She realized that this Soviet underwater complex had to be at some tremendous depth.

Kerenin, through the translator, went on. "That is a decompression chamber, of sorts. You may be familiar with some of its uses. But we have a special use for it. We will slowly begin to equalize the air pressure to the pressure of the sea outside the wall of the capsule. As we do, your husband or whoever he is will be crushed to death. We utilized the ultrasonics to render him unconscious so he could not resist us when he was placed in the chamber. But now . . ."

Natalia looked at Kerenin. Kerenin gestured to a technician. The man stepped inside the open airlock of the capsule, approached John Rourke's naked body suspended there, and wiped John's left upper arm near the tricep. He placed a gun-shaped object against the muscle. She imagined it was something like adrenalin, to revive him. Blood trickled from the tricep and the technician wiped it away neatly, then left the capsule. The airlock was sealed.

"Now he will revive in order that he may be aware of his death agonies. But you have the power to stop this. We will increase the pressure by ten percent and you can watch his torment. We will then increase by two percent at a time. He is very strong, despite the ordeal you have both passed through. He could suffer for hours. But he will eventually reach a point that, even if the capsule is gradually depressurized to normal atmosphere, too much internal damage will have been done and he will inevitably die, or perhaps only be paralyzed. But, if you tell the truth to me in time, he will live. At least for now. Undamaged. Without pain. And if, after the use of truth drugs, I am satisfied with your story, even if he is executed, he will die quickly. I give you my word as an officer."

Kerenin signaled the technicians beside the airlock. And for the first time, Natalia saw the controls for the capsule. One of the technicians began adjusting a diode readout, then pressed a button.

There had to be microphones inside the capsule, because she could hear John Rourke scream over the wind sound of the inrushing air. . . .

Natalia Anastasia Tiemerovna, Major, Committee for State Security of the Soviet Union, had ceased to weep. No more tears remained to her and her eyes only burned and her head ached. She had been forced to stand perfectly erect and perfectly still for what she judged internally as at least an hour, watching as slowly the pressure on the body of the man she worshipped was increased. And he had long since stopped screaming with the pain.

But he was conscious, his face contorting in agony, his body suspended by his wrists, twisting, twitching, as if being hammered at by invisible fists. His hands were swollen and purpling and the veins in upper arms and forearms were distended, purpling as well. The third finger of his left hand would be the first to fully die because of the constriction from the ring he wore as a symbol of his marriage to Sarah Rourke.

So often, she had cried herself to sleep at night wishing that the ring had been worn because of her.

Kerenin whispered beside her, the translator taking up his words. "He is stronger than I had thought. But as we increase by another two percent, I think you will see something spectacular."

She closed her eyes.

She wanted to cry but there was nothing left in her. The fears that their ultrasonics had engendered in her—she had seen John Rourke dying at Kerenin's hands, at Vladmir—her husband's—hands. She had been totally alone in the world, everywhere she looked John Rourke dying; and then she had seen herself, as a very old woman, totally alone. And her loins had still ached for him.

She watched now as she knew she must.

John's body twitched and blood began trickling from both his nostrils and his head lolled back.

Kerenin spoke. "He will die or worse soon."

She answered Kerenin in Russian. "I am Major Natalia Anastasia Tiemerovna of the Committee for State Security of the Soviet Union. I am the wife of Marshal Vladmir Karamatsov, leader of the rebel armies of the Soviet State and operating now in China as part of a continuing war against the few surviving Americans, the government of New Germany in Argentina, and other allied democracies. My husband would sacrifice anything to get me back."

Kerenin spoke not at all for a moment, then, "He loves you."

"He wishes me dead because he is like you, an animal who feeds on pain, evil incarnate. And I chose to fight for what was right and reject the lies I had been taught from my birth. I am the niece of a true Hero of the Soviet Union, General Ishmael Varakov, Commanding General, North American Army of Occupation, following the Night of the War. I am the most valuable prize you will ever obtain. But I will find a way to kill myself, no matter how well you guard me, if you do not release him at once and give him the necessary medical attention."

Kerenin licked his lips. "You will freely submit to drug therapy?"

"Yes—but only if you release him immediately and see to his injuries."

"Who is this man if he is not your husband?"

"Release him, now!"

"First—who is he? Or there is no arrangement, Comrade Major Tiemorovna."

Natalia closed her eyes. She would focus all her mind on one lie only. And perhaps she could save him. "He is a German officer of intelligence. His name is Wolfgang, Colonel Wolfgang—" She searched for a name. She remembered the American soup. "Wolfgang Heinz."

"Bring the pressure to safe entry level and attend to the German officer, quickly. See to it that he is given the best medical attention!"

Kerenin's hands went to her shoulders, his finger tips gouging into her flesh beneath the fabric of her black jumpsuit. "If you lie to me, Major Tiemerovna, his death and yours will be more horrible than anything you could possibly imagine."

The truth was always the best lie, she had learned—at too early an age. She watched John Rourke and now the tears came again.

Chapter Nine

The German J7-V aircraft's subtle droning had lulled her to sleep and she had dreamed.

Annie Rourke Rubenstein sat staring out the window now, the J7-V coming in for its final approach at the boundaries of a strange city. It was called the First City, she knew, and was the disputed capital of China.

Her hands were balling tightly over her shawl and she stared at her hands. She released the shawl, folded it neatly, and placed it on the seat beside her. She crossed her legs, arranging the ankle-length full skirt. It was so dark a gray as to be almost black. She stared at it now. In her dream—and since the Sleep her dreams were not normal dreams, were increasingly more vivid when they occurred—she had seen her father, John Rourke, and Natalia Tiemerovna. They had been found on tables that were of some shiny metal and they were being hurt. She had felt pain. She had felt Natalia in a terrible, unending loneliness.

And when she had awakened from the dream, Annie had known that her father and Natalia were in the greatest danger of their lives and that death was very near to them, almost touching them.

She wanted Paul to hold her very tightly, very badly, very long.

He would not be waiting for her after she disembarked from the German aircraft. There would only be strangers, strangers told to treat her well, to protect her. Paul, her brother Michael, and some small force would be searching for her father and Natalia.

She had to contact them, tell Paul and Michael about her dream.

She closed her eyes, her hands clenched tightly in her lap.

Her mother had been having tea with Madame Jokli, the President of Lydveldid Island. She had asked to see her mother privately. Sarah Rourke had gone with her into the little garden off the library.

"What is it, Annie?"

Before the Night of the War, her mother had called her Ann, never Annie.

"I talked to Paul through a radio link the German commander set up for me. Daddy and Natalia—they're missing." She folded her mother into her arms, her shawl falling from her shoulders.

Sarah Rourke stammered, "What—ahh—"

"I don't know much about it, Momma—but there were signs of a fight, I guess, and they're just gone. Paul and Michael and some of the Chinese are going looking for them. I said I was coming—if you don't need me here?"

Her mother held her at arm's length, and Sarah Rourke's eyes were tear-rimmed. "If you think you can help. I—ahh—"

"You can't go, Momma—not with the baby."

Sarah Rourke's fingers splayed over her abdomen. She took Annie into her arms.

Annie looked out the window, the J7-V into vertical mode, nearly touched down. She picked up her shawl from the seat beside her. It wasn't one of the ones she had crocheted herself during the long years alone with Michael in the Retreat. It was one of the heavy ones, like the women in Iceland used when it was necessary to venture out of the protected environment of Helka or one of the other communities. She placed it on her lap. Beneath the shawl was her pistol belt, the Detonics Scoremaster .45 in one holster, the Beretta 92F military 9mm in the other.

The aircraft touched down.

She undid her safety belt and stood up, taking up the

pistol belt and securing it just below her natural waist. Annie raised her left foot to the level of the seat and hitched up her skirt and slip. When her father had returned from the Retreat he had brought her a present. He had told her it was one of the finest and most practical knives made before the Night of the War. He had given her a special sheath for it, pattered after the Bianchi Leg Holster but designed to carry a knife rather than a gun. It was secured both above and below her black-stockinged left calf, a Cold Steel Tanto. She let her skirt drop as she lowered her leg.

She picked up her shawl, the copilot of the J7-V smiling at her as he passed to open the exit hatch.

She slung her M-16 cross-body beneath her right arm and started from the aircraft.

Chapter Ten

Natalia Anastasia Tiemerovna sat in the chair. It was quite comfortable, really, or perhaps it was only her fatigue and lack of sleep and the tension which now—temporarily, she knew—had eased.

She had seen John Rourke as she had been brought here to Marine Spetznas Headquarters in the same dome as the Headquarters Building and its torture chamber. He had been resting quietly in the infirmary. She had checked his chart. She had enough knowledge of medicine from her own training at the KGB's Chicago School before the Night of the War, and additional training when once she had posed as a nurse in order to perform a termination, to realize that, according to the chart at least, John was being given appropriate care. Vitamin shots, a glucose IV, and mild sedation for rest. He seemed to have suffered no permanent ill-effects.

She had bent over his bed and touched her lips to his forehead, then gone on with Kerenin.

His office was very personal-looking, a Chinese assault rifle on the wall behind his desk, photographs of training companies along the walls, trophies, medals in glass cases.

The medical technician, a woman, was very gentle as she placed the IV. "Does that feel comfortable, comrade major?" The IV would regulate the flow of the truth drugs into her bloodstream.

"Yes—thank you," Natalia told her.

She had asked to be allowed to change from her perspiration-soaked, sand-filled clothes. She had asked for a dress. Dresses did not exist here. She had been given the blue uniform that the civilians wore. Or at least she assumed they were civilians. She had been allowed a shower, but there was no such thing as a hair drier. She had toweled her hair as dry as she could, and refused to wear the blue scarf that was part of the female civilian uniform.

Her shoulders and neck felt damp from her hair and she was slightly cold now.

And already, she could feel the truth drug starting to take effect. She focused on John Rourke/Wolfgang Heinz. She would protect John's identity—protect . . .

Kerenin's voice was very smooth, soft, gentle-sounding. "You claim that you are more than five centuries old?"

She had to be patient with him, Natalia reminded herself on one level of consciousness. "Of course not—we did not age in the cryogenic chambers, major."

"Explain to me what you remember of meeting this John Rourke whom you later joined. And why is he not here?"

She attacked the question immediately. "John Rourke is consulting with the German military high command concerning my husband's strategic posture. You must remember that John Rourke is unofficially considered the leader in the war effort against my husband and his armies. He is the man to whom they all look for courage and inspiration. If he were here—"

"The lighting device found on the person of this Colonel Wolfgang Heinz who accompanied you," Kerenin interrupted. "It bears the Roman letters J.T.R. and a word I am told might be pronounced 'Zippo.' "

"Many of the Germans still smoke."

"What is that?"

"The small cylinders of leaf material wrapped in white paper which I carried. They are cigarettes. I could use one now. The things Colonel Heinz carried are cigars." Her head ached when she thought of John Rourke/

Wolfgang Heinz. "You light them and inhale the smoke into your lungs."

"That is insane."

"It was a habit long years ago, and many of us still cling to it."

"What do the Roman letters and the word 'Zippo' refer to?"

There was a terrible pain behind her eyes. She had been taught to resist drugs. These were strange drugs. "Zippo is the manufacturer's name and the initials identify the lighter more specifically." To defeat a truth drug, one told the truth as much as possible, she had learned—how long ago?

"All right. Your guns—why do they have these birds on the barrels? I am told they are American symbols."

"They were given to me by Sam Chambers, who was the President of United States II."

"What is that?"

"A government formed after the death of the American President during the Night of the War or just afterward. It was headquartered near the border between Texas and Louisiana in the United States." The more truth she could tell, the better.

"How did you meet this John Rourke?"

Thank the Judeo-Christian God Kerenin didn't know John's middle name or he would never have believed the business about the lighter, she thought. Was there time for a prayer? A quick one. Help me, she prayed, help me to save this man who is Your best and brightest hope for the world. Amen. "Yes—I met John Rourke after the Night of the War."

"How?"

"There was a war. No one told us who initiated it. There was an ultimatum from the American President to our Premier."

"This Chambers person?"

"No—he was President after the other President died." She had to cling to the thread. "There was an ultimatum for us to leave Pakistan. We invaded from Afghanistan.

83

Someone ordered the missiles to be launched. We were never told who first launched, the Americans or ourselves. And after the Night of the War, my uncle, General Varakov, was given command of the Army of Occupation and he headquartered in Chicago, a city in the midsection of the United States. My husband was given command of the KGB for the United States. They never got along."

Her uncle and her husband had hated one another, her uncle a decent man, a good soldier, a loyal Communist.

"Vladmir had a list of people he wished killed or incarcerated, among them Sam Chambers, who was the only surviving member of the Presidential cabinet and the next man in line to become the President. My uncle wished him captured alive so that negotiations could get underway to stop the violence, because there was always resistance to us from the first. The American people enjoyed a constitutional right to keep and bear arms for their own defense, and we encountered armed resistance to our regime at every turn."

"Civilians possessed arms?"

"Civilians fought for their country and did themselves proud in the end."

"How did you meet Rourke?" Kerenin's voice insisted.

Natalia told him. "I went into the desert with a man named Yuri who was very adept at portraying Americans. We were set upon by men I later came to call Brigands. Outlaws. They killed Yuri and severely injured me. I killed them. John Rourke and his friend Paul Rubenstein were traveling from New Mexico to Georgia—those are states in the United States—by motorcycle, and they found me after my vehicle became disabled. I would have died otherwise."

"This Rourke is an American, I know. This Rubenstein?"

"Ohh, a fine American, major."

"How did they travel when you were discovered?"

"They traveled by motorcycle. It is like a car and a bicycle. A two-wheeled machine."

"Why did they travel during a war?"

"John is married to a woman named Sarah and they have two children, Michael and Annie. But they were allowed to grow up when John used the cryogenic chambers."

"You are getting ahead of yourself, Major Tiemerovna."

"John was searching for his wife and children and Paul was helping him. They became friends after the crash of the airplane."

"Airplane? You said they traveled by means of these motorcycles."

"On the Night of the War, John was in Canada, a country north of the United States. He was trying to return to his family in Georgia, and the airplane was diverted and the pilot and crew were unable to land the aircraft, and John did it. In New Mexico. The airplane was diverted that far. There were many people killed and many more injured. Paul told me about it all. John set out for Albuquerque, a town. A city. Paul and some other men went with him. To get help. The other men were more interested in saving themselves. Only Paul stayed with John. They found what they could to help and John—he is a doctor of medicine, you know?—worked at a hospital set up in a church—"

"What is a church?"

She told him. "A place that is usually quiet where you go to pray to God."

"God?"

"The Supreme Being who is the ultimate cause of the universe, some say. And He watches over us."

"What does one do when one prays?"

"You ask God for wisdom or strength or courage, you ask Him to help other people."

"A hospital—is this place where you pray?"

"There was a tremendous fire in Albuquerque and there were many burn victims. John and Paul helped however they could. Then they drove a car back to the airplane." And she started humming.

"What are you doing?"

"Paul told me they played a song by the Beach Boys, I

85

think, in the car."

"What are Beach Boys?"

"A singing group. For entertainment. They drove to the airplane."

"The singing group—no—"

"No—John and Paul. But Brigands had attacked the airplane and killed most of the people and kidnapped a stewardess."

"A what?"

"A flight attendant. Usually women. John and Paul fired at them and they escaped. John and Paul burned the bodies of the dead and then went after the Brigands. That was how Paul learned how to ride a motorcycle and shoot a gun. John and Paul faced about forty or so of them. But the woman they tried to rescue was killed. But John chased the killer down and killed him. Then they started to cross the country to get back to Georgia. And Paul had a family in Florida."

"And this is how Rourke and this other man found you?"

"In Texas. They took care of me, took me with them. I think John knew all the time that I was a Soviet agent."

"He found incriminating documents?"

"He was in the Central Intelligence Agency before that."

"What is this?"

She told him. "The CIA was like the KGB, in a way."

"Then he arrested you."

She shook her head and it made her head swim a little. "He helped me. He treated my wound. He restored my body. He shared everything with me. He and Paul. And then we met the Brigands who were raiding all the towns and, to save some prisoners, John fought some of them man-to-man and we pretended to join them. Then this other group came and there was a big battle and the helicopters came."

"A type of aircraft? Helicopters?"

"Yes—a type of aircraft. My husband's soldiers were in them and Paul had been hurt badly and John surrenedered so Paul wouldn't die."

"Then if he was captured, this Rourke—how is it that—"

"I promised they would be released. Vladmir would not release them. I helped them to escape. Vladmir punished me. My uncle tried to have Vladmir killed by John Rourke. And it almost worked. And then I was sent to Florida and—"

"What? You get ahead of yourself again."

"My uncle thought I needed a different assignment."

"What happened to Rourke?"

"We separated. I thought I would never see him again. I had fallen in love with John, you see. And he fell in love with me, but he still loves his wife and he is a very honorable man and so we were never able to . . ." Natalia started to cry.

Chapter Eleven

The Chairman, leader of the First City, had asked her to join him for breakfast. He had sent word by a messenger. Annie had told him that she would be honored, by messenger.

In her suite of rooms there were closets and they had been empty until she had hung in them the few things she had brought with her—a few extra blouses, an extra skirt. The other things—underwear, stockings, the cleaning kit for her handguns and her rifle, the whetstone for her knife—she had placed in the drawers of one of the two lovely dressers in the bedroom.

Another messenger had arrived, asking if she would honor the Chairman by accepting a small and unworthy gift. She had smiled and said yes. Women had returned a few moments later with their arms loaded with clothing. She had seen things like these—in the videotapes her father had stored at the Retreat, in picture books as a little girl, and to a degree among the few very pretty things Natalia had brought with her to the Retreat.

The woman in charge of the other women had told her to select however many or few items she wished. Annie had been unable to comprehend so many things because all of her adult life, with the exception of the time spent in Iceland, she had made all her own clothing. And the habit remained. In Iceland, she had begun making her own clothing again.

She had settled on six very pretty dresses, reasoning that to have taken less would have been rude and that there would never be any hope of taking more with her.

She stood in front of the full-length mirror now, studying herself. She had never seen herself look so—so—so sophisticated, she decided. It was a chong-san, if she remembered the right word. Of green silk—at least it felt like silk—it was sleeveless, high-necked, and came to the middle of her calves, but there was a deep slit up the side, halfway to her left thigh. And the stockings she wore, they were also silk. So was the underwear. Natalia had silk underwear, the only time Annie had ever seen silk.

She had arranged her hair atop her head, held in place with two things that looked like thin spikes and had large gemstones at one end and were very pretty. The stones were also green.

She wore no jewelry other than her wedding ring and her watch. She took off the watch, too mannish. She would never take Paul's ring from her finger.

Annie Rourke Rubenstein heard the knock at her door. "Just a minute!" she called out. The one problem with the dress was that there was no place to hide a gun. She had never gotten used to the idea of a purse, never owned one in her adult life. "Shit," she said under her breath. The gunbelt, aside from being bad manners, would look terrible with the green silk dress.

Annie sat down on the edge of the bed. If they wanted to kill her, they could have killed her while she slept. Or they could poison her at breakfast.

She stood up, opened one of the dresser drawers, and put her gunbelt and the leg sheath for the Tanto inside and closed it. Her father would be angry with her for going unarmed. She closed her eyes. There had been another dream. Her father was calm, she knew. And Natalia was struggling. She had tried contacting Paul. Michael. There was no way to contact them, their radios turned off, she had been told.

Annie stood up and walked to the door, sniffed, made a smile on her face—the lipstick tasted funny—and opened the door.

It was the Chairman himself. She had seen him from a

distance shortly after she had arrived.

"If I may speak with such boldness, you are very beautiful, Mrs. Rubenstein."

"And you are very flattering." She smiled. "There has been no word from my husband or my brother?"

"One can only assume, Mrs. Rubenstein, that all goes well in their attempt to penetrate the encampment of the Soviet leader and resolve this perplexing situation concerning the whereabouts of your father and the Russian woman who is his companion."

"One can only assume, sir."

"And now—please join me. It is a rare thing for me to breakfast with a woman so beautiful." He stepped back from the door and Annie stepped into the corridor, closing the door behind her. She had already made up her mind. If there was no news by midday, she would go after Paul and Michael herself. She could not take another dream.

Chapter Twelve

"How were you given these firearms with the birds you say are eagles?"

"They are American Eagles. Benjamin Franklin wanted the turkey to be the national bird of the United States."

"Who was Benjamin Franklin?" Kerenin asked her.

"A famous American; what they called a 'founding father.' "

"A turkey—it is another bird?"

"Yes."

"Tell me about the guns."

"I was in Florida," she told him. "And it was discovered that the Florida peninsula was about to fall into the sea. An artificial fault-line had been created during the Night of the War. John allowed himself to be captured in order to save as many people as possible by alerting the Cuban—"

"Ahh—Cuba. Our historic ally."

"What was I . . ." Her head wasn't aching as badly, but she was feeling mildly nauseous.

"About John Rourke coming to save people in this place called Florida."

"He came and no one wanted to believe him. And I realized that I had to. And I helped him and there was a massive evacuation. Why was I telling you this?"

"About your guns."

"The President," she said slowly, "of U.S. II gave them to me because he said he couldn't give a medal to me even if he had one."

"How did you escape the Americans?"

"No—the American President gave the guns to me and let me go. There were some people who wanted to—to hurt me. John didn't let them."

She didn't hear Kerenin's voice for a moment, then, "Major Tiemerovna. Tell me. How is it that you came to sleep for five centuries as you said earlier?"

"Vladmir had the Womb planned then Rozhdestvenskiy took it over."

"I do not understand," he said.

She was very tired. She tried to tell him. "After John killed Vladmir—"

"But you say your husband is still alive. Is this another Vladmir?"

"No—everybody thought that Vladmir was dead but some of his KGB Elite Corps personnel took him to the Underground City and—"

"Is this the Womb?"

"No," she answered and the nausea swept over her and she felt herself falling. . . .

John Rourke opened his eyes. He remembered seeing Natalia and then Sarah and the baby and . . . The fear. Kerenin had said that the ultrasonics would make fear possess them. John Rourke had learned his greatest fear's identity. That he would be powerless to prevent the destruction of those whom he loved. Natalia, his wife and their unborn baby, Annie and Paul, Michael. He closed his eyes and an involuntary paroxysm moved along his spine.

There was no need to open his eyes to confirm that he was in a hospital or infirmary. In five centuries, the smell of disinfectant had changed precious little from the days when he had been fresh out of medical school and worked in hospital emergency rooms. That was where he had first met Sarah, only to meet her again years later and marry her.

His secret fear. He knew that it was about to become

reality unless he could prevent it. To be powerless to defend the lives of the ones he loved, called family.

John Rourke tried to move. Every muscle in his body seemed to come instantly alive and simultaneously hurt.

He remembered now.

Some sort of decompression chamber or something like it. A tube and outside he had seen Natalia and he had shouted to her not to speak. That he was alive meant that she had evidently spoken.

Rourke opened his eyes and sat up. There was no guard at the foot of the bed. Hence, there would be a guard outside the door.

He was naked except for a hospital gown. Something else that hadn't changed in five centuries.

Time was of the essence, as the expression went, but a movement too fast might well cause him to pass out. So, very slowly, John Rourke began to move his legs toward the edge of the bed. If he could kill the guard or guards outside the room door, then he could steal a uniform and a weapon, perhaps more than one weapon, then commence to turn things around in one manner or another.

His feet were just over the edge of the bed. The door opened. In the doorway stood two uniformed guards with Sty-20 pistols aimed at him, and between them a medical technician with what passed these days for a hypodermic. Medication? Sedation? Execution?

His watch was still left to him. He had read a novel once in which the hero used his Rolex wristwatch as an improvised set of brass knuckles. But a diving watch might prove invaluable if indeed there were some means of escape, and any value the Rolex would have possessed as a weapon would be essentially lost after its first use. And there were three of them but only one Rolex.

Rourke asked in German, "What is this?" And he gestured to the facsimile hypodermic.

"I do not understand your German language," the medical technician said in the same, curiously sterile Russian Rourke had heard used by all his captors.

The medical technician came closer. Rourke lowered his

93

head, as if groggy, and it was partially true. At the far left corner of his peripheral vision he could see the medical technician nearing him, the two guards ever so slightly lowering their pistols.

John Rourke accelerated his breathing. He needed oxygen in his system. His fists balled tight.

The medical technician said, "Poor fellow. If you could only understand that I am not going to hurt you. A vitamin shot—relax."

John Rourke respected his own profession, no matter who practiced it, as long as it was practiced with compassion. He would not kill this one.

He felt the man's hand at his left upper arm.

John Rourke moved his right hand.

He caught the medical technician's right wrist. Rourke was to his feet, twisting his body a half turn left, snapping the medical technician fully around, Rourke's left forearm at the man's throat, both guards reacting, the muzzles of their Sty-20s rising, Rourke hearing the pneumatic pops as he threw the medical technician toward them, then leaped over the bed, rolling, to his bare knees hard on the cold floor, the medical technician impacting the two guards.

John Rourke was up, moving, his left hand smothering the Sty-20 of the nearest of the two guards, sweeping the weapon downward and away from his own body plane, his right fist crossing the guard's jaw hard, slamming the man against the closed door behind him. Rourke's right hand closed over the guard's gun-hand wrist and he snapped the gun hand upward, Rourke's body twisting, his right shoulder beneath the man's right arm near the elbow. Rourke threw his weight to the floor, the sound of the forearm and elbow snapping almost as loud as a pistol shot, the Sty-20 clattering to the floor.

Rourke flexed his knee toward an upright position, his left elbow hammering back and left, searching for a target. He found what felt like an abdomen, wheeling half left as he let the first guard fall, screaming. Rourke's right arm snapped back and forward, the heel of his right hand impacting the second guard at the base of the nose, breaking it, driving the bone through the ethmoid bone and into the brain, the man's brown eyes locked open in death as his body snapped into the door.

The medical technician—he was starting to his feet, despite at least one instantly visible dart from an Sty-20 in his right chest. Rourke's left fist curled into the front of the man's uniform, drawing him up, Rourke's right fist gently but firmly crossing the man's jaw. Rourke eased him to the floor.

He turned around. The first guard was moving. John Rourke reached down to him, to kill. But there was no reason. He raised to his full height and his bare left foot snapped out, the edge of it catching the first guard at the tip of the chin, the man's head snapping back. Alive.

Rourke glanced at his watch. Less than a minute. If there were a guard in the corridor still . . . But already, Rourke had one of the Sty-20s in his right fist, visually and tactilely feeling for the controls. Magazine release. Gas-cartridge release. Safety. He slowly dumped the magazine. It was transparent plastic and there were nineteen rounds left in this one—Sty-20, he realized. The rounds loaded in the magazine looked almost like conventional 9mm Parabellum cartridges, but where a primer should have been there was what appeared to be a gas-inlet valve of diminutive proportions. The gas cylinder somehow charged the individual shells as they were fired—or perhaps as they were chambered, but that was doubtful. Then some mechanism—there was no time to be more precise—caused the gas in the charged cartridge to be released, propelling the dart, which was evidently contained in some sort of sabot, down the barrel (rifled), the excess gas opening the action and ejecting the spent shell. There was a shell casing on the floor near his feet. He replaced the magazine and turned the pistol toward the bed and fired at the pillow. The plopping sound. No recoil at all.

He would have preferred a real gun.

He took up the second pistol, checked its magazine.

One missing as well. He assumed from his observations that the guns were normally loaded with a twenty-round magazine and it was habitual to keep one round in the chamber.

Neither guard carried anything on his gunbelt which looked like a spare magazine or spare gas cylinder.

Rourke glanced at his watch, his internal clock confirming what the Rolex revealed in analog form—another thirty seconds elapsed. He could not hope to escape in the hospital gown. A quick search of the only cupboard in the room revealed his Levis, freshly washed as he had been. He put down the Sty-20s near him on the bed, quickly ripping away the hospital gown, skinning into his freshly washed underpants, his Levis, his shirt, not buttoning it, zipping the fly of his jeans. To have taken one of the guard uniforms would have been impossible, both men several inches shorter than he, the medical technician the tallest of the three Russians and skinny as a wraith. Rourke stuffed his socks into his pockets, stepping into his combat boots, lacing them up only high enough to stay on, then tying them. He grabbed his handkerchief. There was nothing else.

Taking up both pistols, he started for the door, placing the left one under his right arm, not trusting the safeties of these unfamiliar weapons sufficiently to attempt a holsterless waistband carry even for a few seconds.

The door opened easily under his left hand, John Rourke running his fingers back through his hair, taking the second pistol into his fist and cautiously peering into the corridor.

There was some movement to his left, none to his right, and what appeared to be a dead-end corridor. This was evidently not a hospital but infirmary or infirmary wing habitually reserved for prisoners—the thought of why that was so did not cheer him.

To his left was the way to go. He stepped into the corridor and started walking along on the near side to take advantage of the doorways he passed as marginal cover if that became necessary. Both pistols were along his thighs, held close. Hospitals were busy places, and busy people were generally poor observers, and, not expecting to see a man carrying two pistols, would be less likely to notice if they were carried unobtrusively. He hoped.

John Rourke kept walking.

It would clearly be a case of shooting his way out—to where, he was not certain. But once he was noticed, that would be the only way. Eighteen rounds in one pistol, nineteen in the other, including the chambered rounds. He had no idea of range or practical accuracy, but he doubted either was substantial, certainly in conjunction with the other. He kept moving, having gone half the length of this portion of the corridor, toward the technicians who moved about near what appeared to be a nursing station.

He passed a doorway and the door opened. A man—perhaps a doctor but more likely an orderly from the sheer bulk of the man's muscular arms. The man started to open his mouth to shout, reaching for John Rourke's throat. Rourke fired each pistol as he took a step back, both from the hip, one dart entering the man's left cheek, the second impacting above the right clavicle.

The shout started to come, then died a gurgling death as the man's body slammed hard against the door frame and slipped into a rather ungainly-looking kneeling position. The sedative effect of the darts apparently was directly related to adrenalin, and this man's rush had not come quickly enough to keep him going.

Rourke noted the shooting characteristics of both hand-guns when fired at hip level and kept going, stepping over the man.

He was another two doorways down when he heard the scream from behind him. He wheeled toward the sound. A woman in a hospital gown. To have shot her with one of the sleep darts would have been purposeless and, if she were a patient as indeed she appeared to be, possibly fatal if conflicting drugs were already in her system or she had some cardiovascular difficulty. Instead, John Rourke broke into a dead run.

She screamed again.

He kept running, nearing the nursing station now, two men and a woman starting toward him from its far side. He shot the woman—the rational way to save on ammunition, which would run low shortly—hopefully convincing the two men he would shoot them too.

He reached the end of the corridor, turning left away from the nursing station, hoping for a stairwell or even an elevator shaft.

There was a stairwell, but there were a half-dozen uniformed guards running from it, each of them with an Sty-20 in his fist. Rourke opened fire, downing one of the men instantly with a shot from each pistol, pumping two from the pistol in his right fist into a second man, a third man lunging for him, Rourke backstepping and firing point blank into the man's neck with the pistol in his left fist. Rourke felt something stinging at his left thigh. He shoved the pistol from his left hand into his trouser band, no time for precautions now, tearing the dart from his leg, firing the pistol in his right hand three times into the chest of an oncoming guard. Another dart hit him in the right forearm, Rourke already feeling the effect of the drug as he kept firing, downing another man, tearing out this dart.

The sixth man fired from point-blank range too, a clean miss. Rourke did a double tap with each pistol, and he didn't miss. The man staggered, reeling toward the stairwell, falling and disappearing over the railing. Rourke dropped to his knees.

He shook his head, to his feet now, moving toward the stairs. His head ached and he felt suddenly cold and nauseous, sweat breaking out from his palms, over his upper lip. He inhaled, trying to fight it with oxygen. He fell to the floor, just turning his shoulder into the fall in time to avoid taking the impact with his face. He rolled onto his back. Three or four hospital personnel were advancing toward him—he couldn't be certain, his vision blurring.

He rolled onto his stomach. To his knees. He stood, his body swaying side to side. John Rourke turned toward the medical technicians, a pistol locked in each fist. They stopped, edging back now, drawing back and away from him.

John Rourke felt it start to go, his knees buckling. He remembered to say it in German as the pistols fell from his weakening hands. *"Schiess."*

Chapter Thirteen

Why had Kerenin stopped asking her questions? She wanted to ask him, but then he was asking her questions again.

"You fell in love with this American spy named Rourke then. Why?"

"He is the finest man I have ever known."

"That is absurd," Kerenin said.

Natalia laughed. It felt nice to laugh. "The Greeks and Romans told stories about the days when gods walked on the earth. One god still walks on the earth and he is a man. His name is John Rourke." She realized she was giggling. She tried to remember when the last time was that she had giggled. Not in the ballet. Because they never wanted you to be anything but serious.

She tried to remember if she could still put her hands together in front of her and make the thing that looked like a bubble.

She put her hands together, cupping one in the other. "See my bubble." She giggled.

"Major Tiemerovna—tell me about the end. Before the skies were consumed with flame."

"All right." She smiled. "Well, you see, John is a very special person and Rozhdestvenskiy, the bad man who took over from rotten Vladmir, well, he had these cryogenic chambers, see, and he had all this serum. It was to keep him alive so he could be the czar of the entire earth when everybody woke up again. And my Uncle Ishmael—he got this nice officer and his sergeant and his men to help us and we all got together with this man named Reed—but he was a grouchy man—and we all attacked the place where Rozhdestvenskiy was hiding and . . ." She lowered her voice and giggled. "We took it!"

"What?"

"His serum, silly, and we escaped and Reed—do you know what he did?"

"No. What did he do?"

"He took Rozhdestvenskiy's mountain and he blew the whole thing up like this!" And she clapped her hands over her head and shouted, "Boom!"

Kerenin's voice sounded grouchy too. "So you took this serum and at the place Rourke called the Retreat you used it. Correct?"

"Correct! You are very smart."

"Thank you, Major Tiemerovna. You are very beautiful."

She giggled again.

"Now," he said, "tell me just what happened at the very end."

She drew her legs up under her and sat on her heels. "It was really exciting but it was very sad. It was. We made up injections for everybody in the Retreat. Michael got one. He was so cute. And Annie. She got one too. And Paul and Sarah and me. And I fell asleep and I slept for five hundred years!" She giggled again. "But John—what he did was he climbed out onto the mountaintop and he shot it out with Rozhdestvenskiy, see. Bang! Bang! Bang! Just like that. And John won and he got inside again before the fires burned him all up because the fires were burning the air and everything. And he woke up early and he woke up Michael and Annie and he lived with them for five years and taught them everything he could and then he went back to sleep. Like this, see?" She put both her hands together, palm to palm, fingers extended, then cocked her head to the right and closed her eyes and leaned against them. It felt nice to pretend to sleep.

"Then what?"

"Annie and Michael grew up and Michael went off to look for the Eden Project, and when he didn't come back Annie woke up because she had a bad dream and Sarah—was she angry! Because her little boy and little girl were all grown up now, you know? And Paul and John and I—we went after Michael and we rescued him. Know from what?"

"No. Tell me, Natalia."

"Cannibals. Uh-huh—that's what they were. Cannibals. They ate people. And there were some crazy people who sent people out to be killed by the cannibals and we sort of rescued Michael from them too. And that's where Michael found Madison. He rescued her—but it didn't do any good at all. Madison died." And Natalia started crying.

Chapter Fourteen

Michael Rourke moved slowly forward on knees and elbows, his neck arched to keep his face out of the snow, Paul Rubenstein beside him, ahead of them the lip of a precipice which, if German high-altitude observation data were correct, should directly overlook the encampment of Marshal Vladmir Karamatsov's armies.

They had left backpacks, assault rifles, and most of the rest of their gear some 500 yards back along the route to the top, with Han and Maria Leuden and Otto Hammerschmidt and the small force of German commandoes.

Michael Rourke kept moving, Paul whispering beside him, "Someday we have to find a warmer climate to do this stuff in."

Michael smiled only, kept going.

He reached the edge of the precipice a second or so before Paul, already unlimbering the German binoculars as he stole his first look.

The encampment stretched for acres, crescent-shaped and following the natural pattern of the terrain. The snow seemed less heavy in the lower elevation of the encampment, at least at first glance. To the rear of the encampment was sheer rock face, and beneath and beyond it the sea, whitecaps whipped in what appeared to be a vigorous wind.

Michael button-adjusted focus, the rangefinder giving precise distance to the center of the camp as he focused on it. Hermetically sealed tents were almost everywhere and, where they were not, there were trucks and armored

103

personnel carriers. He could not discern the command tent immediately. He kept moving the binoculars. "Look all the way to your left," Paul whispered beside him. Michael swung his binoculars to the north. A helicopter pad, one helicopter rising in a swirl of snow and ice spicules, two dozen more helicopter gunships anchored against the wind. More would be airborne. "He must have a hell of a lot of that synthetic fuel," Paul observed. Michael nodded. "If we could get to that and destroy it, we'd have him trapped with his back to the sea."

"My dad never said Karamatsov was a brilliant tactician," Michael noted. "But before we can take a try at that . . ."

He let the sentence hang, no need to state the obvious.

"We're gonna have to get down there, Michael. And I don't think either one of us picked up enough Russian from Natalia to be able to understand very much of what's going on."

Michael put down the binoculars and closed his eyes for an instant. He opened them. "Maria. Before the Night of the War, the Russians did quite a bit of archaeological research. She has a reading knowledge. Maybe between us—damn."

Michael Rourke looked at Paul Rubenstein. The smaller man nodded, his face—the torque pulled away and his ears reddening with exposure to the wind and cold—grim and hard-set.

Michael took up his binoculars again. If Karamatsov were at all smart, he would make the command tent as indistinguishable as possible from any other, a wolf hiding amid the flock in the event of aerial attack. But Karamatsov would be near enough to the helipad that he could reach it rapidly in the event that survival became his most important concern. "The command tent," he began. "It has to be near the helipad. Look for the most innocuous thing you can find."

Michael kept scanning the encampment below them.

Then Paul spoke. "Check out the hospital tents. The smaller one in the middle."

Michael shifted his gaze, refocusing, taking a new distance reading. One of the hospital tents, set almost in the exact center of the others, yet with totally unobstructed access to the helipad, had two guards stationed near the opening, one on either side of it. Portable deflection barriers were installed around it and guards stationed at regular intervals ringed it.

"You have a good eye," Michael told his brother-in-law and friend.

"Which one—the right or the left?"

Michael Rourke reached out his left fist and gently punched Paul Rubenstein's right shoulder. "Touché."

"How are we gonna get in there? I found it; you figure that one out," Paul whispered, his voice holding a hint of amusement.

"Standard thing, I guess. How'd my father and Natalia get into the Womb just before the Great Conflagration?"

"You know how."

"Then we'll get some Russian uniforms and play it by ear. And if we're wrong and Dad and Natalia aren't there, we'll find out where they are. And I can get Karamatsov."

"You'll get him, Michael. But maybe not yet."

Michael Rourke didn't speak. Of greatest importance was finding his father and Natalia. Then killing the man responsible for the death of his wife, Madison, and their unborn child. That would be dessert.

Chapter Fifteen

John Rourke's hands were bound behind him and a length of the plastic restraint was around his throat, his neck held arched back with it by the hand of one of the two guards who flanked him close. Natalia Anastasia Tiemerovna, her head aching, her mouth dry, her insides feeling as if her period were a week overdue when in reality it had just passed, spoke to him quickly in German. "Wolfgang. I revealed my identity as a Russian, and yours as a German officer—I am—"

"Quiet!" Kerenin clamped his hand over her mouth.

John, looking as though he was barely able to smile, tried breaking away from his captors. The one guard drew back hard and fast on the cord around his neck, the other punching him in the left kidney. He dropped to his knees, his lips drawn back from his teeth, his high forehead glistening sweat, his eyes glaring toward Kerenin as he coughed, sounding as though he were choking.

Kerenin took his hand from her mouth and she screamed at the Russian. "You promised he would not be hurt!"

"I promised he would be given the best medical attention and he was. He then killed one guard, injured another, and nearly beat one of the medical technicians to death. He escaped his compartment in the Marine Spetznas hospital and shot several guards and hospital technicians with Sty-20s he had stolen. He would be dead at my hands now if it were not that I promised you. His fate is no longer under my control, Major Tiemerovna—

and . . ."

Kerenin fell immediately silent, the triumvirate entering the marble-floored, marble-walled room, unceremoniously seating themselves at the long desk she had seen before.

She looked at John. He had been dragged to his feet, the cord still tight around his throat. He smiled at her, as if to say that somehow everything would be all right. But she knew; this time, it wouldn't be all right. And she was suddenly chilled more deeply than she had ever been chilled.

Kerenin urged her forward, her hands again bound behind her.

John moved forward, no longer fighting them.

The female intepreter was again present.

The man at the center of the triumvirate spoke, the woman beginning the translation—unnecessary though it was—for John. "You have both been adjudged enemies of the State. By her own words, this self-proclaimed former comrade has outlined the systematic betrayal of the ideals of Communism, the Soviet State. If her claims of somehow surviving since before the vicious and unprovoked attack by what was called the United States against the people of the Soviet Union is true, she is personally and collectively responsible for countless deaths, unnumbered acts of sabotage and espionage. And this man is an officer in an enemy force which seeks to destroy Communist forces this woman tells us exist in force on the surface of the planet. He is an intelligence officer, and therefore a spy. The penalty for espionage, of course, in time of war, is obvious. The woman—if her story is true, there could be no penalty horrible enough to properly punish her.

"We are told that she claims that the husband she betrayed for the love of an American . . ." He consulted his notes. ". . . named John Rourke is also alive and is the commander of Soviet forces even now fighting an imperialist alliance bent on the complete obliteration of Soviet Communism. If she tells the truth, it might be useful to the welfare of the State to meet with this Marshal Karamatsov and work with him to advance the cause of

107

Communism on the surface. To that end, it is the judgment of this triumvirate that the woman, who calls herself Natalia Anastasia Tiemerovna, Major, Committee for State Security of the Soviet Union, be held in an appropriate location until such time as contact has been achieved with Marshal Karamatsov and the transfer of this woman to his custody can be effected."

Natalia wanted to scream. And then she wanted to cry. And then to die. She stood perfectly erect, shoulders back and lowered, her chin raised, her eyes unwavering as they stared ahead.

"It is the further judgment of this triumvirate that the man, identified as Wolfgang Heinz, Colonel of Intelligence, the Army of New Germany, shall be taken to the customary place of execution immediately and there shall be meted out the reward for his crimes. You are both allowed a brief final statement."

Natalia spoke quickly, before John could speak and implicate himself still further and perhaps try to save her. "This German intelligence officer has valuable information which my husband would wish to possess. If you kill him, you will anger Marshal Karamatsov. He—"

Kerenin interrupted her, shoving her back. "Comrade Chairman. It is clear the woman wishes to bargain for time."

John spoke, his Russian as faultless as she had ever heard it. "I am John Rourke. And any crimes you claim this woman had committed were done at my order. If there is any punishment to be meted out, I am the one deserving of it. She is—"

Kerenin had nodded, and the cord around John's neck was snapped back so tightly he was forced to his knees, gagging, his face purpling. Natalia tried to move toward him, the two guards who stood beside her grabbing her at the upper arms and shoulders, holding her back. And she realized that if she could convince them, perhaps John would live long enough that . . . "Comrade Chairman! I must speak!"

"Speak," the man said emotionlessly.

108

Kerenin nodded. The pressure on her arms was released. She took a tentative pace forward. "He is John Rourke. I lied to protect him, but I see now that—"

Kerenin shoved her aside. "It is clear, Comrade Chairman, that the woman lies in order to save her own comrade. This man—" and he gestured broadly to John, John on his feet again, but the cord still so tight at his throat that his face was discoloring, "—could not be John Rourke. She told of a man of virtually superhuman abilities, not a common ruffian such as this. I am convinced, comrades," and he addressed them all now, all three of their judges, "that this man is only a German officer. And I am further convinced that this John Rourke of whom she speaks even now works for the undoing of our system. I am convinced that such a man would not be so easily taken. This man—" He stabbed his right first finger toward John. "—must die!"

Natalia fell to her knees, tears welling up in her eyes. "I beg you. All of you. Kill me, or give me to my husband, but—"

"Natalia!" It was John's voice, shouting at her, but she didn't look back, his shout choked off.

"I am guilty of all you have said. I will accept any punishment. But do not kill this man. Please. Oh, please." And Natalia crawled nearer to the desk on her knees.

"Nata—"

She kept crawling toward the desk and when she was as near to it as she could get, the tears flowing freely now, she lowered her head to the floor, her forehead against it. "Please. Please. *Please*—"

She was jerked to her feet, Kerenin's left fist knotted in her hair, her head pulled back unnaturally far, her neck aflame with pain. His eyes bored into her, and she realized that he knew and he didn't care. "The woman is very convincing, comrades. I too have learned this. Request permission to carry out the execution of the German officer Wolfgang Heinz."

"Granted," the Chairman intoned. "And take her away.

I suggest a constant guard that she does not attempt to take her own life."

"Very good, Comrade Chairman, comrades." Kerenin looked at her once again.

She whispered to him, "I'll do anything you ask me to do—anything—please—do not kill him." He let go of her and she dropped to her knees at his feet. She could hear John behind her, struggling with the man who held him. Natalia Anastasia Tiemerovna touched her lips to Kerenin's right boot.

He dragged her up to her feet by her hair. His left hand crashed against her cheek and she fell to the floor.

The guards were hauling her up.

She saw John one more time. She would always know he had loved her. . . .

"You know who I am."

"If I did, I would not say that I knew."

"You want Natalia. But all her husband wants is to murder her in the cruelest way possible. You are playing a loser's game."

Kerenin stopped, drawing Rourke's Crain LS System X knife and placing its point against Rourke's throat. He told the guards, "Wait for us ahead, now!" And the guards moved ahead, leaving Kerenin and John Rourke in the corridor leading from the hall where the triumvirate had passed the sentence of death on Rourke. "If you move, your throat is cut."

"I know that. And you will know you are killing the only prisoner you could possibly have for Karamatsov more valuable than Natalia."

"Yes." Kerenin smiled. He looked down at his hand, which held the knife, then into Rourke's eyes. "I am afraid that I have never been more strongly attracted to a woman in my life than to Major Tiemerovna. I must possess her, even if for a short time. You should be happy. Perhaps I will be so moved that I will find some way of saving her from her fate."

110

"If I thought you could . . ." Rourke let the sentence hang.

"She will hate me for supervising your execution. But perhaps her hate can turn to something else. At least it is a strong emotion."

"Take her to the surface. Find my son. Tell him you saved her life. He is a man of honor and will see to it that you are not harmed. Do not give her to her husband."

"You love her as much as she loves you. Fascinating."

Rourke didn't say anything.

Kerenin did. "I have taken it upon myself to keep a promise, in a manner of speaking. I am showing you mercy in the only way I can. Personally, I would prefer your death to be the worst possible. But, for the sake of Major Tiemerovna, I am electing the alternate form of execution available. I have, of course, taken the time to obtain proper authority for doing so, on a pretext. You have much to thank me for, but little time in which to do it. Keep in mind that I would enjoy personally killing you."

"I will keep that in mind. And may I extend the same wishes."

Kerenin smiled. "From the way she spoke of you, I must say I had anticipated more."

"We all have our bad days." Rourke smiled. "But in the event I should survive, where did you put my guns and my other knife? And, while you are at it, where will you be keeping Natalia?"

"You are trying to live up to the image of infallibility painted of you by Major Tiemerovna. Very good! Why not? She will be in the command module where we are now. In the building on the far left as you enter through the causeway. On our right, as we stand here. And your guns? I would imagine they are in the security complex which is in the main city. The dome furthest away from the submarine pens where you entered the city. You cannot miss it. Any other questions, my friend?"

"How are you going to kill me?"

"Please—leave something for expectation. You will

111

learn soon enough. But now, move ahead. The guards grow restless." He prodded gently with the knife, still at Rourke's throat, and Rourke started ahead, the cord still looped about his neck—he imagined in the event he tried to resist—and his wrists bound behind him with the seemingly unbreakable plastic restraints.

Natalia—she had wept after she had kissed Kerenin's foot to beg for his, John Rourke's, life. He looked at Kerenin once.

Rourke inhaled, exhaled, walked ahead in the company of the guards, two on either side of him, two in front and in back, all Marine Spetznas, all with their Sty-20 pistols drawn. He knew well by now the inevitability of the effect from the darts the Sty-20s fired.

They returned to the artificial sunlight, Rourke squinting against it. One of the Gullwing cars awaited and Rourke ducked his head as he entered behind three of the guards, Kerenin placing himself in the seat just aft of the driver. Kerenin ordered the driver to take them to the pens.

John Rourke didn't like the sound of that, but he liked nothing else here either.

His head ached and he was stiff, the ache the result of having eaten nothing in more than twenty-four hours. But the effect of the drug used in the Sty-20 pistols seemed at least moderately cumulative. He shook his head, wiggling his toes inside his boots, moving his fingers behind him, trying to increase his circulation and burn off the drug as much as possible.

The Gullwing passed through the deactivated energy barrier, the armored personnel carriers and other vehicles behind them now.

He would have one chance at best, and, if he failed, Natalia would die and the world of the surface would be in deadly peril. He would have to make his one chance work to fullest advantage. He began deep breathing, careful that in his debilitated condition he would not begin to hyperventilate. He closed his eyes, summoning energy first to one part of his body, then to another, focusing his concentration on the inner self, cleansing his mind of all but his single purpose and its multifaceted goals.

He felt the motion of the Gullwing, subtle, letting his body rhythm blend with it, the idle, subdued chatter of the guards pushed from his mind.

A quietness came over him, peace. His breathing evened.

The vehicle stopped. He felt the change of rhythm. Slowly, John Rourke opened his eyes.

There was a pneumatic-sounding thwack as the gullwings opened. Kerenin was already stepping out onto the curb. Three guards, then Rourke followed in their train.

The artificial sunlight, however it was generated, was strong here. And he smelled seawater very strongly. Beyond the walkway, there were massive doors and lettered above them in cyrillic the words "People's Institute for Marine Studies."

The guards fell in around him. He asked Kerenin casually, "Taking me for an outing to the aquarium?"

Kerenin laughed. "You might say that, you might indeed.

They entered into a high-ceilinged, formal hall, a bank of elevators at the far right. Kerenin started for them, saying something to one of the guards, the man jogging ahead to signal on the elevator call-button panel.

An elevator, not unlike the one aboard the submarine, opened, Kerenin stepping inside and waiting beside the interior panel, the guards still surrounding Rourke, their guns drawn, Rourke standing at the approximate center of the elevator, waiting for the movement to start. It did, noticeably downward.

The elevator stopped. "Are we below the level for the main portions of the dome?"

Kerenin laughed. "You are incorrigible. Yes—yes, we are. Come—there is more of the tour before—well, before." Kerenin stepped into a dank-smelling, fishy-smelling metal-walled antechamber, three guards, then Rourke after him, the other three guards behind him, then one

113

from in front and one from the rear falling in on either side of him, their Sty-20s pointed at him almost casually.

They began walking down a long corridor, wide enough for two trucks to pass one another easily, watertight doors lining it on the right every few yards.

"We are passing beneath the Institute for Marine Studies and will soon be entering a special section. You are very fortunate. This is a maximum-security area you will be entering."

"I'm flattered." Rourke kept altering his stride to work muscle groups differently, flexing his upper and forearms, moving his fingers, loosening his shoulders as subtly as he could.

At the end of the long corridor there was a more massive watertight door, and beside it something that looked like an alarm switch. Kerenin signaled one of the guards to activate it. It proved to be nothing more than a doorbell. Television cameras mounted over the watertight door—he had noticed cameras in other portions of the complex as well—buzzed and hummed, scanning.

Kerenin identified himself and there was a different sound, like a burglar alarm, but of short duration, the watertight door opening, then swinging outward. Kerenin stepped over the flange, three guards, then Rourke following him, Rourke glancing over his left shoulder at the other three guards.

He looked ahead then, a comparatively narrow walkway at his far left, and directly ahead and extending well away to his right a huge pool.

The interior guards waited at their posts, Kerenin leading the way, the six guards surrounding John Rourke staying in formation as Rourke followed them.

Kerenin began to speak as they took to the walkway at the left. "It is a merciful death which awaits you."

"Thank you."

Kerenin went on, saying, "To guard against the actions of enemy divers, sharks are kept, a great variety of them. Electrodes are implanted in the cortexes of their brains, as I understand it. I am not a science technician. But the sharks are controlled by a central command console. They serve as guards against unwanted intrusion."

"Just fascinating," Rourke told him. He was working to build a scenario and no opportunity could be missed, however meager.

Kerenin turned off the walkway and approached the pool. "Of course, there are other sea creatures perhaps equally as vicious, and sharks as well, none of which are under our control. But when work is being performed outside the domes of the complex, or when the implants are being checked or some reprogramming is required, the sharks which we do control are penned inside here. Beyond those gates." Kerenin extended his hands over the water. Rourke smiled at the Biblical allusion it suggested. There were massive steel or steel-like gates at the far end of the Olympic-length pool.

"And is this their exercise yard?" Rourke asked.

Kerenin smiled. "You might say that. The sharks are programmed to kill; but, of course, they will kill of their own volition, which is why it is sometimes necessary to bring them in." The water of the pool was calm, the surface perfectly quiet. Kerenin turned away from the water, facing Rourke, who now stood behind him. "The prescribed means of execution, lest you think me to be deceiving you, is far worse than this. The sharks will make quick work of you. The other means is ejection into the sea through a missile tube, hands and feet bound and an oxygen breather attached to your mouth. You are crushed to death by the pressure, the internal organs destroyed—a horrible death, I understand."

"Yes—much nicer to be devoured by hungry sharks. I assume you keep them hungry enough, titilate them with human blood in the water?"

Kerenin smiled. "You are the cool one—or so you would have me believe. But I essentially promised Major Tiemerovna that a pressure tank would not be used to kill you, and the preferred method is very similar."

"Rather like Jehovah promising Noah he would never again end the earth by flood," Rourke observed.

Kerenin evidently didn't understand the Biblical allusion. "Now, before we end it," Kerenin continued, "would you care to see the control room?"

"Certainly. I was hoping you would ask." Rourke smiled at him.

Kerenin returned to the walkway, Rourke following him as the guards fell in almost as an afterthought, Rourke urging them, "Come along, comrades." Kerenin glanced at him quickly, then looked away. Was it working? Rourke wondered, hoping. He kept walking.

The walkway ramped upward toward what was evidently the control booth, at the far end of the pool area, as long as the pool and some eight feet or so high, well-lit, fronted with plexiglas or some similar transparent substance. Men and/or women (the short haircuts and unisex attire making it difficult to tell which was which at a distance) were moving about busily inside. Rourke used a long-strided, slow-paced walk to move up the ramp, stretching muscle groups in his legs.

At the height of the ramp, Kerenin signaled one of the guards to admit them to the control booth, the guard opening the door, Kerenin and the other guards passing inside, Rourke in their midst. Rourke nodded at the guard who held the door for him.

The personnel in the control booth continued working at their tasks, as if no one had entered. Television screens were everywhere in banks over each control console, the outside of the domes visible, sharks moving occasionally through the field of view of one of the cameras. "I thought your pets were indoors today."

Kerenin answered good-naturedly, "Recall that I mentioned some of the sharks are not under our control."

"Yes, that's right." Rourke nodded.

Rourke slowly moved about the control room, Kerenin making no attempt to have his progress arrested. Everything was in diode readouts. It seemed dials were a thing of the past here. One group of technicians was apparently responsible for what fell within one bank of cameras, the outer regions of the underwater complex zoned for better

116

management. There were cameras covering the interior of the shark pens as well, Rourke seeing several dorsal fins cutting almost lazily along the surface of the pool beyond the shark gates, beneath a transparent geodesic dome, a departure from the standard architectural style.

There was no control console, other than a smallish unit which evidently controlled the opening and closing of the gates in and out of the pens. "How do you get your pets to come in for the night, Kerenin?"

Kerenin shrugged his shoulders. "Remember the electrode implants I spoke of? They are capable of being used to stimulate a wide range of responses. I was told once to consider them an electronic brain implanted within the brain of the shark, a brain within a brain. But just think! You will very soon have the opportunity of firsthand research—at considerable depth." Kerenin's own sense of humor apparently amused him, so Rourke forced a smile of his own. "Shall we go?"

Rourke shrugged his shoulders, then started back across the control room, joining Kerenin and the guards, calling to the technicians, "I had a lovely time. Thank you."

They left the control room through the same door, the same man holding it, Rourke walking beside Kerenin now, biding his time for the right moment. "What happens if your sharks do attack one of your own men? What would he do to defend himself?"

"I almost do admire you," Kerenin said, laughing. "Very well. Our men carry something not terribly dissimilar to the Sty-20. It has a longer barrel and is a larger caliber. It is called the PV-26. It will kill or disable a conventional shark. But not ours. The same poison is fed these creatures we control in very small doses; and they gradually build up an immunity to it. Otherwise, an enemy diver would simply need to duplicate the poison used in the darts fired by the PV-26 and he or she could easily enough disable our sharks. Their usefulness would be at an end. There are always scout ships on patrol and should any of our own personnel stumble into a potentially hazardous situation with our own sharks, I imagine

117

something could be done."

"You only imagine?"

"I doubt it has ever happened."

They were back to the walkway now, Rourke slowing his pace slightly, Kerenin evidently enjoying the wait.

At last they reached the pool, Kerenin turning toward it, John Rourke beside him. Sharks such as these, Rourke knew, could well have been implanted and controlled in his own original time, made the killing machines of men, but it was hard to imagine anyone so inhumane as to do it—perhaps.

Kerenin stopped at the water's edge.

Rourke eyed the gates. Then his eyes drifted to Kerenin's belt and the one unusual item there. His own knife, the one made for him by Jack Crain five centuries before.

"What sorts of sharks are they? I understand there were several species."

"That I can answer for you easily. Part of our training for the Marine Spetznas includes such things—fortunately only a small part. The name is Carcharodon carcharias."

John Rourke knew the common name. Great White. "How about making it a little more interesting, for us both?"

"What do you mean?"

"Untie my hands. I will at least be able to die fighting. You would want that if you were in my position."

"But I am not." Kerenin grinned.

"It would be a better show." And John Rourke looked away. He couldn't push it.

"Your hands? Hmm . . . You honestly feel you have some chance of escape and survival, do you not?"

"Allow a dying man his delusions."

"You are going to reverse the situation, and somehow miraculously escape and then wreak vengeance on us? Amusing."

Rourke made his nastiest smile. "Are you afraid that I might, major?"

"Keep your weapons trained on him. At the slightest

provocation, fire." Then he looked at John Rourke. He drew the Crain LS System X. "Turn around."

Rourke thought to ask if it were to cut his bonds or stab him in the back, but held off, not wanting to push. "All right." He turned his back to Kerenin, an instant later feeling Kerenin's hand at his wrists, then the coldness of steel; and then his wrists were freed. Slowly, Rourke brought his hands forward, slowly again massaging his wrists. He turned—slowly—to face Kerenin, Kerenin sheathing the knife, but not binding it into the leather with what some called a "peace knot," merely closing the safety strap. "Thank you," Rourke told him quite sincerely. "Thank you, very much, major." Rourke slipped the cord from his neck over his head, holding it idly in his left hand. It was about three feet long.

Kerenin smiled again. There was a post a foot or so from Kerenin, and rising from its top a conically shaped speaker. It was also a microphone, Rourke learned in the next instant. "This is Major Kerenin. Open the gates to the shark pens. Slowly."

Rourke watched the shark-pen gates, but at the far left edge of his peripheral vision he watched Major Kerenin more.

"I met your challenge," Kerenin said, moving a pace closer. Already, Rourke could see dorsal fins moving through the opening made when the shark gates had drawn back on each side. "Will you meet your own?"

"I do not understand."

"I ask, do you intend to jump into the pool, or must you be pushed?"

The gates were completely open now, the number of fins at the far edge of the pool increased.

John Rourke turned to the Marine Spetznas major. "I hate to think of you missing out on anything. And I have become quite fond of your company."

Kerenin's eyes hardened.

"Sharks, the various rays and some others—they are called elasmobranchs. With the smaller ones, of course—say, something the size of what in English we call a 'lemon

119

shark'—they can be instantly disabled merely by inverting them. They become flaccid. Rather like a penis at the wrong moment." And John Rourke smiled. "I would imagine what are called the 'ampullae of Lorenzini'— pores on the head—are the receptor organs for the signals used to control them. Obvious, but ingenious certainly."

Rourke's left hand moved, flipping the three-foot length of cord toward the arc of Sty-20-armed guards, as his hand came back, his fist knotted over Kerenin's right ear, Rourke's left thumb gouging into Kerenin's right eye as Rourke's right hand grabbed for the haft of the Life Support System X. Rourke threw his body weight toward the pool, dragging Kerenin after him by the Russian's ear and Rourke's grip on the knife still sheathed at Kerenin's belt.

They hit the water, Rourke a split second ahead of Kerenin, Rourke's right little finger already having the safety strap popped off on the knife sheath, his right fist drawing out the knife as he and Kerenin dipped below the surface of the pool, Rourke's mouth gulping air, then closing tight. The water was clear. And John Rourke could see the leading edge of the shark pack coming for them, excited by the sudden violent movement in the water. He and the Russian were near the pool's edge and Rourke, still holding Kerenin's right ear, slammed Kerenin's head against the side of the pool, blood clouding the water around them almost instantly.

Time—there was no time. Rourke's left hand moved and his right hand came down, the knife tight in his fist. It was either kill Kerenin or get the sheath for the knife and let the sharks take care of Kerenin's fate. Rourke slicked Kerenin's belt, grabbing the sheath as the belt started to float away, ramming the sheath into his left Levi pocket. Rourke pushed Kerenin's limb body away, diving, impacts from Sty-20s on the surface above him, the darts floating harmlessly down toward him, smudges of their poison clouding around them.

His only chance was the shark gates.

The creatures were all around him now, but above him,

drawn to the blood. Something impacted his left shoulder, almost knocking the air from his lungs, driving him to the bottom. The sleeve over his left arm was ripped partially away, but there was no blood, at least not yet. He kept swimming, propelling himself over the bottom, the water over him alive with their movement, the sleek gray-whiteness of them everywhere. Ahead he could see the shark gates. He kept going, his lungs burning with the exertion. He had been a powerful swimmer ever since his youth, and scuba diving had at times been a sport and at times an occupational necessity during his career with the Central Intelligence Agency prior to his leaving CIA to write and teach on special-weapons training and survival. And neither were sharks a new experience, survival in shark-infested waters a skill he had studied from the best marine biologists and fisherman in the field, before teaching it himself.

But the Great Whites were something else again.

He was at the shark gates, his lungs, his accelerated heartbeat, the wooziness in his head telling him he had been too long below the surface. But he had to get through the gates. And they were starting to close. That meant Kerenin had survived or someone in the control booth had presence of mind enough to attempt to trap him—Rourke—inside the pool. None of the six guards had struck him as being conditioned toward individual initiative.

He started for the gates, a Great White of average size, as the rest of them seemed to be, coming through, directly in his path. It measured roughly fifteen feet from the pointed snout over its triangularly shaped teeth—its jaws were spread wide toward him—to its crescent-shaped tail. Rourke tucked down, the creature's head passing over him, the grey-white of its overall body surface fading into the starker white of its underbelly. As long as he could keep beneath the creature he had a chance, because they habitually attacked upward. He kept moving, the opening between the gates narrowing drastically now. There was a sudden pressure against him and he realized the Great

121

White had flick-turned and was charging after him. To pass through the gates, it was necessary to come upward, a solid barrier beneath the shark gates separating this pool from the one beyond. And now the shark was beneath him.

Rourke changed direction, angling away from the creature, the Great White blocking him from the gates now. Rourke's head broke surface for an instant and he gulped air, the water swelling beneath him and to his left, and he dove under the surface, the Great White slamming against him, Rourke rolling away from it, his right fist still balled on the half of the LS System X. The shark changed course, arcing downward, John Rourke rolling in the water, kicking, forcing himself down, the shark's snout impacting him in the chest, Rourke reeling from the blow, but his reaction saving his life, the great jaws snapping shut inches from his head. He rolled left, the shark's momentum carrying it over him. Rourke bunched both fists over the haft of his knife, only seconds of air left to his lungs after the impact of the fifteen hundred pounds of living eating machine against him. He stabbed the knife upward, into the great creature's white underbelly, and suddenly a cloud of deep red the color of berry juice washed around Rourke, the creature thrashing now, Rourke barely able to hold to his knife. But he couldn't let himself lose it.

The White twisted, Rourke's arms nearly wrenched from their sockets, the creature's head breaking the surface, Rourke drawn up after it, his mouth gulping air as he twisted away, the creature dragging him downward again, its jaws snapping. Rourke wrenched his knife free, the creature twisting round, the jaws coming for him, Rourke slashing the big Crain knife across the dorsal fin, half severing it as Rourke dodged its head, more blood clouding the water.

Rourke looked toward the far end of the pool, the water churning violently, the violence nearing him with an almost incomprehensible rapidity, his mind so concentrated on outmaneuvering the shark that he hadn't realized the basic import of what he had done. Cutting the shark—twice—had signaled the other sharks in the pool, and he was about to be at the center of a feeding frenzy. Rourke propelled himself away, clawing water, a body slamming against him, knocking him against the base wall beneath the gates, another hammering against him and thrusting him forward, Rourke nearly losing his knife.

With all the strength and all the air remaining to him, Rourke pushed himself over the barricade, sideways because of the still-narrowing gap between the gates, sliding through, the shark gates snapping shut like the jaws of one of the creatures themselves behind him.

Rourke made for the surface. Air was his greatest concern now and, as his head broke the surface, his right fist broke the surface as well, the blade of his knife upthrusting. He gulped air, his head twisting from side to side. This was the pool he had seen from the control room, the shark pens. Something brushed against his leg. Rourke didn't take time to see what, hurtling his body across the surface toward the edge of the pool, his left hand reaching it, his right hand then, letting go of the knife on the edge of the pool, his palms downward, his body pumping upward as he rolled out of the pool, his right combat boot soleless. John Rourke sank back and made the Sign of the Cross.

Rourke rolled onto his stomach, his right fist finding his knife. He looked around him. A watertight door on the far side of the pool. A shark cage, empty, beside the pool, a winch over it and a chain secured between the winch and the cage. Rourke drew his right knee up as he got to a sitting position, ripping the laces of his boot free, tugging the soleless combat boot from his foot. His foot, his toes— "Thank You"—and he looked upward. One boot on, one boot off, he climbed to his feet, lurching forward, his breathing still labored, the left sleeve of his shirt gone, the rest of the shirt in tatters. He took the sheath from his left Levi pocket, the leather sodden. He shoved the empty sheath between his flesh and the interior of the waistband of his blue jeans.

He walked the outer edge of the pool, aiming for the watertight door. A noise behind him startled him and Rourke looked back. The shark-pen gates were opening, and the sharks would be entering this pool again, at least some of them beyond whatever it was—he assumed a young Great White—which had nearly claimed his right foot.

Another noise now, Rourke wheeling to his left. A conventional door set back in an alcove was opening, two technicians storming toward him, one armed with some sort of scientific instrument, brandishing it like a club, the other with a chair. Rourke dodged the first man, hacking outward with the Crain knife and opening a wound over the man's upper arm and chest, the man's body crumpling to the concrete-like surface. The second man's chair crashed downward, Rourke taking the blow across his bare left arm and his left shoulder, losing his balance, the man still charging forward as pieces of the chair shattered downward—it was some type of plastic.

Rourke was falling backwards, the second technician's hands going for his throat, both of them hitting the water, the water's surface around them seeming to swell upward, Rourke ramming the knife upward into the technician's abdomen, pushing him away into the gaping mouth of one of the Great Whites.

Rourke was less than six feet from the edge of the pool. The technician screamed as the White's jaws closed over him, the entire right side of his body shaken off as the shark had bitten, the half-torso and head flicked across the pool, coming down with a resounding splash. John Rourke was nearly to the edge now, reaching, thrusting himself upward, rolling left, massive jaws almost obscuring the head of which they were a part, rising from the water behind him, the creature crashing against the water's surface, head over the edge of the pool as Rourke edged back from it. Then the head sank from sight.

Rourke was up, running now, to the watertight door. He wrenched at the opening device, wheeling it counterclockwise, dragging the door toward him, half falling over the flange, no time to look what might be beyond. Behind him was certain death. That he knew.

He stopped, sagging back against the wall, catching his breath. The floor beneath him was marble, like that of the hall of the triumvirate. He looked across the room. This too was a massive hall, but a museum hall, display cases alternating with built-in aquarium exhibits, sea creatures of every description here. He was back inside the Institute for Marine Studies. For an instant, he experienced déjà vu. Natalia's uncle, General Varakov, his headquarters in the natural history museum—his "office without walls," as Natalia had told him her uncle had called it.

John Rourke shook his head to clear it. "The door," he hissed, startled by the sound of his own voice speaking English. He pulled the watertight door shut, spinning the locking mechanism to seal it. He had to brace the wheel, but not with the knife. Aside from the fact that it was irreplaceable, more important under the circumstances was that it was his only weapon.

A display case, and though he felt like a barbarian doing it, he staggered toward the nearest case, using the butt of his knife like a hammer against the flimsy lock on the access opening, the lock shattering beneath the impact, reaching inside then and shoving the stuffed carcass of a manta from one of the pedestals which supported it. He wrenched the pedestal free of the case, unscrewing the flat top piece. What he needed was the tubular section running up from the base, made of steel or something like it to take the weight of the display. Quickly, he passed the bar through the wheel and into the exposed locking bars of the mechanism, effectively sealing the door against opening from the other side.

Rourke started across the museum hall, an alarm sounding in the distance. He broke into a jog trot, all the energy he could muster at the moment. A set of double doors. They were made to look like wood, like the doors leading into the hall of the triumvirate where he had been sentenced to death. He threw his weight against them. They vibrated, but didn't break. There was a gap between the two doors and he shoved the Crain knife into the open space, then brought it downward with all the force he could summon, against the crossbolt, the spine of the knife breaking the grip of the bolt. He threw his left shoulder against the doors and they rocked outward, one partially falling from one of its hinges.

He was in the entrance hall, the elevator bank to his left. If Kerenin had survived, or even if the Marine Spetznas major hadn't, his men would be coming up those elevators, perhaps already were. Rourke forced himself to run, his breathing more regular, some strength returning now. To the elevators, pushing the call buttons. If they were already on their way—Kerenin's men—it would do no good. If they weren't, it would perhaps buy a few more seconds.

He ran toward the street beyond the main doors, the Gullwing transport still there. But as he pushed through onto the walkway, at the far right edge of his peripheral vision, he saw a solitary Marine Spetznas enlisted man, the man seeing him, starting to draw his Sty-20. Rourke hurtled himself toward the man, the two of them smashing down to the pavement of the walkway surface. Rourke's right hand hammering forward and up, the Crain knife gouging in beneath the sternum and into the chest cavity, the man beneath him dead in the same instant, a gurgling rattle issuing from his drooling open mouth. Rourke grabbed the Sty-20 from the sidewalk and was up, running into the street, dodging another of the Gullwing vehicles, running toward the still-parked vehicle he had arrived in. They each had registration tags—he had memorized the number. The gullwings were starting to close. Rourke threw himself down, ramming the Sty-20 ahead of him, firing, then firing again, the body of the driver lurching twice.

John Rourke was to his feet, the Gullwing starting away from the curb as he reached it, extending his left hand with the knife under the gullwing, hacking the primary edge across the left side of the driver's neck. Rourke rolled the body outward, pushing the gullwing up, sliding be-

126

hind the wheel. He had watched as best he could how the vehicle was manipulated. "Here goes," Rourke rasped, the knife and the Sty-20 going to the floor beside the driver's seat, his hands going to the wheel. The vehicle was already in drive or whatever it was, moving slowly forward. He found what he hoped was an accelerator pedal and stomped it, the Gullwing lurching ahead.

Another Gullwing was dead in its path, Rourke cutting the wheel, but too sharply, the Gullwing he drove climbing the curb, bouncing off, back to the street, sideswiping the oncoming vehicle. Rourke recovered the wheel and stomped the accelerator again, the pickup terrible. But he was moving.

Alarm signals were sounding everywhere around him now. . . .

Natalia Anastasia Tiemerovna, her wrists and ankles bound to the sides of the bed, her arms and legs splayed above and below, naked beneath the sheet and light blanket that had been placed over her, felt the corners of her mouth raising in a smile. She awaited whatever Olav Kerenin's pleasure might be with her and she realized that she had endured worse and was powerless to prevent what might happen.

But Natalia smiled because she heard the alarms through the open window, their dissonance music to her. She told herself the alarms could mean only one thing. John Rourke had escaped. He lived.

Chapter Sixteen

Guards were everywhere. John Rourke had critically disabled the Gullwing while smashing through an improvised roadblock, then had ditched the vehicle and run for it. Cameras were everywhere, but their sheer number logically dictated that the images they produced would be computer-scanned rather than observed by human operators.

With little left of his shirt and only one boot, it was imperative that he acquire more suitable attire.

He waited inside a hedgerow with that specific purpose in mind.

To steal just any uniform would have been pointless without the services of a creative tailor to assist him. The majority of the men here were too short in stature. After more than an hour of waiting, freezing as his clothes dried to his body, and after several changes of location, he found his man. But unfortunately his man was not alone, a woman with him.

The combination presented an awkward moral problem, but on the positive side, the woman was tall as well and approximated Natalia's height. And Natalia would need a uniform after he managed to free her. Rourke shrugged.

The man and woman approached, the two of them arguing over the proposed relaxation of rules governing fraternization between members of the opposite sex within the Marine Spetznas, the woman insisting it was clear evidence of moral decadence. They searched the hedges for the missing prisoner—Rourke. He felt relieved somehow that they were not two off-duty lovers out for a stroll, but rather coworkers. And the woman's contention that moral decline loomed on the horizon sounded much too narrow-minded.

Both of them had their Sty-20s drawn, but he was familiar enough with the weapons by now to be able to tell as they neared him that the man at least had the safety of his Sty-20 activated.

It was time for Jack Crain's knife again, but logic dictated another mode of use.

And John Rourke rose from the hedgerow, the order of progression now clear. The man had his safety on, which would mean it would take a split second longer for him to use his gun. Women had higher-pitched voices, and a shout would be a scream and be heard over a greater distance.

John Rourke stepped into the path of the two Marine Spetznas, the Life Support System X sheathed, his right hand hammering the massive two pounds of steel and leather down against the crown of the woman's skull, her body collapsing at his feet as his left hand fired the liberated Sty-20, double-tapping, both darts impacting the man's throat. As the man started to raise his pistol, Rourke used the sheathed knife like a flat sap, slapping it across the left ear and the side of his head. The man went down. Rourke dropped to his knees, testing the woman for a pulse. Her pulse was strong and he judged she would regain consciousness in a matter of moments, however woozily. He rolled back one of her eyelids, confirming that what he had to do next would not be murder. He shot her twice with the darts from the Sty-20, aiming into her left thigh to delay the course of the sedative.

Rourke safed his pistol, then hers, then took the man's pistol, proceeding to drag the man and woman in turn back into the hedgerow. . . .

The Crain knife was under his stolen uniform, the two spare pistols wrapped inside the woman's uniform, which he had neatly folded and then tucked under his arm. Women here wore atrociously unfeminine underwear and he had left the female Marine Spetznas hers. Natalia wouldn't have been caught dead in it. He had used the primary edge of the Crain knife for a makeshift shave, touching up the edge first, moistening his beard with the still-wet trouser legs of his Levis. He had used the polished uniform belt buckle from the male Marine Spetznas as an improvised mirror. Pulling the long-billed uniform cap low over his eyes, John Rourke left the hedgerow, his original Sty-20 in his right fist. He continued "checking" the hedgerow, lest curious eyes should see him and wonder, then left the hedges for the greenway which led down from the roadway bordering the perimeter of the dome toward the nearest of the monorail stations.

Rourke holstered his pistol.

The monorail cars were as gray as the prospects of someone who lived under a totalitarian government such as this, he thought, ascending the low steps toward the diagonally moving sidewalk, the sidewalk rising toward the monorail station platform itself. Men and women in the blue civilian attire passed him by, evidently in a hurry to go somewhere. Rourke, instead, studied the city. The main dome's ultimate height disappeared among the clouds of vapor—it was very humid here—and strikingly plain edifices rose everywhere, the upper floors of some of the taller structures lost in the cloud cover as well. In the distance to his left—he had no conception of cardinal directions here—a portion of the next dome could be seen, more green visible. The suburbs, he supposed.

At the height of the diagonally moving sidewalk, John Rourke stepped onto the platform and began walking its length. When a stare came his way he stared back. In a totalitarian society, the soldier or secret policeman's stare always triumphed. Rourke kept walking. Seeming to ring the city itself, he realized, were a system of downward sloping ramps, soon shrouded in shadow. Access systems to the city sewage system, perhaps. And there were no visible electric or telephone lines. But he wondered.

He almost showed his surprise when a voice addressed him. He turned easily toward the voice instead. A man, perhaps his own height, but very young. A Marine

Spetznas, he stared at John Rourke's uniform and said, "Excuse me, Comrade Sergeant Markov?"

Rourke had never thought to look at his name tag—the officers wore none—but a quick glance at the younger man's uniform indicated that the Marine Spetznas's name was Vishnov. "Yes, comrade?"

"The alert is still in force?"

"Why do you ask, comrade?" Rourke tried to force his Russian to be as accentless as that of the people here.

"My communicator—it must be broken, comrade sergeant." He smiled.

Rourke patted the communicator on his belt. "Mine is not. You are just the man I need, comrade—come with me at once."

"Yes, comrade sergeant. I have never seen you before." They started walking, toward the downward moving diagonal sidewalk.

"I have been on a protracted mission. Tell me—have you been briefed concerning the accomplices of this person for whom we search?"

"I have not, sergeant—are there many?"

Rourke leaned toward him conspiratorily as they took to the walkway. "I have just captured two of them, but I will need your help, comrade."

"Yes, comrade!"

Rourke clapped the young fellow on the shoulder. . . .

He had shown the boy the two still-unconscious, disrobed Marine Spetznas personnel and, while the boy had stared, John Rourke had withdrawn his knife from beneath his uniform and placed it at the young man's throat. Adding still another Sty-20 to his growing arsenal, John Rourke put the boy to sleep with two darts from it and gently eased him to the ground. When everyone had awakened, the boy would be the one least likely to get into trouble, Rourke reassured himself. The other two, after all, were just in their underwear.

At the base of the main dome there was a deep underground complex, the lowest level of the research center—Rourke hadn't asked toward what goal the "research" was directed—and above that the security-police headquarters and offices. The security police wore, he deduced, the differently marked uniforms he had seen since his escape. And in the midst of the security complex was the prison. The boy had not known how many were held there, but had guessed at well over a hundred men and some women. Above this level was the overall dome-maintenance control—sewage, light, water, and the like. And above that, like the frosting on a cake, the interior of the dome, the city itself. A hallway crowned the maintenance level, ringing its circumference. There was a system of elevators allowing access from above to below, but the most direct route, Rourke had been assured, was from below. The ramped tunnels John Rourke had detected from the monorail platform were marked to indicate to which level they extended. Best to go to research rather than directly to the prison. Since the boy had been so insistent on that, Rourke decided that going through research was the last thing he wished to do.

But entering at the prison level might be tricky. He elected to enter via the maintenance level.

And again he walked, passing several of the tunnels until he found one marked for access to the maintenance level. And he turned down the ramp.

It sloped only gently and the darkness here better suited his eyes, always light-sensitive. Without his sunglasses, the artificial sunlight which pervaded the domes was uncomfortable to him. And, although the dampness was heightened, it was cooler here, the outside temperature more like that of a hothouse. If this were Paradise, he wanted no part of it.

Rourke reached the end of the ramp, a small guard cubicle, plexiglas or of a similar material, all that blocked access to the maintenance area. He could hear the hum of machinery and realized he held a certain anticipation for what he would find, the technology that could support all this so far beneath the surface of the ocean.

132

He had no firm idea whether a Marine Spetznas sergeant would have automatic access here and was reluctant to simply walk past the guards. So, instead, he angled his steps toward the guard cubicle. One of the men stepped out, straightening his uniform, the second joining him.

The men came to attention and Rourke stopped. "Comrades!" John Rourke's right hand swung forward and he shot each man once in the neck, and as they staggered back, shot them again, racing toward them, clubbing them down with the Sty-20 pistol before one or both of them could sound an alarm. The cameras here kept to their normal pattern of movement, but Rourke had no doubt that, whether they were monitored by computer or man, an alarm would be sounded in seconds. Rourke left the bodies, taking the Sty-20s first, and made a quick inspection of the cubicle. Nothing of interest except for something that for all the world looked like a 1960s gym bag. Rourke stuffed the uniform he'd brought for Natalia into the bag, putting two of the pistols inside it as well. Two pistols in his belt and one in each fist, the gym bag under his left arm, he started into the maintenance section. And then he broke into a run, alarms sounding now.

He wanted a real gun, better yet two. Having to shoot someone twice and then club him into unconsciousness was inefficient to say the least. He kept running.

He passed through what seemed like a massive sewer pipe, but large enough for heavy truck traffic, then entered into the walkway area which ringed the maintenance level. Kerenin could be anticipating him here after the inquiry about his Detonics pistols, but the prison area was of paramount importance to the rudimentary plan he had formed since the sentence of death had been passed upon him. He kept running, finding the nearest elevator bank, pushing the call buttons for down, then running on, doing the same at the next elevator bank, searching for the stairwells the boy had told him could be found here. The boy could have lied, but Rourke didn't think so.

To his right and below, there lay a vast expanse of machinery—compressors, pumps, generators. And the smell of the steam here made him think that the power base was geothermal, the entire complex located above or (more prudently) near some undersea volcanic vent. Above him, forming a tightly woven gridwork extending as far as he could see ahead or to either side, were pipes of various diameters, some simply servicing fiber-optic telephone systems, no doubt, or electrical wiring, but others transferring live steam to and from the maintenance complex to provide the power to run the machinery. Oh for an explosive device, he thought. He kept running, hitting the call button for another elevator bank and almost directly beside it finding the stairwell.

Rourke started down it, taking the treads fast, two at a time, the alarms louder here but as yet no guards blocking his way. The stairwell came to a landing, then another set of stairs, Rourke continuing downward, peering over the railing. Below him, more stairs. He kept going, to the next landing and beyond and then to the next, wondering if perhaps the boy he had interrogated had cleverly sent him into a trap. Finally, as he peered again over the railing, he saw an end and he quickened his pace, shifting the spare pistols to the rear of his belt so they would not immediately be noticed, holstering one of them, only one gun in his hand now, in his left fist, held behind his thigh, the gym bag in his right hand held by its handles.

He reached the base of the stairwell, quickly trying to orient himself. Ahead and left, he thought, a system of smaller tunnels opened before him. He took the one at the farthest left edge and ran some distance along its length, but it sloped downward and he doubled back, taking the center tunnel now and running. This one did not slope downward and he quickened his pace. The light here was gray, the walls a dully gleaming metallic hue. And as the tunnel took a bend right, he spotted what he thought was his goal. An electronic barrier like that used on the submarine's brig, only vastly larger, more the size of the force field near the entrance to the military dome. Guards were formed on the other side of the barrier. Rourke made no move to evade them, but rather ran straight toward them, shouting to them in their language, "The prisoner has an explosive device and is barricaded near the pumping stations!" And then Rourke thought of something that had been mentioned in passing at his "trial." "He is from Mid-Wake!"

A senior noncom behind the barrier was pulled aside by an officer of junior rank, these men not Marine Spetznas but security. They seemed to confer for an instant as Rourke stopped before the electrical barrier. "Comrades, the destruction could be unthinkable!"

The junior officer and the sergeant ran toward the barrier, the sergeant shouting commands to shut off the power, one of the five enlisted men of the guard detail running into a lighted cubicle identical to the plexiglas structure Rourke had encountered earlier. Rourke watched the position of the guard's body intently without appearing to, he hoped. Rourke started to limp with his left leg.

"Are you all right, sergeant?"

Rourke began to cough, not completely certain of the officer's rank. But Rourke nodded, holding his leg. The officer shouted, "You and you, remain here! Call for assistance!"

Rourke stepped past the officer, inside the energy barrier, the officer, sergeant, and three of the enlisted personnel drawing their Sty-20s and racing along the corridor. John Rourke turned toward the two guards, one of them already starting into the cubicle. Rourke shot the man twice in the back of the neck, wheeling toward the second guard and shooting the man once in the neck and once, a miss, in the left cheek. Both men staggered, starting to fall. Rourke shoved past the one who had been entering the cubicle and stepped inside. "Barricade Control" was clearly marked and Rourke worked the lever, the barrier activating before his eyes. He ran from the cubicle now, the officer, noncom, and their men not yet aware they had been tricked. Rourke picked up the Sty-20s from the two guards he had dropped, then ran.

The corridor split in three sections and the prison, if his information were still holding out, would be in the center

135

section. Rourke had asked the young man where the crime laboratory was, and had been told that it was probably to the left. Rourke took the tunnel to his right. He needed his guns first. He kept running, the alarm sounds diminishing—apparently there was no need for outdoor alarms sounding inside a structure designed to prevent leaving rather than entering.

The corridor ended abruptly, double plexiglas doors lettered "Headquarters Forensics, Committee for State Security" blocking it. "Committee for State Security." Rourke smiled. But it wasn't the old KGB, because clearly here the Marine Spetznas were the power to be reckoned with. KGB here simply meant police.

Rourke stopped before the doors. He pushed against them and they opened into the walls, sliding away on either side of him.

He stepped through.

A man entered the inside corridor. He wore the uniform of the security police. Rourke shot him before he could draw, approached him carefully, shooting him again, then disarmed the man before he passed out. Tossing the Sty-20 into the bag, Rourke kept moving, reading the signs on the plexiglas-fronted doors, at last finding one that indicated evidence might be held inside. He went through.

A lab-coated technician looked up from what appeared to be a modern version of an electron microscope. "Yes, sergeant?"

"Excuse me, comrade—the weapons brought in with the male and female prisoner. Captain Feyedorovitch has requested that I examine them for a moment."

The technician looked affronted. "The weapons will be examined in due course, sergeant."

"But comrade, the woman has revealed that secret information is concealed under the grip panels of each of the handguns. Putting the individual elements together will provide us with valuable data that is vital to security of the submarine pens." CIA had never offered a course in advanced, creative lying, but Rourke had worked with enough self-taught personnel over the years that he could employ the technique when needed. The technician's expression changed from irritation to puzzlement. "It is vital, comrade," Rourke insisted.

"Very well. I have them here." And the technician started toward a bank of plastic-looking locking cabinets. Rourke glanced through the plexiglas toward the corridor. No one was coming yet. The technician opened one of the cabinets. "They are here and I believe they are unloaded, but I can assume no responsibility for that. Weapons are not my department."

"Certainly, comrade. The ammunition—ahh." And Rourke stopped before the open cabinet.

The twin stainless Detonics .45s lay side by side. The magazines were withdrawn, but he could tell they were at least partially loaded, seeing brass through some of the upper witness holes. He picked one of the pistols up and jacked back the slide, raising the slide stop. He stuffed what looked like the fuller magazine up the butt. "What are you doing, sergeant?"

Rourke thumbed down the slide stop, the top round stripping from the magazine and chambering as he turned to face the technician. "I am pointing a loaded, five-centuries-old .45-caliber automatic at your testicles. Where is the rest of it?" Rourke jerked his head toward the cabinet.

"I do not—"

"Such a gun as this will not numb you or put you to sleep. It will rip your genitals from your body and you will die in considerable pain and not all too quickly. Where, comrade?" Rourke punched the muzzle of the little Detonics against the man's crotch.

"The next cabinet!"

"Open it," Rourke ordered.

Rourke turned around with the man, the muzzle of his pistol less than two inches from the man's body. The technician opened the cabinet. Natalia's revolvers. Her speed loaders. Her Bali-Song folding knife. Her holsters. His A.G. Russell Sting IA knife. His compass, the contents of his musette bag, the Sparks Six-Pak of spare

137

magazines for the little pistols.

"All is in order, comrade. Now—the prison—that way?" And Rourke gestured to his left.

"Yes—that—"

Rourke smiled, then raised the pistol quickly, more quickly bringing it down behind the technician's left ear, the man sagging to his knees, Rourke guiding him the rest of the way to the hard floor. He had, after all, been cooperative. Rourke set down his pistol, taking up the second gun, chamber-loading it, dumping both magazines and replacing them with fresh ones from the contents of his musette bag, not bothering to lower the hammers, merely using the thumb safeties. He tucked the partially spent magazines into a compartment of the musette bag, then quickly packed away the rest of its contents. His field medical kit, the snakebite kit, the other necessities he was never without. There were Safariland speedloaders for his Python, but the gun was still on shore. The ammo, however, could be used with Natalia's revolvers. Rourke stuffed the Alessi shoulder rig into the musette bag. He placed the little Sting IA Black Chrome inside the boot top of his stolen footgear, using the chrome belt clip. He threaded the Sparks Six-Pak and his Crain knife onto his uniform belt. Natalia's Metalife Custom L-Frame Smiths he placed into the gym bag, along with her holsters, speedloaders, and other personal items, pocketing her Bali-Song. He slung the musette bag cross-body from right shoulder to left hip.

John Thomas Rourke picked up his pistols, the twin stainless Detonics .45s feeling solid in his hands, the texture of the black-checkered rubber Pachmayr grips, now nearly worn smooth, somehow very comfortable to him.

Rourke looked at the sleeping technician. Being a doctor allowed him to use force without causing permanent injury. "Sleep tight—and thank you." He smiled. And started for the door.

138

Chapter Seventeen

Michael Rourke was very much like his father—plan ahead, improvise on the plan as you go along, cautiously daring. Paul Rubenstein, slightly uncomfortable in his tight Soviet uniform, but for more reasons than its fit, was supposed to be the enlisted man, so it meant that he drove the half-track vehicle, Michael beside him in the truck's front seat. Michael was uniformed as a captain. And the fit of Michael's uniform was much better. Paul Rubenstein laughed. "What's so funny, Paul?" Michael asked him.

"Before the night of the War, I saw a play once. A musical. 'Man of La Mancha.' About—"

" 'Don Quixote'—by Cervantes. I read it."

"Yeah—so did I. Play or book, though—remember the character of Sancho Panza?"

Michael Rourke smiled. "And?"

"I was just thinking—we sidekicks never get the best outfits, do we?" And Paul gestured broadly over his uniform.

"Sidekick?"

"You know—Tonto, Pat Buttram, Smiley Burnette, Sancho Panza—like that."

"I know who Tonto was, of course—and Sancho Panza."

"Same idea, I suppose." Paul laughed. "I'm your dad's sidekick, if you think about it. I never much thought of myself as comedy relief, though. More like Tonto—faithful."

"He was an American Indian."

"You didn't know? The Indians were really Jewish. Braids instead of forelocks, that's all. Look at all the ones

139

who wore broad-brimmed black hats."

Michael Rourke started to laugh. Paul went on. "Yeah—your dad's sidekick, his Faithful Jewish Companion. On loan at the moment to you. Think this will ever end, Michael?" And Paul caught the change of tone in his own voice.

"You mean the whole thing? The war?"

"Yeah. You know, I started keeping a diary, right after the crash there in New Mexico. Before that, really—on the plane when I figured I was probably going to die. And then your dad and I got together and he taught me how to ride and shoot—so what if they were motorcycles and automatic weapons instead of horses and sixguns. He's a good man—the best. If he's dead and we find out who ahh—who—you know . . . If he is, you're gonna have to move awful fast to beat me to the bastard. You know what I mean, Michael?"

Michael Rourke only nodded.

Paul Rubenstein's eyes returned to the track they followed, a road of sorts but only by dint of use, the snow all but gone here, the ruts deep. He imagined they would get deeper when the weather warmed if that ever happened. Winter had gone on forever.

And ahead now, he could see the gates in the outer deflection barrier. Michael called to Maria Leuden and Otto Hammerschmidt in the rear of the truck. "Watch out—we're hitting the first guard post."

Maria's voice came back. "Are you sure you've got it right?"

"No—but we'll find out, won't we," Michael whispered.

Paul began braking, the controls of the half-track truck at first difficult to master, a cross between the German mini-tanks and a standard truck in practice. But the vehicle was slowing smoothly enough.

Paul was suddenly seized with mild panic. Karamatsov's army numbered in the thousands, but what if this guard post harbored someone who had a terrific memory for faces and didn't remember seeing a captain who looked like Michael Rourke?

140

Paul's palms were sweating as he finally brought the vehicle to a stop just a few yards from the passage through the first deflection barrier.

Two guards approached, the senior man saluting. Michael returned the salute smartly, but not too eagerly. Paul mentally shrugged. The guard asked for orders. Paul understood that much Russian. Michael relayed the command to Paul and Paul took the orders from the seat between them and passed them to Michael defferentially, Michael passing them out the window. Maria Leuden, claiming her reading knowledge of Russian was good enough, had read the orders, interpreting the contents as she went. Paul hoped her reading knowledge was as good as she thought.

The sentry seemed to be taking considerable time with the orders. Michael said something in carefully enunciated Russian which Paul only vaguely understood as being an insult. The sentry handed in the papers. Paul breathed. Michael gestured for the truck to be driven on, the sentry stepping back, not checking the rear of the truck—Maria and Otto were hidden behind crates of synthetic fuel there.

Paul eased the vehicle forward, not wanting to appear too eager. It started to stall and he backed off on the accelerator and then fed it gas again. The truck moved forward smoothly.

They were through, heading toward the secondary barrier—but there would be a perfunctory check there, observation having proven that during the intervening hours since they had first reached the camp. They were inside. He thought that it was probably true—the Lord watched over fools, drunks, and Irishmen. And add to that Jewish sidekicks.

Chapter Eighteen

There was another energy barrier, directly blocking John Rourke's way into the prison complex at the center of the security level, three guards armed with Sty-20 pistols on the opposite side of the barrier. He approached at a brisk walk, both hands behind him, the twin Detonics mini-guns cocked and the safeties off.

"Halt! Identify yourself!"

Rourke doubted the Sty-20s would successfully penetrate the energy barrier, but was confident the loads in his pistols would—identical duplicates of the load that had been his favorite before the Night of the War, the Federal 185-grain jacketed hollow point. There was no time like the present to search for scientific truth, he decided. He stabbed both pistols toward the man who had spoken over the crackling energy barrier and fired, the barrier crackling maddeningly for a moment, the guard's body rocking back and skidding across the floor, twisting over onto his front, a smudge of blood where the exit wounds had contacted the floor surface.

Rourke shouted to the two men left standing. "Comrades—lower the barrier and let me pass and you will not be killed. Now!"

Rourke could see the barrier control on the wall to his right, their left, no plexiglas cubicle here. The two remaining guards exchanged glances. John Rourke took a step closer to the barrier. One of the two men shouted to him, "If we do not lower the barrier, you will not be able to get inside."

"If you do not lower the barrier, you will not live past the count of ten. Either of you. One . . . Two . . . Three . . . Four . . ." The guard nearest the barrier control hesitated, but the second man didn't. He went to the barrier control and activated it. The barrier crackled and vanished. John Rourke stepped through, saying, "Close the barrier now. Do it." The same man activated the control once again and the barrier crackled to life.

John Rourke thumbed up the safety on the Detonics .45 in his right fist, ramming it into his belt. He drew the Sty-20 he still carried in the uniform hip holster. He dropped the safety. "I am a man of my word, comrades. Sit—both of you. Hands behind your heads. Now—or it is this!" And Rourke gestured with the Detonics .45 that was still in his left hand. Both men sat, hands behind their heads. Rourke shot each in turn once with the Sty-20 and, as the men started to recoil from the impacts, shot each of them again to keep them asleep for a long time.

One of them fell back and, a second later, the second man fell.

Rourke safed, then holstered his own Sty-20, relieving the two sleeping guards of theirs, the gym bag that had been under his arm getting two more of the pistols. He went to the man he'd shot for real, taking the dead man's pistol as well, placing it in the bag, which went back under his arm. Thoughtfully, the Russians had provided him with a map, a layout of the prison center on the wall beside the barrier control. Cell blocks, interrogation rooms, re-education centers, medical research. The last smelled. Rourke studied the map a moment longer so he could place its significant points firmly in his short-term memory, then started moving again—toward medical research.

There would be guards arriving at any instant, even if the prison were largely automated, as he suspected. The gunshots would have been heard. He broke into a run. His stomach growled and he tried to remember when he had last eaten. But he kept running. . . .

Olav Kerenin, his head pounding with pain, his left arm, like his head, bandaged, but the arm the result of a brush with death from one of the sharks, leaned heavily against the side of the Gullwing he had commandeered, his own stolen, since found, crashed. "Where is he!" He hammered his good right fist against the vehicle's roof, Boris Feyedorovitch beside him, talking into a communicator. "Well?"

Feyedorovitch's voice was calm. "Olav—you should rest. I can settle this matter."

"What did you learn?"

"Very well—gunshots. Live ammunition. As you suspected, he has evidently penetrated the security complex."

"I increased the guard—how could—"

"There have been several personnel found already whom he has shot with sedative darts. There is substantial reason to believe he is dressed as one of us."

"But—how substantial?"

Feyedorovitch almost groaned. "Three of our personnel were found in the hedges not far from Monorail Station 17, two of them stripped of their uniforms, the third—"

"Two?"

"One of the Spetznas stripped of his uniform is a male of approximately the same height as this Wolfgang Heinz or whoever he is. The other guard was a female. Approximately the same size as the female prisoner. I checked. May I suggest—"

"What?" Kerenin snapped.

"May I suggest, comrade major, that security be asked to put out search teams. We do not have enough Marine Spetznas personnel available to us to cover all three domes—and if he has already left the security complex, we will not know for several minutes more."

"No," Kerenin said simply. Then he started under the Gullwing, telling Feyedorovitch, "Coordinate from here. I go to my quarters. If he plans to attempt to free the woman, he will come there." Kerenin could not bring in

144

security. If it were learned that he in fact knew this Wolfgang Heinz to be the American John Rourke—if the triumvirate were to discover this . . . Kerenin shouted to his driver. "My quarters! Quickly!"

Chapter Nineteen

John Rourke heard the new alarms starting, his left hand on the door handle for the room marked "Medical Research." The plexiglas in this door was frosted over. He pushed the door inward, letting it swing. He could see a typical laboratory beyond and, with one of the Detonics pistols in each fist, stepped through, dodging left. But no one appeared to be inside. The lights were on. There was a strong smell, like acid.

In Russian, he called out, "Is anyone here?" He heard muted sounds from the far end of the laboratory beyond what looked to be more or less standard double doors, the kind that swung open and closed. Rourke started toward the doors, passing ranks of large plastic cabinets of the type in which his and Natalia's weapons had been kept.

He was almost to the double doors, thinking that perhaps he had made a moral misjudgment of the Russians. He heard it an instant before it happened and started to dodge, something enormously heavy impacting his left arm and throwing him down to the floor, the cocked and locked .45s skating from his hands across the smooth hard floor. As he rolled right, he saw it—a man, huge by any standard, lunging for him. Rourke started for the Sty-20 in his holster, the man's ham-sized hands on him, wrestling him up from the floor, shaking him so violently that Rourke couldn't reach the Sty-20. Rourke's right knee smashed up, impacting the man's crotch, the grip on Rourke's upper arms loosening, Rourke falling away from him, skidding back across the floor.

John Rourke drew the Sty-20, fumblingly, his arms tingling from the man's vise-like grip. He was at least six feet six, and the chest was so large Rourke couldn't estimate it. He had seen adult black bears in the Georgia mountains that looked smaller and less formidable—and friendlier. John Rourke pushed himself to his feet, the Sty-20 finally in his right fist. The gym bag had fallen to the floor. The big man—in white tunic and white pants, a laboratory worker perhaps—had a beaker in his hand and threw it, Rourke ducking, the beaker shattering against Rourke's right hand, the Sty-20 falling as Rourke's flesh started to burn.

Acid.

John Rourke lunged toward the laboratory sink inset at the center of the table that ran the length of the room down its center, with his burning right hand hurtling a double of rack of test tubes toward the man as the charged, the man swatting them away. But Rourke had the water turned on, his right hand beneath it now, flushing off the acid. The man's body slammed into him, Rourke's abdomen taking the impact against the lab table top, Rourke's left elbow smashing back, hammering into the bear-sized man's abdomen, a rush of sickeningly sweet breath against Rourke's left cheek and the left side of his neck. Rourke's left leg snapped back, the heel of his liberated Marine Spetznas boot contacting bone as Rourke slid between the man's body and the counter top.

The flesh of John Rourke's right hand had stopped smoking, but the pain was killingly intense. He backed away.

The big man turned toward him. He reached to a rack running down the center of the laboratory table, taking down first one, then a second hypodermic, the syringes of huge proportions and opaque, the needles themselves several inches long. He gave each needle a test squirt, opaque liquid geysering from the needle tips. As the liquid contacted the floor, the floor started to burn.

John Rourke reached to his belt for the Life Support knife.

147

The giant charged, the needles plunging toward Rourke's face, Rourke dodging left, the skin of his right hand blistering now and one of the blisters popping, Rourke involuntarily sucking in his breath against the pain. But in his right fist he held the knife. There was no opening and Rourke edged back. A solid jab from one of the needles and he would be dead.

The man came at him again, surprisingly agile for someone so massive, and clever too. Because as John Rourke feigned with the Crain knife, the man anticipated him and stabbed outward with the hypodermics, Rourke swatting at him with the knife just to keep him away.

Rourke's eyes found his guns on the floor. He edged toward them, nearly tripping over the Sty-20 that had been bathed in acid along with his hand. The gun was partially melted away. But it was some type of plastic for the most part, he told himself. His right hand was blistering more now.

The big man charged and Rourke threw himself left, onto the floor, skidding across it, his left hand grasping one of the twin Detonics stainless pistols, his left thumb sweeping behind the tang, dropping the safety, sweeping back as he rolled, the big man diving for him now. John Rourke fired, then fired again, the man's body lurching, but still coming. Rourke fired again and again, then emptied the two remaining rounds into him, the man staggering. Rourke shoved the pistol into his belt, the slide still locked open over the empty magazine, both hands going to the haft of his knife. Some of the blisters on the back of his right hand burst as Rourke swung the steel, just sidestepping one of the acid-filled hypodermics, the knife's primary edge contacting flesh, Rourke's full body weight behind it, the momentum of the huge man who wanted him dead pushing against it. The head severed, blood spurting in a red wash, Rourke turning his eyes away from it, his fists still locked on the knife. Rourke fell to his knees. The head rolled past him on the floor.

Rourke hauled himself to his feet. His second pistol. He crossed the room, nearly losing his footing in the blood.

He picked up the second pistol, giving it a quick visual examination. It was undamaged. He clenched it tight in his left fist as he moved toward the still-running sink, immersing his hand beneath the jet of water, tears welling in his eyes from the pain.

He set his loaded pistol down beside him, water splashing on it, but the steel of the little Detonics pistols was as rustproof as the case of his Rolex watch. He was shivering, but kept his hand beneath the water. He inspected his forearm—no blisters there, and apparently no contact from the acid. He took the empty pistol from his belt, buttoning out the magazine, taking a fresh one from his musette bag, inserting it one-handed, pushing it home against his left knee. He worked the slide stop with his left thumb and the slide snapped forward. He raised the safety and set the little .45 beside the first one. The empty magazine he dropped into the musette bag. His eyes scanned toward the door. No one yet.

His left hand searched the musette bag. Medical kit. He needed his full bag but that was somewhere on the land above as well.

A B-complex shot—he administered it to himself, first cleaning the skin with an alcohol swab. It was a reusable syringe and he replaced it in the kit. He twisted open the cap on the hollow handle of his knife. He found the German painkillers, taking four of them, because of the pain and because of their weakness, with a mouthful of water cupped from the sink in his left hand. The water tasted processed, but was clear.

There was a cup beside the sink, half-filled with water, and there was no sign of settled sediment. He shook his head. The German spray was both an antiseptic and healing agent. He closed his eyes against what was to come, then sprayed his right hand, a scream involuntarily issuing from him, floaters over his eyes from the pain. He sagged against the laboratory sink top, feeling faint.

Rourke opened his eyes. He had covered all of the blisters.

"Bandage," he hissed.

From the small medical kit, he took the necessary items and began to wrap his hand, flexing it despite the pain because he would need both hands soon again.

The hand bandaged now, he replaced the remaining elements of the emergency medical kit in his musette bag, picking up his knife again, washing the blade of blood beneath the spigot, then wiping it dry against his trouser leg. He sheathed the knife, securing the safety strap only.

Rourke stabbed one of the twin stainless Detonics into his belt, the other taken up in his left hand.

He started for his original destination, the double swinging doors. He caught up the gym bag in his bandaged right fist, pain again washing over him.

John Rourke lurched through them, the pistol balled tight in his left fist.

When he saw what lay beyond them, Rourke murmured, "Mother of God."

There were cages, and inside the cages were men.

Some were Chinese, but others were not. White men. Black men, some of them obviously in terrible condition, growths on their bodies, skin rashes covering large portions of their flesh, others with dazed expressions.

And Rourke heard a voice above the moaning sounds, the Russian sounding terrible. "What are you planning for us now, you bastard?"

John Rourke turned toward the sound of the voice. A tall, well-built black man, his clothes some sort of uniform once, but now in rags. The color of his skin was gray, bespeaking poor health.

Rourke called back to him. "Russian is not your first language, and certainly not your best. What is your language?"

"Fuck you!"

Rourke grinned. The epithet had been in English, the accent American. John Rourke started for the cage. "Say that again and as soon as you're well enough, I'll kick the shit out of you," Rourke told him in English, smiling, stopping just before the cage.

"What the hell kinda trick is this?"

"You an American?"

"Damn right I am—and proud of it."

"Music to my ears, buddy," and John Rourke began inspecting the lock on the cage as he continued to speak. "Keys? Where are they?"

"You really—"

"My name's John Rourke. The uniform's 'borrowed.' This bag is filled with Sty-20s and a couple of .357 Magnums. Ever heard of those?" The man didn't answer. "How about a .45?" Rourke gestured with the Detonics mini-gun in his left hand. "I pledge allegiance, to the flag of the United States of America and to the republic for which it stands, one nation—"

The black prisoner joined him. "—under God, indivisible—"

Another voice joined and then another, some of the voices so feeble-sounding they seemed barely human. "—with liberty and justice for all."

There were tears in the black man's eyes. Rourke felt a shiver along his spine.

The black man said, "I don't know where they keep the keys."

"Then stand back—take that mattress and cover yourself with it and get in the corner of the cage. I'm shooting the lock. Go on and hurry."

The man drew back, catching up the mattress, taking shelter in the farthest corner of the cage as John Rourke leveled the Detonics toward the lock and stepped back a few paces. He took aim, averted his eyes slightly against the possibility of flying debris, then fired. The noise was earsplittingly loud, and as Rourke looked toward the lock plate, it seemed heavily damaged. "Come on, buddy— push!" Rourke grabbed a handful of bar and mesh, the man inside the cage bracing his right shoulder against it. "Now!" As Rourke pulled, the black man pushed, the lock snapping and the cage door swinging open, Rourke moving back to catch his balance.

The black man almost sprang from the cage. "Who are you? You're not from Mid-Wake."

"I'm not from Mid-Wake—I don't even know what Mid-Wake is except something that some of these Soviets are afraid of. I'm an American. And there are a few left like me. I can't take the time to explain it all now. And I don't feel like wasting ammunition on the rest of these cage doors so if you're up to it, look for the keys or a pry bar."

"What happened to your hand—they been experimenting on you too?"

"No—big guy out there. Built like a bear—"

"A bear? How the hell would you know what a bear looked like except out of a book or a vid-tape?"

John Rourke smiled. "I got into an argument with one once. But that's another story. You need help or can I stay by the door out there and wait for company with this?" And Rourke raised the little Deltonics .45 in his left hand, flicking up the safety.

"I can do it."

"Figured you could—here . . ." And Rourke dropped to his knees beside the gym bag. He took out one of the Sty-20s, the man recoiling from it. "Take it—I'll put the rest out on the floor here. Watch out, though—they're not all fully loaded and I haven't found a spare magazine in this whole damn place." Rourke set the pistols out, caught up the bag in his bandaged right hand and rose to his full height, a little woozy still from the pain.

"Thanks—I think," the man said. He extended his right hand. Rourke gestured with his bandaged right, then gambled, putting the Detonics in his belt and extending his left hand inverted. They clasped hands.

"You're welcome, I think." Rourke grinned.

Then he started through the doors and across the laboratory to guard the main entrance to the lab.

Chapter Twenty

Maria Leuden felt terrified, and tried to evaluate the source of her terror. She was alone in the back of a Russian army truck, hiding beneath a tarp surrounded by containers of synthetic fuel. The truck was surrounded by at least several thousand Soviet troops because she was in the midst of the principal Soviet encampment. Michael Rourke, Paul Rubenstein, and her fellow countryman Otto Hammerschmidt had left the truck shortly after Paul had driven them in, leaving her behind despite the uniform they had stolen for her. And it was even a woman's uniform. But Michael had told her that now she might be in danger. That she should stay in the truck. She should wait.

She had been raised to believe that women were equal to men in all things, but that women should defer to a man's judgment when necessary. She had considered it necessary and deferred. She was beginning to regret it.

Her chief fear was for Michael, although she feared for them all. Both Paul and Otto had become good friends since she had first flown from New Germany to Lydveldid Island and joined the pursuit of Vladmir Karamatsov. But Michael had become her lover. His wife had just been murdered, along with his unborn child. And together with Hammerschmidt and Michael she had gone to Egypt in pursuit of some mysterious weapon of destruction, her skills as an archaeologist and authority on ancient Egypt her only qualification.

She was no soldier, no adventurer.

She had learned both the hard way.

She had been drawn to Michael instantly, and moved by the sadness which pervaded every element of his being.

And one night—after many nights when she had fallen asleep thinking of him—he had come to her, made her his.

If this insane war ever ended—

Maria Leuden had no choice but to wait, hope. . . .

Midday. Annie Rourke Rubenstein stood on the terrace overlooking the First City, listening for the knock at her door.

And at last it came.

She ran to the door, unaccustomed to the higher heels of the Chinese shoes and nearly falling, reaching the door, sagging against it, opening it, smoothing her dress against her thighs, her fingers splayed with tension as she stepped back. The Chairman himself had come again. "Mrs. Rubenstein. I thought that I should tell you personally." Her heart skipped a beat. "There has been no word from your husband, your brother, or any of the rest of the rescue party, including our agent Han."

"Then I'm going, sir."

"I wish you would reconsider, Mrs. Rubenstein. It could be very dangerous."

She inhaled, lowering her shoulders. "Maria Leuden went with them."

"Doctor Leuden accompanied them simply because of her reading knowledge of the Russian language. That is the only reason."

Annie looked him straight in the eyes. "I'm going. Alone if I have to."

"Not alone then. But it will consume some time in order to mount a second expedition, Mrs. Rubenstein."

"Not too much time, Mr. Chairman." He merely nodded and turned back into the corridor. Annie closed the door behind him and flattened her hands against the joint of door and frame, leaning her face against the backs of her hands. Her father had told her that persistence in the face of adversity was a virtue. And she had read that a virtuous woman was more valuable than rubies.

Olav Kerenin entered the room and she realized she had fallen into sleep, dreaming. "Major Tiemerovna?"

She looked at him. "Would you unbind me? I have to go to the bathroom."

"Your heroic John Rourke has temporarily escaped death."

"I assume he would. I still have to go to the bathroom," Natalia told him. He had drawn the shades or curtains, she realized, and the room was nearly dark.

"I wish to have you for my woman."

"Apparently you leave me little choice," and she tugged at the bonds at her wrists and ankles which held her on her back in the bed.

"I would make you take me now, but he will be coming here. If he makes it this far. I have men stationed everywhere. And I will wait for him myself outside this door. So, I am afraid, I cannot unbind you at the moment, Major Tiemerovna. But after he is dead, before I must surrender you to your husband, Marshal Karamatsov, I will have you."

"And when I tell Vladmir he will have you killed."

"Somehow, Comrade Major Tiemerovna, that does not matter to me at all." He opened the door and the light beyond was bright and flooded over her on the bed, and then the door closed and the room was darker than before.

Natalia closed her eyes. "Don't come for me, John—save yourself."

Chapter Twenty-one

He had detected movement at the end of the corridor
and the alarms within the prison had stopped sounding.

Rourke heard the black man's voice coming from behind him. "The alarms stopped."

"They know I'm here."

"Then we're trapped—shit!"

"Yeah—but we have weapons—and we have this." John
Rourke had not been idle while he waited for the man he
had released to release the other prisoners held for experimentation.

"We're not being captured again. Any of us."

"We have this," Rourke repeated, pointing toward a
large plastic container on the laboratory table.

"What's that smell?"

"This." Rourke smiled. "Know anything about chemistry?"

"Not much."

"To become a doctor of medicine—that's what I am by
trade—at least in my day you had to study chemistry. So I
mixed a few chemicals available here. That's a firebomb.
But it won't do us much good if there isn't more than one
way out of that corridor out there."

The man looked toward the doors, then at the container
of combustible chemicals. "Just deeper into the prison."

"How many men in there?"

"You mean . . . Yeah," and the man grinned.

Rourke looked toward the swinging doors which led from the room in which he had found this man and the others caged. And now the others were coming, those in better condition helping those in poorer condition, in all almost a dozen of them, each man clinging to some sort of weapon, one of the Sty-20s or a pry bar or simply a bar rooted out of one of the cages.

Rourke peered through the door into the corridor again. "We'll have to move rather quickly. The men who don't have anything more than clubs can take charge of the men who can't move too well. Anybody speak Chinese?"

There were five Chinese among the freed men.

"No—but we learned to talk a little bit among ourselves at nights. I can tell 'em what you want. You're a doctor?"

"Yeah—but I used to be with the Central Intelligence Agency—a long while back."

The black man laughed, but his eyes didn't. "You're bullshitting me. I read about the CIA. That's from before the Great War."

"Is that what you call it?" Rourke was moving the improvised firebomb nearer to the door. "At Mid-Wake? Where's that?"

"You get us out of here, you'll find out. And I'm buying the first drink."

"You're on." Rourke nodded. "But after we clear the prison, there's somebody else I still have to free."

"Rourke—that's your name?"

"How about yours?" Rourke asked, the container in position now, ready to be used.

"Aldridge, Samuel Bennett, Captain, First Battalion, B Company out of Mid-Wike, United States Marine Corps."

Rourke looked at him, knowing the look was odd. "I thought you guys were extinct."

"Just been layin' low—Doctor."

"Get the guys up here, Sam—we gotta boogie."

Aldridge began speaking in a mixture of American standard English and what sounded like heavily fractured Chinese baby talk, but the men started forward, separating so the ones armed with Sty-20s were bunched together

157

and the ones armed only with blunt instruments were helping those who couldn't walk too well.

They gathered round Rourke near the door leading from the laboratory into the corridor. "Sam, you translate as needed. Here's what we're doing. This jar has a combustible mixture in it. I'm gonna roll it into the corridor and toward our friends down there," and he jerked his left thumb in the direction from which he had originally come to the laboratory. "Whoever best knows his way around the prison, take the lead in the opposite direction, because once that container is near enough to our Soviet friends, one bullet in it and the thing should explode if I did it right. And I'm pretty certain I did. Whoever the leader is, take off and the rest of us will follow. We want to reach the main prison compound or whatever so we can spring the people in confinement and swell our ranks. Anything you come across that you or one of the guys we free can use as a weapon, grab it."

"Not just guys, Doctor Rourke. They got some women down there too. And they should be ready to fight like hell because the guards like to—"

"I understand," John Rourke whispered.

Sam Aldridge completed the translation, one of the Chinese stepping forward, a Sty-20 in one hand, a bar from one of the cages in the other. His forearms were blistered and blood drooled from the right corner of his mouth, and when he spoke Rourke saw that the man's gums were hideously inflamed. He pointed to himself and to the corridor, saying something in the fractured English-Chinese patois of the prisoners. Aldridge started to translate it, Rourke preempting him. "He'll lead us. Tell him thank you."

Aldridge started to speak, but the Chinese managed an awkward but sincere-sounding, "You bet, man." Rourke clapped the man on the shoulder, then drew the first Detonics for his left hand. Then flexing his right fist, the pain coming in a brief, heavy wave, he drew the second one, the double Alessi shoulder rig taken from the bag and in place.

"Captain Aldridge—you get the honors. Give it a good roll; I'll cover you with these."

"Your hand—I can handle a regular firearm."

"So can I," Rourke assured him.

The Chinese man with the bleeding gums and blistered arms stood beside the door. Aldridge opened the door, Rourke nodding. Aldridge shoved the container through, then turned it on its side. Nothing leaked out. "Now, Sam," Rourke said calmly, stepping into the doorway.

The black U.S. Marine captain started the great jar rolling, the thwacking sounds of Sty-20s being fired toward them, Aldridge tucking back, Rourke firing both pistols simultaneously, the normally moderate recoil of the little Detonics pistols sending a wave of pain through his right hand, Rourke tucking back, the jar exploding, flames belching from it in all directions, screams from the far end of the corridor. Rourke stepped into the hallway, both pistols ready, shouting to Aldridge, "Take that bag and don't lose it! Now go for it!"

Flames were everywhere in the corridor now, the ceiling afire, Soviet personnel, their uniforms, their bodies aflame, trying to leap to safety, screams filling the air. Rourke heard the sounds of Sty-20s being fired around him, Aldridge and other escapees shooting at their enemies. "Save your ammunition. Move out!"

"You heard the man! Hustle! Hustle! Go!"

John Rourke turned away from the flames, shoving past some of the more injured men, getting up beside Aldridge and the Chinese who had agreed to lead them. The corridor here took a sharp bend and Rourke shouted to Aldridge, "Slow 'em up and you and I take that corner first in case we have company!"

"Right, doctor!" And Aldridge shouted his commands in English, then a Chinese equivalent. The pack slowed, Rourke safing the pistol in his left hand, reaching into his musette bag. There had been enough chemicals and the proper container for one more surprise. "What's that? Another firebomb?"

"No—it's a gas—should render them nauseous. But it

should dissipate quickly and there's not much of it. If we use it, we wait about thirty seconds and hold our breaths and run. Got it?"

"Yes, sir."

They were at the bend, Rourke edging forward along the wall, the flames behind them spreading, the screams dying. The fumes from burning building materials in the corridor were getting thicker, Rourke coughing, his eyes tearing. He blinked, then peered around the corner, ducking back. "They're waiting for us," Rourke snapped.

"Lemme see," Aldridge volunteered.

"Wait a minute." Rourke drew his knife, the polished section on one of the blade flats that was designed for use as a heliograph mirror-bright. Rourke angled it right, then told Aldridge, "Look in there."

"A dozen of 'em—but all prison security it looks like."

"I've been wondering why the troops weren't out myself. How big's the regular security force?"

"Couple thousand at least. Could be a lot more."

"Know a nice guy named Kerenin?"

"The Marine Spetznas field commander?"

"That's the one. Watch out," and Rourke took the grenade-sized container of gas, his left arm snaking around the bend into the corridor toward the security guards. There was a sound of glass shattering, the thwacking sounds of Sty-20s being fired toward him, then coughing, wretching sounds. Rourke was already counting seconds, the timing for the gas to dissipate an educated guess.

He reached thirty seconds and shouted, "Hold your breath, squint your eyes against the stuff, and drill everybody with your Sty-20s, then take their weapons and run for it. Let's go!" Aldridge was translating as they ran, Rourke into the corridor first, the twin stainless Detonics pistols blasting from each hand.

The security guards were either kneeling, prostrate, or leaned against the corridor walls. A few of them tried firing their pistols, Rourke downing four of the men, Sty-20 rounds from Aldridge, the Chinese, and some of the

160

others downing the rest of the guards.

The escapees used their clubs and Rourke could not have stopped the wholesale killing if he had tried—or wanted to. Twelve Sty-20s with nearly full magazines were distributed among the men, Aldridge with one in each hand now.

Rourke stepped over a dead man and past a puddle of vomit, then signaled the others. "Let's go!" And he broke into a dead run down the corridor, Aldridge nearly even with him, the Chinese just beside Rourke, his gums bleeding more badly now from the exertion, some of the blisters starting to drain.

As Rourke ran, he rammed fresh magazines up the butts of his pistols, depositing the partially spent ones in his musette bag.

He kept running, the corridor playing out, the Chinese who was guiding them signaling that they should slow, Aldridge shouting back the command in English, the Chinese doing the same in Chinese to the other Chinese among the escapees.

At the end of the corridor, John Rourke could see a rough barricade erected, prison guards on the other side of it.

Rourke signaled a complete stop. He knew the Sty-20s well enough by now and he started toward the barricade, intending to keep out of range. Aldridge and the Chinese man flanked him. Rourke called out to the guards in Russian. "If you surrender your arms and assist in the release of all prisoners, I will personally guarantee that you will be neither abused nor killed. Otherwise, the powerful explosive devices and poisonous gases we utilized against the corridor guards will be turned against you and you will be slaughtered to the last man. You have ten seconds."

"You're lyin' in your teeth," Aldridge rasped.

Rourke, without moving his lips, hissed, "If they go along, okay. No killing."

"Yeah—yeah."

Rourke began counting aloud in Russian, ticking off

the seconds.

And then part of the barricade fell away and the first of the guards stepped out, hands raised, his Sty-20 in his fist. From inside the two-tiered complex that formed the prison itself, cheering started, rolling toward Rourke like thunder.

Chapter Twenty-two

It had been necessary to physically restrain some of the female prisoners to prevent them from killing their former jailers. But Rourke was able to enforce his word, the guards now locked in their own cells, many of them stripped of uniform parts to compensate for the rags and tatters of their former prisoners. There had been two dozen guards and there were now two dozen additional Sty-20s added to the collective arsenal, plus several long wand-like implements that seemed to be a creative combination of riot stick and electric cattle prod.

Among the prisoners were whites and a few blacks, these, Rourke learned from Aldridge, taken in the continuing war between the Russians and Mid-Wake, the Americans and their Russian enemies having battled beneath the sea for a period Aldridge described as "centuries." Most of these personnel were from captured and subsequently destroyed Mid-Wake vessels, some few divers on intelligence missions. The Chinese, Rourke had assumed and further observation confirmed, were prisoners taken during the attacks by the mysterious raiders to whom the Chinese authorities on the surface had referred.

Rourke stood on a table top, one of the Chinese from among the prisoners a fluent English-language speaker, like Michael's friend Han. As Rourke spoke, the Chinese woman translated. "Soon, there will be more security police, Marine Spetznas—more Soviet personnel coming than we can hope to handle. We must leave here at once. Taking everything that can be useful as a weapon. Captain

Aldridge will lead you to the submarine pens and you can commandeer a vessel or vessels and try for this place called Mid-Wake. You'll be safe there, you Chinese. We are all allies now. But the diversion you people will create will allow me to get to another part of the complex and attempt the rescue of my friend who is still a prisoner, a woman like some of you, with perhaps the same fate in store for her." The 120 or so armed escapees, some of them showing the marks of repeated beatings and near starvation, fell totally silent. "If my friend and I reach the sub pens in time, we'll join you. But don't wait for us. Just make as much mayhem as possible and you'll help us best."

There was a shout, then another and another, and soon all around him were shouting. And then the shouting became a chant, odd-sounding in both languages. But beautiful. The chant was "Freedom! Freedom! Freedom!"

Chapter Twenty-three

Using the prison guards as shields against conventional firearms would have been effective, but against the Sty-20s, when the worst that could result would be an impromptu sleep and a headache, it would have been pointless. So they left the guards locked in the cells and, Rourke leading, the Chinese guiding them, they started from the cell blocks, Aldridge telling Rourke that it would be the first time in more than two years for some of these men that they had left the prison. Aldridge himself had been confined for more than two months, most of that time in one of the cages of the research laboratory.

As they moved through the corridor, at each turn expecting interception, Rourke queried Aldridge concerning the nature of the experiments conducted on the prisoners.

"The Russians seem to love those dart guns of theirs— the Sty-20s. Best I can figure is they're working to come up with new poisons for them. I've actually seen prisoners strapped against a wall and then shot with as many as a half-dozen rounds, medical technicians checking pulse rates, heart rates—stuff like that. Feng—the fellow with the bleeding gums . . ." Aldridge gestured toward the man who was their guide. "Feng was shot twice a day for better than a week. And the first day, his gums started bleeding."

"What about the blisters on his arm? How'd he get 'em?"

"A different thing, I guess. Just regular injections. He

165

got two injections and then they just left him, and pretty soon the blisters started appearing and splitting and there was pus and everything oozing out of his arms. We tried helping him by giving him part of our water rations—but when they realized we were doing that, they moved his cage further out so none of us could reach him. And then they put him in a smaller cage, underneath two larger cages, and took away the pots those guys used for toilets, and the guys tried, but after a while they couldn't help it, and—then the infections on his arms got worse, ya know, and . . . They hate the Chinese. I guess because the Chinese fought against them during the Great War. More than they hate us. Man, I don't know. But I know none of us are ever going back inside," and Aldridge jerked his head back toward the cells.

John Rourke kept walking.

They were nearing the confluence of tunnels which he had originally seen when entering the security level. The Chinese who was their guide stopped for a moment, apparently considering which of the tunnels to take. Rourke told the English-speaking Chinese, "If it's of any help, after I penetrated the security level, I reactivated the energy barrier. Tell him, please."

The Chinese nodded, translating, the first Chinese listening attentively, then pointing toward the third tunnel. Again, they started ahead, unable to run because of the injured among them, but keeping a brisk pace. One of the Marines started singing the Marine hymn. He had a terrible voice, but in a moment others were joining him, the confluence of voices almost pleasing. Rourke wondered if, in the days of "the halls of Montezuma" and the pirates of Tripoli, anyone could possibly have envisioned United States Marines escaping an enemy city underwater in the Pacific five centuries after a war which nearly destroyed all of humanity—when men decided to unleash the power of the sun against each other.

The tunnel was cooler and darker and damper, the sounds of their footsteps there like drums rapping some out-of-time tattoo, Rourke gradually getting those imme-

166

diately around him to quicken the pace.

He knew they were being monitored, security cameras buzzing and whirring as they walked into their scanning range.

They were nearing the end of the tunnel. "Could those APCs they have get down here?"

"I don't think an armored personnel carrier would make it."

"Sam, what's the thing they'll think we'd do?"

"Escape to the perimeter of the city. Why?"

"Let's try to outsmart them." Rourke turned to the English-speaking Chinese. "Ask our friend if there is a means of getting from this dome into the Institute for Marine Studies. And, if there is, where is it?"

The Chinese translated as they walked, sounding slightly out of breath from the exertion. Rourke was inwardly amazed that some of these men had been able to walk even this far.

After a moment, the man guiding them responded, the English speaker giving a running translation. "There is a service tunnel from the maintenance section above. It is very narrow. But when he was first brought here, prisoners were used in the maintenance service to replace piping sections which carried steam to the other domes, because the work was considered very dangerous. Some men died there. If a pipe were to break while we traveled through the tunnel, we could all die."

Rourke closed his eyes for an instant, exhaling, opening his eyes. "This is what we do. Since we haven't encountered resistance so far, I'm going to assume, unless circumstances prove otherwise, that they're waiting for us outside. In the open air, so to speak. If we get into the Institute for Marine Studies, is there a direct route into the sub pens? Does anybody know?"

A woman's voice answered. "Hey—I do!" And Rourke turned toward the throng following him, a short woman with short blonde hair shouldering her way to the front of the mob. "I know. When they brought me here, they took me past the shark pens and they hung me in the water—

upside down. They almost drowned me—and then some of them—well . . ." And she drew a deep breath.

Rourke nodded. "You came out in Marine Studies?"

"Yeah—a lot of stuffed fish and a big marble hallway? Yeah."

"When we get that far, you lead the way. What's your name?"

"Martha."

"Martha—that good with you?"

"Yes," she agreed. Her cheeks were darkly bruised and part of her left earlobe had apparently been ripped or bitten off and the little finger of her left hand was twisted, as if broken and never set, just healed. He wanted to embrace her. Instead, he walked with her beside him.

And he wondered what was happening to Natalia Anastasia Tiemerovna. . . .

Feyedorovitch had assembled some 1200 of the Marine Spetznas, so many personnel on duty with the fleet that it had been impossible to put together a larger force.

He stood on the greenway near the hedges where the two disrobed Spetznas had been discovered along with the third, younger victim of this Wolfgang Heinz. Coming up the greenway from the road beyond, walking as he always did, as though he had filled his pants, was Viktor Metz, head of security, head of the KGB.

"Boris. I must talk with you."

"Viktor, certainly. Never fear. The Marine Spetznas have the situation in hand."

Metz removed his black uniform cap and ran his left hand back across his thinning hair. "I consulted the Chairman. I asked him, Boris, why the Committee for State Security was not called in. This is a police matter, Boris."

"The missing man was a prisoner of Marine Spetznas."

Viktor Metz shook his head. "That is another thing, that only one man is responsible for such mayhem. Who is he?"

"I am given to understand, Viktor, that his name is Wolfgang Heinz and he is a German intelligence officer. They must train their men well. But we have him trapped. Even if, as we believe, he has released the prisoners held in detention, not even their considerable numbers will have a chance against us." And Feyedorovitch clapped his left hand against the AKM-96 assault rifle.

"High-power weapons beneath the domes? Do you realize—"

"I realize full well, comrade," Feyedorovitch interrupted, "that I have a responsibility to the people and to my men. This Heinz, or whoever he is, has firearms. We know that. And he uses them with considerable skill. Tapes of surveillance-camera runs have shown that all too well. He should have in his possession at least four cartridge arms and a considerable supply of ammunition. Primitive arms, yes—they fire cased ammunition! Yet effective. It would take considerably more than a few stray rounds from our AKM-96s to puncture dome material. At least I should hope so."

It was warm today and he disliked Viktor Metz intensely and that only heated him more. And full battle gear was habitually uncomfortable under the domes because of the humidity.

"Why have the police been excluded? I demand to know, Boris!"

Feyedorovitch considered fleetingly what would happen to him if, by accident, his AKM-96 discharged and the resultant catastrophe claimed the life of the head of the KGB. "I act only on the orders of Comrade Major Kerenin. And I would assume, based on your remarks of a moment ago, that the comrade major has the approval of the triumvirate. Therefore, until I am notified otherwise, this remains a matter for the Marine Spetznas. Look—"

And Feyedorovitch gestured beyond the greenway toward the ramps entering the tunnels. Armored personnel carriers were placed at regular, close intervals, men clustered around them, all armed with assault rifles. "No matter from what level they exit the prison, even if they go to the

169

maintenance level above or the research level below, they will be trapped. The entire main dome is ringed. Their only way out. If they wish to remain inside the prison for weeks, they can. But they will starve to death. And, lest you be concerned, I have dispatched teams of my best men to the walkway surrounding the maintenance level, to prevent full access to that level and any resultant sabotage."

"You did not allow firearms there!"

Feyedorovitch grew tired of being patient. "They are armed with PV-26s. If they can kill sharks, they can kill men. But I have entrusted each team leader with one AKM-96, in the event its use is at once safe and necessary. Each man knows the penalty for bad judgment. So, my friend," he said smoothly, "rest easily. Come. I have a field mess set up. We can perhaps have some refreshing drink while we await the inevitable."

Metz shook his head, grumbling, but Feyedorovitch started toward the mess shelter, knowing Metz would soon enough follow. The fellow had no choice. . . .

John Rourke edged back into the stairwell, the men at its top having betrayed their presence with idle chatter. He withdrew into the main hall and joined Aldridge and the other de facto leaders of the escapees. "We have a problem. Not insurmountable at the moment, but a problem nonetheless. Guards posted at the top of the stairs. And so I would imagine there are guards posted on the walkway surrounding the maintenance level. They obviously don't want us up there interfering with things, which is all the more reason to go. Probably just enough of a force to contain us down here, they think. Likely something similar on the research level below, perhaps not. If we wish to get to maintenance in order to sabotage the electricity and cut off their cameras and then utilize that tunnel, then we have to take out whatever force has been implaced there."

"How?" Aldridge asked.

"Funny you should ask," Rourke smiled. "Are you

conversant with the concept of a 'scavenger hunt'?" Aldridge didn't answer immediately. . . .

John Rourke had planned ahead. In anticipation of a situation such as this, with a confined space that was a corked bottleneck, he had formulated a strategy. All that remained was to find the necessary tools with which to bring that strategy to fruition. And the tools were arriving. With Aldridge and the English-speaking Chinese and the woman named Martha as team leaders (he had spared the ill Chinese who was their guide the added exertion), he had commissioned expeditions into portions of the prison already secured. In the cell-block area, there had been a cage similar to the ones used in the research laboratory, but apparently for punishment, considerably smaller, as if designed to confine a man or woman in an upright position. Some of the escapees confirmed that it had been used in just such a way. Sometimes prisoners were simply placed in it in a normal standing position, at other times forced to enter the cage upside down, spending long periods inside the cage as a form of torture, leading to days of added misery after release as a result of the confinement.

Along the corridors and in the cellblock area there had been what appeared to be chemical fire extinguishers, and this had been confirmed for Rourke as well.

When the cage was brought back, Rourke realized its construction was perfect for his idea. Assigning Martha to oversee assembly, he had two dozen of the Sty-20 pistols secured between the vertical and horizontal portions of the grillwork grid, the butts of the Sty-20s wedged between the cage sections, then tied into place with strips of cloth from the already tattered clothing of the escapees.

The haft of John Rourke's Crain knife was bound with twenty-three feet of 180-pound test cord. A certain skill was required to wind the cord to form a handle surface, and he had learned that skill from Jack; but no skill at all was required to unwind it. He unwound a sufficient length

171

of the it so that the cord could be passed through the trigger guards of each of the Sty-20s mounted together, four groups of six. Because of the stirrup-style triggers, like those found on a typical .45 automatic as opposed to the double-action revolver-style triggers found on such guns as the Browning High Power and Beretta 92F 9mms, the Sty-20s were ideal for the procedure.

Meanwhile, Aldridge supervised preparation of a plexiglass-wall section taken from the guard cubicle near the energy barrier which was used to restrict entrance to the security level.

Utilizing the web belts taken from some of the overpowered prison security personnel, the cage, fitted with the four groups of six Sty-20s, was secured to the plexiglas-wall panel. Other belts were improvised into straps bound round the plexiglas panel.

The device constructed, John Rourke stood at the head of the mob of escapees. "Here is what we're doing. I'm going into the stairwell first, using my pistols. I'll lay down some fire to send them back into cover, allowing the people utilizing our little gadget adequate time to get into position at the base of the stairwell.

"The 'gadget,' as I called it, is designed to function as both a weapon and a shield. The Sty-20 pistols were positioned in the cage gridwork so that they would be secure but also so that they would have sufficient clearance for slide operation. Four people will maneuver and fire the device. As these four people proceed up the stairwell, they will be protected from enemy Sty-20 fire by the plexiglas shield, but able to fire four separate batteries of six Sty-20s against our enemy. Once they reach the top landing, they'll take up a defensive position and retrieve any additional Sty-20s from any incapacitated security personnel or Marine Spetznas—I didn't see the uniforms clearly. The Sty-20s mounted on the device can then be reloaded as much as possible with fresh magazines.

"Meanwhile," John Rourke continued, "the fire-extinguisher brigade will move into position at the top of the stairwell. The device will be taken into the corridor for no more than twenty seconds, fired for a few volleys, and, as enemy fire starts, the device will be withdrawn. Any commander worth his salt will press the apparent advantage and close, with the withdrawing force. That's when the fire-extinguisher brigade goes into action. As soon as a substantial number of the enemy force is in the stairwell, open fire from that grillwork structure over the stairwell. And I'll be up there too in case some of them start firing back, or in case there are any live-ammunition guns in the bunch. If they do start to employ live ammo, stay clear because the only chance we'll have is for me to take out whoever is using the guns. Any questions?"

One of the women from the center of the group—black, pretty, Rourke bet, when she wasn't dressed in rags—called out, "Do you think we will bump into real guns?"

Rourke looked at Aldridge. "Do they dare under the dome?"

"Yeah—I think so. But they really love these Sty-20 things, so they'd probably only use them for backup. An emergency."

"Any other questions?" Rourke asked.

There were none. "All right—four volunteers see Martha here and give using the device—" and he pointed at the plexiglas shield with the cage and the Sty-20 pistols "—a dry run. Check that the pistols are all empty before you do. Don't forget to check the chambers."

As the mob started to break up, Rourke took Aldridge aside. "Sam—give me the operating characteristics on their assault rifles. Just in case we get hold of one, I want to know what to look out for."

"Right. It's called the AKM-96, and it's a short-action firing 4.86mm caseless projectiles. Kind of a slow cyclic rate. Which is good. The projectiles are armor-piercing and spin. I don't know if you're into old weapons besides those .45s of yours, but it's like the M-16 assault rifle used five centuries ago, before they changed the rifling. The projectile turns into a little saw blade, basically. It's what they used to call a 'bullpup.' There's a thumbhole in the stock and the action is set back from the trigger guard.

The carrying handle has a built-in optical sight."

"What's the magnification?"

"None—just a battle rifle, and it's never used for sniping or for much of anything over two hundred yards for sure. Forty-round magazine and the magazines are disposable. Magazine attachment is nice and positive. It's a good battle rifle. I like ours better, but theirs is good."

Rourke smiled. "If we get out of here like we plan, you'll have to show me one of yours."

"Hell, doctor—I'll buy one and give it to you. They owe me a coupla months back pay with hazardous duty and combat on top of it."

"You're on," Rourke grinned, clapping Aldridge on the shoulder. . . .

John Rourke stepped into the stairwell, his right hand hurting maddeningly, but a stainless Detonics pistol in his right hand just as in his left.

He edged toward the stairs, peering upward, wanting to start out with a clean shot—it would induce more terror, what he needed now. Shooting almost straight up was a poor proposition at best.

He could just see one of the men posted at the top of the stairwell now, the right arm and right side of the chest cavity. Although Rourke was for all intents and purposes ambidextrous, he was still right-handed and, despite the injuries to his right hand, felt more confident of a one-shot hit with that hand considering the difficulty of the shot. His left thumb swung behind the tang of one of the pistols, upping the safety. He stuffed the pistol into his belt, shifting the other pistol from his right hand into his left, flexing the hand at once to work out the stiffness and to inure himself to the pain that he would experience when he made the shot.

The bandage he had wrapped over the hand was soaked through with a mixture of blood and what smelled like pus. He shifted the little .45 back into his right fist, closing his hand over the nearly smooth Pachmayrs. He cupped his right hand into his left, closing his eyes against the pain for an instant, then edging further out into the stairwell.

The target was gone. He waited.

Rourke would periodically lower his pistol, periodically take his eyes off the height of the stairwell.

Then . . . Rourke saw the man now, a Sty-20 held lazily in the right fist, the right arm over the railing, the right side of the chest cavity exposed.

"Good-bye," John Rourke whispered, his right thumb whisking down the safety, settling just below the mating of slide to frame, the first finger of his right hand starting to move slowly rearward, taking up the slack. Because of the angle from the target at which he stood and the height of it over him, Rourke held high. If the bullet impacted the precise point of aim—which it most certainly would not—it would enter the right shoulder near the base of the neck. He was hoping for a center-of-mass hit to the chest.

There was no more slack left and he held his breath in his throat. The normally mild recoil sent tremors of pain along his right forearm, his ears ringing from the gunshot in the confined space, a scream emanating from the top of the stairwell, a Sty-20 clattering along the stairs and down, angered shouts. Then the body came, tumbling, John Rourke dodging back, the man dead before he hit the floor, the body bouncing once, arms and legs flapping like wings from an injured bird, then still.

Rourke drew the second pistol, firing both pistols now toward the height of the stairwell, a useless fusillade of Sty-20 projectiles peppering the base of the stairwell, Rourke emptying both pistols, shouting, "Now!"

The team with the combination weapon and shield was already into position, and now they started up the stairwell, not firing yet, another fusillade of Sty-20 fire coming at them, the darts bouncing harmlessly off the plexiglas, the team already to the first landing. Beside Rourke now were the men and women of the fire-extinguisher brigade. Rourke started up the stairs, the fire-extinguisher brigade behind him, both his pistols reloaded. There was precious little ammunition left for them, considering the enormity of the task ahead once clear of the prison. He took the stairs three at a time, hanging back as he reached the first landing, the team beneath the plexiglas shield opening fire now, the volley of Sty-20 fire launching toward the height of the stairwell, curses shouted in Russian, the static of a communicator briefly heard.

Rourke took the communicator from his own belt. The idiots were using the same frequency. He shook his head in disbelief. He monitored the signal. They were Marine Spetznas at the height of the stairwell, apparently part of a larger unit that was guarding the maintenance level. And the Spetznas commander on the communicator now was calling for the AKM-96s to be broken out.

John Rourke started running up the stairs, three at a time, nearly dead behind the team operating the volleying Sty-20s from behind the shield, the height of the stairwell nearly clear now, Rourke edging past them, firing the Detonics pistols, dropping two more of the Spetznas, the last half dozen fleeing for the doorway, Rourke dropping two more of them. "Into the walkway now!" Rourke flattened himself against the wall beside the doorway, the fire-extinguisher brigade climbing up into the grillwork over the stairwell, readying their "weapons."

The team behind the plexiglas shield charged into the corridor, the thumping of Sty-20 darts against the plexiglas shield, then the sound of live gunfire. "Withdraw! Withdraw!" Rourke commanded, the shield team ducking back, Rourke noticing one of the team with blood coming from his right arm, the arm limp at his side. "I'll see to it in a minute if we live that long," Rourke told the woman. "Get some pressure on it. Martha! Take her position!"

Martha came forward, getting behind the shield, some of the others reloading the Sty-20s as Rourke started clambering up into the grillwork. "As soon as they're inside, get the hell away!"

There was another burst of automatic weapons fire from the walkway/corridor outside, and Rourke hissed to his companions in the grillwork, "Wait until I open fire. And try to avoid hitting me with the crap in those extinguishers because I'm going down after the assault rifles. Be ready!"

Rourke was loading the last of the magazines from his musette bag into his pistols. All he had left were the ones in the Milt Sparks Six-Pak and the spare box of fifty rounds in his bag. It could go fast, all of it.

The first of the Marine Spetznas burst through from the walkway, chunks of wall surface breaking away under the three-round bursts from their AKM-96 assault rifles, another of the shield team hit, then another, this one going down, Martha shouting, "Break off now!" The shield team fell back. Rourke, a .45 in each fist, opened fire into the men below him, four of them with AKM-96s, Rourke backshooting them because it was the easiest way, one of them turning toward the grillwork to open fire, Rourke putting a double tap into the man's wide-open mouth.

His pistols empty, Rourke stuffed them into his belt, the slides still locked open, then dropped from the grillwork, the fire-extinguisher operators spraying white chemical foam over the Marine Spetznas below them, Rourke's right foot finding the face of one of the Marine Spetznas, kicking the dying man into unconsciousness as Rourke's hands wrestled the rifle from the man's grip. There was a shoulder-slung bandolier of spare magazines and Rourke took it.

Rourke found the selector, the weapon still on full auto as he started for the doorway, more of the Marine Spetznas suddenly filling it, but armed only as far as he could tell with the Sty-20s. Rourke opened fire, spraying the AKM-96 into the nearest bodies. Marine Spetznas fell, Rourke stepping over the dead, continuing to fire, the rifle equipped with what Rourke had grown up calling a "jungle clip," a device clamping two magazines together.

As Rourke emptied one magazine, he buttoned it out, not inverting, but shifting the spent magazine right, ramming the full one up the well, working the bolt release by guesswork and overall weapons experience only, then opening fire again. Darts from Sty-20s impacted the wall surface around him and he ducked back, firing again into more of the Marine Spetznas.

And now Aldridge was beside him, one of the AKM-96s almost alive in the U.S. Marine's hands.

Together, Rourke and Aldridge advanced into the walkway corridor. Marine Spetznas were closing from both sides, most armed only with the Sty-20s, some few with AKM-96s. Rourke's rifle was empty and he rammed the flash-deflectored muzzle into the eye of an advancing Spetznas, killing him. A fresh magazine from the bandolier. Rourke rammed it up the well as the spent one fell away, firing the dead man's weight from him, advancing.

Martha's team with the plexiglas shield and volley-firing Sty-20s was onto the walkway now, flanked on either side by more of the escapees armed with fire extinguishers, more men and women filling the walkway behind him now as Rourke glanced back, some armed only with pieces of their cages, or using empty fire extinguishers like cudgels, some using the riot stick cattle prod devices and just beating at their enemy.

The enemy AKM-96s were opening up from a defensive line formed along the walkway near steps leading down to the maintenance-level floor, Rourke shoving through the throng of escapees, advancing, Aldridge beside him again, advancing to reach the assault-rifle-firing Soviets before their weapons could do their work.

One of the Soviets went down, then another, Rourke's left upper arm feeling a hit tearing across the bicep. He kept going. Another of the Soviets went down, trying valiantly to hurtle his assault rifle out of reach of the escapees. Rourke sprayed him again, kicking the rifle toward the escapees so it could be picked up and used. Someone picked it up—he didn't know who—because he heard the rifle opening up, more of the Soviets, now fleeing down the metal steps toward the maintenance floor, dropping.

John Rourke reached the head of the steps, ramming a fresh magazine into his expropriated rifle, hosing the steps below him, Marine Spetznas turning to fire up at him,

Rourke killing them before they could. Aldridge jumped the railing to the maintenance floor below, firing into the fleeing Soviets. Rourke, his left upper arm cramping on him, flipped the handrail along the steps, jumping only half the distance Aldridge had, coming out of it in a roll, firing out the AKM-96 into the backs of a half dozen of the Soviet defenders.

His rifle was empty. No time to reload now, one of the Spetznas hurtling his body at Rourke, his bare hands going for Rourke's throat. In his left fist John Rourke had the big Crain knife, and he rammed it through the man's abdomen up to the double-quillon cross guard, then shoved the body away, ramming a fresh magazine up the well of the AKM-96, firing again.

A good fifty of the escapees, some of them wounded, had made it down from the walkway now, some of them using the steps, some hurtling themselves onto the backs of Soviet fighting men below them. There were pockets of hand-to-hand combat everywhere, Rourke bracing his right foot against the stomach of the man he'd stabbed, wrenching his knife free. The knife in his left fist, the nearly fully loaded AKM-96 in his right, he waded into the thickest of the fighting, a short burst to one man, a downward slash from his knife to another.

He kept going.

Screams of death filled his ears, the escapees taking no prisoners as they finished the Soviets who had been their tormentors. As Rourke turned away from shooting one of the Spetznas who had been locked in combat with a woman escapee, he saw another of the escapees—a Chinese—ramming an electrified riot stick down the throat of his Russian adversary, the Russian's face purpling, the Chinese kicking the Russian repeatedly in the face until the body stopped moving.

Rourke stood where he had stopped. He looked from side to side. Some of the Russians were still being finished off. But the battle had been won.

Bodies littered the floor, were draped over the walkway railings and over the handrails for the steps, prisoners and their former jailers as well.

He had tried earlier to determine which pipes carried the electrical current that supplied the domes and which were the emergency circuits. He crossed toward the locked control panels at the center of the maintenance level, studying the piping in greater detail now. As he walked, he loaded a fresh magazine up the well of the AKM-96, let it fall back on its sling, then began reloading magazines for his pistols from the spare box of 185-grain JHPs in his musette bag. Six rounds to one magazine, then he loaded it up the butt of one of the twin Detonics pistols. Six rounds to another, then up the butt of the pistol. In turn, he worked the actions, chambering fresh rounds, lowered the hammers, and holstered his guns in the double Alessi shoulder rig he wore. He continued reloading magazines, some of the spares that were loose in his musette bag, taking from the rapidly depleting box of fifty, reloading partially spent magazines as well.

He stopped before the locked control panels. Aldridge joined him. "Open that," he told the black Marine captain.

"Sure, doctor." Aldridge stepped back from the panel doors and fired a burst into the locking mechanism, the thin substance, metal-like, that formed the cabinet cracking. Aldridge rifle-butted the lock away. Rourke approached the panel, studying it.

"It looks like these control the main power supply for the domes and these control the emergency power supply. Now we'll need emergency lights on to get through that passageway into the Institute for Marine Studies. That leaves two other systems—this and this. Now, if you look here at these diode readouts, only the main system is showing a fluctuation in power. And this one. The emergency system is just on and that's all, ready to kick in. And this one—the one I mentioned a second ago—it's got less leading out of it but is evidently in use. Must be for the electronic monitoring system. And having it on a different circuit board only stands to reason. Agree?"

"Ohh, sure." Aldridge laughed.

"All right. So—we cut this one and the main power supply is off and the emergency power supply kicks in. And I bet when we do, this other one that's in reserve kicks on. If everything here is geothermal, they won't be running anything off fossil fuels, synthetics or nuclear. You agree?"

"Everything's geothermal here. That I know."

"So—if the geothermal energy supply just cuts out, they'd be up shit's creek without a paddle. Assuming they assume that won't happen, then they need a power source, probably off batteries, that'll allow them to have the power to restart their machines and generate power to restore full power. This should kick on then." Rourke shut off the main system. There was sudden, inky blackness, but only for a second, and shouts and muted screams from the survivors of the battle. Emergency lights came on with an audible click, red like those used at night in submarines to allow for maximum visual acuity when going onto the surface. Rourke could see the panel again. "All right. Both of these reserves are activated. Now—we switch off this." He closed down the one original panel that still had unchanged power levels. "And we kill the surveillance cameras. Now—watch which one of these goes to a higher reading and hope it's the one for the emergency start-up power."

His gamble worked. "All right," Rourke whispered. "Now—we kill this and they can't restart their generators without a lot of fooling around and—more important for our purposes—they can't see or hear us as we hit the trail." Rourke shut down the third panel. The emergency lighting still worked.

"Damn," Aldridge whispered. "What now? I mean, all they gotta do is turn on those switches and they're back in business."

"Nope. Help me follow this piping in and out. Then we cut through the piping—yeah, it's not metal. Some sort of fireproof plastic substance. We cut through it with these," and Rourke gestured to the AKM-96. "Got somebody good with electricity?"

181

"Besides you?"

"Yeah." Rourke grinned.

"Yeah."

"Good. Get whoever it is to crosswire the three dead panels so when they start connecting things they not only start connecting things wrong but they electrify the panel. Get my idea?"

Aldridge laughed. "You wanna job in the Marines when we get back?"

"No—but thanks anyway. I'm too old to enlist."

"You thirty-five or so?"

"Add five hundred years to that and you're almost there," Rourke told him, then started walking the piping, Aldridge doing the same. Tracking the piping took almost ten minutes, but when they were through, Rourke was satisfied and Aldridge went off to find his electrician.

Rourke took the communicator from his belt. He walked away from the area near the panels, getting as far away as he could from the moans of the injured and dying. His doctor's instincts told him he should be treating these people, but other instincts told him that if he didn't secure what remained of the operation as best he could, all of them would be dead and he would have helped no one.

When he was a sufficient distance away, he opened the communicator, depressing the push-to-talk button. Aldridge joined him and Rourke touched his finger to his lips to signal the Marine officer's silence.

Rourke spoke into the communicator. In Russian. "All dead here. Some kind of—of chemical weapon. Coming to surface by way—by way of—of research level tunnels. Followed them." Rourke coughed into the communicator. "Stop them—stop them, comrades." Rourke left the circuit open for a moment longer, breathing heavily into it, then released the push-to-talk button.

"I speak Russian. That was cute." Sam Aldridge grinned. Aldridge's left arm was bleeding, but not badly, the cut long but not appearing deep. Rourke realized it was the first he had noticed it.

182

"Yeah, well—hope they believe it. Let's do what we can quickly for the wounded and then get the hell out of here."

Aldridge nodded, starting back with Rourke.

As they passed the electrical controls, gunfire was starting, the pipes which carried the electrical feeds being severed. Rourke noticed a woman, as disheveled-looking as any of the rest of the escaped prisoners, but pretty nonetheless, working to cross-wire the panels.

As they returned to the base of the steps leading down from the walkway, there were still moans, cries for help. John Rourke found the nearest of the seriously injured and tried to do what he could. All around him, men and women from among the escapees were either caring for the injured as he was or arming themselves from the weapons of the fallen.

Rourke glanced at the face of his Rolex. Time was running out for them to escape—and perhaps too for Natalia. "We move out in five minutes!"

Chapter Twenty-four

Michael Rourke returned the salute, walking purposefully but not quickly toward the half-track truck where they had left Maria Leuden hidden among containers of synthetic fuel, Paul Rubenstein and Otto Hammerschmidt walking at his left in descending order of apparent rank. It amused Michael slightly that the only one of the three of them who was an actual military officer wore the lowest rank. He had noticed that Karamatsov's army seemed rank-heavy, and in a quick conference in hushed tones Captain Otto Hammerschmidt had confirmed that deduction.

The sky was darkening, not from the hour but from what appeared to be an approaching storm. And in the comparatively short time since they had left the truck, the temperature had noticeably dropped.

Michael walked on, nearing the truck, whispering to Paul beside him. "We're going to have to take turns watching the command tent until my dad and Natalia show—" But he was cut off, an officer of major's rank approaching, Michael stopping, his blood turning colder than the air temperature. Michael came to attention, saluted, the major hurriedly returning the salute, barking orders that were totally incomprehensible, then leaving as abruptly as he had come, Michael saluting again, the major not returning it at all this time.

"What the hell was that?" Paul whispered.

Hammerschmidt, coming nearer, his voice a guttural hiss, said, "I didn't like the sound of it."

Michael shrugged, starting for the rear of the truck. There were other vehicles parked in long ranks on either side of it and behind and in front of it. It would take some jockeying to move the vehicle and he was grateful that at least it looked as though the truck could be moved when needed.

Michael looked from right to left. There were people running throughout the encampment, vehicles starting up. He was beginning to get bad vibes. He threw up the tarp covering the rear of the truck and started to clamber up. Then he heard Maria Leuden's voice. "Michael—if I understood that voice out there, he was ordering Paul and Otto to the assembly area at the front of the camp. Some emergency and he required personnel. I think. And if I'm right and they don't show up—"

Michael Rourke cut her off. "Hang on." He threw down the tarp.

Paul looked at once nervous and resigned. "If we've gotta hang around here for maybe another six hours or so, we don't have any choice, Michael. Next time that officer sees me or Otto or you for that matter, we're in deep shit with him and all of a sudden the center of attention we can't afford."

"You are suggesting we go?" Hammerschmidt asked, his voice tinged with urgency.

"I don't see a heck of a lot of choice in the matter, Otto. Michael?"

"You don't speak Russian—what the hell are you gonna do?"

"We're just enlisted guys, right? Whose gonna ask us anything?"

Hammerschmidt answered for Michael. "Other enlisted men—that is who. This could be suicidal. But I agree, we have no choice. Michael?"

Michael Rourke licked his lips. "Yeah—but check it out. If it goes sour, have a way out. Don't get in over your heads. It looks like . . ." And Michael glanced toward some of the running men. They were in full battle gear. There was appropriate equipment in the truck for Paul and for Hammerschmidt. "They may be planning on being gone for a while, guys."

"If we hide in the truck and that major realizes we didn't show up or sees us after he gets back—ohh, boy." Paul's eyes were pinpoints of light.

"Go for it—get your gear." Michael looked around them to be certain they were not observed, Paul and Otto Hammerschmidt disappearing into the rear of the truck. Michael clambered in behind them. Hammerschmidt was stuffing his German service pistol under his uniform tunic. Paul was checking the battered old Browning High Power he habitually carried—had carried, he had told Michael, since that first battle near the crashed jetliner when Paul had first joined with Michael's father—how long ago?

Maria Leuden, in the gray half-light there in the rear of the truck, looked sick with worry. She hugged Hammerschmidt, and then Paul. "This is madness."

"You're tellin' me?" Paul grinned. He was stuffing all the spare magazines he had into his pockets. "This is crazy, but we don't have any choice."

"Just don't get on any airplanes, guys."

"We're gonna have to play it straight, Michael—otherwise it'll lead that major back to you, and when your dad and Natalia do show up here, there won't be anybody to get 'em out. We'll be cool."

Paul slipped a black-hafted Gerber MkII fighting knife under his tunic as well, Hammerschmidt doing the same, having adopted the knife as his own after Michael had given him one. "Gonna be up to you and Maria now," Paul said, starting for the rear of the truck bed. "Maybe I shouldn't say this, Michael, but I will. I know you want Karamatsov dead for causing the death of your wife and the baby. But that isn't why we came here. Right?"

Michael Rourke clapped his and his father's best friend on the shoulder. "Right. You've been hanging around with my father too long. You're beginning to think like him."

"I'll take that as a compliment."

"That's how I meant it." Michael Rourke clasped Paul Rubenstein's right hand for a moment, then released it. Then he shook Otto Hammerschmidt's hand as well. "Ahh—"

"I know." Paul grinned. " 'Dark of the moon,' right?"

"You've got it."

Rubenstein started through the tarp, Michael calling to him and to Otto Hammerschmidt. "When you guys get back, don't hang around here too long looking for us. We may have already pulled it off. If you don't see us, rejoin Han and his men on the high ground."

Paul only nodded, Hammerschmidt shooting Michael and Maria a salute, then following Paul out of the truck. Maria stood beside Michael Rourke. "We might never see either of them again," she whispered, a catch in her voice.

"We'll see them. You stay in the truck. I'm going back to check on the command tent again. They might be looking for female enlisted personnel out there too. So lay low."

"Lay low?"

"Hide!" Michael smiled. He touched his lips to her forehead and started for the tarp covering the rear of the truck, but her arms came around him and she kissed him hard on the mouth and he held her tight against him for an instant longer. He had lost one woman that he had loved, always would love. He didn't want to lose another. "Hide—do it!" And he left the truck, checking the positioning of the two Beretta pistols under his tunic. He had the uncomfortable feeling he might need them soon.

Chapter Twenty-five

The Chinese with the bleeding gums and blistered forearms had led the way before, but now the woman named Martha had joined him, Rourke and Aldridge keeping to the rear of the mass of humanity for the first several minutes after they had entered the service tunnel, to guard against attack. But after they were well inside the tunnel, Rourke delegated some of the other escapees who had picked up AKM-96s to guard the rear, then with Aldridge worked his way forward.

The deeper they trudged into the tunnel connecting the maintenance level to the Institute for Marine Studies, the hotter and more humid it became. Pipes were everywhere along the ceiling and walls and even along the floor, pipes carrying live steam in and electrical energy out, some of the pipe joints dribbling scalding-hot water, the floor awash in water several inches deep.

They kept going. Rourke took the gym bag back from the young black woman who had volunteered to carry it for him. Her name was Lisa. She was a corporal, like Aldridge a United States Marine. "Who are you after? I mean, must be some friend." And then she laughed.

"What's so funny?" Rourke asked her.

"I was just thinkin'. You did all this for us and you don't even know us. I could see you riskin' your life for a friend."

"She'd do the same for me, Lisa."

"A 'she,' huh?"

Rourke smiled. "That's not why."

188

"You tell me something, Doctor Rourke?"

"If I can," Rourke said, stepping over a knot of pipes in the growing jumble of pipes, the water deepening too.

"How come all the good guys are always spoken for?"

Rourke didn't know what to say to her. . . .

The red lights, the rising vapors, the wet-earth smell of the place and the intense heat were like the vision of hell John Rourke had conjured in his mind when he had first read Dante. Each time the service tunnel took a bend, he kept expecting to see Virgil standing just beyond and inviting Rourke and the escapees to take the complete tour. Rourke had already decided he would decline the opportunity.

And also beyond each bend, Rourke expected to see Kerenin's troops waiting. It would not have taken a genius to guess the route Rourke and the others followed, Rourke realized. It was the only logical alternative. But as John Rourke had often realized, before the Night of the War and since, simply because something was logically obvious there was no reason to suppose it would be perceived as such.

They kept moving, Rourke again checking the luminous black face of his Rolex, smudging steam away from the crystal with his thumb just to read it, neither the darkness nor the red light sufficiently intense to read it easily. And so, when he read the time, he had to hold his wrist up to where it nearly touched one of the ceiling-mounted emergency lights. And time was running out for Natalia, he realized. If Kerenin harmed her, he thought . . . And Lisa, still walking beside him, between him and Sam Aldridge, interrupted his thoughts. "You're gonna break off from us and try and penetrate the officers' complex?"

"Yeah." Rourke only nodded. The water made slapping sounds as he walked through it, the liberated Soviet boots leaking like sieves now.

"You're gonna need a backup, doctor. You did me a good turn. I'll do one for you. They had me up to the

189

officers' quarters once. Hosed me down. Gave me one of those tacky-lookin' blue pantsuits the women wear around here and let me air-dry while they transferred me. Some of the officers—sometimes they like something exotic, you know. Guess they figured black was exotic. But I saw the place real good. I can help."

"I can find my way," Rourke told her good-naturedly. "But thanks for volunteering."

"You just don't want any help."

"That's not it," Rourke told her.

"Good—then I can go with you. Me and my new buddy." And she slapped her open left palm against the forward portion of her AKM-96's bullpup stock and the assault rifle rattled. . . .

The tunnel opened ahead, the clouds of steam less intense and already a certain coolness in the air, Rourke shivering once as they walked on. Soon, he told himself. And inside his head, he almost whispered to Natalia, "Soon." John Rourke quickened his pace. . . .

Paul Rubenstein remembered Michael's warning not to get aboard any airplanes. As he looked at Otto Hammerschmidt, he thought the German commando captain must be thinking the same thing. But there were aircraft waiting in the distance across the hardpack of the snowfield over which he, Hammerschmidt, and about 250 armed Russian soldiers marched. To board the planes? That seemed obvious.

Trucks had taken them from the main camp to one of the smaller camps, Paul judging the travel distance as about two miles from the main camp. They had passed through the camp, tents erected there, but ordinary tents, not the fancy, hermetically sealed, climate-controlled kind used by the German forces and the similar ones used by the Russian forces. And there was a large crater around which the trucks transporting them had traveled, the crater scooped out with mounds of snow-splotched dirt near the rim and heavy construction equipment parked beside the mounds.

And there were actual buildings, in various stages of construction, but all the shells at least looking nearly completed. And then there had been the trucks bearing the gas which Karamatsov had unearthed in Egypt and used against his own people to overthrow the government of the Soviet Underground City, the gas which acted only on males, causing them to become enraged animals obsessed only with killing.

Paul had turned his eyes away from the hole in the tarp through which he had viewed this and tried to think what it reminded him of.

As he marched now beside Otto Hammerschmidt in ragged formation toward the airplanes, he still tried to remember but could not. . . .

Annie Rourke Rubenstein slid her holsters forward a little and dug her hands into the slit pockets of her ankle-length, heavy woolen skirt. She was becoming impatient with waiting for the Chairman's promised escort.

The Chinese guards inside the tunnel, which lay beyond the monorail platform on which she stood with a lovely, English-speaking Chinese girl, had more than once stared at her. The strange race, she supposed, or even the heavy clothes. Particularly the guns. The Detonics Scoremaster .45 her father had given her was at her right hip, the Beretta 92F 9mm at her left. The rest of her gear—her backpack, her heavy coat, her heavy shawl, her M-16— was piled on the platform near her.

"Ma-Lin?"

"Yes, Mrs. Rubenstein?"

"How long have we been here?"

"Five minutes, I believe." And the Chinese girl consulted her delicate-looking watch by rolling back the storm cuff of her jacket. "Indeed. It is five minutes almost exactly since we disembarked from the monorail."

Annie nodded. Ma-Lin wore heavy pants and a heavy sweater and a light, storm-sleeved jacket over the sweater, a knapsack and a long, heavy-looking, fur-ruffed coat on the platform near Annie's own gear. "You didn't have to come with me. I'm a married woman. I don't need a chaperone."

Ma-Lin smiled. "I was ordered to accompany you by the Chairman himself. And I was greatly honored to be chosen, Mrs. Rubenstein."

"Do you work in Intelligence?"

Ma-Lin only smiled.

Annie felt the corners of her mouth turn down. An escort that wasn't coming. A chaperone who was a spy. "Great," she murmured.

"What is great, if I may be so bold, Mrs. Rubenstein?"

"What?"

"What is great?"

"Nothing's great."

"Then why—"

"I'm getting angry—and not at you. My husband and my brother are out there somewhere and they're looking for my father and one of my 'family,' who are also out there." A monorail car was coming in to the station. "And I'm just supposed to stand here and be calm and ladylike. That's a pile of bullshit. And I'm just about—"

She wheeled toward the arriving car, the sound—not one of the mechanical ones—startling her, somehow filling her with hope. It was the sound of a dog barking.

Hrothgar, bounding toward her, almost knocking her over as the animal stood on its hind legs, trying to lick her face.

And then she saw him, his green tunic, the high boots, the staff that was almost as tall as he was. The Icelandic policeman Bjorn Rolvaag. He stood, filling the doorway of the monorail for an instant, then stepped from the car to the platform, the car shaking behind him, his massive weight gone from it. His voice was calm, even, and he smiled at her.

"Annie."

Behind Rolvaag were a half-dozen Chinese troops in what looked like full cold-weather field gear.

Rolvaag whistled faintly, quickly, and Hrothgar bounded away from her, toward him. And she ran into Rolvaag's arms and let him hug her tight.

Chapter Twenty-six

Lisa, the U.S. Marine corporal—John Rourke had never caught her last name—crouched behind one of the specimen cases, a solitary red light illuminating the museum hall. The doors leading into the entryway were still open, the way Rourke had left them after making his escape from the shark pens.

Rourke touched the woman on her bare left arm, then started forward in a low crouch, the AKM-96 tight in both fists. They had entered through a back door leading from a narrow stairwell into a small office, perhaps the office of the curator, a partially completed exhibit drawing on the desk along with trays of paperwork. When they had entered the gallery, Rourke had noted with satisfaction that the watertight door he had secured between the shark pen area and the display hall was still secured.

They had left Aldridge and the remaining escapees to continue on toward the submarine pens and escape, Captain Aldridge vowing that once he and his band had reached the dome beneath which the Soviet fleet was housed, they would create the noisiest and most attention-getting diversion possible.

Martha had estimated the travel time, unless they encountered serious resistance, as under fifteen minutes.

Rourke stood beside the doors now, the entry hall just beyond. He had counted seconds, not trusting that there would be sufficient light by which to view the face of his watch.

"Now," he whispered, stepping through the doors slowly, the Soviet rifle in a hard-assault position.

He started to turn toward Lisa, to call her out, but the

black Marine was beside him. A bank of three red emergency lights bathed the entry hall in blood-tinged gray shadow, the entrance to the walkway and street beyond nearly as dark.

And suddenly, Rourke realized what he had done. In disabling the primary lighting system, he had turned off the artificial sunlight, however it was made to work, which illuminated the domes. Outside, beyond the doors, it was "night."

Hugging the wall as he moved, he started for the doors, Lisa beside him. As yet, there was no sound of the diversionary action promised by Aldridge. "Don't worry," Lisa hissed beside him, the top of her curly-haired head not quite even with his shoulder. "Captain Aldridge'll deliver, doctor. Pretty soon, you're gonna have one hell of a disturbance."

"We're gonna need it," Rourke told her.

He had formulated a plan, if it could be called that. But he needed panic for it to work.

They were beside the doors leading to the walkway now and as he reached to touch the doors, he heard the sound of an explosion. . . .

Natalia had been allowed to leave the bed, Kerenin sending in two female Marine Spetznas, both women powerfully built and armed with Sty-20 pistols. She had been given nothing to wear, and so she had wrapped the blanket from the bed around her, then used the bathroom. After all the time waiting, it was difficult to do what she had to do, the presence of the two armed women making it worse. One of the women smiled at her. It was not a smile of friendship, but more like a smile of lust. Natalia told the woman, "You would have to kill me first, sergeant. And then Major Kerenin would be very angry with you." Natalia had closed her eyes then, pretending no one was there, at last relieving herself.

The women flanked her now on either side as they started back from the bathroom along the small hall toward the bedroom. If these were a senior major's accommodations, she would not have been eager to see enlisted barracks.

The moment the two women had first entered the bedroom, the smiling one watched while the other woman cut the bonds which had trapped Natalia in the bed—for how long?—Natalia had determined this might be her best possible chance for escape. The unsmiling woman wasn't that much taller than she, although considerably heavier. But the uniform would serve.

Her blanket tight around her now, she stopped beside the bedroom door, the smiling woman reaching past her to open the door. An alarm sounded, from somewhere beyond the confines of the apartment. The smiling woman hesitated, looking toward the apartment door further along the hallway. Natalia did not hesitate.

The blanket would have to fall.

Natalia's right hand caught the smiling woman's right wrist, Natalia's right knee smashing up into the elbow joint, the heel of Natalia's left hand hammering up and out against the base of the second woman's nose, killing her instantly. The smiling woman screamed, falling away, a Sty-20 pistol in the woman's left fist, a curse on her lips.

Natalia wheeled half right. Still unsteady on her feet, her right hand went to the doorknob for support as the sole of her left foot snapped out, catching the smiling woman's gunhand and knocking the pistol clear of her grasp, the Sty-20 skidding across the bare floor. Natalia's left foot slapped out again, the heel of her foot contacting the smiling woman's throat, crushing the larynx. The smiling woman gasped, choked, Natalia getting her balance as the door knob against which her right hand rested fell away and she herself started to fall, inward, into the bedroom.

Her right shoulder hit the bedroom floor.

To her feet—almost. The muzzle of an assault rifle, inches from her face. "Major—you are very good!" Kerenin's voice. Natalia started to go for the muzzle of the assault rifle, but there was a popping sound and some-

196

thing struck her right breast and she screamed.

She got to her knees. She could see Kerenin's booted feet, hear him whisper. "We have a variety of special-purpose rounds for the Sty-20, major. The one I just used is a special psycho-de-inhibitor that is combined with a mild muscle relaxant. The sensation is supposedly quite pleasant, really."

Natalia threw herself across the floor toward him. And then she started to laugh as she spread out her arms like wings and cooed, "I am flying!"

Kerenin was talking to her, but she didn't understand about what. But she knew that his hands were on her breasts. . . .

Paul Rubenstein's feet were cold, just standing there in the snow within fifty yards of the cargo helicopters. Their rotors had shut down. The windows were steamed and he could not see inside.

The abrupt major who had stopped Michael, Otto (beside him in the ranks now), and himself had two other officers with him, the junior officers shouting commands Paul Rubenstein could not understand. The forward ranks broke off left and the ranks just in front of him and behind him started right, Paul joining the men around them, Hammerschmidt still beside him. He ran, not knowing where, but as part of a herd, after a second or so detecting some order in the chaos. The leading ranks had broken up by squads to ring the cargo helicopters to the north side of the field, and the element Paul and Otto Hammerschmidt were part of doing the same with the helicopters on the south end of the field.

Semicircles were formed near the cargo doors, the doors opening now. Junior officers were everywhere, shouting commands, running from one squad to the next, Paul, Hammerschmidt beside him, joining the rest of the men in their squad in fixing bayonets, then going to high port.

The cargo doors opened.

Men. Women. Children. They were all Chinese. They

were all naked. They were all pushed through the cargo doors and into the snow.

Paul Rubenstein felt tears welling up in his eyes.

He now knew what the camp they had passed reminded him of.

Inside himself, under his breath, he whispered, "God of Abraham, let this not be so."

But he knew that it was.

More orders were shouted, Hammerschmidt's elbow prodding him, and Paul advanced on the naked people, their bodies shaking in the cold like leaves in the wind. Rifle butts were hammered into naked backs, kicks were leveled against naked legs, spittle was fired from the mouths of some of the Soviet soldiers into the startled, frightened faces. And the naked people—there were hundreds of them, some of them crying, some of them talking as though they were trying to say this was all some terrible mistake, some of them as saucer-eyed as an epicanthically folded eye could be—were prodded forward across the snow, the helicopter crews shoveling human excrement from the insides of their machines. Women held infants, the infants' bodies blue-tinged with the cold, some of the infants trying to suckle.

Gradually, the naked people were all herded together as they marched on, close to one another, Paul realized, for warmth. A woman fell, dropping her baby, and Paul started toward her to help her, stopped, realizing what he was doing, another of the guards running toward her, kicking at her, brandishing the bayonet toward her baby. The woman caught the baby in her arms and ran stumbling into the herd.

"God of Abraham," Paul said again under his breath. He was a Jew marching naked human beings through a snowfield toward a death camp.

And his body shook with rage. . . .

"What are you doing, Boris Feyedorovitch!?"

As Feyedorovitch jumped inside the Gullwing, he

198

shouted back to the KBG head, "I am using my brain instead of waiting for orders! Try it sometime, comrade!" And he shouted to his driver, "The submarine pens. Now!"

The Gullwing started ahead, bumping across the greenway and over the curb, just missing one of the armored personnel carriers Feyedorovitch had ordered to the pens as well.

He spoke to his driver, but he was really thinking out loud, he knew. "We have been tricked. That radio communication. This Wolfgang Heinz or whoever he is—he speaks Russian, I would wager. And he tricked us. Curse him!" And Feyedorovitch started to laugh. Whoever he was, this tall, lean, courageous man had so far outsmarted all of them. And Olav Kerenin would be hard put to explain it all away. "Faster!" And the Gullwing moved ahead. . . .

John Rourke stepped through the doorway from the People's Institute for Marine Studies and onto the walkway. Alarms were sounding, even more loudly, it seemed, than before. The street between the walkways was jammed with fast-moving Gullwings, most of the Gullwings—they had running boards—with armed men hanging from either side of them. And many of the soldiers carried AKM-96 assault rifles. He tucked back into the doorway. "What the hell do we do now, Doctor Rourke?"

He looked down at Lisa and smiled. "Join all the happy people. Come on." Rourke left the doorway, crossed the walkway to the street.

As the first likely-looking Gullwing passed, he jumped for the running board, his assault rifle slung under his right arm, shouting, "Come on!" to Lisa. But there was no time to look to see if she was coming. As he reached the running board, his right hand grasped the right ear of one of the men clinging to the Gullwing there, just beneath the level of his helmet. Rourke snapped his right arm back, his right hand alive with pain but still functional. The man fell away, the Gullwing bouncing as the vehicle careened over the man's body, a stifled scream, then no more sound. Beside him, another of the soldiers was grabbing for him.

As Rourke turned to struggle against him, he saw the woman Marine. She was clinging to the soldier's back, her fingertips gouging into his eye sockets. "Grab onto something else!" Rourke commanded. She obeyed. Rourke's left elbow moved, impacting the hapless Russian in the face, the man's body falling away to the road surface.

Lisa clung to the Gullwing's roof with both hands now. On the opposite side, the driver's side, one of the three Russians who clung there was trying to level a Sty-20 pistol, Rourke ducking as it fired. Clinging to the Gullwing with one hand only now, Rourke's battered right hand found the butt of the little Detonics pistol beneath his left arm pit, ripping it from the leather, his thumb working back the hammer. As the man with the Sty-20 readied to fire, Rourke fired first, the top of the Russian's forehead suddenly a mass of ugly red; and then the Russian was gone. One of the other two men jumped, landing just behind the Gullwing, to his knees. The AKM-96 that had been slung across the soldier's back came up, firing. Glass or whatever it was that formed the rear windshield of the Gullwing shattered, the third Russian soldier taking part of his comrade's burst, falling away. Rourke shouted to Lisa, "Duck!" He stabbed the little Detonics toward the man, bracing it on the roof. As he readied to fire, the soldier with the assault rifle was struck, another Gullwing crashing against him.

"Doctor!" Rourke looked toward the woman, hands grabbing for her from inside the Gullwing, Rourke's right hand punching downward with the Detonics. As he swung back and out, he could see inside the Gullwing. A half-dozen armed men and the driver. This was no surprise. Rourke opened fire through the window opening, killing the man reaching for the woman Marine with a single shot into the throat, the man's eyes going wide open as his body snapped back. Inside the Gullwing, an AKM-96 opened up and there were screams, the glass of the front windshield exploding outward.

Rourke emptied his little pistol into the Gullwing, Lisa beside him, hanging on one-handed as well, the muzzle of her liberated AKM-96 stabbing through the shot-out glass near her, firing short bursts into the vehicle. The Gullwing was swerving erratically now, sideswiping other vehicles in the roadway, Rourke changing handholds and grabbing Lisa, pulling them both tight against the Gullwing now, the passenger vehicle just missing an armored personnel carrier by inches. The driver was still alive—Rourke could see him. The pistol Rourke had shoved into his belt was empty. But the second one under his right armpit wasn't. Rourke drew it with his left hand, thumbed back the hammer and fired through the open side window, the Gullwing driver's right temple dotted red, the head snapping away, impacting the raised glass on the driver's side with a slapping sound, blood smeared there as the head slid away.

Rourke shouted to Lisa. "Get that door handle beside you! Quick!"

She had it, the Gullwing rising, the driverless vehicle accelerating now, heading straight for the rear end of an APC dead ahead of them. Rourke looked back and Lisa was gone and for a moment he thought—the Gullwing was slowing. He heard the woman Marine shouting, "I made it!" She had slid through the opening. Being small could be an advantage.

The Gullwing doors were almost completely open now and Rourke swung inside, bodies of dead Russians littering the seats and floor. "Turn us around! We're going the wrong way!"

"Yes, sir!" Rourke nearly lost his balance as the Gullwing, the doors still closing, U-turned in the middle of the street, sideswiping another Gullwing. Gunfire was coming toward them now, assault rifles, bullets pinging off the bodywork. Another window shattered.

Rourke grabbed up an AKM-96 from the hands of a dead Marine Spetznas noncom and rammed the muzzle through the shot-out rear windshield. He crouched in the seat, ready. A burst of automatic weapons fire. Rourke pegged the source. The open top hatch of the APC they had nearly crashed into. Rourke fired back. "Step on it, huh?"

"These things don't have any guts, doctor."

"Pretend they do—put it to the floor and drive, lady!"

He fired out the AKM-96, the APC slowing, the top hatch closing. He wanted one of those. "Think this thing would keep rolling if we knocked the doors off, Lisa?"

"Knock the doors off?"

"Hit the door controls—do it!" Hurriedly, Rourke began to relieve the dead Marine Spetznas personnel of their weapons. Two more AKM-96s, six Sty-20 pistols. But most importantly, spare magazines for the AKM-96s. He stuffed as many of these as he could into the magazine carrier beside his musette bag, then took a second magazine carrier from one of the dead men and began filling it for Lisa.

He looked over her shoulder as he knelt behind the driver's seat. "Those two APCs with the third one behind them—the one with the hatch open?"

"You're not—ohh, my God."

"I'm glad to see religion has survived with your culture. Now, thread the needle right between those first two. If the doors go, they go. We need to be able to clear out of this fast. Got any idea how many guys they have inside one of those APCs?"

"Too many, I bet, doctor."

Rourke felt himself smile.

She was threading the needle. "Take your right hand off the wheel for a second," he ordered, crouched beside her now. When she did it, he slipped the shoulder strap for the magazine carrier over her hand, along her arm, and over her head. "Just a little something for you. Many happy returns," Rourke told her, eyeing the two APCs. "Close your eyes when we hit and step hard on the gas," Rourke told her. Almost—now, and Rourke's left arm passed across her back, sheltering the woman Marine as

202

best he could with his own body, his right arm going up to protect his face.

The open Gullwing doors were being torn away. He could feel it in the vibration of the vehicle, hear it in the sound of metal or something like it against something even harder. And he could smell smoke. As the doors went, Rourke opened his eyes, shards of the glass-like substance all around them. Lisa was screaming. "Are we out of it?"

"Step on it—right for that third APC, then cut left and just do what I do." The Gullwing was on fire somewhere and he couldn't tell where. Rourke rammed fresh magazines up the butts of his pistols, lowered the hammers, holstered them, checking the trigger-guard breaks that held them in the leather especially carefully. A spare AKM-96—he slung it cross-body behind his back like the first one. He grabbed up two of the Sty-20s, no time to check them, just safing them as he rammed them under his belt.

They were almost to the third APC, Rourke shouting, "Cut the wheel left—now!"

The Gullwing swerved hard left, Rourke coming up out of his crouch, almost losing his balance, but holding it. He was beside the ragged aperture where the right-side Gullwing door had been, jagged metal or whatever it was all that remained. "Close as you can to that APC, Marine!"

The Gullwing swerved right and Rourke jumped, his hands reaching for one of the handholds along the side of the bodywork, his right hand finding one, his right arm almost wrenched from its socket. But he held, Lisa jumping out after him, Rourke's left fist knotting into some of the rags she wore as she started to fall away, holding her for the extra instant it took while she found a handhold. She had one and he let go. He started for the top hatch, praying it was still open.

As Rourke reached the top of the APC's superstructure, the top hatch was closing. He threw himself toward it, both hands going to the exterior hatch opening, his body weight throwing back and away from the direction in which it was closing. "Lisa! Get some fire in there now!"

Assault-rifle fire, short bursts again and again, and suddenly the pressure on the hatch was gone, Rourke almost skidding back across the top surface. To his knees now, the APC bumping and jostling, over the curb, sidewiping a doorway, bouncing away. Rourke threw himself over the open hatch cover, ripping both pistols from the leather. "Ohh, for a grenade," Rourke rasped, stabbing both pistols down the open hatchway and firing them out, screams from inside, the sounds of bullets impacting metal and whining away as richochets.

"Gimme room, doctor!" Lisa knelt beside him now, her AKM-96 pouring death into the APC below them. Rourke rolled onto his back. Bullet impacts clanged off the superstructure. They were being fired on from one of the other APCs, its top hatch open.

Rourke thrust both empty pistols into his belt beside the Sty-20s he'd taken along just in case. He swung one of the AKM-96s forward, rolling onto his stomach, firing a couple of fast bursts toward the source of enemy gunfire, the other APC's hatch closing.

He edged toward the fully open hatch lid of this APC, taking a deep breath. He stabbed the AKM-96 down the hatchway and fired a short burst, tucked back. There was no answering fire and Rourke swung his legs over the hatch and down. "Wish me luck, corporal." He dropped, through the hatchway, his head banging against something, both hands going for the Sty-20s at his belt.

He fell to his knees. The interior of the APC was rigged for red, but in what light there was he could see nothing but dead bodies and unmanned control panels. "Get inside and close it and lock it after you!"

Rourke moved forward, nearly banging his head again, shoving a body from behind the wheel, the machine rolling, twisting under him, around him as he sank behind the controls. There was no steering wheel, only levers. And at the center of the control console was a video screen. Rourke started working the levers, the machine aimed dead on for another of the APCs, Rourke moving the levers frantically now, sideswiping it, the APC stalled for an instant, then moving again. He found the accelerator with his foot. He found what he thought was the brake and tapped it gently. The APC slowed. He stomped the accelerator and the vehicle surged ahead.

"You in, Lisa?"

"Right behind you, doctor," he heard her answer.

"Hang on." There was a curve ahead and Rourke punched aside a Gullwing on his right and went half over the curb and onto the walkway. He needed rearward visibility. "See if there's some way of seeing what's behind us."

"Yes, sir."

Rourke started slowing down, playing the levers until the APC started arcing. "Rear controls, doctor—there's a video screen. Just a bunch of Gullwings and some APCs. I think this is the biggest they got that goes on land."

Rourke only nodded, working the levers and making the arc now, slamming aside another Gullwing, one of the APCs suddenly looming up in his path. "How we doin' behind us?"

"Just Gullwings."

"You wouldn't know how to find reverse, would you?"

"No—what—ohh my—"

Rourke hit the lever that had been arcing him left all the way now, shouting, "Hold on to something—tight!" as he stomped the brake, the APC skidding, the rear end fishtailing right. Rourke stomped the gas again, feeling the impact as he saw it on the video screen, his APC sideswiping the oncoming vehicle. But his APC was still moving and in the right direction now, toward the military command center.

And suddenly he experienced a sick feeling in the pit of his stomach, rising into his throat. What if Natalia weren't there? Or, what if she were—He shook the thoughts away and stepped on the accelerator hard.

Chapter Twenty-seven

The German aircraft which had brought her carried them now, Annie seated with Ma-Lin, the only two women, the only two who spoke English.

"This Mr. Rolvaag—you have great affection for him?"

Annie looked at the Chinese girl and told her, "He saved my life. Yes. I have great affection for him."

"I see," and the girl fell silent. She was about Annie's own height, and their figures, as best Annie could tell, were not unalike either. Ma-Lin's hair was almost as black as Natalia's hair, and her eyes were a deep brown. She had high cheekbones like actresses Annie had seen in her father's videotapes at the Retreat always had, like she had never had.

"Do you want me to tell you about it?"

"It would be rude of me to—"

"Not if I volunteer to tell you. It wouldn't be rude then. There was this man. You know we're fighting the same war we fought five centuries ago. Well, there was the Eden Project. It started out as a group of people from all of the democracies, men and women of all races. One hundred and twenty, in all. It was a doomsday project."

"Doomsday?" Ma-Lin repeated, as if searching for meaning for the term.

"When the end of the world came. Like your city."

Ma-Lin nodded.

"They left on the Night of the War, as we call it, when the missiles were already falling. And then the crew, the commander, all of them—they opened their sealed orders. Aboard the six space shuttles—reuseable spacecraft," Annie amplified. "But aboard the six space shuttles there were cryogenic chambers and there was a supply of cryogenic serum. The majority of the people aboard all six space craft were already in cryogenic sleep. They'd thought it was just another practice drill for deep space travel, all they were ever told it was supposed to be. But the sleep chambers they were in—"

"Cryogenics?"

"Ageless sleep, I guess you could say," Annie told her. "Like your famous father and yourself and the others."

"Yes—like my famous father," Annie agreed.

"I understand," Ma-Lin said softly.

"So," Annie told her. "The sleep chambers were already programmed, just like computers, to awaken the crew automatically in a little under five hundred years. I'm surprised nobody went insane when they realized what was happening. Are you one of the Chinese Christians?"

"Yes. I am Christian," Ma-Lin affirmed.

"Then you know the story of Noah and his Ark. It was like that. One hundred and twenty nearly perfect people with a vast library of the earth's knowledge and principal species of use to mankind cryogenically frozen as embryos, to be revived and allowed to develop. Everything they needed to start a new world. And five centuries later, they returned.

"But the old world was still around," Annie whispered. "Karamatsov—the Soviet KGB commander. He had wanted to rule the world. He had worked to bring about World War III. A lot of people—good people—a lot of Russians and Americans and everybody else had died because of him, and he was still around. He had his army and his helicopters waiting for the Eden Project when the shuttles started back into their landing sequences. My father and my husband—my husband almost died.

"But the Eden Project shuttles landed finally, safely," Annie said at last. "And after a while, it was realized that Karamatsov had even had the gall—"

"Gall?" Ma-Lin shook her head. "I do not know this word."

"The nerve, the audacity."

"Audacity." The girl nodded.

"But a kinda bad audacity," Annie told her. "He'd put one of his own men aboard the Eden Project shuttles. There was a big battle when the Russians attacked the German soldiers who were helping us and the Eden Project personnel—"

"And the Germans had a community similar to ours, but in a place called Argentina in South America," Ma-Lin said, as if reciting a fact learned from a book.

"Yes. My father helped them and they helped us. And there was this real big attack." Annie gestured with her hands. "And during the attack, this guy named Forrest Blackburn, who really was a KGB agent all along, had tried framing Natalia—"

"He had a picture of Major Tiemerovna?"

"No." Annie laughed. " 'Framing' means to implicate with false charges."

"Yes! I understand."

"Okay—anyway, he tried using the battle as a cover for his own escape. He kidnapped me and stole a helicopter. He kept me all tied up and he was telling me how he was going to rape me and if—if I didn't let him, then he'd kill me or give me to the Russian soldiers he was going to and let them all take—take me." Annie shivered. She had shivered then too.

"And Mr. Rolvaag, the policeman with the dog and the green clothing—he saved you from this other man?"

Annie shook her head. "Maybe from something almost worse—I don't know. But Blackburn needed fuel and supplies and he stopped and he opened up a Soviet supply cache buried before the Night of the War. He refueled the helicopter and we went on. He had to stop for the night. And he stopped in Iceland. There was just nothing there—just—just—ice and cold and I was terrified. And when he came at me in the night, I took his knife and I killed him with it." Annie stopped talking and looked out the window, realizing that her body was trembling and her voice was trembling too. . . .

There was an officer's mess tent but Michael Rourke avoided that, instead walking past the command tent as often as he dared as part of an irregular patrol of the camp he had established for himself.

As yet there had been no sign of his father or Natalia. It was on his third pass of the command tent that he stopped.

Standing in the flap of the command tent he saw the "Hero Marshal," a man sane men would call a murderous animal. Vladmir Karamatsov, in shirt sleeves and dark slacks and high boots, a shoulder holster under his left arm, stood at the opening to the command tent.

Michael judged the distance.

Karamatsov just stood there.

The distance was under twenty yards.

With either or both of the military Beretta 9mms under his uniform tunic, Michael Rourke could have taken him at twice the distance.

The man on whose orders his wife, Madison Rourke, and his unborn child had been murdered just stood there. He was speaking with a colonel, the two of them just talking.

Michael Rourke started to reach under his tunic, one of the buttons opening under his gloved fingers.

His father, John Rourke, had told the story once or twice of a man he had known who had, before the United States had entered World War II, had the opportunity to kill Adolph Hitler. The man had been standing less than thirty feet from the Beast. The man had been armed, had killed before when he had had to kill. But his orders were not to kill Hitler.

Hitler had lived, lived to slaughter millions.

Michael's right hand was beneath his tunic now.

His fingers curled around the butt of one of the Berettas. He wore tight-fitting, thin gloves. He had shot while wearing them. Often. They would not inhibit his marksmanship.

The man Michael's father had told him about had been a Jew and after the war, when the truth of what Hitler had done was no longer hidden, the man had taken the same gun he had carried that day when he could have shot Hitler and shot himself. He had not killed himself, Michael's father had told him, but instead he had shot himself in his gun hand so that the hand would be forever useless.

The last time his father had seen the man, he had worked for one of the agencies which had searched the world for the missing war criminals. His right hand was withered and dead.

Michael's fist tightened on the butt of the Beretta.

Karamatsov still stood there, talking, orating perhaps on his greatness, his plans for world conquest.

Vladmir Karamatsov just stood there.

Michael Rourke wondered if someday he would shoot his own right hand.

But he had come as a rescuer, not an assassin. He turned, walked away, but looked over his shoulder once more. Not to memorize the face. He would never forget it, would see the face in his dreams.

He whispered to Karamatsov, "Someday, I'll be back—as an assassin."

Michael Rourke walked away.

Chapter Twenty-eight

Captain Sam Aldridge ignored the fact that some of his people were not part of the Corps. He also ignored the fact that some of them were not even Americans, and those for the most part spoke no English.

He raised the AKM-96 in his right hand and shouted, "Marines! Follow me!" And he broke into a dead run toward the fences which barricaded the submarine pens, Marine Spetznas personnel barricaded behind the fences, packing crates, and the bodies of their fallen comrades used as cover now.

He kept running, the men and women around him shouting, screaming, their weapons firing. The defenses here were impressive, but built to repel any attack which might come from the huge lagoon beneath which the submarines and the Scout subs traveled to enter and leave the Russian stronghold. The defenses were not designed to thwart an attack from behind, from within the stronghold. And as he opened fire now, his first two bursts cutting down a Marine Spetznas officer, he was not oblivious to the fact that, had his soul inhabited a Russian body, he might have been one of them, one of the Marine Spetznas. He was convinced that being a Marine, a fighter, was his karma, in his blood.

He kept running, to the locked fence now, his Marines with him, swarming over the fence gates now, a slug in his thigh—but only a grazing wound, he told himself. He was at the top of the fence, flipping it, dropping down onto the back of a Russian armed only with a Sty-20. The Russian took the impact, Aldridge told himself, his right knee hurting him. Aldridge was up, his rifle butt splitting the Russian's skull. His people were over the fence and he started forward again, toward where the Scout subs were kept. He could run one of those, he thought, and so could most of his people. But to take one of the monster subs would have been hard enough, to run it impossible without the skills.

With the Scout subs, maybe at least a few of them would actually get away. He kept running, shouting, "Come on Marines! This isn't some damn walk to the chow line! Hubba-hubba!"

Ahead, he could see the water. . . .

There were armored personnel carriers streaming from the dome for the military complex, but the energy barrier had to be down, John Rourke told himself, cutting the levers into a sharp right and stomping the APC's accelerator pedal all the way to the floorboards. The APC's rear end fishtailed. Lisa knelt beside him, holding onto him as he had made the turn, but now reloading his pistols for him. "We have guns like these. The officers carry them for ceremonial stuff, like parades. I didn't think anybody actually shot 'em."

"Just think of me as an antique collector," Rourke told her, his eyes riveted to the video screen by which he guided the APC.

The tunnel leading from the command complex was nearly choked with APCs, and Rourke was going against the flow. "Hang on again—I'm using the sidewalk. The only way." And Rourke angled the massive vehicle right, bouncing the curb, sweeping aside a Gullwing that had evidently pulled onto the sidewalk for safety. The Gullwing flipped up and rolled into the path of an oncoming APC. Rourke kept driving. He could see the point

212

where the energy barrier could be activated, a Gullwing coming through.

Rourke kept driving. "What the hell are we doin' when we get inside?"

"Straight for the officers' residences on our left. I get out and go inside after Natalia and—"

"Hey—that sounds like a Russian name."

Rourke grinned, but kept his eyes on the video screen. "She's a major in the KGB—but she retired five hundred years ago, and she was on our side even before that."

"What?"

"You'll like her—don't worry. But you stay—" He sideswiped another APC, the jar to the superstructure of their vehicle and to his body bone-shattering.

Rourke kept driving. "You stay inside and wait for me. Gimme about ten minutes tops. If we're not out, we won't be coming out."

"I got your magazines loaded. You're just dead even. No more of that funny ammunition in the box."

"Right. How are you for activating some of the weapons console on this sucker, huh?" Rourke took both pistols back from her in turn and stuffed them into his belt, the Sty-20s discarded already. He didn't have time to shoot people twice and then wait around for them to fall asleep.

"I can do it. These aren't too different from some of our stuff. If I could read the damn language."

"Whatchya need, Lisa?"

"That one." And Rourke took his eyes from the video screen for a split second. "That's fire control. The one next to it arms the system. You guys got death rays yet?"

"Death rays?"

"When I was a kid I used to see Buster Crabbe as Buck Rogers. He was transported into the future and they had death rays."

"We don't have any death rays. Neither do the Russians."

"Maybe it's a good old-fashioned cannon. Any idea?"

"Wanna find out?"

"Sure," Rourke told her. "But common sense mitigates

against it. Right now we're an APC going against the flow of traffic, maybe for some reason. We open fire, we're the enemy. So hang in there."

The energy barrier was dead ahead, some kind of Marine Spetznas traffic cop waving them to stop. Rourke regretted the fact the vehicle didn't have a horn. He kept driving, the Marine Spetznas jumping aside just before the APC Rourke drove would have flattened him, Rourke crashing against the plexiglas booth for the guards and pitching it into the roadbed. He kept driving, but slowed, waiting for a break in the Gullwing traffic so he could cross and get to the far side of the dome.

"Those things just keep coming."

"Officers who don't want to miss the chance for promotion in battle. The hell with it—hang on again," And Rourke worked the levers to cut the APC into a hard left, crossing the flow of traffic now, batting aside the Gullwings, the APC slowing, then lurching ahead.

"You're drivin' over it!"

"Only because it was there." He brushed aside the last of the Gullwings and was on open road, the officers' residence he wanted dead ahead, just as he had remembered it, just as Kerenin had told him.

If Natalia was there—he closed his eyes for an instant and prayed. If Natalia was there, Kerenin would be too. If he hadn't been killed by the sharks. Rourke stomped his foot to the floorboards, the APC's engine whining. . . .

Annie said, "I'm sorry—but just talking about it then . . ."

"There is no need for you to continue, Mrs. Rubenstein."

"Maybe I should continue, though, Ma-Lin." Annie licked her lips. "After Blackburn tried to—well—after that, ahh—I was scared to death and there were these sounds out there in the snow. I was making myself pants out of one of the blankets and I was going to try to find some way out. But I knew I was the next best thing to

214

dead. You see, I didn't know how to fly the helicopter but I knew enough to know I couldn't get it off the ground. And I knew there just couldn't be anybody alive there—in Iceland, I mean. And I saw this thing—I'd gone outside, you know? How maybe sometimes you're too frightened to go out and look at what's frightening you but you're more frightened not to?"

Ma-Lin smiled, Annie realizing she had struck a responsive chord in the girl. "Anyway—so I went outside. I had Blackburn's pistol and I know how to use a gun. My daddy taught me. So I went out, and I don't really remember what happened to me. I was just so terrified that I couldn't think and all of it was like a nightmare. But I woke up and I was in this cave and I was under all these quilts and there was a fire going and there was this dog—Rolvaag's dog, Hrothgar. And there was this man. It was Bjorn Rolvaag. He saved my life. He found me out in the snow. I would have frozen to death, but he found me, saved me. And he took me to his city."

"The Hekla Community inside the volcano," Ma-Lin noted.

"Yes—Lydveldid Island. My mother's still there. She's carrying a child—just like Madison did," and Annie Rourke Rubenstein closed her eyes. "Madison," she whispered. . . .

John Rourke already started hitting the brakes as the APC rolled over the curb and onto the lawn fronting the officers' residence. "Remember—stay here."

"I came along to help you find your way inside—remember? I was there."

Rourke looked at the Marine corporal. "Lisa," he whispered. "I thought it over. You go inside there, you might never come out again. I couldn't have gotten this far without you and if you stay with the APC and I do get Natalia out, then at least we've got a chance to reach the submarine pens and maybe make it out. If I leave this thing unattended, I can't count on it being here to get us

215

out. You understand?"

"Yes, doctor," and she leaned up to him, her arms going around his neck tight, her lips touching his cheek. He held her for an instant. "Don't get killed."

"I don't intend to." Rourke smiled. "You're a good Marine and a fine woman. Now, hang tough and give me ten minutes. Need my watch?"

"No—I can keep track of the time."

Rourke released her and started up through the hatchway, Lisa calling to him, "All clear forward—and aft too. At least on the video screens."

Rourke kept going, calling back to her, "Lock the hatch from the inside and check that all other entryways are secure."

"Yes, sir!"

Rourke slammed the hatch behind him and moved across the APC's superstructure, one AKM-96 slung beneath each arm now, a full carrier of magazines and both Detonics pistols loaded and ready to go, the Crain Life Support System X hanging at his left side. He made a mental note to find high-tensile-strength nylon cord if he got out of this alive so he could rewrap the haft of the Crain knife fully. He jumped from the superstructure of the APC to the grass which fronted the officers' residence.

The entire military command dome seemed almost empty. A Gullwing was trying for the tunnel, perhaps to join the battle by the submarine pens. The red emergency lights were a little brighter here, and there were more of them. He broke into a dead run for the main entrance. Lisa had told him one valuable piece of intelligence as they had eluded the APCs on the street and made for the tunnel leading into the dome here. All field-grade officers were given top-floor apartments. Kerenin was a major. . . .

There were a half dozen of the Scout subs at dockside in the pens and Aldridge—after setting up a ragged but, he hoped, sufficiently effective defensive perimeter—had asked for volunteers who felt they could crew the little subs. There was a sufficient number to handle half again as many subs as were available. He had ordered them to board, assuming the Scout subs were empty of crew but not taking any chances, sending a party armed with AKM-96s ahead into each of the craft first.

He had been mentally logging the minutes. Rourke was taking his sweet time rescuing his friend.

And Aldridge made a decision. "Martha!"

"Captain!" The woman ran from the edge of the dock toward him, one of the Soviet rifles in her right fist. "Sir?"

"Look—I got somethin' to do. You're in charge here. You got the rank for it anyway with me gone. Now—get everybody aboard the Scout subs and pull in your defensive people when the last hatch is gonna close, then get away from the docks so you're ready for the deep-water passage. Make a formation so you can defend each other, then get through that tunnel into the lagoon for the main sub pens. If you encounter one of the Soviet monster subs, get the hell out. If you don't, wait for me as long as it seems practical."

"Where you going, captain?"

"After Rourke. Like he said about the lady. She woulda done the same for him. Well, he did the same for us."

"Need some volunteers?"

Aldridge grinned. "Didn't you ever learn, Martha? Only assholes volunteer." Aldridge slipped his rifle forward on its sling and broke into a jog trot toward the fence. When he reached the fence, he looked behind him. The Chinese who had served as their guide, two of his Marines, and another Chinese, the one who spoke English and was probably some kind of spy, were tailing after him.

"What the hell are you doin' here?"

It was the English-speaking Chinese who spoke. "You are their commander, not mine. And, at any event, we volunteered. These rifles are useless once our people are aboard the small submarines. So . . ." The Chinese smiled.

217

Aldridge just shook his head and kept moving. . . .

There were two Marine Spetznas guards at the desk inside the foyer beyond the plexiglas doors. Rourke had crouched beside a hedgerow, seeing them although they were unable to see him. There would be other entrances, but the guards would need terminating in any event in order to make an effective escape.

Rourke moved from the hedgerow, firing a burst from an AKM-96 toward the joining of the two doors, chunks of the plexiglas and the locking mechanism falling away, his left foot kicking in against the doors, the doors swinging open. As he stepped inside, he fired an AKM-96 in each fist, cutting down the two guards as they rose from their desk.

Beyond their desk were potted plants, a table, two chairs, and a couch, all very modern-looking, then a corridor with elevator banks on both sides, and at the end of the corridor a doorway marked "Stairs."

Rourke ran for the stairs.

It was all too easy and he knew he was walking into a trap—or rather running into one. . . .

Her tongue felt thick, but she could talk a little and she called out in the red-tinged darkness to Kerenin. "What did—did you . . ."

"I did not rape you. There was no time. Lie still. I know he is coming. There is an armored personnel carrier parked outside and I heard gunfire in the hall. He is coming."

Natalia tried to move, but she was tied to the bed again, her wrists and ankles bound. "John!" She screamed his name. And Kerenin only laughed. . . .

Feyedorovitch climbed into his Gullwing again. The Scout subs that had pulled away from the docks would have all of the escapees aboard. He leaned forward, telling his driver, "The military dome—and hurry!"

From his belt, he took his communicator. "This is Captain Feyedorovitch of the Marine Spetznas. I request a frequency link with Naval Defense. Quickly. This is maximum priority." The submarines could get them, even if the Scout subs made it out of the lagoon and into open water. It took some time for the submarines to launch, and they could make no real speed in the lagoon, the Scout subs easily able to outmaneuver and outdistance them. But once they were out of the lagoon, there would be no chance of the Scout subs evading the larger craft or defending themselves against the superior weapons which would be used against them.

But he knew that one man would not be aboard the Scout subs. He was beginning to think there was no Wolfgang Heinz of German Intelligence. This had to be the John Rourke of whom the Russian woman had spoken. And this John Rourke would not leave her behind.

He got his frequency cleared, "I must speak with the duty officer for the submarine pens immediately. This is Boris Feyedorovitch, Marine Spetznas Captain, and this is a maximum priority communication. I repeat—" But already, he was being switched. . . .

Aldridge had circled around to the far side of the Scout sub pens, and there were more than two-dozen armored personnel carriers there, some of them already withdrawing. So far, he thought, so good.

The crews of the APCs stood about their vehicles, their expressions ranging from intensity to boredom, their individual weapons leaned against the sides of their vehicles or slung over their shoulders.

"That one," Aldridge whispered, gesturing toward the APC nearest his five volunteers. It had a clear means of getting from the pens onto the street and the crew looked particularly vulnerable. He thought of the old expression about a marriage made in heaven.

"Do what I do, unless I do something dumb—move out." He started ahead, angling between the hedges which separated the drive which ringed the dome from the greenway on which the APCs were parked. There was no traffic on this portion of the driveway, all non-military traffic barred, he assumed, because of the military emergency.

Aldridge stopped, signaling the men with him to do the same. He wondered if Martha had thought to inquire if all the volunteers could swim, because that was the only way, if they pulled it off, they would reach the Scout subs. He knew his own people could. Citizens of Mid-Wake were taught to be as at home in the water as on dry land from birth. If the Chinese guys couldn't, they'd learn fast enough.

He slung his rifle back. He gestured with his hands toward the six crewmen of the APC. His volunteers nodded, understanding, he hoped, that without total silence all was lost.

Aldridge started from the hedgerow, breaking into a crouching run, eyeballing the largest of the six men and taking him as his own target. The Marine Spetznas started to turn toward him, as if sensing him. The Russian started to open his mouth, as if to cry out. Aldridge slammed his full body weight against the man, hands going for the throat, thumbs closing over the windpipe. . . .

Feyedorovitch took his AKM-96 from the seat beside him. Once they had turned into the access tunnel, he had realized he was right, seeing the wreckage of several Gullwings and the destroyed guard kiosk.

His driver turned the Gullwing toward the officers' quarters on the far side of the dome, where Comrade Major Kerenin was barracked.

"Stop the car—now!"

The Gullwing skidded, stopped, Feyedorovitch activating the doors himself, stepping out, his AKM-96 in his right hand. An armored personnel carrier was parked on the grass which fronted Kerenin's quarters, the vehicle's engine still running.

Boris Feyedorovitch started laughing and he couldn't stop, really didn't want to stop.

Chapter Twenty-nine

John Rourke had reached the top floor without encountering resistance, the only shots fired his, after he had entered the building.

He stood just inside the doorway leading from the stairwell, the dim light perfect for his eyes, less perfect for the eyes of his adversaries—he hoped.

Rourke opened the door, swinging it in toward him, stepping away from it as it opened and framing himself just inside the doorway so he could see along the length of the hall. The nearest door bore the name of another major. Rourke almost felt like writing the Soviet High Command a thank-you note for being so accommodating as to place names on the apartment doors.

He reached into the case in which he had the spare magazines for the AKM-96s, extracting one of the partially spent ones he had used when he had entered the building. With his right thumb—the pain in his right hand was something of which he was barely aware, despite its intensity—he edged a half dozen of the caseless 4.86mm cartridges from the magazine lips. He put the magazine away in the case and hefted the six cartridges. He hurtled them into the hallway, across the slick-looking tiled floor.

Nothing happened.

John Rourke glanced at his Rolex. Three minutes gone, seven or so until Lisa, if she followed orders, would take the APC and run for it.

He stepped into the hallway.

Slowly, keeping to the stairwell side, he walked ahead. In American reckoning, this was the seventh floor. On the way up, he had peered through the small, reinforced plexiglas window in each door and seen nothing, no activity. It seemed the same here. He was beginning to think Kerenin had lied. But at the time there would have been no purpose.

"She has to be here—she has to be here," he repeated under his breath.

John Rourke stopped.

He saw the right combination of cyrillic characters— Olav Kerenin, Major.

It was the door at the end of the hallway, commanding the entire hall.

And finally, John Rourke thought he understood.

He stepped away from the wall, swinging the second AKM-96 forward as well now.

He stood in the hallway. "Kerenin. I finally got here."

He heard a scream—Natalia, calling his name, her voice sounding pained somehow. He walked ahead. "Kerenin. Come on."

He kept walking.

Kerenin's door swung open inward and Rourke stopped in mid-stride, his body tensing.

"If you want the woman, John Rourke—come and get her. Now!"

John Rourke started walking again.

Natalia screamed, "John—he's waiting for you—" There was the sound of an automatic weapon triggering a short burst and Natalia screamed again.

John Rourke broke into a dead run for the door, knowing he was doing what Kerenin wanted, not caring, throwing himself through the doorway in a roll, gunfire ripping into the wall inches from his head coming from the end of the apartment's narrow hallway. John Rourke fired both assault rifles and was up, throwing himself against the opposite wall. It was darker inside the apartment. "You missed me, bastard!"

"I did not miss her!"

John Rourke fought to control his breathing. His palms sweated. His mouth was dry. He licked his lips and edged forward. "If you killed her, kill yourself now because it will be easier for you than having me do it." He kept edging along the hallway wall, the rifle in his left fist stabbed forward into the red-tinged grayness, the rifle in his right hand raised slightly and almost against the wall.

"Are you coming for me, John Rourke?"

"I am coming for you, Olav Kerenin."

And suddenly the narrow hallway was bathed in brilliant light and John Rourke could see Kerenin in the doorway, an assault rifle in his fists. Rourke stepped away from the wall, his eyes squinted against the sudden brightness, and he fired, both assault rifles simultaneously. The image of Olav Kerenin shattered, glass fragments flying as the—a mirror—as the mirror exploded. At the far left corner of his peripheral vision, John Rourke saw the open door and started to wheel toward it and at the same time throw his body left, but Kerenin's assault rifle opened it, John Rourke feeling as if something were hammering into his chest and abdomen, his body slamming back against the hallway wall as the assault rifles fell from his grasp. Rourke's body skidded along the wall, another burst, Rourke's left leg swept from under him, and he fell, both hands going for the twin stainless Detonics pistols, his right forearm taking a hit, but his fist still grasping the little .45. His left hand stabbed forward as Kerenin stepped into the hallway, then his right, Kerenin wheeling toward him, the muzzle of Kerenin's AKM-96 coming up.

"You were easier to kill than I thought you would be. Two full-length mirrors and a field floodlight. Now the woman is mine."

John Rourke fired both Detonics pistols simultaneously, double-tapping them, then again, Kerenin's body slamming back along the wall, his AKM-96 discharging into the floor. Kerenin's rifle fell from his grasp, clattered to the floor.

In English, the words coming hard through the pain, John Rourke hissed, "Kiss your ass good-bye, motherfucker!" Both Detonics pistols bucked twice in his fists, Kerenin's eyes blowing out of their sockets, chunks of blood-flecked brain matter spraying against the wall behind him, the body flopping to the floor, the arms still vibrating, pulsing.

John Rourke sagged against the wall.

He looked down at his stomach, the uniform tunic blood-drenched. His left lung ached and it was hard to breathe. These were mortal wounds, he realized. Maybe if—and he laughed, blood rising in his throat, and as he coughed, blood sprayed against his hand.

He leaned his head heavily against the wall.

He had very little time until loss of blood would bring on unconsciousness and then death. The Detonics pistol in his left fist. He let it fall to the floor, moving his left hand over his left thigh. More blood. But he didn't think anything was broken.

The leg should still work.

Rourke leaned forward, pain surging through him, his eyes squeezing tighter against it than they had against the light.

"Natalia!"

There was no answer.

Rourke forced himself to his knees. His little Detonics pistols—one was still in his right fist, the other on the floor beside him, the stainless steel of the two pistols splotched with his own blood.

No artery was hit—he would have been under a quicker death sentence if it had been. He found spare magazines for the pistols and, from force of habit, saved the emptied ones. "Michael," he whispered. Michael could use them if Natalia got away. She could give them to Michael. He lowered the hammers on the fresh-loaded pistols, wiped the blood from them against his right thigh, and holstered them.

The two AKM-96s he had dropped. Rourke started to crawl toward them, coughing again, more blood this time, his head swimming, dizziness seizing him. He closed his eyes, waited until the dizziness passed. He crawled, at last

225

reaching the first, then the second of the assault rifles. He safetied each of them, slung them cross-body this time so they couldn't be lost to him. The wound in his right arm was bleeding only slightly—a flesh wound, he told himself. It seemed to extend along the length of his forearm. He wondered clinically what had happened to the bullet— or was it still inside him? It really didn't matter. There were enough bullets inside him already. One more wouldn't . . .

Rourke pushed himself to his feet, falling against the wall, coughing, blood spraying along the wall.

He pushed away from the wall, his left arm reaching out, his left hand pressing hard against the wall for support.

Awkwardly, he stepped over Kerenin's body, nearly fell, then stopped, leaning heavily against the bedroom door frame.

Natalia. Her perfect right cheek bruised, a rag balled in her mouth. But her head was moving. "You were right. We aren't getting out of this one. Not together anyway." And John Rourke collapsed toward the bed onto which she was tied.

Chapter Thirty

As he had fallen onto the bed, she had opened her eyes. And she had wished she were dead.

His left hand moved, the knife he had gotten for his son but his son had not needed in his bloodied fingers. For a moment she had been afraid for herself and she was ashamed of that. He moved the knife, perilously close to her. But in the end, he brought the primary edge of it down against the headboard where her left wrist was bound and severed the plastic cord and she was free.

"John! John!"

"Bag strapped to my back. Clothes for you. Your guns. Take my stuff. Give my guns to Michael. The knife—you keep the knife. Tell—tell Sarah—tell her—I always—she knew." His head sagged forward and the knife fell, the flat of the blade against her bare left arm. She took the knife in her left hand and cut her right wrist free, then freed her ankles. Naked, she moved her body into a fetal position beside his head and held his face against her breasts. . . .

"You and you—go ahead along each side of the corridor. Slowly. Carefully. Stop before entering Major Kerenin's apartment."

The men moved out, their AKM-96s in hard-assault positions.

Feyedorovitch stayed inside the doorway, waiting. He had heard the gunfire from Kerenin's floor, known what it had to be, then assembled a dozen men from the headquarters offices, and out of the dozen he had four armed with assault rifles, his own making the fifth, the others armed only with Sty-20 pistols.

Inside himself, he wondered who had won. John Rourke? He smiled at the thought. . . .

Natalia had packed the abdominal wounds with the blanket, folded into a tight, thick rectangle, then secured it over the wounds with the uniform belt he wore. The wound along his outer right forearm she bound with strips cut from the bedsheet, spraying it and the abdominal wound with the German antiseptic-healing agent taken from Rourke's musette bag. The leg wounds she bandaged like the arm, spraying them as well. Neither the leg wounds nor the wound to his arm were even potentially fatal unless they were just allowed to bleed. But the abdominal wounds. They were fatal. She knew that.

She had dressed quickly then in the uniform he had brought for her, buckled on her L-Frame revolvers, taken her Bali-Song knife.

She took both AKM-96s from him and started for the hallway door to make certain the way was clear.

Natalia fired a burst from each and tucked back, gunfire ripping into both of the apartment hallway walls. She fired back and ran along the hallway, back toward the bedroom.

"John—you must get up."

He was still conscious. She knew that. "John—get up."

He raised his head, looked at the Rolex on his wrist. She had taken back her watch from Kerenin's dresser, where he had put it. Apparently he had kept it as a pretty bauble to give some woman. "John!"

"You have two minutes. A woman—black—U.S. Marine Corporal. That APC out on the lawn. She'll wait for another two minutes."

"Bullshit." Natalia took his knife, one eye going to the bedroom door for a moment, then sheathing the knife, securing the safety strap.

228

She had sometimes regretted her height. It had kept her from the ballet, sometimes made clothing awkward. When mini-skirts had been popular, she had looked like she had nothing but legs. But now she was thankful for it. As she drew him up from the bed, her own height made it easier to hold him up, his left arm drawn over her shoulders.

"Forget me. Tell Annie I love her. Tell Michael the same. Tell Sarah I always loved her."

"Shut up, John—you can tell her yourself."

And John Rourke's left arm pulled tightly around her and her face was next to his. "And I love you—I never loved anyone the way I love you. Leave me a gun and I'll hold 'em off. Get out through the window. There's a balcony out there. You can work your way down."

"No."

John Rourke kissed her, harder than he had ever kissed her, then pushed her away from him, her body slamming against the wall, the breath knocked out of her. "Leave me. I'm dead."

She pushed away from the wall and walked up to him. "No you are not! You taught me never to give up. So, goddamnit, you can't either!"

Natalia Anastasia Tiemerovna grabbed his left arm. He was weaving, about to collapse again. She hauled his left arm across her shoulders and started for the window. . . .

Aldridge turned the stolen armored personnel carrier into the tunnel, little traffic except for Gullwings, the plexiglas guard booth at the end of the tunnel all but destroyed, the energy barrier down, he hoped inoperable. "Hold tight—we're goin' through!" He stomped the accelerator and aimed for dead center in the tunnel, the few Gullwings swerving away to give him wide berth, the APC sideswiping one of them, hurtling it against the tunnel wall.

Aldridge cleared the tunnel, seeing an APC parked on the grass near the officers' residence on the far side of the dome. He cut left. It was ringed by four Gullwings, men visibly hidden behind the Gullwings. And as he watched, the APC's cannon opened fire, one of the Gullwings exploding, a fireball belching toward the dome roof. At least two men were firing assault rifles toward the APC, uselessly, he knew.

"Let's get our weapons systems onto those Gullwings," Aldridge ordered. He'd bet Lisa was inside the defending APC. And on his video screen now, he saw something happening on the top floor balcony of the officers' residence beyond the little firefight. "My God—I think that's Rourke—"

Chapter Thirty-one

John Rourke started to fall, Natalia whispering beside him, "I have you, John," and as she helped him to remain upright, he touched his lips to her hair. He closed his eyes tight against the pain, almost stumbling again, walking with her.

He reassessed his wounds. She had staunched the bleeding of the abdominal wounds. And there were no exit wounds. Which meant the projectiles were still inside him and would have done considerable damage. The prognosis was still the same—death. But it was easier now to go along with her than to further delay her by insisting that she leave him behind. He would likely die on the way down, or certainly inside the APC if they made it that far.

"How are you feeling, John—don't slip away from me—please!"

"I'm fine—much better. You—you always were a good nurse," he reassured her. "How much further?"

"Not much further—getting through that window was the tough part, wasn't it?"

He looked around them, not remembering getting through the window at all. They were on the patio-like balcony, entered from Kerenin's apartment. There had to be a doorway to it—but he hadn't seen where that was. The emergency lights were still on and that was good. Aldridge, Martha, the Chinese—all of the escaped prisoners would be long gone by now, but Natalia was amazing in her adaptability and her wealth of technical knowledge. She could steal one of the little submarines he had seen coming into the lagoon and she could get away. He knew she could get away.

"All right—we're at the railing, John—now—I have to make some sort of harness so I can get you down. The slings from the rifles will do it, I think."

He nodded, licking his lips. His mouth was terribly dry. There was a second APC down there now, on the grass. "Was there cannon fire a minute ago?"

"Yes—that APC—the girl you spoke about. She vaporized one of the Soviet cars—she must be pretty good. I can't wait until you introduce us. You'll do that, won't you, John?"

"Yes—of course."

"Good—now I'm counting on you. Don't forget."

"I—ahh—"

He leaned forward, against the railing—it was at waist height.

"Careful—let me do this now—you just stand still, John."

"Yes, Mother." He laughed, and as Natalia started putting the harness of rifle slings around him, she kissed him on the cheek. He heard something, shaking his head and turning around. "They're in the apartment, Natalia. Get outta here."

"Not without you."

Rourke turned himself around, leaning against the railing now. "Gimme—gimme a rifle."

She had two of them—his? His, he told himself. She handed him one.

The window shattered and Natalia started to throw herself in front of him and John Rourke pushed her aside, shouting, "Jump for it!" as he lurched toward the window, the light brighter than it had ever been. He fired the AKM-96. The two men in the window fired back, bullets ripping chunks out of the concrete of the balcony surface, Rourke still firing, Natalia's assault rifle opening up. Rourke kept firing, one of the men down, Rourke's rifle empty. He threw it down and started to reach for the twin stainless Detonics pistols. The second man went down.

And he saw Feyedorovitch and at least two other men coming through the window and Natalia screamed. "John!" Why had she screamed? Feyedorovitch had an assault rifle. Rourke couldn't bring his arms up enough to get to his guns. He was trying—he knew he was trying. Natalia screamed his name again or was it the same scream? Feyedorovitch's rifle fired. The stupid little Sty-20s fired.

John Rourke's head suddenly hurt very badly and he knew he was falling backwards. Natalia was running toward him, in slow motion and she was moving her mouth, saying something he knew but he couldn't hear the words, just the tremendously loud explosion inside his head. It just kept going on and on and on and he was falling, Natalia's fingertips touching his fingertips and then they weren't touching and the blur in front of his eyes was suddenly faster and he saw the wall of the building and he saw Natalia looking down at him and he thought she was screaming and then everything just stopped and there wasn't anything anymore at all.

Chapter Thirty-two

"I think he's dead, captain."

"Damnit, we didn't come this far—"

"They got the woman—I know that. But I didn't hear any more gunfire."

"Fuck it—we're takin' him with—move it, Marines!"

Aldridge shoved Lisa Belzer into motion, tears rolling down her cheeks.

"Get back in that damn APC and follow orders—you and you," he shouted to the two Chinese, "get in there with her. Keep tight on us." Aldridge clambered up the APC's superstructure, two of his Marines still hauling Rourke's body out from beneath the trees through which he had fallen from the top floor of the officers' residence. Rourke's face was covered with blood and if he was breathing, Aldridge couldn't detect any sign of it. No pulse in the neck. "Shit," he snarled, shouting to the Marine he'd left inside his APC. "Lay some rounds on that balcony—now!"

He didn't want to kill the woman that Rourke had died trying to save, but he didn't need his men shot either. The APC's cannon roared and Aldridge covered his ears with his hands, the superstructure vibrating under him. Lisa and the two Chinese were into the other APC, the hatch closing.

Aldridge reached down, his two men passing up the body, and he caught it under the armpits. Rourke had been a big man and heavier than he looked. But dead-weight was always heavier. He hauled him up, the two men scrambling up onto the superstructure, one of them helping him. "In the hole, move!" The second Marine dropped through the hatchway and Aldridge dragged Rourke's body across the superstructure, gunfire coming at them now from the balcony—or what was left of it—and bullets ricocheting off the APC's superstructure. He was tempted to leave the already dead man behind, but he couldn't bring himself to. The body would be flushed out into the ocean to feed the fish. The man deserved full military honors at Mid-Wake. And as Aldridge began stuffing the body through the hatchway, he vowed inside himself that if he got out, so would Rourke's body.

He had him down and shouted, "Careful with the body. No sense breaking bones!" His father had died in combat and so had his younger brother, and his brother's body had been a mass of broken bones after it had been dragged back and never looked right in the coffin. His mother had said that.

Aldridge pushed the second Marine through ahead of him, then, his feet almost on the other man's head and shoulders, he threw himself down after him, swinging the hatch shut under a hail of gunfire. "Blow that damn balcony to hell!"

"Yes, sir!" The APC vibrated around him and he lost his balance, caught himself, then threw himself into the control seat, gunning the engine. The second APC with Lisa Belzer running it was already moving. She was a gutsy lady. If she ever got herself promoted, he could ask her out sometime. But it looked bad an officer and a— and Aldridge started laughing.

"What's so funny, captain?"

"You wouldn't understand," and Aldridge worked the levers and the APC started rolling forward and left, Lisa's APC ahead of them, Aldridge stomping the accelerator and, following her, aiming the APC for the tunnel. . . .

She had crawled from where she had fallen, chunks of debris raining around her, her revolvers in both hands, her left leg already numbing from the Sty-20 round she'd taken.

She saw him for an instant, her consciousness going.

His body had caught up in some trees and, even as she watched, it had slipped from the boughs which had cradled it and fallen to the ground below.

There was no movement.

There was no life.

She had turned away from him, firing her revolvers as they had charged toward her, getting two of them at least until the rifle butt came and impacted the side of her head.

She lost her guns, but not consciousness—adrenalin, she thought. "Kill me!"

John Rourke was dead.

Natalia Anastasia Tiemerovna knew she had died inside too. . . .

Aldridge turned out of the tunnel, Lisa's APC dead ahead of him and moving fast. He hit the radio controls and could pick up somebody named Feyedorovitch calling for everything and everyone available to rendezvous at the lagoon. Aldridge worked the levers and swerved the APC into an almost too-tight hook onto the right side of Lisa's APC, then accelerated, his rear end fishtailing, evening out, passing her now. "How we doin' behind us—speak to me!"

"Corporal Belzer's APC is accelerating too, captain—she's right on our tail. Don't see anything—belay that—got five—make that six APCs just turning out of the tunnel and about the same number of Gullwings."

"These guys never give up, do they?" Aldridge shouted back rhetorically—he knew they didn't. His people and their people had been fighting the continuing battle of World War III since the night that it all went down, almost 500 years if he remembered his dates right. They never gave up. You killed them and more came. You blew up one of their submarines and there was always another one. And now—they had missiles. The nuclear ones just like five centuries ago. And they'd win—he felt the pres-

236

sure around his eyes. He kept driving. He'd led a commando raid against the Stalin, one of the big ones, one of the monster submarines, and they'd ridden the damn thing almost into port to place their explosives and hit the missile factory, but they hadn't made it, had been gassed, and he'd awakened a prisoner and they'd started playing with him with electric shock, with sensory deprivation. His dreams had become more horrible than being awake, and that was saying a lot.

There was a line of Gullwings blocking the roadway and there was an APC behind them. "Take the cannon—that APC," he shouted to the Marine beside him who had worked the gun against the balcony. "Kill it!"

He floored the accelerator now, realizing that even electronically controlled guns would have a harder time hitting a faster-moving target.

"Fire, damnit!"

The cannon fired, smoke and fire engulfing three of the Gullwings, the enemy armored personnel carrier firing back. Aldridge swerved his machine hard right. When the explosion came, he almost lost control, skidding, jumping the sidewalk, sideswiping the building walls on his right, every bone in his body feeling as if it were vibrating. The APC fired again, Aldridge shouting, "Shoot now!"

His gunner fired as the Marine at the rear monitoring the video screen there shouted, "They got Lisa Belzer! God damn 'em to—aww, nothin'."

The road surface beside the enemy APC turned into a rising fireball, gushing toward them and away from them along the tunnel ceiling, Aldridge keeping the accelerator to the floorboard, through the fireball, past the enemy vehicle.

"Disabled—what! Get specific!"

The man called back. "Corporal Belzer's APC got flipped over on its side and rammed into the far tunnel wall. The superstructure's half blown away. They got her, captain—the motherfuckers!"

"Let's see they don't get us," Sam Aldridge called back lamely. There were tears welling up in his eyes. He could

237

never ask her out now. "I'm sorry, Herb," he said. And he glanced at the Marine beside him. "You making it, Bernie?"

"Yes, sir—making it—just."

Aldridge could see the fence ahead. There were Gullwings there and there were troops behind every imaginable sort of barricade and there was a phalanx of APCs closing from the right.

He cut left, jumping the curb, punching the Russian machine through the fence leading to the main sub pens. He was starting to slow since he was traversing ground now and not a hard road surface.

"APCs closing fast, captain," the man at the rear called out. "Those other six are still dead behind us."

"Just pray the guns in the Scout subs are waitin' for us and be ready to move."

"How about the dead guy, sir?"

Aldridge looked at Corporal Bernie Richter. "The body goes with us—right?"

"Yes, sir!"

Aldridge could see the tunnel between the Scout pens and the lagoon dead ahead, nothing blocking it except two Gullwings. "Vaporize 'em, Bernie!"

"You got it, captain!"

The cannon fired, the pulse of the thing making the superstructure vibrate, the two Gullwings vanishing in a ball of flame the next instant. Aldridge drove through the flames, knowing he couldn't stop now.

"Gettin' a readout off the rear tires, captain—they're hot—on fire!"

"Hang in there, Herb!"

He realized his knuckles were going stiff on the levers which controlled the APC, his neck aching, his eyes burning him because he couldn't blink. It was a narrow walkway here, not made for traffic at all. He bounced a curb, was in the tunnel.

"Be ready!" Come on, baby, he almost said aloud to the machine. He was starting to lose the steering.

The lagoon was dead ahead, another APC there. "Fire

around it—make a ring around it—do it now!"

The cannon fired, then again and again and again, the APC almost out of control as Aldridge slowed her, the lagoon less than a hundred yards ahead, just beyond the dock. "Now!" He stomped the brake and skidded, "Hold on to something tight!"

The APC fishtailed, the rear end sweeping right, Aldridge bracing himself. If he did it just right, maybe they wouldn't die just yet.

He felt the impact. "You hit the thing, sir!" It was Herb shouting from the rear of the APC. "She's—she's gone over, into the lagoon!"

"Out!" Aldridge hit his seat-belt release and slid from behind the controls, their APC smoking now, on fire. Flames were starting from some of the overhead panels, and he could smell burning insulation. He grabbed up Rourke's body—one of his two men had strapped it into one of the other seats. He hit the seat-belt harness release and it sagged toward him. Aldridge shouted to Bernie Richter, "Up the hatch—watch for enemy fire and he grab him."

"Right, sir!" Richter disappeared through the hatchway, Aldridge realizing Herb Koswalski was helping him with the dead man. "Ready, sir!"

"Just thrills me no end you're ready, corporal!" Aldridge pushed, the Marine with him lifting, and they had Rourke's body through the hatchway.

"Got him, sir! We got company—those damn APCs!"

Aldridge was the next one up, the AKM-96 going ahead of him.

They were ten yards from the water.

Aldridge jumped from the smoldering superstructure to the dock, shouting, "Pass him down!"

His two Marines slid Rourke's body down, Aldridge getting the tall, lean white man over his right shoulder. It was stupid, hauling a dead body. He did it anyway, running, his two men outdistancing him, dropping into kneeling positions beside the water at the end of the dockside. Gunfire tore into the dock bumpers. Aldridge heard an explosion—one of the APCs firing—and felt the dock vibrate under him.

"Into the water, guys! Hubba-hubba!" Aldridge tossed his rifle away and jumped, letting the body slip from his shoulder as he impacted the water, tucked down.

He had never liked diving. He opened his eyes. Rourke's body wasn't floating.

As Aldridge's head broke the surface, he started to drag Rourke up. "He's alive, damnit! All right!"

Assault-rifle fire peppered the water around him and grabbed Rourke across the chest and under the left armpit and shouted, "If you can hear me, take a deep breath, Rourke!" Aldridge pulled Rourke with him under the surface, air escaping Rourke's mouth in great bubbles. Aldridge felt something hit the water's surface. The APCs firing, he knew. He dragged Rourke with him, breaking the surface, gulping air, drawing Rourke's head toward him, rocking the head back, forcing air into Rourke's lungs from his own.

Two of the monster subs were crossing the lagoon, a deck gun firing. Aldridge could see Richter, but not Herb Koswalski. "Herb! Where are you? Koswalski! Koswalski?"

"Captain!"

Aldridge swallowed water, choking as he twisted in the churning lagoon, one of the Scout subs coming dead on for him. But he could see Martha on the deck, another of the escapees at the deck gun. The deck gun opened fire, long volleys, the noise of the thing deafening. She had disobeyed orders being in this close. He'd kill her after he kissed her.

A line—he couldn't reach it, swam toward it, the line snaking out again, this time his right hand catching a whole coil. He twisted the coil around his upper body and Rourke's, shouting, "Reel us in!"

The water around him exploded again and he dragged himself and Rourke under, the sound even more deafening beneath the waves.

He was being dragged up and he pushed Rourke's head

240

to the surface. "Get him first—he's still alive or he was a second ago!" Aldridge slipped the rope from his own body, shoving Rourke up under the rail, Martha and another woman and a Chinese reaching for him. "Get him some mouth to mouth—but he could have a shot-out lung—be careful!"

Aldridge was halfway up himself when the hands reached for him and he fell forward to his knees onto the deckplates.

APCs were firing from the dock and the monster subs were closing, both their deck guns firing now. "Richter and Koswalski? You see 'em?"

Martha turned away from him, snaking out the line again, and Aldridge vomited up water across the deck plates, then looked after her. Richter and Koswalski, something wrong with Richter, the same rope that had reeled him in hauling them in now. He grabbed the rope and started to pull.

Richter was passed up first—his left arm was limp and his mouth was trickling blood. Koswalski—as Aldridge and Martha reached down to him, the deck guns of the monster subs opened up again, Koswalski's body jerking, slamming against the Scout sub, then falling away.

"Koswalski!"

"He's dead, Sam—come on!"

Aldridge looked at Martha, then back to the water—he could see Koswalski, floating face down.

Aldridge clambered to his feet, lurching toward the deck gun, shoving the Marine away from it, swinging it round. "Eat shit, you bastards!" he started pumping the deck gun, the pounding of it something he could feel inside himself.

Martha—she was hitting him with her little fists. "Damnit, captain! You gonna stay up and swim?"

He looked at her and started to laugh. "Lieutenant— you got balls!" He secured the deck gun, then headed for the main hatch.

Chapter Thirty-three

"Sonar's picking up Soviet Scout subs, Captain. But the odd thing is that it looks as though their own Island Class submarines are pursing them."

Sebastian's dark chocolate-colored hands were splayed over the illuminated plotting board which dominated the control station.

"Sonar—talk to me."

"Sir, I've got four Soviet Scout subs proceeding at full flank speed but rather erratically, it appears. I have three Island Class—correction—four Island Class submarines in the classic Soviet pursuit formation. None of the Island Class submarines is dragging a sonar array."

"Very good, Lieutenant Kelly—keep on it."

He swung his chair left. "Communications—what are you getting, lieutenant?"

"I'm starting to get low-frequency transmissions on the Soviet distress band, Captain. But the signal is too weak, sir. I can't make anything out of it."

He turned his chair toward the Warfare Station. "Lieutenant Walenski—what's the status on the torpedo tubes?"

"Forward torpedo status—numbers one and four empty, numbers two and three loaded with High Explosive Independent Sensing, Captain. One and four can be loaded. Aft torpedo status—numbers one through four loaded with HEIS, Captain."

Louise Walenski had confirmed what he already knew. "Very well, lieutenant. Order forward torpedo tubes one and four loaded with HEIS as well."

"Aye, Captain."

He looked back to Sebastian. "Commander Sebastian—anything further?"

"Negative, Captain—still monitoring."

"Order the ship to Battle Stations, Mr. Sebastian."

"Aye, Captain. Ordering the ship to Battle Stations." Sebastian reached down the intraship communications microphone. "Now hear this. Now hear this. Battle Stations. I repeat, Battle Stations. This is not a drill." The klaxon sounded.

He got out of his chair and moved aft between the sonar and computer stations, Seaman First Class Tagachi at periscope station. "Mr. Tagachi—attack periscope."

"Aye, Captain," Morris Tagachi responded, activating the control panel. He was already at the attack periscope, folding down, the tube rising. At this depth it was hard to see anything even with vision intensification and computer enhancement. But just off the starboard bow, he thought he could make out one of the great hulking shapes of the Soviet monsters. He snapped the handles back to closed, not bothering to tell Tagachi to lower the periscope.

"Captain—I have their position. Precisely twenty-three degrees off our starboard bow, moving north by northeast at forty-one knots."

"Thank you, Mr. Sebastian. Sonar?"

"Aye, Captain?"

"Tell me about their engines."

"Into overdrive, Captain. Not at maximum."

"Very well."

Sebastian looked up at him from control deck.

He stood beside his chair at the con. "Navigation."

"Aye, Captain," Lureen Bowman answered.

"Plot an intercept course with those Scout subs. After you've brought her about, go to all ahead full, lieutenant."

"Aye, Captain."

"Engineering."

"Aye, Captain."

"Saul—notify me immediately if the starboard reactor

243

starts acting up again and put everything into the port reactor. We're going to need speed with that wolfpack out there."

"Aye, Captain."

He took the three steps down onto the control and navigation level, not bothering to study Sebastian's console, but rather staring forward onto the composite video screen which dominated the forward bulkhead. He could make them out almost as clearly as he had through the attack periscope, which wasn't very clearly at all. He turned and looked back at Sebastian. "What do you think, Sebastian?"

"I don't have the data to support anything beyond sheer supposition, Captain."

"Gimme me some sheer supposition then."

Sebastian's powerful shoulders shrugged and the corners of his mouth turned down. "Sheer supposition, Jason. All right. I'd say somebody—persons unknown—has stolen several of the Scout subs and is being pursued. At this juncture, that's all I can discern."

He nodded. "Sonar!"

"Aye, Captain."

"Have Soviet vessels fired torpedoes yet?"

"Negative, Captain."

"Notify me immediately if they fire."

"Aye, Captain."

Jason Darkwood stared at the composite video screen, wishing that at least once in a while it would provide the impetus for some brilliant flash of insight. Especially now. It wasn't cooperating. He stepped around Sebastian's console and pulled down the microphone out of the overhead. "This is the Captain speaking. In answer to your unspoken questions, the answer is, 'No, I don't know what's going on.' We have several Soviet Scout subs which are apparently being pursued by Island Class submarines which we cannot outfight, but which we can outrun and definitely outmaneuver. I will keep you informed. Captain out."

He secured the microphone, turned toward the con, and

ascended the three steps, then sunk into his seat. The fingers of his right hand tapped on the armrest. He closed his seat restraint. "Navigator."

"Aye, Captain."

"How are we coming on the intercept course?"

"We should be immediately astern of the four Scout ships in—make that three minutes and forty-five seconds, Captain Darkwood, at the present course and speed."

"Thank you, lieutenant." Darkwood stared ahead into the composite video screen, all the hull-mounted cameras both fore and aft, above and below computer-controlled to produce a solid image. "Communications—bring up aft projection on the screen."

"Aye, Captain—you have aft projection."

The picture had changed almost instantly. He saw nothing else suspicious within visual range and there was no need to call for split-screen imaging. The intercept course would put them in the line of fire of the lead elements of the Soviet Island Class wolfpack—by his watch and the digital readout built into the left arm control of his seat—in a little less than two minutes.

"Communications—forward visual display."

"Forward display now, Captain."

Forward display showed the four Soviet monsters clearly now, closing along their starboard side with the Scout subs. "Navigator." He could never quite bring himself to calling a woman "Helmsman" and "Helmswoman" sounded downright ridiculous.

"Aye, sir."

"On my signal be prepared to bring us hard about to port and cut speed to half flank speed."

"Aye, sir."

"Saul."

"Aye, sir."

"Have your people in Engineering deliver a pig of lubricant to aft torpedo room on the double, sealed just tightly enough she'll burst when she hits the water."

"Aye, Captain."

"Lieutenant Walenski."

"Aye, Captain?"

"Pull the HEIS out of aft torpedo tube four and make preparations to load the pig of motor oil."

"Aye, Captain."

"Sebastian—work with Lieutenant Bowman on a cripple course—get Mr. Rodriguez on it."

"Aye, Captain," Sebastian answered. "Lieutenant Rodriguez—have computer plot a damaged-vessel course—I assume the portside reactor, Captain?"

"What?" His attention had gone elsewhere. "Yes—portside reactor it is, Sebastian. You get my drift." He hit the com switch on the right arm of his chair. "Sick Bay."

"Sick Bay, Doctor Barrow."

"Margaret, this is Jason. If what we're doing works, we'll be taking in those Scout subs into our own Scout sub bay. May be some injured personnel."

"I'll be ready, Jason."

"Right." He shut off, then back on to break the connection. "Security."

"Security, Lieutenant Stanhope."

"Darkwood."

"Yes, sir?"

"I'll want full security moving to the Scout Sub Bay on the double—be prepared for anything since I have no idea what to be prepared for."

"Yes, sir!"

Jason Darkwood clicked off. "Sonar—any word on torpedoes yet?"

"Nothing happening, sir. They have us on their sonar, that's all."

"Still keep me informed." He rotated his chair forward and his eyes met Sebastian's. His black first officer was laughing. "Yes, Sebastian?"

"It was the battle of Miners Reef, wasn't it? Your father—"

"Yes—my father against Admiral Suvorov. But that was forty years ago and I doubt seriously that any of our friends out there are heavy into American History. At least let's hope not, hmm?"

"Then you *are* planning your father's maneuver."

"The 'Ruptured Duck' was what he liked to call it, Sebastian." He checked the timepiece in his chair console. Thirty seconds until intercept. "Navigator—be ready for that maneuver."

"Aye, Captain."

"Lieutenant Walenski—ready with that oil pig in aft torpedo tube four?"

"Aye, Captain—ready to fire on your command."

"I'll be giving that command shortly." He looked forward. "Navigator—do it now."

"Aye, Captain—hard to port and reducing to half flank speed. Cutting in Mr. Sebastian's computer program."

"Very well. Communications?"

"Aye, Captain?"

"Those signals any clearer?"

"They're being jammed, sir—but what I'm making out sounds like it might be English."

"After all this trouble, I certainly hope so. Broadcast this message to the Soviet Scout subs. 'United States Attack Submarine Reagan calling Scout subs. We're attempting to come to your aid but must break off. Godspeed.' Sign it Jason Darkwood, Commander, Captain of the Reagan. And send it quick. Keep repeating it until I say otherwise."

"Aye, Captain."

He looked at Sebastian. "Think we could make one of the Island Classers come after us? How about two?"

"Then you have embellished your father's famous maneuver?"

"About to embellish, actually."

"We could fire at one of them—but of course unless we move out quickly we'll be—"

Darkwood let himself smile. "Engineering. While keeping revolutions at current speed, gradually bring off line starboard reactor, then at my signal bring both reactors to maximum and kick into overdrive on the screws."

Saul Hartnett pushed both hands back through his thick, black hair. "You want us to take off like a bat out of hell, don't you, Captain?"

"More or less." He looked away, saying, "Navigation hold present course but on my signal take us straigh through the middle of the concentration of enemy vessels You won't have time for computer—make sure we get i right, Lureen, or I'll have the people that own this boa really pissed with my estate."

"Aye, Captain."

Sebastian spoke. "If my calculations are correct, we wil reach a speed of forty-five knots in seventeen point nin seconds. May I advise Collision Quarters?"

"Good idea—alert all hands."

"Alerting all hands to Collision Quarters, Captain.' Sebastian pulled down his microphone and gave the order the klaxon sounding again, but with a different series.

Darkwood cranked his chair to his right and back looking over Julie Kelly's shoulder at the sonar display Sonic impulses were translated into computer imaging and made visual on the various screens before her. He could see the Soviet wolfpack, tighening up on the Scout subs apparently little interested in the Reagan. "Sonar—b ready with some crippled-ship noises."

"Aye, Captain."

Jason Darkwood turned his chair around to face for ward, his eyes riveted to the composite video screen in th forward bulkhead of the Command Deck. "Navigator— implement the maneuver."

"Implementing maneuver, Captain."

"Engineering—start taking that starboard reactor of line."

"Starboard reactor coming off line."

"Warfare—you have the order to fire that pig."

"Aye, Captain. Firing pig through aft tube four."

Tom Stanhope's voice came over Sebastian's speaker "Lieutenant Stanhope to the bridge. Please notify the Captain that Security is in place in the Scout Sub Bay.'

Sebastian glanced up at Darkwood and Darkwood nod ded, his eyes intent on the video display. "The Captain has the word, Mr. Stanhope," Sebastian said.

"They're following us . . ." Two of the Soviet Island Class submarines had broken off from the wolfpack to outflank the Reagan. "Navigator—tell me when we're right between them."

"Aye, Captain."

"Lieutenant Walenski—have cluster charges ready to fire off port and starboard sides amidships on my command."

"Preparing cluster charges to fire off port and starboard sides amidships on your command, Captain."

"Sonar—give 'em our noise."

"Making noise now, Captain."

"Captain." It was Lureen Bowman. "We are exactly equidistant to all four Soviet Island Class vessels."

"Hold her steady, Lieutenant. Louise—ready with those cluster charges?"

"Aye, Captain—cluster charges are ready."

"Fire cluster charges now. Engineering—give me everything you've got now. Navigator—complete the maneuver."

A ragged chorus of assents began and ended, the Reagan already accelerating, Darkwood slapped back by the G-force as if it were some invisible hand, the display on the composite video screen a gray blur for an instant while the cameras adjusted focus. Darkwood shouted, "Communications—belay that fake message and signal the Scout subs to draw out of our immediate vicinity and be ready to dock with us and abandon ship."

"Aye, Captain."

"Mr. Sebastian. Plot a firing pattern based on our present trajectory utilizing aft torpedo tubes one, two, and three. Warfare—what's the status on those cluster charges."

Sebastian started to respond, didn't. Louise Walenski called out, "Eighty-two percent impact ratio on starboard package, eighty-one percent impact on portside package."

"Good. Engineering, how we holding out? Anything melt yet?"

"Pretty good, Captain."

249

Margaret Barrow's voice came over the com line. "Jason—what are you doing up there?"

"Taking a ride, Margaret. How's Sick Bay?"

"I almost had a patient throw up all over me."

Darkwood didn't know what to say to that. He clicked the com line to kill it, called to Saul Hartnett, "Engineering—complete that report."

"Both reactors on line, Captain, starboard reactor getting a little hot but nothing even near critical."

"Navigator—cut to full flank speed and bring us hard about to port. Don't bother responding."

He turned his chair left. "Warfare—aft torpedo tubes ready?"

"We have Mr. Sebastian's program, sir. Ready on your command."

"Excellent. Navigator—full overdrive—right through the middle of them again."

"Aye, Captain, going to full overdrive."

"Warfare—I want forward torpedo tubes one through four ready to fire on my signal—you'll have it in . . ." He glanced at the video screen and at the digital time display on his console, ". . . ten seconds."

"Aye—"

He cut her off. "After firing forward torpedos, give me another set of cluster charges just like before. Then on my signal fire aft torpedos with Sebastian's program."

He didn't wait for an answer. "Navigator—on my firing command, that is your command for every ounce of speed we've got."

Lureen Bowman started to respond. He cut her off. "Warfare—fire forward torpedoes now!"

"Firing forward torpedoes, Captain."

"Now the cluster charges." The G-force came again, this time harder than before.

"Firing cluster charges, Captain."

"Sonar—watch your ears."

"Thank you, Captain."

"Let's have Sebastian's aft torpedo program—now!"

"Aft torpedo program implementing, Captain."

"Navigator—get us the hell out of here before the concussion ruptures us."

"Aye Captain, employing evasive maneuvers."

The Soviet Island Class submarines were taking cluster charge hits and simultaneously beginning their own evasive-action patterns.

"Sonar—back on line?"

"Aye, sir."

"Tell me how our friends are doing."

"Island Class submarines off our stern have sustained what sounds like at least one direct hit—torpedo. There's—I think two of them are in trouble, sir."

"Captain," Andrew Mott called out.

"What is it, Communications?"

"Two of the Island Class submarines have just collided, sir, according to their transmission."

"Ha, ha, ha!" Darkwood leaned forward in his seat, despite the G-force, saying through his laughter, "Mr. Mott—please convey our compliments and condolences to the commanders of the Island Class submarines so afflicted."

"Aye, Captain."

"Warfare—what have we got?"

"Cluster charges off starboard eighty-six percent with wide dispersion. Cluster charge package off portside eighty-four percent with wide dispersion as well. Forward torpedoes one and two still traveling. Numbers three and four have impacted. Computer currently assessing damage to enemy vessels. Aft torpedo three is off my instruments and may be down. One and two have impacted. Computer assessing damages, Captain."

"Excellent." He turned forward. "Navigation—reduce to full flank speed and maneuver to evade enemy response—"

Sonar interrupted him. "Sir—a wire-guide torpedo of theirs was fired. The only one so far. Coming after us at forty knots on a trajectory to impact us amidships on the portside in ten seconds and counting."

"Navigator," Darkwood called, "belay that previous

order. Everything we've got and fast! Engineering—help her out! Sebastian, plot the duration time on that wire-guide."

"Plotting now, Captain."

Darkwood looked at the video screen. The Pillars of Woe were straight ahead, chimneys of undersea rock extending several hundred feet toward the surface, scattered at irregular intervals for several nautical miles square, beyond them a deep trench, within the trench a volcanic vent, part of the system which provided geothermal power to the Russian domes. "Lureen—hold as much speed as you can and take her through the pillars on my commands."

He unbuckled his seat restraint and started forward toward the video screen. "Sebastian, advise the crew to maintain Collision Quarters."

"Advising the crew to maintain Collision Quarters, Captain."

"Sonar—how close is that wire-guide?"

"Twelve seconds and staying right on us, sir."

"Give me word if the gap gets below ten."

"Aye, Captain."

Darkwood grasped the forward rail with both fists, his eyes intent one the video screen. "Lureen—we're doing it."

"Aye, Captain."

"Ten degrees right rudder." A chimney was dead ahead, but the gap between it and the one off their bow was tight. "Back one third. Five degrees left rudder. Maintain reduced speed. Five degrees right rudder, ahead to flank speed." His head was beginning to ache. "Right rudder ten degrees, back one third. Left rudder five degrees. Shoot me some air—up fifty feet," Darkwood ordered.

The Pillars of Woe were tight here and the only way through was to come up, over, and dive. "Ten degrees on the bow planes," he commanded. "Level bow planes and ten degrees right rudder. All ahead full. Flank speed now." The Reagan had dipped inside the heart of the Pillars of Woe, frightened-looking undersea creatures hastening out of its way. "Sonar? Tell me about the wire-guide."

"Still twelve seconds out, Captain."

"Back on one third, rudder amidships. Sonar! Give me a count."

"Twelve seconds to impact, Captain. Eleven. Ten. Nine. Only seven now, sir. Six. Five, sir. Four—"

"Navigator—twenty degrees on the bow planes, ten degrees right rudder, all ahead full." .The Reagan lurched violently, angling upward, Darkwood holding tight to the railing, legs braced against the deck. He licked his lips, eyeing the Pillars of Woe. "All back. Rudder amidships!"

He felt the shudder, the chimney off the port bow trembling, tumbling. "Sonar—tell what's happening."

"Wire-guide detonated fifty yards off the port bow, sir."

"Engineering—damage report."

"Aye, Captain. Checking for damage."

Hartnett began reciting the litany of ship's departments, soliciting for damage reports.

Darkwood leaned against the railing. "Sonar—any new friends to report?"

"Negative, sir."

"Navigator—you've got the helm. Sebastian—keep an eye out for the Island Classers and get a rendezvous set with the Scout subs. I'll be in Scout Sub Bay. You have the con."

"Very well, Captain."

Darkwood started aft, past Sebastian's station and up the three low steps and past his chair, between the sonar and computer consoles. Morris Tagachi was still at his post by the periscope controls. Darkwood shot the young man a grin as he stepped into the shaft for the utilitarian but efficient vertical conveyer, his feet positioned on the step, his left hand on the strap. Already, he was moving downward.

He could hear Hartnett informing Sebastian that damage reports were negative and then all sounds from the bridge faded.

On the next level below he stepped out, moving around the conveyer shaft and aft toward Sick Bay. Sebastian would signal for permission to step down from Collision Quarters as soon as they were out of the Pillars of Woe. But Battle Stations would be maintained until whoever was aboard the Scout subs was brought aboard, the Scout subs were gotten well away from the Reagan and destroyed, and the Reagan was well away from the Russian domes.

Sick Bay was just ahead and he turned the companionway and entered the reception area, no one apparently sick since all but one of Margaret's Barrow's on-duty nursing staff seemed engaged in conversation. One of the staff called, "Attention!"

"As you were." Darkwood just shook his head. The woman was a Marine who had cross-transferred into Navy and she always did that. If every time he walked through the ship everybody stopped what they were doing and came to attention, nothing would ever get done. Formality was fine, but had its limits in practicality.

He entered Margaret's surgery, not having seen her through the windows in the Sick Bay door. She was sitting at her desk. "Is all of this over with, Jason?"

"Well, more or less. Tell that ex-Marine out there to knock it off with calling everybody to attention whenever she sees me."

"I think she likes you."

Darkwood nodded his head. "Ohh boy!"

"You ready to take on your passengers?"

"Whoever they are. I thought you might want to come along."

Lieutenant Commander Margaret Barrow stood up from her desk and smiled at him. "Some cheapshot date."

"Stick with me afterward and I'll buy you a cup of coffee in the officers' mess."

"Yuch." She laughed, starting through the still-open surgery door and into the reception area. He followed her and they made their way back along the companionway toward the vertical conveyer. "Who do you think these guys are?"

"In the Scout subs? If we're lucky, escaped prisoners.

But that's pretty much stretching it. But they do speak English. Could all be some kind of setup. I've got Security down there."

"What would I need Security for when I'm with you?"

"Can't argue with logic like that." He laughed, following her onto the conveyer. He looked down at her as they were carried along. Her hair had always been one of her best features, dark brown with lighter highlights when the light was just right. Just a little past the nape of her neck and not really within regs, but she was a doctor and doctors were notorious about regs. He remembered how her hair had smelled, even though it had been a very long time. Like roses.

She stepped off the conveyer and he followed after her. As they passed a squawk box, he heard Sebastian coming over the intraship. "Bridge to Captain. Bridge to Captain."

"Just a second, Margaret," he told her, depressing the push-to-talk switch on the squawk box. "This is the Captain."

"Captain Darkwood. Request permission to step down from Collision Quarters. We have cleared the Pillars of Woe."

"Permission granted. Maintain Battle Stations."

"Of course, Captain."

"I'm just about to reach Scout Sub Bays, Sebastian. Keep me informed as necessary. Darkwood out." He walked on, Margaret waiting for him a little further along the companionway, near the entrance to the reactor complex. He hurried past it with her, and where the companionway reached a T intersection, he took the right passageway, leading toward the Scout Sub Bays. "How about dinner when we get back to Mid-Wake? I promise to be good."

"You always promise to be good—but you never are."

"I know, but you wouldn't want me to change after all these years."

"Just dinner?" She smiled. The companionway lights danced in the green of her eyes. "Hmm?"

"Well, a drink or two maybe. How about it?"

"Jason Darkwood looking for Platonic companionship?"

"Plato has nothing to do with it and he was probably homosexual anyway. And if companionship is all that's available to me at the moment—"

"That's just the trouble, Jason," she interrupted. "You'd want more and so would I."

He touched her right elbow with his left hand. "Maybe I'm saying we can try again."

"Maybe I know you're saying that, Jase. Dinner—but just that for now."

"Dinner—agreed," Darkwood told her.

They had reached the Scout Sub Bays. They always reminded him of a vast auditorium but without seats. On the starboard side of the Reagan, they occupied the entire central section of the lower level, the height of the overhead some thirty feet here, the Reagan's Scout Class vessels secured here on rails to be brought into position for transfer through one of the two massive airlocks into the sea. But all three of the Scout subs were locked down and the activity by the air locks was that of the Marine Corps Security detail under the command of Lieutenant Tom Stanhope. When Sam Aldridge had been MIA'd, Darkwood had requested that Stanhope, Aldridge's second-in-command for the Marine Unit, be temporarily placed in charge. Darkwood realized it was simply his reluctance to accept the finality of death. He and Aldridge had attended the Naval Academy together, had been friends ever since, and when Darkwood had been given command of the Reagan, and with it the prerogative of staffing it with his pick of available officers, the two he had picked were Sebastian and Aldridge. He had been told it was a curious choice. Someone had even asked if he didn't like people of his own race, Sebastian and Aldridge both being black. Darkwood had considered it fortuitous that the person who had asked that question had been male, approximately his own size, approximately his own age, and of neither greater nor lesser rank. All those factors taken into consideration, he'd punched the man in the mouth.

But it had been a curious choice. Sebastian, though in superb physical condition and an accomplished man of violence when necessary, abhorred violence and was best described as cerebral, although someone six foot six and slightly over 220 pounds was rarely considered that.

Aldridge was—had been, Darkwood mentally corrected—about his own height, a little over six feet. And, though Aldridge was a gifted scholar, he hardly gave that image. He looked and acted the consummate man of action. Within Mid-Wake's closely knit black community, it was said that Aldridge and Sebastian were distant cousins, something both men vehemently denied. In an environment like that of Mid-Wake, it was almost an oddity not to be related to half the people you knew or worked with. Saul Hartnett's mother was Darkwood's aunt and sonar specialist Julie Kelly was the daughter of Hartnett's father's brother. Darkwood had always wondered if that made him and Julie Kelly cousins of some kind.

He and Margaret Barrow were not related at all—they had sat up until three in the morning once confirming that by comparing genealogies, another common pastime at Mid-Wake. As they neared the air locks now, he advised Margaret, "Why don't you take the stairs to the observation platform and wait there. Just in case."

"I'm a Naval officer and I'm a doctor—so in both cases I belong right here." She smiled at him.

"Yes." Darkwood smiled back. "But you're only a lieutenant commander and I'm a commander, plus I'm the Captain of this ship, and why don't we consider my request a direct order?"

"Aye, Captain," she snarled, and broke off from him and ran toward the stairs leading up to the platform.

Darkwood watched her over his shoulder for a moment, then continued on, Stanhope starting to call his detail to attention, Darkwood saying, "As you were, gentlemen."

"Captain, the Scout Sub Bays are secure."

257

"Somehow I knew they would be, Tom—loan me your communicator."

"Here you go, sir." Stanhope took the radio from his belt pouch and handed it to Darkwood.

Darkwood depressed the push-to-talk button. "Bridge, this is the Captain. Sebastian—anything new on the Scout subs?"

"We have not been able to get a cleaner transmission from the Scout subs, Captain. For that reason, I would advise caution lest it should prove to be some Russian trick. Docking, if they understood our transmissions and allowed our remote interlock, should begin in less than a minute. I was about to inform you of that."

"Consider me informed. Once we get whoever it is aboard, I'll have Stanhope notify you as soon as the Russian vessels are clear of our docks and Lieutenant Walenski can practice her marksmanship."

"I will advise Lieutenant Walenski, Captain."

"Very well—Captain out," and Darkwood handed back the radio. "Deploy your men, lieutenant. I'll only be observing."

"Very good, sir."

Darkwood wanted to say something, didn't, drew back instead, and waited a respectable distance from the Marines and the air locks. He glanced up toward the observation platform. Margaret looked like she was angry—at least a little—and he wondered if dinner was still on.

When he had first been given command of the Reagan, he had personally involved himself in everything. He had learned that wasn't the right way. Taking virtually direct command of the helm when they had successfully attempted to elude the wire-guide torpedo had been necessity. He knew the Pillars of Woe better than anyone on board. But after a few awkward experiences, he had learned that the function of command truly was the delegation of authority, and ever since he had learned that lesson, life for everyone aboard the Reagan had been easier, most particularly himself. It was using this logic which had determined that he did not stop at the arms

258

locker to avail himself of a weapon. That was what he had the Marines for.

There was a loud thud and the computer's voice came over the loudspeaker. "Docking in Air Lock One accomplished. Equalizing pressure now." The computer sounded like an English butler from one of the five-centuries-old movie tapes he had seen, and rumor at the Academy had always been that indeed the voice had been synthesized from such old films. But the English the machine "spoke" was, indeed, lovely.

Darkwood watched. He waited.

Stanhope had drawn his pistol. His Marines had their assault rifles ready. Darkwood had not reminded them that a serious firefight could put holes in the Reagan's hull, perhaps, and that then the sea would rush in and the hull, its integrity gone, would rupture and they would all die. Hopefully Stanhope and his people remembered. Darkwood had learned that as well—it was wise to assume everybody might be an idiot but not that they actually were. But, on the other hand, some unpleasant surprises were permanent in duration.

The computer voice came again, announcing Air Lock Two was also equalizing pressure. The interior door of Air Lock One started fanning open.

Darkwood realized he was balling his fists and getting ready for something, although he wasn't sure what. He locked his hands behind him, instead, like some sort of admiral.

"Captain—Air Lock One is opening, sir!"

"Thank you, Mr. Stanhope." Darkwood wanted to add that he was neither blind nor deaf, but didn't.

The air lock door opened. Through it stepped Sam Aldridge, thirty pounds lighter, dressed in rags, and visibly wounded.

Jason Darkwood suddenly felt tears fill his eyes.

He was running across the deck, shouting, grabbing Aldridge and almost crushing him as he embraced the man. None of this was very Captainly, he thought absently. "Sam—my God, man!"

259

"I know, Captain—I look like shit."

And Aldridge embraced him too. Then Darkwood and Aldridge both came to the realization that two grown men, both officers, hugging each other—and Aldridge was crying too—looked terribly dumb, and they stepped away from one another.

Aldridge saluted. "Permission to come aboard, sir."

"Oh, hell—I suppose so." Darkwood laughed.

Aldridge grinned, then turned toward Tom Stanhope. "You don't have these Marines snap to when a superior officer comes up to them?"

"Ahh—well—Ten-Hut!"

Stanhope saluted. Aldridge saluted, then clasped Stanhope's right hand. "Tom—you haven't changed a bit." He looked at Darkwood. "Sir—I have several wounded personnel aboard and one of them, a civilian, is critical."

Darkwood nodded, turning around and shouting toward the observation platform, "Margaret!"

But she was already on her way. Darkwood shrugged mentally. It was hard to get someone to remember you were her Captain when you had been her lover. But now he looked at Sam Aldridge. "A civilian?"

"Name is John Rourke, Captain—and that he isn't dead already is some kind of miracle. Here . . ." Aldridge ran back toward the air lock. Two men and a woman, one of the men a Marine and the other a Chinese—a Chinese?—were carrying on a makeshift litter a man of roughly his own size and build, the man wearing a ripped and much-bloodied Soviet Marine Spetznas sergeant's uniform, some sort of double shoulder holster with pistols hanging in it and a knife as huge as a short sword.

"A civilian?"

"He's a doctor. And he's an American. He's not from Mid-Wake and he's about the bravest man I ever met, Jason."

As Darkwood neared the stricken man, Margaret Barrow ran past him. Closer to the man now, Darkwood could see that some of the man's wounds had been bandaged, clumsily it appeared. But in the field . . .

260

"Jason—I need this man in Sick Bay as fast as possible. And I need people to meet me down here with—"

She had interrupted his thoughts. He interrupted her stream of orders. "Stanhope—see to it that Doctor Barrow gets everything she needs down here on the double. Get some of your men, under Doctor Barrow's direction, to assist with the other wounded. Sam—point out the most obviously serious. Then get those Scout subs away from here fast so we can blow them up and get ourselves away from here." He looked at Margaret. "All right—can facilities aboard the Reagan meet your foreseen medical needs?"

"Negative on that—not with this man. If I started telling you everything that's wrong with him just by looking at him, he'd be dead by the time I finished."

"Right." Darkwood sprinted across the deck toward the squawk box, Stanhope's belt radio already in use up to Sick Bay. He reached the squawk box on the far bulkhead and hit the push-to-talk button. "Bridge, this is the Captain. Sebastian. Be ready to implement the most expeditious course possible to Mid-Wake. There are injuries down here requiring medical facilities beyond our onboard capabilities. As soon as the Soviet Scout subs are away and destroyed, implement it at once."

"I will proceed to carry out your orders, Captain."

"Sebastian—Aldridge is alive. He's back."

Sebastian didn't answer for a moment. "Please convey my felicitations to Captain Aldridge and that I look forward to congratulating him personally on his escape."

"I certainly will—Captain out." Darkwood leaned against the bulkhead for a minute. A civilian American doctor named Rourke, armed to the teeth. A hero. But where was he from?

Margaret Barrow was administering a shot to him while one of her nursing staff was getting an IV going, his stretcher already in motion toward Sick Bay. From the man's apparent condition, there might not be much time to get the answers.

And somewhere at the back of his mind, it all sounded

familiar. A doctor of medicine named John Rourke who was a hero's hero. Something from the early history of Mid-Wake.

He hit the squawk box again. "Computer. This is the Captain."

"Voice print identity confirmed. Proceed, Captain Darkwood."

"Identify name John Rourke, doctor of medicine. Involved in some heroic action in the early history of Mid-Wake."

"Processing."

Darkwood waited.

The English butler voice came back through the squawk box. "Rourke, John Thomas, Biographical Extract: Rourke, John Thomas, doctor of medicine, weapons expert, survival expert, former case officer prewar United States Central Intelligence Agency, presumed deceased during period of atmospheric fires which consumed earth surface and destroyed terrestrially based life-forms following massive ionization effect as result of nuclear exchange during World War III. Exploits of John Thomas Rourke chonicled by Commander Robert Gundersen, USN, after his vessel, the USS John Paul Jones, docked at Mid-Wake following commencement of World War III. Gundersen—"

Darkwood knew the rest of the story. He had studied it in history classes. And he smiled at the thought as the stretcher with the severely injured, almost certainly dying man passed him. Of course, this couldn't be the real Rourke, just a similarity of names. What made him smile was that he had flunked a history test because he had spelled Rourke with an *a* rather than a *u*.

His past was coming back to haunt him.

He still had the computer on the squawk box. "Computer. Physical description of Rourke, John Thomas."

"Processing," it answered, interrupting itself.

Then, "Rourke, John Thomas, physical description as follows: exact quotation from Commander Gundersen's memoirs entitled 'A Warrior's Recollections.' " The computer gave the publication data. " 'John Rourke stood well over six feet tall, lean, well-muscled. A high forehead, but naturally so because his hair was thick, healthy, dark brown with a touch of gray when I knew him. He was soft-spoken, and I remember he seemed to move with the grace of a cat, and both his speech and his manner implied that there was tremendous energy beneath the surface of this man, as I later found out there was indeed, a tremendous energy coupled with immense, almost super-human self-control. Rourke's hands were the hands of a pianist or a surgeon, and I later found out that he was indeed both, although I only had the opportunity to witness the results of his surgical abilities. He was light-sensitive, he once told me, which accounted for the dark-lensed aviator-style sunglasses he wore whenever he was in natural daylight. The sunglasses, a thin, dark cigar, and his Detonics .45-caliber pistols were his trademarks. These pistols—two of them worn in a double shoulder holster and with black rubber grips—were always with him, and his abilities to save life with his surgical skills seemed at parity with his abilities to end life with these pistols as his instruments. John Rourke epitomized many things to me—courage, tenacity, resolve. Over the years, my early impressions of him have only deepened to conviction. He was the finest and truest American I have ever met, bar none. May God rest his soul.' Physical description of Rourke, John Thomas, ends."

"Thank you, computer—request satisfied." Darkwood broke into a dead run, shouting over his shoulder to Aldridge and Stanhope, "I'm going to Sick Bay if you need me!"

He ran into the companionway, and at that intersection took a left. Maggie Barrow and her people would have taken the freight elevator. They'd be there by now. He took the vertical conveyer, swinging out of the shaft as it reached the upper level and running along the companionway toward Sick Bay.

He entered the reception area. Office equipment was being pushed aside to make room for the wounded being brought in. "Captain—can you give me a hand?" one of the nurses called out. He nodded only, throwing his weight behind the desk, helping the woman move it across the deck and against the bulkhead. "Thanks, sir."

"Anytime, Helen."

Darkwood entered the surgery, Margaret already at work. He hung back, his eyes searching and finally finding what he had sought. The man's Russian uniform and his weapons were piled in a corner and Darkwood went to the pile. The uniform was one of the newer ones, ballistic fabric used in its construction. But soft body armor did little to protect against an assault rifle. He picked up the knife. He drew it from the scabbard. The blade was easily a foot long, and marked on the left flat was "LIFE SUPPORT SYSTEM X" with a circled "R." It was a twentiety-century manufacturer's trademark symbol. There was the word "CRAIN," the circled "R" symbol again, and beneath it the stick figure of a bird. Ornithology had never been his passion, but he assumed the figure represented a crane. He flipped the knife over. On the rightside blade flat, just beneath the massive double-quillon guard, the steel was marked "Prototype," and beneath that "01." He resheathed the knife, making a mental note to get Louise Walenski to have one of her Warfare people oil the knife and do something with the sheath. It looked to be actual leather and was sodden.

He took up the double shoulder holster. It was leather as well. He looked at the actual holsters and they were marked "Alessi." He assumed it to be a manufacturer's name. It took a moment to deduce how to extract the guns from the holsters, but he did so one at a time, prying apart the snaps which closed the pistols into the holsters by securing through the respective trigger guards.

The pistols were of bright metal, presumably stainless steel or titanium, very much like the knife. The grips were black rubber, checkered, but much of the checkering worn smooth. With use, he presumed.

A quick glance at the muzzles—he had always been interested in antique weapons—confirmed that these were

.45s. A chill moved along his spine. He did not attempt to disarm the weapons, handling them carefully instead. The guns were nearly each other's twin. The one from the holster that would have ridden beneath the right arm was marked on the left slide flat "DETONICS .45," and in smaller print beneath it "COMBAT MASTER." The right slide flat bore no markings. The second pistol. The top line on the left slide flat was as the first, but the words "Combat Master" were engraved in script beneath it. He turned the gun over. On the right-hand slide flat, beneath the ejection port, there was a facsimile signature engraved. It read "John Rourke."

Jason Darkwood set down the pistols. A descendant of the original man spoken of in Gundersen's memoirs? Or somehow . . .

Darkwood exhaled heavily as he crouched there in the corner. As he stood up, he heard one of the nurses assisting Maggie Barrow saying to her, "Doctor Barrow— did you see this? It's a vaccination mark, I think."

"Come on—they haven't used vaccinations that produce a mark like that on the arm—let me see that—damn. It can't be a vaccination mark. That'd be like finding an operational compact disc player outside the New Smithsonian. Help me with this retractor."

Jason Darkwood looked back at the two guns there with the pile of blood-stained clothing. "Holy shit."

Chapter Thirty-four

Paul Rubenstein stood in the gathering darkness, watching as the last of the people from the cargo helicopters was herded into the camp. He, Otto Hammerschmidt, and about three dozen others from the contingent of Soviet troops under the command of the abrupt and—Paul had learned—heartless major had been detailed to guard the interior of the fenced perimeter within which the meager tents were enclosed. The tents were now packed with naked prisoners. Paul doubted there was room in the tents for anyone even to sit, let alone lie down.

Several times throughout the afternoon, Otto Hammerschmidt had grabbed his arm and held him back—several times when there had been whippings, beatings, when mothers had been forced to trudged naked through the snow carrying their howling and dying infants.

And Paul had waited.

Reason had told him that to act rashly would be to act uselessly. The prisoners who were destined for extermination would not be served by his martyrdom, but rather by intelligent action.

Otto Hammerschmidt stood beside him, slapping his hands against his upper arms, stomping his feet against the cold. Paul Rubenstein was numb to it.

The massive concrete structures at the far end of the camp—which his Jewish heritage and gut reaction told him were crematoriums—were at the moment devoid of activity. But, throughout the last hours of the afternoon, there had been considerable activity there. Piping had been laid and the segments of concrete had been sealed against leaks. The temperature was dropping now with the sun, and he wondered how many of these people would survive to die the next morning.

And he had no intention of waiting that long to find out.

"We have to arrange an escape for these people."

Otto Hammerschmidt had said it and Paul Rubenstein looked at him oddly. A German and a Jew posing as Russians and guarding a death camp together. "What do you have in mind, Otto?" Paul whispered, looking back into the camp. The major was nowhere to be seen now and, aside from the crying of infants, the occasional scream, all from inside the tents, there was only the growing howl of the wind.

"We find the strongest among them and get them to help us. We arm them—"

"What will the rest of the guards be doing, Otto?"

Hammerschmidt swore softly. "I suppose we must do it ourselves."

"Yes." Paul Rubenstein looked toward the crematoriums because he had heard engine noises. And he closed his eyes against what he saw. He recognized the cylinders of gas being brought near them on huge trucks now. This was no modern variant of Zyklon B but, however unimagineable, something even worse. These were the same type of cannisters that had carried the gas Vladmir Karamatsov's forces had used against the Soviet Underground City, the gas which only affected males, working with their hormonal structure to turn men into blood-lusting creatures of destruction.

He had seen it work. Seen men turn on their female comrades, even each other, killing until they themselves were killed or died of exhaustion from their murderous rampages.

It was this gas that Karamatsov was planning to use on his helpless prisoners. Perhaps as some test, or perhaps only because he wanted to watch it.

Chapter Thirty-five

Sam Aldridge took a gulp from his coffee cup, medicinal whiskey Jason Darkwood had expropriated from Sick Bay. "Go slow on that stuff, Sam."

"Yeah," Aldridge breathed.

Darkwood stood up and walked from the small sofa across the cabin to his desk, turned around to face Aldridge again, and leaned against the desktop as he spoke. "So—what happened?"

"Everything?"

"Tell me about this Rourke guy."

Aldridge laughed. "He made some joke about being five hundred years old—God bless him. He risked his life for us like crazy—then this. Shit."

"You said he was going back after a woman."

Aldridge nodded. "Must be some woman. Maybe one like him. Wherever he's from."

The few old planes that were left had gone out in search of terrestrially based life and, aside from some data concerning the Chinese—never anything conclusive—there had been nothing. No evidence. But perhaps that was why some of the planes had never come back, Darkwood mused. "You think he's telling the truth, Sam? I mean, about being a five-hundred-year-old American?"

Sam Aldridge had been sipping at his whiskey and now he swirled it in his coffee cup, setting the cup down, Darkwood watching him intently. "Well, Sam?"

"Remember Lincoln's remark when they told him Grant was a whiskey-drinker? Well, if John Rourke's five centuries old, I'd like to know his brand of whiskey too. That man's good. He is so good it would scare me to death if he was a bad guy, ya know? He's like a machine—deadly efficient. But compassionate too. I gotta say, if Rourke's an American, however old he is, he's the finest American I've ever met."

Darkwood was struck by his friend's words—almost the same words used five centuries ago by Commander Gundersen to describe the original John Rourke. Were they really one and the same?

The com box on his desk buzzed and he hit the switch. "Darkwood here."

"Jason—this is Maggie. I've gotta talk to you."

"My place or yours?"

"Mine—I've got too many people down here to leave them for long."

"Rourke—he's, ah . . ."

"That's what I've gotta talk to you about. How much longer until we dock at Mid-Wake?"

Darkwood consulted his watch. "A little over an hour. Will he make it that long?"

"Come down and talk to me about it. They're waving me over to another patient now. So take about ten minutes, Jase."

"Right."

The transmission was gone and Darkwood stared at the com-box for a long time afterward. . . .

He had given her more than ten minutes and still had to wait for her once he had arrived in Sick Bay.

He sat in her private office now, watching as she poured herself a glass of her own medicinal whiskey. "Want some?"

"Looks bad for the Captain to drink on duty—but you go ahead."

"Doesn't look too hot for the ship's medical officer either—but what the hell." She took a long swallow from a coffee cup and set the cup down, then scrunched up onto the top of her desk and tucked her legs up, pulling her uniform skirt down over her knees.

"Is he gonna live?"

"I don't know. I think he's built like a rock. And he's been shot before. That's evident from some scars. That's in his favor, because shock and trauma can be just as big killers. Those new Soviet uniforms with the built-in soft armor took the spin out of those 4.86mm rifle bullets, so the bullets just penetrated and never exited, and they didn't do as much internal organ damage as they could have. He lost a lot of blood. Some of the bullets I just flat out can't get out—with these," and she raised her hands toward him, backs outward, fingers splayed. "Someone who specializes in delicate surgery and has the right team assisting—maybe she could. I don't know. I mean, anybody could take 'em out and kill him. The head wound was just a deep graze. The acid burns on his hand will heal quickly enough. Apparently that spray Sam mentioned that was found in his shoulder bag is some kind of combination antiseptic and accelerated healing agent, like our Dermi-Flex 2. Even smells similar. The arm wound isn't much. But the abdominal injuries—shit. I lasered the bleeders but I couldn't get half the bullets out—couldn't get near them."

"Maggie," Darkwood said softly. "That's not what's bothering you."

"No." She took another sip from the coffee cup. Darkwood was beginning to feel out of place. Aldridge. Now Margaret Barrow. Everybody had a coffee cup except him. "Do you have your appendix?"

"Of course I don't. Nobody has an appendix anymore. Just a useless organ that can work like a time bomb inside you."

"The appendix has been removed from every infant born at Mid-Wake in the last four centuries."

"So—so he still has an appendix. Did you remove it?"

"No—I didn't think I had the right to and as far as I could tell there was nothing wrong with his anyway. My nurse found a vaccination mark—"

270

"I was there."

"There hasn't been any such thing as a vaccination mark for centuries, Jase."

"A vaccination mark and a healthy appendix don't make him five hundred years old either."

"No—but he's not one of us, he's not a Russian. I can tell their surgical procedures a deck away. And he's not Chinese."

Darkwood leaned back against the bulkhead. "Then he is a surface dweller from some other American community. Do you realize what that means?" He pushed away from the bulkhead and walked across to stand beside her. She rested her head against his chest. "It means we're not alone," he told her.

Five hundred years old or middle thirties like the man looked to be. An American. Not from Mid-Wake. But from the surface of the earth.

Jason Darkwood touched his fingers to Maggie Barrow's hair and she looked up at him, her green eyes tired looking but pretty. "Hold me—tight." And she stood up and came into his arms.

He held her tight. . . .

"I was speaking with one of the Chinese, through Machinist First Class Wilbur Hong, Jason. According to the Chinese—who was not terribly eager to speak with a non-Oriental but did appear comforted at having Mr. Hong translating—the Chinese have quite a flourishing culture on the surface. The Chinese knew nothing of our mysterious friend Rourke, but did know that others may well exist on the surface as well. There are at least two Chinese cities and possibly a third, though that is likely only rumor. The First City, as this Chinese calls his homeland, is most curious in its design, rather like the petals of a flower, the various segments of the city in fact being called petals—"

"Sebastian—I'm interested in all of this, really. But right now I'm more interested in our friend in Sick Bay."

271

Darkwood sat in his command chair, Sebastian hulking over him as he spoke, the familiar noises of the Reagan's bridge something Darkwood found himself oddly aware of, keenly aware of, as if a background for his thoughts. "This man Rourke, Sebastian—he is evidently from another culture like our own, but a surface culture."

"I would be more inclined to think of it as a culture more similar to that of the Chinese, in many respects more in touch with the reality of existence far beyond our own scope."

"Reality of existence?"

"For five centuries, Mid-Wake has battled the Russians here beneath the sea, and for five centuries both we and they have had precious little time for concerns other than survival. But, most curiously, the Chinese endured several centuries of peace, it appears from my brief discussion with the escapee who accompanied Captain Aldridge and the others here. We have advanced in the ways of war, but perhaps the Chinese and what other terrestrial cultures there may be have advanced in other ways. For the dead, on the surface, the war ended. For those who survived, as did the Chinese it would appear, the war ended as well. But for ourselves . . ."

Jason Darkwood looked up at his friend. "Generation after generation, your ancestors and mine."

"I have always found it rather ironic that our ancestors were scientists dedicated to advancing the possibilities of living and working beyond our planet and we have been forced in order to survive to live, in effect, beneath it. Men and women of peace forced to become a warrior culture . . ."

"We have art, learning—we do only what we have to do to survive, Sebastian."

"At what cost, Jason? For generations, we have not seen the sun except for rare visits to the surface within the past century by heroic persons willing to attempt to fly outmoded aircraft in a so-far-vain search for others of our kind—a vain search until just a few short hours ago. And perhaps we have indeed found other Americans, potential

272

allies and friends, but we may also lose them forever if this man Rourke dies, as it appears he might."

"Your point," Darkwood said, hearing in his own voice a testy quality he hadn't consciously intended.

"My point is pointlessness. If we someday defeat our Soviet adversaries, what will we do then?"

"Return to the surface, I guess. It's habitable now. We've been sure of that for the last century almost. But we can't return to the surface while the Russians remain a threat. They wouldn't dare use their nuclear missiles here in the ocean. It would be sheer madness."

Sebastian smiled strangely. "Then why have they developed them, Jason? In anticipation of destroying us after we have destroyed them? That is a logical absurdity. They intend surface conquest. The testimony of the Chinese with whom I spoke made it abundantly clear that his people have been plagued by our Soviet adversaries for some time, the ultimate goal perhaps conquest of the Chinese city on the surface, the technology they possess. Why go to the surface in order to struggle when you can go as a conqueror, with a city and all that one might require already waiting for you?"

"That's an intriguing theory. And if the Russians were to do that, we couldn't stop them unless we fabricated nuclear weapons of our own, if we had the opportunity."

"Yes." Sebastian nodded somberly. "Built nuclear weapons. We threaten and they threaten and eventually they strike first or we strike first and the world is once again in ashes. What will we have achieved then?"

Jason Darkwood had no answer to that.

Chapter Thirty-six

The darkness was like velvet now, and the stars were very bright as they always were in the thinner atmosphere since the Great Conflagration. And the temperature had dropped drastically. As she shifted her weight in the saddle, the blanket she had cocooned around her upper body and draped over her legs began to slip and she rearranged it.

There was a shape, gray against the blackness, and she recognized it as one of the German field tents. Ma-Lin rode sidesaddle beside her and, for the first time in at least a mile, spoke. "I believe we approach the encampment."

Annie Rourke Rubenstein looked at the girl and nodded. "I believe you're correct. I know women did it for hundreds of years, but how can you ride like that? I'd be scared to death I'd slip off."

"I will show you, if you like."

Annie smiled at the thought, picturing herself in a long dress and fancy hat and veil, riding off to the hunt like something out of a videotape movie or a book. "All right. I'd like to try it, but I don't think I could ever get used to it."

"Is it not uncomfortable riding astride, as you do?"

"No—you get used to it. I haven't ridden in a long time—a very long time. But—it just seems natural."

Ma-Lin smiled. Ma-Lin smiled quite a bit.

Annie turned her little horse—the Chinese horses seemed smaller in stature than Western horses—up along a defile, the gray shape taking more definite substance now.

There was a flash of light where the tent flap should be, and for a brief instant she saw a figure profiled in it. She kept riding, slowing her horse as the ground rose, then reining in a few yards away from the tent, Ma-Lin and the Chinese soldiers a respectable distance behind her. At her left was Bjorn Rolvaag, his dog Hrothgar over his saddle. Rolvaag looked so ill at ease on horseback that perhaps, Annie thought, Ma-Lin should teach the huge Icelandic policeman how to ride sidesaddle. The thought was amusing. Rolvaag half fell from the saddle, his dog bounding away from him. Annie stayed where she was.

The figure from the tent approached, a lantern in one hand, a pistol in the other. She could see his face clearly now as he belted the pistol and raised the lantern toward her.

Annie had been told by the Chairman that his personal representative with the Rourke-Rubenstein party sent to penetrate the Soviet base camp was an intelligence agent named Han Lu Chen.

He was a smallish man, wiry-looking and with an air of toughness, but with a warmth in his eyes that she liked. "So—you are Mrs. Rubenstein. It is an honor to meet a woman whose father, husband, and brother are all men of such great courage."

She had flown by J-7V, traveled by one of the German jeep-like vehicles—its technical designation something which continually eluded her powers of recall—then ridden the last five miles on horseback. And she was tired of politeness.

"Yes—and you are Han Lu Chen."

"Yes." Rolvaag's dog was sniffing at Han's high boots and the Chinese bent over to stroke the animal behind the ears, saying something in his own language which she could not comprehend. Then he reached up and took hold of the reins of her horse. "Your brother and your husband and Dr. Leuden have not been heard from in several hours. There is no reason to suppose that something is

275

amiss, yet there is no reason for rejoicing. Please join me in the tent for refreshment."

"I didn't come here to be refreshed. I came to look for my husband, my brother, and then for my father and Major Tiemerovna. But there's no sign of them either, is there?"

"There is no sign. It is cold out here. Please—may I help you to dismount, Mrs. Rubenstein?"

She only nodded, not that she needed help, sluffing off the blanket and draping it across the front of the saddle, then rising in the stirrups and swinging her right leg up and over, stepping down, Han's hand at her elbow. She was shivering without the blanket, the heavy shawl and the coat beneath it usually more than adequate, but not now after sitting for the past five miles with the cutting edge of the wind so terribly cold.

Han led the way inside, and as he moved his lantern she realized there were two other tents.

The interior of Han's tent was just as she had expected, warm, comfortable, and yet militarily austere. All at once she was warm and she took the shawl from her head and shoulders and folded it neatly, still standing just inside the hermetic seal. "I see that the rider who went on ahead of us has briefed you," Annie said quietly.

"That you wish to rescue your husband and brother and Doctor Leuden, assuming they require it."

She opened her coat and swung back the coattails on both sides. The gesture worked for men. At her right hip was the Detonics Scoremaster .45, at her left hip the Beretta 92F. "I assume they require it."

The Chinese looked at her for a moment, then smiled. "May I offer you refreshment, Mrs. Rubenstein?"

"I will feel more refreshed when I am given information."

"Very well, madame." She liked the sound of that word. "The Russians are very strong here. Some while ago, helicopters were brought in, very large machines; and my men were able to detect that people were being carried in aboard them. The people were young and old, male and female. There were children. All of them were naked. A force of Soviet soldiers herded them across the snow. I presume to some sort of short-term internment and perhaps eventual death. Much is going on in the Soviet base, but from the distance which prudence dictates, it is impossible to tell in great detail. It is clear that something must be done and very quickly, Mrs. Rubenstein. But what? Without the data that would have been the natural result of the foray made by your husband, your brother, and Doctor Leuden, I am like a blind man standing in the middle of a great hall with bottomless pits on all sides, into which I will easily fall if I take one false step."

"You have a nice way with words, Mr. Han." Annie stood her ground by the doorway. "But we have to do something. One thing I learned from my father was that it is better to move forward with prudence than to stand still."

"Your father—he should have been Chinese."

"It is my sincere hope you will be able to discuss that interesting observation with him at some future date. Get me as close to the Russian camp as we dare and then we'll figure out what to do."

"Very well, Mrs. Rubenstein," and Han bowed slightly to her.

"But before we go, may I use your bathroom?"

He smiled and gestured toward the portion of the tent where she knew the chemical toilet would be. As she started toward it, she considered that men did not know how lucky they were to be able to urinate standing up in the middle of nowhere without getting their legs wet.

Chapter Thirty-seven

The entire thing was a disaster, Michael Rourke was beginning to realize. He had come in search of his father. So far, he had lost his best friend, Paul Rubenstein, and if he were not extremely careful, he would lose Maria Leuden. And the realization grew by the day that he loved her very much.

His father had taught him to persevere, but that sometimes that meant withdrawing and taking a different approach. It was time for a different approach now.

He had started walking back toward the truck, Maria in her Russian uniform beside him. "We're leaving here," he said almost under his breath.

"What? But your father and Natalia—and what about Paul and Otto?"

He stopped walking for a moment and looked at her, his eyes passing over her then and shifting about the camp. "Paul and Otto know that we might already have gone. They'll get out. And anyway, I'll be coming back. This isn't the way. I know where Karamatsov is, and if he knows where my father is, I'll convince him to tell me. And if he doesn't, all of this is useless anyway. Walk with me to the truck and don't stop for anybody. And if something goes wrong, you get on that truck and drive like hell. I can take care of myself."

"Perhaps I know that you can," she answered, then began to walk.

Progressively, over the past several hours in the camp, hours spent moving about, searching for some clue that his father and Natalia had either arrived or soon would, Michael Rourke had been becoming more uneasy.

Aside from the obvious factor that this was a Soviet camp and to be caught here would mean quite literally a fate worse than death for both of them, there was something else, almost intangible, in the air. Nervous looks in the eyes of the officers and some of the senior noncoms, idle chatter among the men that he could not understand but which sounded—somehow on edge.

The truck was in sight now and Michael quickened his pace slightly, the number of trucks parked here increased from when he had last been in the area. "You drive—only stop if I tell you to," Michael hissed.

"Yes, Michael," Maria whispered.

She started for the driver's side of the cab and Michael started for the rear of the truck, to make certain that nothing had happened there and to get to the passenger seat. He was halfway back along its length when he saw the major he had seen earlier, the man whose orders had precipitated Paul and Otto's leaving.

Michael saluted. The major didn't return it. The major began talking. Michael tried to look interested. The Major's eyes . . .

Michael licked his lips.

The major took a step back, his hand going to his belt for the pistol there.

There was no choice.

Michael's left hand snapped forward, the gloved middle knuckles formed into a ridge of bone, impacting the base of the major's nose, breaking it, driving the bone up into the brain. It was a technique his father had taught him for silent, virtually instantaneous killing. The bone in the nose would break the ethmoid bone and . . . The major's body started to collapse, blood smearing out beneath his nostrils and across his upper lip, Michale's hands reaching out, catching the Soviet major under the armpits, and propping him against the side of the truck.

In the next instant, Maria Leuden was beside Michael, her voice a frightened whisper. "I saw in the mirror—

Michael!"

"Get back in the truck," Michael ordered, looking around them now to see if the deed had been witnessed. There was so much activity that for the moment at least, the killing seemed to have gone unnoticed.

Michael's left arm went around the major's waist, his right hand at the major's right elbow, and he propelled the dead man toward the rear of the truck, moving his lips as though in conversation, but merely reciting the Gettysburg Address under his breath. By the time Michael had him to the rear of the truck he was into Hamlet's soliloquy.

Nothing unexpected in the truck bed. Michael looked around himself. No one watching that he could detect. He shoved the major against the truck, then bent low, letting the major collapse over his left shoulder, then packed the body into the rear of the truck. "Sleep tight, Mother." Michael grinned, then closed the tarp. The truck's engine started and the belch of the exhaust shocked him for an instant.

He resumed his circuit around the truck, ready to reach under his uniform for the twin Beretta pistols. But there was no provocation for it.

He climbed up into the cab beside Maria, the engine purring nicely now.

"Drive carefully, slowly, so you don't attract attention. But don't stop for anybody unless I say so."

"Yes, Michael."

She started the truck moving. . . .

The track along which they had entered the base camp area was glutted with traffic now and Michael told Maria Leuden to take the turnoff toward the helicopter pads. In the distance on their right there was brilliant light. "What is that, Michael?"

"I don't know—be ready to slow down or stop. Keep going for now." He debated whether to unlimber his pistols for faster use or keep them concealed. He decided on the latter for the moment, his eyes still drawn toward the light.

And a childhood memory returned to him. His father and mother had taken him and his sister to a traveling carnival or circus—he couldn't remember which. And they had ridden all the rides and his father had won prizes for both of them at the sharpshooting concession on the midway and then it had been time to go because of something or another—maybe school the next day. He couldn't remember that. But he and Annie had sat in the back of the station wagon, Annie hugging the stuffed dog their father had won for her, he and Annie both looking back toward the carnival, his stomach hurting a little from the mixture of cotton candy and soda pop. But Michael hadn't wanted to disclose the stomach ache to his father or mother because they had both warned him that he had been eating and drinking too much.

And he remembered how all the lights there in the middle of a dark nowhere at the edge of some Georgia cow pasture had made it look as though a spaceship had landed or something. And these lights now. Not a spaceship, certainly, nor a carnival or traveling circus either.

"Slow down a little, Maria," he told her.

The lights shone down from guard towers and bathed the fences in glare, the fences made of barbed wire or perhaps some modern-day Soviet equivalent. There were tents inside the rectangle of wire and yellow-white light. But beyond the tents, inside a smaller fenced area, he could see massive structures of concrete and beside these, parked, trucks, the cabs linked to the massive cylinders of gas . . .

"Holy God," Michael Rourke whispered, realizing what it was that he saw.

Chapter Thirty-eight

Boris Feyedorovitch stood at attention before the three bored faces of the triumvirate.

The face in the middle changed expression and words came from between the flaccid lips. "The Sverdlovsk has been retrofitted with the new surface-searching scanning array, I have been given to understand."

"Yes, Comrade Chairman. I believe this is true."

"The woman who claims she was an officer of the Committee for State Security and is the wife of this Marshal Karamatsov—she lives?"

"Yes, Comrade Chairman. She was overpowered by use of Sty-20 pistols. Even now, she is regaining consciousness."

"She is well-guarded?"

"My own men, Comrade Chairman."

The eyes in the face seemed to wander for a moment. "It is our decision," the Chairman said, his eyes appearing to refocus, "that you be given personal charge of the following mission. Utilizing the enhanced capabilities of the Sverdlovsk, locate the base of this Marshal Karamatsov. Take to him a photograph of his wife. Entice him to return with you that a possible alliance to our mutual benefit may be discussed. His land armies, if indeed they exist, could well be the missing element we have required for our conquest of the Chinese and eventual conquest of whatever other peoples may have survived on the surface. Giving him his missing wife and telling him of the death of his nemesis, this Rourke person, may indeed be the means of approaching him. This Rourke, the American—he is dead indeed?"

"He could be nothing else, Comrade Chairman. I personally shot him in the head. He was already wounded. There was much blood found in the late Colonel Kerenin's apartment, and the blood was typed to indicate that it was not Kerenin's. Colonel Kerenin died valiantly, Comrade Chairman."

The Comrade Chairman said nothing for a moment.

"You are now a colonel and will replace Colonel Kerenin as commander of the Marine Spetznas. The Sverdlovsk awaits you, colonel."

Boris Feyedorovitch stiffened his back. "Your orders will be carried out, Comrade Chairman."

But the eyes were already all but lifeless again.

Colonel Boris Alexeivitch Feyedorovitch smartly executed an about face and strode from the great hall. . . .

An ambulance monorail had been waiting on the emergency track for them as soon as the Reagan had docked in the sub pens, had sped along the blue tentacle of the marine and naval studies area with the dying John Rourke in a life-support tube. It breathed for him to save the exertion of energy. It monitored heart and other vital signs, as well as brain-wave patterns. Robot servos were poised over him, laser-targeted, controlled entirely by the computer which ran the life-support tube, ready to inject adrenalin or other substances which might preserve life until he reached the surgeons. She had sat with the tube-tech, watching Rourke's face. It was a strong face. A handsome face. And she had had a hard time imagining this man dead, but logic and her own medical experience dictated otherwise. "Can Remquist do the operation?"

"Yes, doctor, I believe he's scheduled for it as soon as the support work-up is done."

"I wish you didn't have to wait for that. Everything's in those records and what isn't can be tapped into off the Reagan's medical console."

"That's not my decision, doctor," the tube-tech said, flashing his even white teeth. He had a cap job and she had never found that appealing in a man. He had curly hair, as Jason Darkwood had, but she had curled her own hair often enough to recognize the difference between beauty services and natural. His was beauty services all the way. Jason's hair—it was a dark brown—had that disorganized, rumpled laziness to it that was real.

She realized she was disliking the tube-tech because he was telling her what she had known he would tell her, and that it made no common sense at all that a dying man should be denied treatment until tests she had conducted were conducted again to the satisfaction of a man who was a genius as a surgeon and a total failure as a human being.

She had observed Doctor Wilson Remquist at his work on several occasions when she herself had been a student. He worked tirelessly to save his patient, not for the sake of the patient but because of the challenge factor. So perhaps he would work in that manner to save the life of this enigmatic Rourke, because in her medical career she had never seen someone so close to death yet still alive.

The ambulance had used the emergency rail all the way until reaching the Hub, then diverted from the emergency rail, which had been under repair there, to the defense rail, then back to the emergency rail after leaving the Hub, and along the yellow tentacle toward medical.

In a long, even stretch there in the yellow tentacle, she had looked behind their car and seen a car speeding after them on the defense rail—it would be Jason, she knew.

The emergency platform at the hospital complex was ready, the tube transferred and expedited away, Maggie Barrow led to a computer console to begin the forms necessary for Rourke's admission and treatment.

But all the while, she had not been able to concentrate on the forms—not that they required that—but rather had

284

thought of Rourke. Was he five centuries old?

And then Remquist had come. He didn't remember her. But who did remember one student out of so many? "You're Commander Barrow?"

"Yes, doctor," she had answered, for Remquist, despite his manner, the title reverential.

"Gave me a tough one, Doctor Barrow. But we'll see if I can pull it out of the fire." Remquist had already turned and started to walk away.

She hadn't realized she was speaking until she heard her words. "He isn't an 'it,' Doctor Remquist. He's a man."

"What did you say, miss?"

"I said that your patient is a living human being, not just another challenge to your consummate skills, doctor."

Remquist looked at her oddly. "I'll try to remember that." And he walked away.

She felt like shit. . . .

The hum of the monorail underscored Jason Darkwood's silence. Maggie Barrow wondered if perhaps his silence had derived from her own and she decided to break it. "I've been lousy company. I'm sorry. I'm just thinking about that poor man Rourke."

Jason smiled at her. His brown eyes were pretty, always had been. "You did all you could."

"What I said to Doctor Remquist. How the hell could I have said that?"

Jason looked at her, his left hand reaching out and covering hers, which were in her lap. "It was the truth, wasn't it?"

"Of course it was the truth—but—"

"If Sebastian were here, he'd doubtless tell you that the truth is always the truth and denying it as such is the ultimate stupidity. Which is why, of course, Sebastian has very few friends." Jason grinned and she felt herself smiling, and then she laughed a little.

"You're mean to say that."

"But, truthful, nonetheless. So Sebastian would be

285

compelled by his own worship of logic to commend me for the statement, wouldn't he? As I commend you for speaking up to that pompous ass."

"How do you know Remquist is a pompous ass?"

"You told me one time when you'd had too much to drink."

"I didn't think you listened to women when they were drunk."

"Hmm." He smiled. "There were other things to do, of course. But you did seem interested in talking."

"And what did you do—what 'other things'?"

"Listened. That's all I did."

She laughed. He was a good listener, but he was a better lover. He was as close to perfect as she'd ever found, or for that matter thought she ever would. And he'd gotten to be a better listener too. "Are you trying to get me angry with you?"

"Now, talk about logic. 'Angry with' me is a totally silly way of putting it. The construction implies that we would get angry together, like going for a walk together or making love. No—I don't want you angry with me or without me. I don't want you angry period. I'm sorry about that dinner."

" 'When duty whispers lo thou must . . .' "

"But speaking for myself alone, of course." Jason smiled. "I haven't been classifiable as a youth for some time—sad to say."

"Why do they want me at this meeting?"

"I think Command and General Staff wants to ask you if in the considered medical opinion of Navy Lieutenant Commander Margaret Louise Barrrow it is conceivable that such a person as a five-hundred-year-old man could indeed exist. And then I have a feeling they're going to send us after his girlfriend just in case she's five hundred years old too. Sounds like fun to me."

She never liked it when he acted flippant because he wasn't really that way. But she knew why he was sounding that way now. "They'd want you to send a team in to penetrate the Russian city."

"Yes," he said, standing now, tugging down the tunic of his uniform dress whites.

She stood up with him, the monorail beginning to slow, the Administration Hub station visible ahead. She asked him, "How's my hat? I hate these things."

"It's fine—your hat's fine."

Wearing her uniform hat always meant putting her hair up, which was the only way the hat fit, and working in the submarine service she had long ago gotten out of the habit of keeping her hair in regs because it never mattered. When she had shore leave, the Reagan in port for a refit or for a long break between assignments, she avoided all official functions that required a uniform and stuck to things like blue jeans and sundresses. When she had first heard the term—sundress—when she was just a little girl, she had asked her mother why people wore special dresses for something that you didn't see. Her mother, a computer specialist, had never left Mid-Wake, never seen the sun. She had not seen the sun until she had gone on the survival course at the Naval Academy. The sun had felt so hot, it had further bemused her why anyone would wear a dress designed to expose bare skin to its harshness.

When her mother had been dying, she had sat at her mother's bedside and told her mother about such things as sun and wind and salt spray, and her mother had remarked that the world beyond Mid-Wake sounded like Paradise. Margaret Barrow had deduced early on in her life that the world outside Mid-Wake once was Paradise, and that the Biblical story of the Garden of Eden could well have been a prophecy foretelling man's destiny rather than an apocryphal tale of his origins. But she had never said that to her mother. As she positioned her uniform shoulder bag, smoothed her uniform skirt, and considered the ridiculousness of wasting time to put on special clothes for a few hours just to see people who knew you didn't normally dress that way at all, she realized that Jason Darkwood was the only person to whom she ever told her private thoughts.

Jason put on his uniform hat and smoothed his hair

back at the sides. The monorail stopped. "Here we go, Maggie," he whispered, then touched his hand at her elbow as she started to step from the monorail car and onto the platform. . . .

Each tentacle was a different color. Blue for Naval and Marine, of course, yellow for Medical/Dental, Educational, and Food Services, indigo and violet for the primary living areas, red for Security/Detention, green for Agriculture/Animal Husbandry—she wondered now as she always had why white had been chosen for the Hub. Perhaps they had run out of colors.

They entered the office of the Chairman of the Joint Chiefs and she stopped for an instant.

The President was there.

"Commander Darkwood. And Doctor Barrow. It is an honor to meet two of Mid-Wake's finest officers."

The President came around the Chairman's desk and extended his hand to Jason Darkwood and Jason—who had saluted—dropped the salute and took it. Then he extended his hand to her and she found his grip firm, warm, and dry. "Mr. President," she said, feeling her cheeks flushing a little as he looked at her. Jacob Fellows was not only the President of Mid-Wake, but one of the most handsome men she had ever seen. And she found that his image on television didn't do the man justice. Steel-gray hair and eyes to match in a face that looked chiseled by Michelangelo.

"If the Chairman of the Joints Chiefs doesn't mind," Jacob Fellows said, "I'll do the talking."

"Certainly, Mr. President." Admiral Rahn beamed.

She licked her lips. Jason looked perfectly at ease, but she knew him well enough to know that he hated this kind of stuff. But it went with commanding the Reagan.

"All right then—both of you—sit down, please."

Jason held a chair for her and she sat down, tugging her skirt over her knees, Jason preferring to stand, beside her chair.

"Very well," President Fellows said, perching on the edge of Admiral Rahn's desk. "We have a situation I understand might prove of immense importance to the citizens of Mid-Wake now and in the future. Commander Darkwood. This man John Rourke. Tell me about him."

"The Commander of my Marine Assault Force, Captain Samuel Aldridge, was MIA. All of a sudden, he's back and Captain Aldridge claims that this John Rourke is responsible. I have no reason to doubt Captain Aldridge, and indeed anything Captain Aldridge would say I would swear by."

"I've read Captain Aldridge's preliminary debriefing out of your computer, commander." His eyes looked at her. "Doctor Barrow. Could this man really be the John Rourke spoken of in our history?"

She swallowed hard. She wasn't a scientist any more than any normal doctor was. "I don't know, Mr. President. He's obviously not from Mid-Wake, and what evidence I was able to glean during my examinations indicated that he was not Russian."

"Explain, miss."

"Certainly, sir. With our culture and theirs—the Soviets, I mean—having no interchange whatsoever, certain procedural matters have evolved along similar but significantly different lines. I could tell from surgical scars, old wounds—no Russian doctor cared for him. And then there's the vaccination mark."

"What's a vaccination mark?"

"In the old days, children were routinely given vaccinations against possible disease threats, as are all of our children, of course. But they were given a vaccination—or an injection—against smallpox, a disease which hasn't existed in five centuries and has never existed here. By the latter portion of the twentieth century, the practice had been discontinued almost entirely. Certainly, any surface culture which did survive in underground bunkers might well have included persons so vaccinated, but since the disease was so rare it would seem likely that it would not have been encountered and vaccination would not have

289

been restarted."

Admiral Rahn spoke. "Could it be that, if this man named Rourke is just a contemporary man sent on some sort of exploratory mission, he would have been vaccinated against this smallpox just in case?"

Maggie Barrow assumed the Admiral had addressed his question to her. So she tried to answer it. "Highly unlikely, sir, since it would have been necessary to have a smallpox culture in order to immunize, and there would be no reason to suppose that smallpox vaccine would have been considered a survival necessity. The disease was in virtual worldwide remission at the time World War III broke out."

"And it couldn't be anything else but this smallpox vaccine that caused this scar, Commander Barrow?"

She turned here eyes toward the Marine Commandant, General Gonzalez. "No, sir. Not to my knowledge."

"But your knowledge isn't all-consuming. Correct?"

"Yes, sir. But I believe, sir, that medical history records would bear me out."

"They do, Doctor Barrow," the President said. "And I like an officer who sticks to her guns even when she's up against superior rank." Jacob Fellows clapped his hands together loudly. "So—we have a man who is very likely five hundred years old. Which is impossible, but we can worry about that later. He sustains mortal wounds in a vain effort to save a female companion. If he dies, this remains an enigma, fascinating but fruitless. But if this woman is five centuries old—just supposing—what if there's a whole colony of them? Hmm? What do you think, Commander Darkwood?"

She looked up at Jason. His brown eyes seemed to hold a hint of amusement. "I don't have any opinion on the five-hundred-year-old theory, but I agree that this woman this man had attempted to save must be of some importance. Beyond his emotional attachment to her, of course."

"Would you, commander," the President asked, "attempt to save a female comrade against impossible odds?"

Jason Darkwood didn't answer for a moment, but then,

290

"I would, sir. Some females more than others."

The President grinned. "You're a straightforward man, commander, and I like that. How about you attempting to do what this self-proclaimed John Rourke was unable to do? What are the chances of getting inside the Russian sphere of influence, extricating a female prisoner, and getting her back out alive?"

"Statistically, Mr. President?"

"However you wish to express it."

"Forgive my bluntness, Mr. President—but the chances are zip. Which doesn't of course preclude doing it."

Admiral Rahn cleared his throat loudly.

Jason Darkwood went on. "From what Captain Aldridge said, this man John Rourke, or whoever he is, was exceptionally gifted at what might be loosely termed commando work. I doubt anyone I could muster would be that good. So, if Rourke or whoever he is failed, I have no reason to suppose that I or any of the men under me could do the job any better. If he is the real John Rourke spoken of in the history by Commander Gundersen, he'd have vastly more experience than we could imagine. If I recall the story correctly . . ." And Jason Darkwood stopped talking. "Sir—has anyone checked the Gundersen memoirs in detail other than for the name of John Rourke?"

"Damnit—you're right." The President leaned over the desk and pushed the com-box button marked "computer," and the voice of Mid-Wake Central Computer came over the speaker. It was a sexy-sounding woman's voice. Maggie had felt flattered when Jason had told her once that the voice sounded almost as good as hers. "This is the President."

"Confirming voice print." There was a pause, then, "Voice print confirmed."

"Consult the memoirs of Commander Gundersen, computer. Is there mention of a woman having accompanied John Rourke?"

"Processing." There was another slight pause, then, "Affirmative."

Jacob Fellows hesitated for a moment. "Computer.

291

Pertinent data only concerning the woman."

"Data as follows. Female, Tiemerovna, Natalia Anastasia, Major, Soviet Committee for State Security (KGB), physical description as follows: approximate age late twenties, height approximately five-foot-eight, Gundersen memoir classifies woman subjectively as—this is quote: '. . . as beautiful as some statue of a goddess, with eyes more blue than the sea.' Physical description Tiemerovna, Natalia Anastasia, Major KGB, ends."

"Computer—anything about her skills?"

"Processing." There was a pause, then the sexy voice came back. "Extract—skilled with firearms and edged weapons and in unspecified martial arts discipline/disciplines. Data exhausted."

"Thank you, computer." The President switched off. "What if that's the woman?"

General Gonzalez began, "With all due respect, Mr. President . . ."

"I know." Jacob Fellows smiled. "Who needs another Russian? But if I remember the story correctly, this Russian woman helped John Rourke to defeat some barbarians or something and a group of military traitors, and then prevented the use of a very substantial atomic weapon. Apparently, she wasn't all bad."

Admiral Rahn spoke. "If I may, Mr. President. As you may be aware, I taught history at the Academy on and off over the years. The Rourke story was something I never put great store in, but if my memory serves, somewhere in Gundersen's original manuscript there is a reference to this Russian woman being someone with whom Rourke was obviously in love."

Jason spoke. "If I may, Admiral Rahn, were there any details about Rourke himself that might not be readily apparent from the computer files?"

Maggie looked from Jason to the Admiral. "As a matter of fact, there were a few things, commander. I seem to recall that Gundersen made a great point of telling how fantastic a fighter this John Rourke was, and that he was, of course, a doctor of medicine, an ex-Central Intelligence

Agency man—things like that. And Gundersen gave Rourke some sort of magazine case to use with Rourke's handguns. They were .45s, in those days, if memory serves."

Jason Darkwood spoke. "This John Rourke had two guns, which were marked Detonics .45s, on his person. In addition to other items of gear, there was a case which held six—"

"How many, commander?"

"Six magazines for his pistols, admiral."

Admiral Rahn crossed the room, looked at the President. "May I, sir?"

"By all means, Admiral."

Admiral Rahn hit the computer button on the com-box. "Computer. Admiral Rahn."

"Confirming voice print." Pause. "Voice print confirmed."

"Computer—extraneous data in Gundersen memoirs. Name of gift Commander Gundersen bestowed on John Rourke."

"Processing." Pause. "Milt Sparks Six-Pak for carrying of spare magazines for matching pistols called in Gundersen memoir Detonics .45s."

"Thank you, computer." Admiral Rahn switched off. He looked at Jason.

"That was part of the man's gear, sir," Jason Darkwood said softly.

The President spoke. "Gentlemen—and Miss Barrow. It appears we have a five-hundred-year-old man who has sustained perhaps mortal wounds in an attempt to rescue a five-hundred-year-old woman who is his lover. Quite romantic, but if my meager knowledge of twentieth-century history serves, it was a period marked by extreme romanticism juxtaposed with radical cynicism, and so perhaps our Doctor Rourke and his KGB major weren't as odd as they might seem to us." Maggie thought it was beautiful, that a man would love a woman for five centuries and willingly give his life to save hers. "I suggest we dispatch the Reagan, Admiral Rahn, General Gonzalez,

Commander Darkwood. And I further suggest that the Reagan be commissioned to extricate this woman at all reasonable costs."

"My sentiments exactly, Mr. President," Admiral Rahn said vigorously.

General Gonzalez added, "As always, Mr. President, the Corps is ready for whatever the challenge."

"Darkwood? You game for it?"

"Yes, Mr. President. It seems like a job that needs doing."

President Jacob Fellows laughed. "I knew your father, commander. I did my military service as an enlisted man aboard the old Reagan and served under him. I remember hearing him say that. You remind me of him. How is your mother?"

"Dead, sir."

"I saw her once. She was a lovely woman."

"Thank you, Mr. President."

"Anything you need for the mission, you've got. Good luck." The President extended his hand and Jason took it, and Maggie Barrow sucked in her breath hard and felt fear wash over her, and it made her cold.

Jason Darkwood would never ask his crew to do anything he wouldn't do himself. And that meant he'd penetrate the Russian domes and he'd probably die and she would grieve him until her own death. She stood up, shook the President's hand, saluted whom she had to salute and fell in at Jason Darkwood's side—where she wanted to be forever. . . .

Natalia Anastasia Tiemerovna had made her decision. Escape was impossible, and with John dead, there was no point to life at all.

When the time came, as she knew it would for just a very brief fragment in time, she would kill herself.

She had become what she had never wanted to become—a woman emotionally barren without the man who was the center of her universe.

294

There were no more tears left and she sat silently, wrists and ankles shackled, on the edge of the bed in the gray detention cell, and waited for her one chance to alleviate her sorrow. Perhaps John Rourke was right and there was a God and somehow there was a life after death. If there was, all the more reason to hurry into death's arms. . . .

Annie Rourke Rubenstein edged along on knees and elbows, her stockinged legs feeling the snow working into her boot tops under her heavy woolen skirt, the 9mm Beretta in her right fist, the holster on her right hip still filled with the Detonics Scoremaster. Han was only a few feet ahead of her, and it wasn't that he crawled faster, but rather that he had started ahead of her.

Han stopped at the lip of the rise and she joined him an instant afterward, giving a quick glance to the terrain below, rolling onto her back, brushing the snow out of the tops of her boots, and then rolling back onto her stomach. He handed her a pair of binoculars. "They have special light-gathering properties, Mrs. Rubenstein."

She took the binoculars in her left hand, not holstering the pistol from her right hand, but instead stuffing it into the pocket of her coat. No "special light-gathering properties," as Han Lu Chen had put it, were necessary to observe what most attracted her eye. A quadrangle bathed in yellow light, a smaller quadrangle near to it, also brightly lit, but, rather than tents occupying its center, concrete structures; and parked beside these were truck cabs hitched to trailers which were gleaming gas cannisters. "Do you see that?"

"Yes—you refer of course to the brightly lit area."

"I know what those tankers are filled with."

"This fuel which your machines utilize?"

"No—not that. A gas that turns men—only men—into homicidal maniacs who'll kill anyone. Karamatsov is going to use that gas like he used it before. Maybe against your people. I don't know. We have to get down there and steal it."

"We would need special equipment." He lowered his glasses as she lowered hers. "If this gas is a weapon such as you describe, it would be insanity to go near it."

"It's like I describe. It makes men insane. Animals."

"Then we will need protective clothing and other specialized equipment. I will—"

Annie cut him off. "You might need it. I don't. Three trucks. And I can drive one of them. Ma-Lin—she can drive a truck, can't she?"

"Yes—but . . ."

"Well?"

"The third woman—who?"

"She's right down there with my brother and my husband and with Otto Hammerschmidt. Marie Leuden. All we've gotta do is find her. If we steal his gas and he does have my father down there and Natalia, too, Karamatsov will be so busy going after us that you and the rest of the men can get in there and get Daddy and Natalia away and free. Karamatsov wouldn't risk losing the gas and our having it to use against him."

"How can a gas only have such terrible effects upon men and not women?"

"I'm no scientist. It's hormonally related." And Annie let herself smile. "Men may be stronger, taller, or anything else. But this one time the best man for the job is a woman, my friend."

"Marshal Karamatsov still seeks the missiles that may remain and he wishes to utilize this gas—perhaps to form an army of madmen to unleash against us." It was as if Han were thinking out loud. "Yes—you are right, Mrs. Rubenstein. You are your father's daughter too, I think." And Han Lu Chen's face seamed with a smile. . . .

Maria Leuden sat stock still behind the wheel of the truck. She had pulled it off to the side of the road and was waiting now in darkness, the engine running but even the running lights turned off, Michael gone to investigate the brightly lit, fenced area. What he had called it had filled her at once with terror and revulsion.

He had called it a "death camp," and every German for five centuries had grown up knowing the phrase. Men like Deiter Bern, whom John Rourke, Michael's father, had aided in bringing democracy to New Germany, had openly spoken the words as a condemnation of National Socialism. The men who had attempted to suppress Bern and others who spoke of freedom had said the death camps were a myth propagated by the forces which had worked to destroy the Third Reich and wished to subvert the Fourth.

She had never believed the words were just descriptive of some myth, and she had eventually learned they had been reality. And it had terrified her. "Death camp." She spoke the words under her breath, and the words chilled her more than the night and her fears for Michael and her loneliness, and she clutched the Beretta 92F American military pistol close against her chest, her knees locked together hard in her pants, and she could hear her heart beating.

Chapter Thirty-nine

Michael Rourke had learned from his father that brashness was at times the best form of subtlety. He stood at the gate leading into the smaller of the two quadrangles and said nothing, rather looking impatiently at the guard who was coming up to open the gate. If the guard who opened the gate or one of the other guards spoke, he would have to act as imperiously as the late major had, because there was no way he could answer.

The guard swung open the gate and Michael started walking, the guard approaching him, saying something. Michael turned and looked at the man as though he were looking at the lowest creature of which he could possibly conceive. The guard backed off and Michael walked on, hearing an unfinished protest from the man, then nothing more. He walked toward the three trucks with their gleaming tank trailers, his left hand held casually across his abdomen, the button of his uniform tunic open so he could get at the Berettas. . . .

Paul Rubenstein and Otto Hammerschmidt beside him walked toward the smaller fenced area, where the trucks were parked and men hovered about them and the concrete gas chambers near them like worker bees buzzing in the hive.

There was one hope only, Paul had realized. But there were three trucks and only he and Otto Hammerschmidt to drive them. That was the problem. Hammerschmidt whispered, "This will not work without a third man to drive the third truck, Paul."

"I'm thinking—I'm thinking," Rubenstein hissed.

There was an officer approaching them. "Great," Paul Rubenstein snapped. He quickened his pace, Hammerschmidt doing the same. He could hear the crunch of gravel and dirt under his own borrowed boots and Hammerschmidt's, and now he heard a third set of feet following after them. He reached under his uniform tunic for his Gerber, glancing toward Hammerschmidt, Hammerschmidt nodding almost imperceptibly.

Paul stopped and wheeled toward the approaching officer, the Gerber half out of the sheath that Paul had stuffed beneath his uniform.

And then he saw the face of the officer.

He slid the Gerber back where it had been and walked toward the officer, saluting briskly, his voice barely a whisper as he said, "You scared the shit out of me."

Michael Rourke returned the salute and whispered, "What the hell is going on here?"

Hammerschmidt said it. "This is a death camp, Michael. Those cannisters of gas are here, we believe, to be used against the Chinese who are held in the main compound. We were planning to steal the trucks, but we're a man short."

"You aren't now." Michael smiled.

"Where's Maria?" Paul asked.

"Back with the truck. We can get her on the way, drive like hell for where we left Han, and hold them off until the Chinese and hopefully some Germans arrive."

"We have to free those people," Paul insisted. "Some of them won't make it through the night. They're all naked."

"The gas first," Michael said. "Then we can maybe utilize the resultant confusion to—"

"Stay right where you are, gentlemen!"

The voice was in English. Michael's expression froze. Paul Rubenstein didn't turn toward the voice.

The voice came again. "You are surrounded. I am Colonel Nicolai Antonovitch. John Rourke, Paul Rubenstein, and the third man—I place you all under arrest. If you move, you will be shot!"

"He thinks you're your father," Paul said between his clenched teeth.

"Then they aren't expecting him here. This was all—"

"Relax," Paul hissed.

Michael slowly turned toward the sound of the voice. Paul turned toward it as well. They were surrounded, Paul could see instantly. At least two dozen men with Soviet assault rifles. And standing just inside the circle they made was a tall, good-looking man holding a pistol, the pistol held lazily in his right hand as if only for show.

"This great John Rourke and his companion Paul Rubenstein. The Hero Marshal will be pleased. You . . ." He gestured limply with his pistol toward Otto Hammerschmidt, who stood between Paul and Michael. "Who are you?"

Hammerschmidt's heels clicked together. "I am a German officer, Captain Otto Hammerschmidt, sir!"

Paul's mind raced. Antonovitch—one of Karamatsov's senior officers, like Krakovski, the man they had killed on the train during the fight for the missiles. The names of Karamatsov's staff officers had been in one or another of the Russian dispatches taken from Soviet patrols since this had all begun.

Michael spoke. "Do you think, colonel, that my two friends and I came here alone? I suggest, colonel, that if you know my reputation as well as you recognize my face, you might consider the fact that it it you, not we, who is in considerable difficulty at this moment."

Michael was bluffing them. Like father, like son, Paul thought. And if this Antonovitch had mistaken Michael for his father—they looked enough alike to be virtual twins—there was perhaps a chance.

Colonel Antonovitch spoke. "Where are your legions of followers? But perhaps more to the point, Doctor Rourke, where are your son, daughter, and wife—and where is Major Tiemerovna?"

It was Michael's ball, Paul knew.

Michael ran with it. "I suggest, colonel, unless we bring this situation to a conclusion rather quickly you will very soon find out where the rest of the Rourke family is. Suffice it to say, colonel, they know where you are." And Michael smiled.

"You suggest an impasse, then, Doctor Rourke?" Antonovitch called back.

Paul was having the feeling this man wasn't easily bluffed.

"I suggest nothing," Michael called back to him. Paul's eyes drifted to Michael. Michael was slowly opening his tunic. To get at his guns? Paul felt a shiver run up his back. "We came for the three trucks of gas and to effect the release of the people you have incarcerated in your little death camp, colonel. We intend to leave with the three trucks and to secure the release of your prisoners. We can do that in one of two ways. Either you and your men step aside and let us get to the trucks and then you order the internees released, or you die and we get to the trucks anyway and we simply release the internees. Either way, you've lost."

Pauls's feet were sweating inside his boots.

And then he heard his wife's voice. "You heard my father!"

Paul's eyes snapped toward the sound. Annie. A pistol in each hand, stood on the other side of the quadrangle fence, flanked on one side by a Chinese woman armed with one of the Chinese Glock-17 pistol, on the other side by Bjorn Rolvaag and his dog, Rolvaag's staff in the man's mighty fists. A few paces away from them were two Chinese soldiers, armed with assault rifles.

And now he heard another familiar voice. "I suggest, colonel, that you take Doctor Rourke's words seriously." The voice was Han Lu Chen's. "The Chinese army takes very unkindly to Chinese citizens being interned under any conditions, certainly by you."

Paul called out, "Hi, Annie!"

"Paul . . ." Her voice sounded as though she were suppressing terror.

Hammerschmidt spoke. "My men are in position, as well, Han?"

"They await your orders to fire, Captain Hammerschmidt."

There were no Germans unless this was a bona-fide miracle.

Michael spoke again. "I'm moving to the trucks. If you attempt to stop us, well—I wouldn't, if I were you."

Paul heard Annie call out. "Daddy—Ma-Lin and I are ready to drive the trucks out of here. And Maria's with us too."

Paul turned his head toward the fence—Maria Leuden had joined them there. How Annie had found her—but Annie seemed capable of virtually anything, Paul reflected. She and the Chinese girl Paul assumed was Ma-Lin and Maria Leuden, who had just stepped into the corona of light, started toward the gate leading into this smaller compound, Annie's pistols still in her fists, the Chinese girl still armed, Maria Leuden with one of the Beretta 92Fs. Paul swallowed hard.

Michael Rourke started walking slowly toward the trucks, not drawing any weapon. And Paul knew why. There was a substantial chance that Antonovitch would know what guns John Rourke carried and somehow make the connection that this was Michael rather than Michael's father John. And what John Rourke could get away with, perhaps no one else could.

"John," Paul called out. "Otto and I are right behind you." Very slowly, so it wouldn't appear to be the opening move in a gunfight, Paul extracted the battered Browning High Power he had carried almost since the Night of the War. He kept it tight in his right fist, beside his right thigh, as he started walking. Otto Hammerschmidt shifted his assault rifle forward.

"Colonel—tell your men to allow the ladies inside through the gates and to leave the gates open."

"You will never escape here alive."

Michael stopped walking, turned, stared at Colonel Antonovitch. "I won't?" And he started walking now straight for the KGB Corps colonel. Paul stopped, the High Power still at his right thigh, his eyes going to the gun Antonovitch held. Perhaps Antonovitch was one of the Elite Corps personnel who survived the Sleep with Karamatsov, or perhaps the Russian only had a fondness for more substantial-looking weapons than were made today. The gun in his right hand was some kind of Smith & Wesson double-action revolver, dully gleaming, stainless steel.

Michael stopped a yard from Antonovitch. "You have six shots. Maybe you'll get me with them before I kill you. But I seriously doubt it. Now—order your men to drive whatever rolling stock they have to just outside the gates of the main compound and then assist the internees to board the trucks. Order your men to get whatever blankets or warm clothing they have and provide these to the people as they board the trucks. Annie and the other two women will be driving Karamatsov's gas outta here, right between those trucks with the internees and you. Anything goes wrong, Annie and the other women will make the gas tankers blow, and every man within a couple of square miles will be a homicidal maniac as soon as he gets a whiff of it. If you and I aren't dead already, we will be. But most importantly to you, Karamatsov's whole army might be destroyed. Now the question you've gotta ask yourself is this: would the Hero Marshal be less unhappy losing a bunch of unarmed people he was going to kill anyway and a couple of truckloads of his precious gas, or losing his whole army?" Michael hesitated a moment. Antonovitch said nothing. "Well? What's it gonna be?" Michael asked, his voice low.

Antonovitch began barking commands in Russian over his left shoulder, Paul Rubenstein tensed. He didn't understand and neither did Michael, but posing as John Rourke, Michael was supposed to understand. When Antonovitch finished, a junior officer and two noncoms breaking off from the ring of men surrounding them, Michael said, "Why don't you join me in helping the ladies aboard the trucks." Annie had already reached the

303

center of the compound, Maria and the Chinese girl with her. Paul fell in beside his wife, Annie smiling up at him. They kept walking, Michael and Antonovitch just ahead of them.

The ring of armed men opened and they passed through. Annie said under her breath, "He's pretty good."

"What are you doing here?"

"Looking to help my husband and my brother. And looks like I got here just in time. We found Maria and the truck when we were coming down for a closer recon, and she told us about you and Otto playing Russians and about Michael going off to check this place out. We realized there wasn't any electronic security around the perimeter here, and we crept in just close enough to see and hear and not so close we'd get caught in the light. You guys are lucky."

Paul Rubenstein wanted to kiss his wife very badly, but there would be time later—maybe.

They kept walking.

Michael and Antonovitch were beside the furthest forward of the three trucks, Michael speaking again. "Now—if your people follow us, that'll be a bad move. The Chinese and German forces are in position to cut you to pieces. And if it gets too heavy, the ladies will break off in three separate directions with the trucks and blow them. Not a one of you will live. Do you understand?"

Antonovitch could say something directly to Michael in Russian, and Michael would not be able to respond and the whole thing might be blown, Paul knew.

"You have won the day—or should I say 'the night'? But your time will come, Doctor Rourke."

Michael stepped onto the running board at the side of the truck cab. "You keep believing that." Then he called over his shoulder. "Paul—Annie! This truck. I'll ride with Maria. Otto—you and the Chinese woman—let's move!" As Paul and Annie started for the first truck, Michael called out, "Paul—Otto—we'll leave these trucks and take some of the other Soviet rolling stock as soon as we get through the gates." Michael turned toward the fence.

"Han—get enough people onto those trucks the Russians will be loading. Have Captain Hammerschmidt's men keep the colonel and his people in their sights until we're well away. You and the rest of the people by the fence, climb on board those other trucks with us."

"Yes, Doctor Rourke!"

Paul glanced toward the fence, Han disappearing from the light, calling out orders that could only be partially heard. He wondered if the Chinese had any of their spiritous liquor with them. If they made it out alive, he wanted a drink. . . .

Vladmir Karamatsov had been watching the newly promoted Captain Serovski for some time. When Ivan Krakovski had been murdered by John Rourke and his band of killers, Karamatsov had promoted Serovski and given the young man provisional charge of Special Operations for the KGB Elite Corps.

Karamatsov studied the maps on his desk, then threw down his pen in disgust and exhaustion, the yellow light of his lamp giving him a headache.

They had been so close. Krakovski and the Elite Corps had seized control of . . . He took up the journal in which Ivan Krakovski had written, the journal left in Krakovski's helicopter and brought back by one of the survivors.

"I have taken personal charge of navigation for the fleet of six helicopter gunships, trusting no one with the coordinates given me by the Hero Marshal.

"For a short while, the fleet of gunships has passed under the teeth of the blizzard, but now, the snow swirls around us maddeningly, crusting over the bubble. I am taking the controls of the gunship for a time to relieve the strain. The windshield wipers race crazily, but cannot compete with the rate of snowfall and wind-driven snow as it lashes against the machine, the five other machines barely visible even by their running lights.

"The Hero Marshal has told me that the cache of some

thirty Chinese weapons is near the city once called Lushun, in what had once been a mine, the interior of the mine shaft reinforced with concrete and steel and capped like something the Hero Marshal calls a 'well.'

"It is cold, and colder still from the feeling of fear which, I admit, consumes me. The machine is buffeted by winds I estimate at gale force, and the controls must be manipulated with the greatest of precision, not just to keep on course, but to keep from being thrown into an uncontrolled spin with the machine destroyed.

"I have ordered all pilots by radio to transfer controls to their copilots for periods of at least thirty minutes while they rest from their ordeal.

"I will find the coordinates, but if the storm intensifies, I doubt we shall be able to take off. And the Hero Marshal and the destiny of the Soviet people depend on me. . . ."

Krakovski had fought to the end aboard the train on which he had loaded the Chinese nuclear weapons. This Karamatsov knew. And Krakovski and the train and all aboard it had been hurtled into the sea, the weapons lost forever. The sea there was very deep, Karamatsov thought.

There was a knock on the pole of his tent and Karamatsov closed Krakovski's journal. "Who is it?"

"It is Captain Serovski, comrade marshal."

Karamatsov leaned back in his chair. "Come in, Serovski."

Serovski entered through the hermetic seal, snapped to attention, and saluted. Karamatsov nodded, saying, "Why do you disturb me?"

"Forgive me, comrade marshal, but—but there is something very strange happening."

"A problem with the prisoners?"

"No, comrade marshal. None of which I am aware. But the base radar is picking up something coming in almost beneath the level of the waves below us.

"What?"

"It must be some sort of aircraft, yet it is too massive unless some sort of squadron—"

Karamatsov was up, moving, grabbing the shoulder holster for the old Model 59 Smith & Wesson in his right hand, his parka in the other, running past Serovski, the younger man at his heels now as Karamatsov exited the tent.

He glanced to the east, toward the sea, the sun beginning to rise there. And as he looked, he blinked.

A dark shape was blacking out the sun. . . .

Annie Rourke kept the Soviet truck's accelerator as close to the floor as she dared now, to the east a gray line which she knew would be dawn, no lights of pursuing vehicles present in the sideview mirrors at all. Had this Russian colonel, Antonovitch, given up?

She kept driving . . . .

Tanks were moving into position along the coastline, the dark shape clearly visible now. But impossible. It was the sail of a submarine. But no submarines existed and none so large as this. It towered as high into the air as a small office building. And the whitecaps that were crashing off its bow as it drew nearer bespoke a length that was impossible.

Vladmir Karamatsov stood beside the turret of the most centrally located of his tanks. A voice startled him, breaking his concentration.

"Comrade marshal!"

He looked down. It was Serovski. "You are to be with the Elite Corps, captain—why are you here!"

"Comrade Marshal—word from Comrade Colonel Antonovitch at the test site."

"Test site—the camp?"

"Yes, comrade marshal."

"I cannot be bothered with such as that now! Later—rejoin your men."

"But, comrade marshal—"

"Later—rejoin your men! Do not illustrate to me that I

307

have been mistaken in advancing you to greater responsibility. Go!"

Karamatsov returned his gaze to the sea.

The black shape which fully broke the water line now was something no power on earth could possess.

Chapter Forty

Michael Rourke had jumped from the truck when he had ordered it to slow. Armed with his Beretta pistols, the knife old Jan the swordmaker had crafted for him, and one of the Soviet assault rifles, he had run off into the night.

It was the one chance.

If John Rourke's whereabouts were unknown to the Russians, then John Rourke might be lost forever. And their only chance at victory over the Russians would be to kill Vladmir Karamatsov.

The snow was largely beaten down here by the truck traffic, and where it was not and had drifted high, the going was slow. He had stopped to urinate once, then continued on, consuming a high-energy snack that he had stashed in a pocket of the Soviet uniform he still wore. When he slowed to navigate difficult terrain, the cold consumed him. But he kept moving.

On Karamatsov's orders, a Soviet suicide squad had penetrated Mt. Hekla in Iceland, and as a result his wife, Madison, pretty Madison, and their unborn child had been murdered.

It was Karamatsov who, before the Night of the War, had worked tirelessly to bring about Armageddon so he could rise from its ashes as master of the world.

It was Vladmir Karamatsov who now controlled the most powerful armies on the nearly barren earth, and who was clearly willing to risk the total obliteration of mankind in order to achieve victory.

It was Karamatsov's men who had attempted, under the leadership of one of his KGB Elite Corps officers, to seize thirty nuclear warheads from the Chinese arsenal which had remained unused during the Night of the War, his intent clear: nuclear blackmail or nuclear death.

With his father, John Rourke, and with Paul and Natalia and the help of Chinese forces, they had stopped Karamatsov's KGB Elite Corps, sent the Chinese train carrying the missiles to the bottom of the sea, and narrowly escaped with their lives.

Karamatsov. The gas which Annie, the Chinese girl, and Maria Leuden drove through the night had been Karamatsov's secret weapon for destruction, a gas which drove men mad and made them turn on each other and kill like vicious animals.

It was time Vladmir Karamatsov died.

When the Russian colonel, Antonovitch, had mistaken Michael for his father, his heart had died. If the fate of John Rourke and Natalia Tiemerovna were unknown to the Russians, then they were gone.

Michael Rourke kept running.

How would he tell his mother, Sarah Rourke, even now pregnant with John Rourke's child? And how would he tell his sister, Annie?

But she would know—Annie would know.

Michael Rourke kept running, the ground rising as it neared the sea, the sky amber tinged and yellow.

He kept running.

At the height of the rise, he stopped.

Karamatsov's encampment was below.

And beyond it, in the sea . . .

"Oh my God," Michael Rourke sighed, then dropped to his knees in exhaustion and despair.

Chapter Forty-one

Sebastian moved quietly down the companionway, Lieutenant Mott, the Communications Officer, having the con. It was either Louise Walenski, the Warfare Officer, or Andrew Mott. Seniority was of no concern. Louise Walenski was a competent officer, and so was Mott. Louise Walenski's sex had not colored his judgment either. But Warfare Officers, by their very nature, tended to rely on force, and Sebastian distrusted force except as a last resort. The only others aboard the Reagan of equal rank to Sebastian were Lieutenant Commander Saul Hartnett, who was off duty and, like Jason Darkwood, sleeping, and Lieutenant Commander Margaret Barrow, and Medical Officers were not to be considered for command duty on a vessel of war.

Sebastian stopped at the compartment door and knocked.

He waited. As he had anticipated, there was no answer.

He let himself in, the total darkness of the compartment cresting over him as he closed the door behind him. But he knew Jason Darkwood's quarters well. He closed his eyes, counted to ten to let his eyes become accustomed to the change in light, then opened his eyes and moved slowly yet easily enough across the compartment to the desk, turning on the lamp there. It was what had been called a "Banker's Lamp" and was of brass, or more likely some look-alike substitute, and had a green translucent shade. A fondness for antiques was commonplace among the citizenry of Mid-Wake, although the only true an-

311

tiques were relics of the first generation of scientists who had inhabited the colony, or those items which from time to time had been recovered from what were called "treasure vessels"—sunken ships that were not radioactively dangerous, with hulls that had survived undersea pressure sufficiently so that they could be explored with some degree of safety.

Sebastian had always found the love of antiquities rather maudlin, considering the circumstances of Mid-Wake's genesis and continued existence.

There was adequate light now from the desk lamp and he proceeded to the personal area of the compartment, a small non-essential bulkhead separating it from the official Captain's Quarters, the door open. He stopped before it and rapped the knuckles of his right fist gently against the jam.

"Commander Darkwood. I'm afraid it is time for you to awaken."

There was a grunting noise, presumably Jason Darkwood's recognition of the fact that he was being awakened.

"Sebastian?"

"It is I, Jason. You requested to be awakened in three hours. I am complying with your request."

"Thanks—thank you. There's some coffee that'll warm up beside my desk. Interested?"

"Thank you. I presume you are?"

"Yes—if you don't mind."

A light went on and Sebastian turned away from the doorway and back to the desk. There was a microwave coffee pot plugged in on the small credenza behind the Captain's desk, and Sebastian worked the controls after first making sure that there was indeed enough coffee for one. There was adequate coffee for four, and Sebastian assumed that would mean for one cup for him and the rest for Jason.

There were two cups, clean.

He sat down opposite the desk and waited, hearing the noise of the shower. There was a hand-held video player on the desk and since it was not regulation equipment, he assumed it was used for entertainment value. He picked it up, holding the earphone beside his right ear as he activated the controls. He noted the diode counter so he could return the tape to its proper position.

It was a film from five centuries ago. An enormous library in the rather primitive videotape formats of the day had been transported to Mid-Wake for the entertainment of the first inhabitants. The tapes had been copied and enhanced down to the present day, the only way people of Mid-Wake could even come close to knowing what it had been like on the earth of their forebears.

This was a film featuring the famous actor John Wayne, the namesake of the only other ship in the Mid-Wake fleet which matched the rather astounding capabilities of the Reagan. It was, unfortunately, in dry dock after narrowly surviving an encounter with three Island Class Soviet submarines. The Wayne had the capabilities of the Reagan, but not the same Captain.

In this film, John Wayne was an Irish-American who had returned to his native land and was attempting simultaneously to adjust to the radically different environment while wooing a very young and charming Maureen O'Hara. Sebastian had seen the film several times.

"How do you like the movie, Sebastian?"

Sebastian looked up, pushing the stop button, then beginning the rewind. He had set the controls so the tape would return to the position it had been in originally. "I find the film to contain one of John Wayne's more sensitive portrayals, Jason, as you know. It has always been one of my favorite films."

Jason Darkwood was naked from the waist up, the hair on his chest starting to gray a little, unlike the curly—still wet—hair of his head, which was not graying at all. Jason consulted his wristwatch. "Time flies when you haven't slept for thirty-six hours."

"I find the deepest sleep the most restful, Jason."

"I would have enjoyed experiencing it more fully. Everybody else up?"

313

"Your penetration team is well-rested and even now preparing for the attack."

Jason only nodded. The coffee had long since been ready and Jason went to it. "Want a cup?"

"Yes, thank you."

As Jason Darkwood poured—it smelled satisfactory—he asked, "What do you think about Sam Aldridge?"

"He is a fine officer."

"That's not what I meant and you know it, Sebastian. Should I pull him from this?"

"Doctor Barrow has pronounced him fit for restricted duty, and yet he seems adequately suited to normal duty by his very bearing and demeanor. But with a Marine, that is difficult to gauge. He is the best man for the job."

"I know that or I wouldn't have overridden Margaret's decision and decided to take him along in the first place."

"I would think you are seeking to expiate what you and you alone perceived as guilt and/or responsibility in the affair which resulted in his unfortunate capture."

"If I had gone with—"

Sebastian interrupted. Since he almost never interrupted anyone, he assumed it would be forgiven. "I should beg to differ, Jason. Had you accompanied Captain Aldridge on the mission which resulted in his capture and incarceration, it would merely have resulted in *your* capture and incarceration. The mission to sabotage the Soviet nuclear-missile effort was ill-conceived at best. Admiral Rahn is a brilliant strategist, but equally well-known as a terrible tactician. It is his lack of ability in tactics which resulted in Captain Aldridge's fate, not the fact that you did not accompanying him."

It was pleasant speaking with Jason at times like these—he was a man of supreme discretion and nothing said in confidence was ever betrayed.

"You think I shouldn't go now then?"

Sebastian looked at his superior officer. He accepted a cup of coffee from him. "I am afraid that your analysis of the situation is undeniably correct. You and you alone have discovered a secret means of entry to the Russian domes. And Captain Aldridge, of all the personnel aboard the Reagan, has an intimate knowledge of the domes once inside. It appears that you are each other's indispensable man and there is no alternative but that you both go. I would prefer it otherwise, as would all of those who count you as a friend."

Jason Darkwood crossed from the far side of the desk, set his coffee cup down, and extended his right hand. "Sebastian. Thank you."

"Thank you, Jason."

The Captain of the United States Attack Submarine Ronald Wilson Reagan raised his coffee cup. Sebastian raised his. They clinked the cups together. "Here's to coming back to drink more of this god-awful coffee."

"And here," Sebastian intoned, "is to the pleasant company with which to consume it."

"Amen."

Chapter Forty-two

John Rourke opened his eyes.

"They had told me you were about to awaken, sir."

Rourke turned his head toward the voice. There was light and shadow, light through nearly closed venetian blinds, the origin of the voice in shadow. His throat was dry as he spoke. "I hadn't quite pictured the afterlife exactly this way."

There was a rich, genuine-sounding laugh. "I am Jacob Fellows, sir, the President of Mid-Wake."

John Rourke closed his eyes, opened them again. He could see the image that belonged to the voice more clearly now. His lifelong light sensitivity had, as a biological trade-off, always enabled him to see better than the average person under low light conditions. The speaker—this Fellows—was tall and broad-shouldered, though sitting. And evidently he was possessed of a thick head of hair from the silhouette of his head. "President?"

"Yes, sir. Would you please identify yourself for me?"

John Rourke licked his dry-feeling lips. "What happened to Sam Aldridge?"

"He's aboard the United States Attack Submarine Ronald Wilson Reagan, his mission to attempt the rescue of the woman you were trying to—"

"Natalia," Rourke whispered. It flooded back to him. He had made it as far as Kerenin's apartment, there had been the shootout in the narrow hallway and he had been suckered by the trick with the mirrors, and even thought he had killed Kerenin . . . "I'm a doctor—my self-diagnosis was that I was dying from my wounds."

"Perhaps in your own era you would have, sir. May I please have your name?"

"John Rourke. Why are you so interested?" Rourke was beginning to feel something in his abdomen—not pain in the true sense, but more of a heightened awareness.

"Did you ever meet a Commander Gundersen?"

John Rourke closed his eyes. "He was a submarine commander. I got shanghaied after some crazy guy pretending to be on a special mission for U.S. II gutshot Natalia. The only way to save her life was to use the medical facilities aboard his vessel."

"He remembered you as well, and also this woman Natalia. Are you the same John Rourke who was born in the twentieth century?"

"Who else do you . . ." He was too tired to argue and he closed his eyes. . . .

Jason Darkwood stood in the Scout Sub Bay before the airlock door. Surrounding him were Sam Aldridge and Tom Stanhope and their Marines. Sebastian stood beside him, and Darkwood noticed Maggie Barrow on the observation platform. Like his men, he was already into his black double-layered diving suit, the inner layer to maintain constant atmospheric pressure for his body, the outer layer designed to compensate for the pressure of the sea around it.

"Several years ago, by accident really, I discovered a means of entering the Soviet domes. The details don't really matter at this juncture. Suffice it to say I was inexperienced enough to get myself caught between their attack sharks and some of their Marine Spetznas divers on Iron Dolphins." There was a portable computer-linked light board behind him, and he took the laser pencil and began to move it over the tactical diagram of the Russian city, his movements on the smaller board enhanced and enlarged on the larger board, the Marines repositioning themselves in order to more accurately observe.

317

"Now, each of us learned the available data on the Soviet domes back when we were in training. There are three large domes—to my right here, the main dome, which was the original dome when the Soviets first entered this environment before World War III and they were still being supplied by the Soviet base at Cam Ranh Bay in Vietnam. The actual working city itself is located there, and beneath the main level are three other levels, consisting of maintenance, security, and research, this latter a bio-medical facility utilizing prisoners as lab animals.

"Immediately to my left here is the central dome," and he moved the light pencil over it. "This is a suburban area, mainly for workers in the main dome, military personnel, and the like. There are schools here, some light industry, etc. And to the front of this dome as we face this representation is the Marine Studies area, equipment storage, and the like. Now—between this dome and the next is a smaller dome which contains the shark pens and the control room for the sharks. A passageway here leads into the largest of the two small domes, where the lagoon is located through which their Island Class submarines and their Scout subs enter and exit. The dry-dock facility is here, etc. Behind it and still under this dome are the Scout sub pens. The machinery needed for maintaining the air pressure which keeps the lagoon at a steady level is here. The actual factories wherein the Soviet fleet ships are built and maintained are here. This is probably the most militarily heavy area and also the least secure, since the very presence of their submarines makes them think that no one would attack here. Behind this dome is the larger dome, where the far suburbs are located. Businesses, schools for the upper class—political functionaries at the upper levels, scientists, high-ranking military officers, high-ranking entertainers, and the like."

Jason Darkwood moved the light pencil back to the approximate center of the dome complex. "Leading out more like a large tunnel than an actual dome here is the military-command complex. Living quarters here and here, a small detention area used for special interrogations, the military-office complex. This area is highly secure as well. But I'll draw your attention back to the submarine pens. It is here that several years ago I found a means of entering the Soviet domes. I informed Mid-Wake authorities of the presence of this chink in the Soviet armor, so to speak, and they elected to save it for a rainy day."

Darkwood put down the light pencil. "The 'rainy day' is here, gentlemen."

Chapter Forty-three

"I am Doctor Remquist. I have been asked by President Fellows to speak with you concerning the results of the operations I performed. As one physician to another, I am pleased to report that the operations were an unqualified success, however difficult."

"I know I should have been dead," John Rourke told the man. Rourke was sitting up in a chair, and the venetian blinds were open and he could see Remquist quite clearly. Penetrating eyes, a firm jaw, and a smile of satisfaction. "You must be quite a surgeon and medicine here must have made some enormous strides."

"I have a reputation for insufferable immodesty, but I'll admit you are correct on both counts. I am quite a surgeon, and I suppose by comparison to the medicine you studied five centuries ago our capabilities here might seem like magic or witchcraft. Five centuries of constant warfare have made medicine a critical profession, and we can save people now and restore them to a fully useful life who only fifty years ago would have been doomed to death. I always enjoyed medical history. I know that cancer was a dreaded disease in your day. Today, we are able to inoculate against the common forms and cure those that get past us. The stability of our population at Mid-Wake represented at once a unique challenge and a unique opportunity. We were able to accelerate the research processes to what you might well consider an astonishing degree. But as to your operations.

"The Soviet uniform you wore actually saved your life," Remquist said easily. "The Soviets have only recently begun manufacturing their uniforms out of a bullet-resist-ant material. It was unable, of course, to stop rifle projectiles at such close range, but it slowed them down to the point where they did not spin as they entered your abdominal cavity, and to the point where they did not penetrate sufficiently to exit. That, my dear colleague, saved your life, admittedly as much as my skill. Whoever originally bandaged you and stopped the majority of the bleeding saved your life at that stage of the game. Lieutenant Commander Margaret Barrow, the Medical Officer of the Reagan, the submarine that brought you here, is a finely competent physician in her own right. Her emergency care, her laser suturing, her perception of the seriousness of your wounds, and hence her restraint also saved your life. Had anyone besides myself operated, had you lived you would have been paralyzed from the waist down for the rest of your life. Try one and one-tenth centimeter from the fifth vertebra for delicate, hmm? We used laser techniques you would be totally unfamiliar with to close your wounds and at once sterilize them, promoting very rapid healing from the inside out—just as it should be, of course. In your day, I venture to say several weeks of hospitalization would have been in order. But not today. By tomorrow morning, the colostomy bag will be unnecessary and you should be able to walk with aid and some care. The IV—"

"It would have been nice if modern medical technology had bypassed that."

Remquist laughed. "Yes. So far, no. But—by tomorrow the IV will no longer be needed. The IV is feeding you a synthetic substance which works with the body to promote rapid healing. I venture to say that in a few days, your wounds will be all but healed and you will feel more physically fit than you have for some time. Had you noticed lately any sort of overall slowing down, tiredness?"

John Rourke looked at the man. "Yes."

"What had you self-diagnosed?"

"You weren't just making idle professional chitchat, were you? With that talk about cancer?"

Remquist gestured expansively. "You are the luckiest

man I ever met, Doctor Rourke. You had a type of cancer I have only read about, one that dated from the days immediately following World War III. You have what appears to be an abnormally strong constitution, and I know you have not lived for five centuries, so you must have utilized some form of cryogenic sleep."

"I did."

"That put the disease in remission. Thyroid cancer. But it came back, as it often will. You would have been dead inside of six months if I had not discovered it."

"You mean . . ."

Remquist stood up, slapping his hands against his thighs as he did so. "You are cured. You should find rather rapidly a return to your full vigor. I wouldn't advise going around near high-level sources of radiation again. In that manner you could always give it to yourself again. But, barring that, you are cured. This woman the crew of the Reagan has set out to rescue. I would advise that she and any others who might have survived with you be checked for the same condition. It was one of the most insidious forms of that disease. But now it is easily cured."

John Rourke extended his right hand. "Thank you, doctor."

"My true pleasure, doctor. And now—you rest, hmm?" Remquist shook Rourke's hand and left the room.

John Thomas Rourke leaned his head back in the chair. In the past several weeks, he had realized something was very seriously wrong. And he had tried very hard to ignore it. It was why he had restocked the Retreat, among other reasons. But he had found himself feeling progressively weaker, exertions that he would have taken in stride now telling on him heavily. Occasionally, even a loss of strength resulting in a temporary loss of balance and a fall. The weakness would come on him in a wave and then pass. But the waves had come increasingly more frequently.

Oftentimes, he had heard the expression "given a new lease on life," and now it appeared that he had been given exactly that, death almost the price of the lease.

If—once Natalia was freed, she as well as Michael,

322

Annie, Paul, and especially Sarah would need to be checked. Especially Sarah with the baby.

There was much to do. Karamatsov needed to be stopped. Forever. And the earth needed to be rebuilt. It was now only a battlefield.

He felt a little tired and accepted the inevitability of that. He was, after all, restored. And he would need his full energies for what lay ahead. . . .

Jason Darkwood and Sam Aldridge entered the water together, the Scout sub's underhull air-lock hatch whooshing a surge of air and water around them, Darkwood keeping his wings folded still to prevent them fouling in the strength of the current, propelling himself ahead instead by the force of his flippers and gloves. The readouts on his helmet told him the Hemo Sponge was working properly, which was outstanding since it was the only way he could breathe.

He rolled over in the water, backing away now from the Scout sub air lock, Aldridge still beside him, the rest of the commando team exiting the air lock. Their own equivalent of the Soviet Iron Dolphins would not be used because the slightest mechanical noise might betray their presence to the sensing equipment of the Russian domes.

Darkwood rolled over again as the Marines fell into formation in a wedge behind him and Aldridge. He flexed his wings and moved out, the vision-intensification unit in his helmet showing the Pillars of Woe dead ahead. . . .

A motorized launch was released from the monster-sized submarine and was moving toward shore under a white flag of truce.

Through the German binoculars he had taken from the truck—Maria Leuden had brought them with her—Michael Rourke could see clearly now in the morning light. The submarine had surfaced several hours ago and the number of tanks and men Karamatsov had assembled

323

overlooking the water had grown steadily. Michael had no idea if there had been radio contact. But he was assuming that at least some action had been taken concerning the escape from the death camp, because approximately a half hour after Michael had reached the rise overlooking the Soviet camp and the water beyond, six truckloads of soldiers and two tanks and one armored personnel carrier had been dispatched in the direction of the compound from which he, Paul, Annie, and the others had extricated the internees and from which Annie, Maria, and the Chinese woman named Ma-Lin had driven the trucks of the deadly gas.

Vladmir Karamatsov still waited at the shoreline with dozens of his huge tanks arrayed there around him, as if the tanks would have had a chance against the submarine. Such a vessel would have been capable of enormous firepower. If he had judged correctly the bore diameter of the deck gun most clearly visible, it was at least thirty-six inches.

The boat—appearing to be of the same material as the submarine itself—skimmed over the water's surface, into the breakers beneath the overlook where Karamatsov's army waited.

As the launch had been released, a flag had been raised from the submarine's sail. The flag bore the Hammer and Sickle. . . .

Vladmir Karamatsov made a decision. It was based on necessity. Antonovitch was pursuing the accursed Rourke family, and Serovski was too junior an officer to be sent on a mission such as this.

This was a Soviet ship, and such technology as must be behind a vessel of such enormity could be invaluable in an alliance, deadly in an adversary situation. And since there were two Soviet governments he knew of on the earth—his own and that of the Underground City—it would be well for this new Soviet ship, and the power behind it, to ally with him rather than his adversaries.

He would go to meet it.

"Serovski—if anything happens unexpectedly, I will rely on your initiative. Send with me six of your best Elite Corps personnel."

The wind was high and cold and Serovski answered over it, "Yes, comrade marshal."

Karamatsov considered changing into full uniform, but he had never liked uniforms and, after all, was a Soviet marshal and could dress as he pleased.

He stepped down from the turret and stood beside the tank for a moment.

The skiff or whatever it was called, this motorized launch displaying the white flag of truce, had passed over the breakers and was nearly to shore. "Serovski—I need the men now!"

"They await, comrade marshal." Karamatsov turned around. Serovski stood immediately behind him with six men in full Elite Corps battle gear. "They are my very best, comrade marshal."

Karamatsov only nodded to Serovski, looking past the ambitious and usually competent young captain at the six anxious young faces. "Comrades. No doubt what lies before us is an historic meeting of the greatest importance. You must be particularly vigilant that all goes well. We believe these persons from the submarine to be Russian, like ourselves. But until we are certain that the fire of true Communism burns within them as strongly as it does within ourselves, we must remain at the highest level of alertness. With that understood, follow me."

Karamatsov opened his coat to more easily get at his pistol, and started walking past his tanks. He glanced back once as the six Elite Corpsmen fell in behind him. He heard Serovski's voice. "The Hero Marshal passes!" And now, from the open tank hatches, from the men beside the tanks as well, from the officers who commanded them, salutes were raised. And then it started, Serovski's voice, then others joining it. "Hail to the Hero Marshal! Hail to the Hero Marshal! Hail to the Hero Marshal!" The chant rang in Karamatsov's ears as he started down the trail from the precipice overlooking the sea, men in dark blue uniforms with high boots and near-ankle-length greatcoats soaked with spray flying open in the wind disembarking the launch and walking onto the beach.

Karamatsov threw back his shoulders, running his fingers through his black hair, inhaling the salt air, the spray fresh on the wind.

"Hail to the Hero Marshal! Hail to the Hero Marshal! Hail to the Hero Marshal!"

The men of the launch in their high-peaked uniform caps stopped a few meters in from the pounding surf, their evident leader a man tall and straight and dark-featured.

Vladmir Karamatsov strode toward him, the chant still on the wind.

"Hail to the Hero Marshal! Hail to the Hero Marshal! Hail to the Hero Marshal!"

The men of the launch in their high-peaked uniform caps stopped a few meters in from the pounding surf, their evident leader a man tall and straight and dark-featured.

Vladmir Karamatsov strode toward him, the chant still on the wind, "Hail to the Hero Marshal! Hail to the Hero Marshal! Hail to the Hero Marshal!"

Marshal Vladmir Karamatsov stopped at the base of the path. He waited.

The leader of the party from the submarine and one other man approached, the second man bearing the white flag of truce.

The leader stopped a meter away and saluted smartly. "Comrade Marshal Karamatsov. May I present myself. I am Colonel Boris Feyedorovitch of the Soviet Union— comrade marshal!" And he held the salute.

Karamatsov returned the salute with equal sharpness. "On behalf of the Armed Forces of the Soviet People, I welcome you, colonel," Karamatsov lowered the salute and then the leader of the newcomers followed suit. Karamatsov stepped forward a pace, as did the man who said his name was Feyedorovitch and his rank was colonel.

Karamatsov hesitated, and then extended his arms in

embrace, Feyedorovitch doing the same, both men holding the embrace for the briefest instant, Feyedorovitch planting a kiss on Karamatsov's left cheek, Karamatsov doing the same to Feyedorovitch as the chant began again from above, "Hail to the Hero Marshal! Hail to the Hero Marshal! Hail to the Hero Marshal!"

And Feyedorovitch stepped back a pace, raising his right hand in salute, proclaiming, "Hail to the Hero Marshal!"

Vladmir Karamatsov very much regretted the loss of Colonel Ivan Krakovski at this moment. Krakovski, the poet and historian, the chronicler of these days of greatness. It would be sad indeed if this moment were not set down for the future, however brief in duration the future might prove to be.

"We come, comrade marshal, from the great Soviet State beneath the sea."

"Welcome to my earth," Karamatsov told him.

"Hail to the Hero Marshal!" The chant went on.

"Comrade marshal. I have a present for you. A small token of our friendship to you."

"Where is this token?" He had heard the admonition to be wary of Greeks bearing gifts, but his curiosity was oddly piqued.

Colonel Feyedorovitch snapped the second finger and thumb of his right hand and a third of these Russian strangers marched forward, carrying in his hands a casket roughly the size of a typical doctor's bag. The man stopped at rigid attention beside Feyedorovitch. "If I may, comrade marshal?"

"Please, colonel. Open it."

The officer dropped to one knee in the sand, Feyedorovitch turning to him, opening the lid of the casket.

Vladmir Karamatsov drew in his breath so deeply he realized it must have sounded like a gasp.

Inside the casket were three items he well recognized.

Two brightly polished stainless-steel .357 Magnum Smith & Wesson Model 686 revolvers, the four-inch barrels flatted, and on the right barrel flats of each, both pistols positioned in the velvet-lined casket with the muzzles pointed in the same direction, American Eagles. And beneath them, partially opened, a skeletonized, handled butterfly knife.

"Those are my wife's custom revolvers and her Bali-Song knife."

"I understand, comrade marshal, that you are most interested in the fate of Natalia Anastasia Tiemerovna, Major, Committee for State Security of the Soviet Union. And one Doctor John Rourke."

Karamatsov stepped closer to the casket, taking the revolvers from it and holding them up before his eyes.

"Major Tiemerovna is held in our city awaiting your pleasure. The American, John Rourke, is presumed dead, his body taken away by our enemies, also Americans. The major is yours, of course, and my superiors would like to propose an alliance in order to better prosecute our separate wars against our common enemies."

Karamatsov swallowed hard, closing his eyes. Antonovitch had reported that John Rourke had been responsible for the breakout at the internment camp. But there had been no sign of Natalia.

And these were indeed her weapons.

Vladmir Karamatsov opened his eyes. "John Rourke has been seen here only hours ago. He appeared well."

"That—that is impossible, comrade marshal. I—I shot him in the head and witnessed his body fall seven levels down to the ground. He had already been seriously wounded in the abdomen and there was considerable blood loss. His body was dragged away by his American and Chinese accomplices."

"And Natalia? Where is she?"

"In a detention cell at our city beneath the domes, comrade marshal. She is unharmed and awaits you."

"With eagerness?"

"No, comrade marshal. With great fear, I think. And she too believes as do I that this Rourke is dead."

"And you bring me these weapons so I will come with you to retrieve her?"

"Yes, comrade marshal. I can assure your safety. You would be our honored guest, a true Hero of the Soviet Peoples, comrade marshal."

Vladmir Karamatsov studied the revolvers in his hands. They were undoubtedly hers. The knife still partially opened in the velvet-lined casket—it was hers as well.

But was that all that was velvet-lined?

Was it a velvet-lined trap as well. . . .

Michael Rourke could see Vladmir Karamatsov clearly through the German field glasses. And he could see the revolvers in Karamatsov's hands. "Natalia's?" he whispered into the wind. And—in the box . . . Was it a knife? Natalia's knife? The Bali-Song she always carried and used with such great deftness?

If these men from the submarine had brought these weapons to Karamatsov, why? As an enticement? A peace offering?

He closed his eyes. "Think, damnit!" he ordered himself.

The raids from the sea spoken of by the Chinese.

Mysterious commandoes. He had seen them himself at the power station. These Russians?

His father and Natalia had been walking by the sea when they had vanished. Signs of a fight. "Think," he whispered into the wind. These Russians?

He had to know.

Chapter Forty-four

They had rendezvoused at the campsite Han had used and now all of them had returned except one.

"Where the hell did he go, man!?"

Paul Rubenstein looked at his wife and then at the Chinese soldier. Ma-Lin approached. "Mrs. Rubenstein—may I perform some service by translating your question to this soldier?"

Paul looked at the Chinese girl. "I think my wife wants to know what happened to her brother, Michael Rourke." He looked at Annie. "Isn't that right?"

"Yes," she almost hissed.

Paul looked at the Chinese girl. "Yeah—that's what my wife wants to know all right."

The Chinese girl nodded and proceeded to interrogate the Chinese soldier. Paul Rubenstein looked at his wife. She had said nothing about the fact that the Russians evidently knew nothing concerning the whereabouts of her father and Natalia, which could well mean they would never be found. He would personally refuse to accept that as finality until his dying day, and he knew that both Annie and Michael would do the—

"Miss—quickly. What's the soldier saying?"

The Chinese girl turned to face him, smiled politely, maddeningly, slowly. "Young Mr. Rourke ordered this man to retard the progress of the vehicle which he drove so that he—young Mr. Rourke—might exit the vehicle successfully. This soldier last saw young Mr. Rourke moving with apparent haste toward the coast and the encampment

330

of the Soviet Army."

"Holy shit," Paul snarled, breaking into a run, Annie right beside him, running for the half-track truck Maria Leuden and Michael had used, Paul shouting to Annie, "You're not going!"

"They've got my father and now they've got my brother—the hell I'm not!"

Paul Rubenstein stopped, grabbed Annie by the upper arms, and almost threw her off her feet, shaking her for an instant. "And what the hell good is it going to do if all of us get killed or captured, huh? Tell me that! Would your father want that? Would he want that son of a bitch Karamatsov to win just because there wasn't anybody left to fight him? And what about your mother and the baby she's carrying? Tell me about how she's gonna do if your father is really dead and if they get Michael and then they get you? How the hell is she gonna do, huh? You are not going—not—not at all! You will wait here, guard those damned trucks with Karamatsov's poison gas, and then get them back safely to the First City. You'll take charge because somebody's got to. Understand me, Annie!" He was shouting. He was screaming. He didn't care. He loved her too much to let her run off and be a fool and die—like he was planning to do.

"If you die—you're hurting my arms—I love you—hold me, Paul." Paul Rubenstein took his hands from her and stared at his hands for a long minute, then folded her gently into his arms and touched his lips to her hair.

"I won't die—I promise," he told her, having every intention of not dying but feeling somehow that he was lying and that the last thing he would ever tell her he didn't want to be that—a lie. "I love you," he told her, raised her face, and kissed her mouth lightly, softly. Then he started for the truck, slinging his Schmeisser forward and extracting the magazine and giving it a good swat on the spine into the palm of his hand. He reinserted the magazine.

He looked back at Annie once, then climbed aboard the truck. He started the engine, put the machine into gear, and cut the wheel sharp left and stomped the accelerator hard.

The last thing he had told her hadn't been a lie. . . .

John Rourke had decided that things could not wait for tomorrow and he had called the nurse, a pretty black woman in her early thirties with long hair that fell into gentle waves at her shoulders. "I'm getting up and walking today. Now—you can call Doctor Remquist or you can call anybody you like, but I'm walking. So—either help me or when I fall on my face you can say you were a good nurse and didn't help me because you were following orders. What's it gonna be?"

"Are you really the John Rourke I read about in the history books—the guy Gundersen spoke of?"

"I guess I am."

"You could cost me my job."

"Tell them I intimidated you."

"Did all men look as good as you back then?"

John Rourke didn't know how to answer that one and he just smiled.

"You just put both hands on my shoulders and I'll get you to stand up and then we try it with your arm around my shoulders. If I get fired, I'm gonna enjoy it, Doctor Rourke."

"What's your name?" She wore no name tag.

"Ellen'll do."

"Ellen. Thank you."

"You let me know how that surgery feel once you stand up and we'll see if you're thanking me." She leaned over him. Her hair smelled like perfume. "Now—hold onto me."

"If you say so." He smiled. "It's a tough job but—"

Ellen laughed as he stood up and almost fell against her. "I know—somebody's gotta do it. Come on—stand up."

John Rourke stood to his full height. His abdomen hurt, but not extraordinarily so. "So—take me for a walk,

332

Ellen."

"Why don't I take you for a walk, Doctor Rourke?"

"Good idea." He started to walk—the first step almost killed him. But the second step wasn't quite that bad.

Chapter Forty-five

Paul Rubenstein abandoned the half-track when he thought he had gotten too dangerously close to the Soviet encampment to risk using it anymore. And then he started to run.

Several times he was forced to stop, to hide in the rocks and wait as a Soviet patrol passed by or a Soviet helicopter gunship passed overhead. And then he moved on.

At last he reached the overlook, Karamatsov's encampment below and beyond that the sea. Michael would have come here first to assess his chances, then moved down into the camp. To get Vladmir Karamatsov. And Paul had reasoned that from this vantage point he too could perhaps assess his own chances of finding Michael Rourke before it was too late—or backing up Michael Rourke after it was too late.

"Why did you die, John?" Paul Rubenstein said, looking skyward as he approached the edge of the precipice in a low, crouching run. It would be up to him now, he realized. Michael, certainly, but Michael would need a friend if he lived. And if Michael died.

Paul Rubenstein had always prided himself on personal honesty—even more than in his interaction with others in his assessment of himself. He was not the man John Rourke was, could never hope to be. Much that he had learned he had learned from John Rourke. His father and mother, God rest their souls, had raised him to be a decent and caring man, someone who could not only survive in the day-to-day world of the twentieth century, but could achieve, do. But John Rourke had taken over his education when so much of what he had learned suddenly no longer had a place in the world. John Rourke had taught him at once to be strong enough to survive in a world that had reverted to barbarism, and taught him too how to retain the compassion and humanity his parents had considered so vital.

As he edged now on knees and elbows toward the lip of the precipice, he swore silently that when someday he and Annie had children, he would tell them everything he remembered about John Rourke so they could carry John Rourke with them always and know their heritage.

He moved forward the final yard or so, the Schmeisser in both raised fists.

Paul Rubenstein slumped forward.

It was the size of an aircraft carrier, or larger. But it was a submarine.

He knew his mentor's son well.

The submarine. The raiders who had attacked the Chinese power installation, like the raiders the Chinese had spoken of who came from the sea and mysteriously returned to it.

If John and Natalia were alive, whoever controlled this submarine knew their fate.

He didn't look for Michael, because he knew where Michael was or would soon be if such were possible. And he had to be there too.

Paul Rubenstein twisted round and began crawling back from the lip of the precipice, and as soon as he felt he was far enough away, he raised up to his feet and, crouching, ran, the Schemisser still in his fists. If John Rourke were still alive . . .

Chapter Forty-six

Vladmir Karamatsov sipped at his vodka.

"Tell me how you know that these weapons belong to my wife, colonel, and what convinced you that you had killed John Rourke."

Colonel Boris Feyedorovitch, his hat removed, his short, curly black hair still bearing its impression, had not touched his vodka after the toast. Karamatsov wondered, perhaps, if vodka were no longer a cultural artifact of Soviet civilization where this man came from.

"I was leading a raid against a Chinese power installation along the coast and when I returned, this man and woman were prisoners."

"How did the raid go?"

"It—ahh—it went badly, comrade marshal—it went . . . Of course!" Feyedorovitch jumped to his feet, his chair falling over with a loud cracking sound behind him, Karamatsov's guards storming through the hermetic seal and into the tent.

"Leave us!" And Karamatsov looked into Boris Feyedorovitch's face.

"At the power facility, comrade marshal. There was a man who was all but physically identical to John Rourke. He carried two pistols, but not the shiny little automatics like John Rourke. And he dressed identically to John Rourke. He—he had a revolving-cylinder gun as well. He and another man who was shorter than he but fought very bravely—"

"The other man—describe him, colonel. And sit down,

336

please."

Feyedorovitch picked up his chair, righted it, and, almost as though his mind were totally consumed with something else, sat down. "The other man—yes—he—ahh—he was not as tall or obviously muscular as this twin of John Rourke, but he was a very courageous fighter. He—"

"This other man's appearance. Was his hair thinning?"

"Yes—John Rourke and this man who looked just like him had high foreheads, but hair as thick as yours, comrade marshal, or mine. But this other one—he dressed very much like the man who was John Rourke and this other man he fought beside. But his hair was much thinner. Ahh—"

"Weapons. Did he have a weapon that looked at all singular to you?"

"It was a submachine gun, comrade marshal. I had assumed that, and after my return from the mission, I consulted with several references and was able to place it as a submachine gun certainly. It looked to have more fluidity in its design than—"

"Could it have been a Schmeisser, a German MP-40?"

"I do not know these terms, comrade marshal."

Karamatsov sipped at his vodka. "The man you describe—the one with the peculiar gun, is a man named Paul Rubenstein. He is a Jew."

"What is a Jew, comrade marshal, if I may ask in order to better understand?"

Karamatsov indulged the officer. He was, after all, a guest. "Are you familiar with the concept of a God?"

"I have heard of this, comrade marshal."

"Jews believed they had a God who was unlike any other, the true God. Christianity grew out of Judaism when one of their number proclaimed that he was the Son of God, the same God as the Jews had. They were a bothersome race of self-styled intellectuals and in the years prior to the Night of the War, they were quite militant, even possessed of their own country called Israel, although not all of them lived there. This Jew Rubenstein is the

337

compatriot of John Rourke. I would very much like to have him as well. But, you say, this Jew fought beside the man who looked just like John Rourke?"

"Yes, comrade marshal."

Karamatsov poured another small glass of vodka for himself, not offering any to Feyedorovitch, who had still not touched his drink since the toast. "Tell me—were their any detectable differences between this man you say was Rourke and the man who looked like him? You said, I believe, they could almost have been twins. Why almost?"

Feyederovitch seemed to consider that, his dark eyes shrouded beneath heavy lids. And then he raised his eyes. "The one who fought beside this Jew, comrade marshal—he was somehow—somehow younger-looking. John Rourke had some slight grayness present in his hair, and yet—although I could be mistaken—I recall no impression of this with the other man. But I was looking only from a distance and through—"

"And you say," Karamatsov persisted, "that the one you said was John Rourke was killed while attempting to rescue my wife from your Colonel Kerenin?"

"Yes, comrade marshal. He was to have been executed, but fought his way out of the—"

"What kind of guns did he carry when he was arrested?"

"Small, as I said, comrade marshal. And he secured them at some time during his flight from the Marine Spetznas guards and used them unfortunately to great effect."

Karamatsov drew his pistol from the shoulder holster he still wore. "Were the pistols dark in color, like this?"

"No, comrade marshal. The pistols the other one who looked like him had were very much like that weapon which you hold, comrade marshal. But perhaps a little longer. And that other man had a very loud revolving-cylinder gun that was brightly polished. Stainless steel or titanium perhaps."

"And the man you claim was the real John Rourke. His pistols were not dark like this?"

"They were shiny, comrade marshal. The muzzles had very large bore diameters. But they were automatics of a primitive design such as yours—forgive me, comrade marshal."

Karamatsov let himself smile benignly. "No, colonel. There is nothing to forgive. This is quite old. It has a story. Would you like to hear it?"

"Yes, comrade marshal. You honor me."

Karamatsov set down the pistol beside the bottle of vodka and sipped at his fresh drink. "This is a Smith & Wesson Model 59, the earliest version of Smith & Wesson's large-capacity 9mm pistols, unless, of course, one counts the preproduction guns made for use, reportedly, by the American SEALS."

"Seals, comrade marshal?"

"American forces, perhaps in some ways similar to your Marine Spetznas units, only of course dedicated to the furthering of American Imperialism. But this pistol—it was stolen along with several others for use in those days in America—this pistol has been with me since Before the Night of the War. In a place called Athens, Georgia, I met with John Rourke and we faced each other and we drew our guns. He was an American gunman all his life and he 'outdrew' me."

"Comrade marshal?"

"The Americans had a peculiar custom on their frontier a century or so before the Night of the War. Two men, both armed, would face each other in the street of their town, and at an agreed signal they would remove their guns from their holsters as rapidly as possible and each would attempt to kill the other. John Rourke and I did this. He won." Karamatsov sipped at his drink. "I was so badly wounded that even Rourke, a doctor of medicine, gave me up for dead. But some of my faithful Elite Corps conveyed me to emergency medical aid, then killed the doctor who gave it in order to safeguard my person. I was transported to—" He almost mentioned the Underground City in the Urals, where Soviet civilization had survived for five centuries while the earth had been uninhabitable.

But it was not time to mention that.

"The Underground City, Comrade Marshal?"

Karamatsov sipped at his vodka. Natalia had talked. "Yes. Yes, colonel. There, I was restored to my full vigor and I took personal charge of the Underground City's defenses, the training of its KGB. And then, I slept. Cryogenic sleep. And I slept for two reasons. I knew that the earth would not be habitable on the surface for five centuries. And I knew that somehow John Rourke would survive the fires which swept the earth clean. And I wanted him. By cruel subterfuge he had subverted my wife from her post of honor and trust. He had made her his mistress, while deceiving his own wife. And I knew that someday I would meet John Rourke again and kill him with this pistol." He raised the pistol from the table. "You may have deprived me of that pleasure, or you may not have. Someone was here—whether it was John Rourke as has been reported or his son, Michael, it is of little consequence now. Because Natalia will tell me the truth. I have ways of convincing her of the error of her ways and eliciting the truth from her."

"We have drugs, comrade marshal—"

"I have ways older than drugs, colonel." Marshal Vladimir Karamatsov stood.

Colonel Feyedorovitch stood up as well.

Karamatsov holstered his pistol, then looked into Feyedorovitch's dark eyes. "I will not return with you to your city beneath the waves. I would be placing myself at perilous disadvantage. But I will dispatch one of my most trusted officers to accompany you and retrieve my wife. If all goes well and this matter is carried out in good faith, I will gladly entertain a delegation of your leaders for the purpose of reuniting the Soviet peoples and forming an effective alliance against, as I believe you have put it, our common enemies. Are these terms acceptable? Because they are the only terms I shall allow."

Feyedorovitch did not answer immediately and Karamatsov guessed that likely he was forcing the young colonel to overstep his prescribed authority. "Very well, comrade marshal. But I can assure you that if you were to accompany me yourself, your safety would. . ."

Karamatsov smiled. "Colonel—you show promise. But, there is one thing you must learn. We discuss the future of the world here. I have much to gain from an alliance with your leaders. And they have much to gain from an alliance with me. Such negotiations are never based on a footing of mutual trust but rather on mutual need. If your leaders perceive that my death would advance their purposes, then, quite justifiably so, they would engineer my death, despite the sincerity of your protestations or whatever you have been told. Just as I would cause their deaths should such serve my purposes. Keep that in mind. And see to it to the best of your abilities that my officer and his entourage return safely with my dear wife. If you value your own life."

Feyedorovitch didn't speak. . . .

Michael Rourke's father always preached the doctrine of planning ahead, but Michael told himself he could not have planned for swimming in the sea toward an enemy submarine when such things as submarines were thought no longer to exist and no submarines had ever existed of such enormous size.

But he had done the next best thing to planning ahead, compensating for deficient planning.

The only way to reach the submarine short of stealing the launch which had brought the vessel's officers to shore was to swim. But the sea would be icy cold. Salt water would damage his pistols beyond repair perhaps but, of more immediate concern, could possibly render his ammunition defective.

He had compensated for these difficulties.

The quartermaster tent he invaded now was the answer to all his difficulties. Bags made of polyurethane or some modern equivalent of it were utilized in field storage of some types of comestibles. These looked to be dehydrated grain, but more likely were potatoes. He emptied two of these bags and wiped their insides as clean as possible, stashing both Beretta 92F pistols in one and their spare magazines in another. He took a third bag and emptied it, dusted it out, and placed both already sealed bags inside the third. His knife sheath went inside this third bag as well. But the knife he kept free. It was stainless steel, and inside the hollow handle there was a small container of lubricant with which he could treat the steel after its bath in salt water. It would be best—if he got that far—if he could find fresh water to bathe the knife in first, but he would have to wait and see.

The knife was what he had used to gain entrance through the extended and poorly guarded camp perimeter, killing an enlisted man of approximately his own size and then taking the uniform, wiping the blood off the uniform collar with snow. Michael wore that uniform now. But once aboard the vessel, if he made it that far, he would need dry clothes because there was no telling where he might hide and there was no telling the duration of the voyage once the vessel did "set sail."

He borrowed from the quartermaster stores again. The KGB Elite Corps personnel had special battle-dress utilities, entirely black, two-piece, not unlike the few sets of battle-dress utilities his father maintained at the Retreat. He took these, fresh socks, and a fresh pair of boots, and used more of the supply of poly-bagged potatoes to provide carrying cases for them that would be proof against the water. Either the Russians provided their own underwear or the quartermaster had skillfully hidden his reserves. Michael shrugged off the concern. He found the modern Soviet equivalent of a duffel bag and shoved everything inside, the Soviet battle rifle and the knife given him by old Jon the swordmaker his only accessible weapons.

Circumstance—activity in the bustling camp and a large patrol returning, perhaps after, he hoped, fruitlessly searching for Annie, Maria, Paul, and the others—kept him in the quartermaster tent for at least fifteen more minutes by the face of his Rolex. But at last, he was able to exit the tent with his duffel-bagged gear.

He moved obliquely toward the sea. . . .

Paul Rubenstein crouched in the rocks, his eyes on the solitary guard who stood lazily beside the half-track truck. Paul knew that he had guessed correctly and that Michael was ahead of him. The body of a dead Soviet soldier, his uniform gone, had confirmed that.

But this guard and his vehicle, perhaps newly in the area and not an obstacle Michael had been forced to contend with, had trapped him here.

It would have been easy enough to kill the man with a shot from the battered High Power beneath his own stolen uniform, but a shot would have alerted anyone within hearing distance and not only confound his own plans but perhaps Michael's as well. Where the man stood and the direction in which he faced precluded creeping up on him and using a knife.

Paul looked at his watch.

"Shit," he almost said aloud. . . .

Annie Rubenstein and Maria Leuden crouched together by high rocks looking down onto the terrain below, the trucks carrying the gas which drove men insane with murder parked behind them under camouflage netting. The base camp Han had established still stood, but only three of the Chinese soldiers guarded it. Hammerschmidt had insisted, and Han had agreed, that the trucks and the majority of personnel be moved to more commanding ground that could be better defended if the Soviets came. And there was no reason to suppose they would not.

A radio message could not be risked lest their position be too soon betrayed, and so Han and one of his men had taken horses and set out to rendezvous with the German crew of the J-7V to summon military aid and German cargo helicopters with which to transport the deadly gas.

If all went well, she had no idea what would be the fate

of the gas.

Maria Leuden, changed back to her own clothes—green slacks that looked like they were made of wool, a heavy sweater, and a lightweight but warm hooded parka—shifted her position, then spoke. "We should have gone with your husband, after Michael."

"Paul told me not to—and he was right. The more of us who go in, the more there'll be to get out. I wanted to go anyway."

"And bowed to your husband's wishes then?"

"Yes."

"Why?" Maria Leuden asked.

"If you and Michael had a difference of opinion and it was irresolveable, what would you do?"

"I—I suppose I would. . ." And she let the sentence hang with a sigh.

"Two people with diametrically opposed views concerning the same specific subject can't both be right, can they? Even allowing for differing perspectives on the problem, in the final analysis one perspective and the perception which it affords will be the more correct one if either of them is correct at all. True?" Annie asked.

"Yes—I suppose so. Yes."

"Then whose opinion should be heeded? And you can't say the most logical one, because each of the two persons with divergent opinions will automatically consider their own opinion the most logical. And especially if the alternatives are both somewhat irrational. As in this—stay here and wait for an attack or go into the enemy camp to help someone who has decided to take on the enemy leader. So whose opinion should be acted upon?"

"You mean, in the final analysis, should the woman acquiesce to the man even though she thinks he may be wrong?"

"I mean that, but not quite. I mean if neither opinion is, as you perceive it, clearly a correct choice, then who in a relationship between a man and a woman should bear the ultimate burden of decision? Say, for example, I had gone against my husband's wishes and been killed as a

344

result after entering the camp or before entering it or whenever. Even though I was the one who insisted on going, he would still blame himself for not forcing me to stay behind. Or, on the other hand, say I stay behind and he finds that if I'd come, things would have been easier. He's going to have to bear the burden of his decision either way, isn't he?"

"But you will too," Maria said earnestly.

"Women don't have to prove themselves in the same way men do, don't have to perceive everything as a challenge to themselves in the same way men do. What if I went and because I did, everything worked out perfectly. We'd all be happy with the results, but yet Paul would know that he'd made the wrong decision and that if I hadn't gone against his wishes everything might well have worked out badly. He'd lose—as a man—either way, wouldn't he?"

"I think you are a psychologist, Annie."

"When Paul and I decided to marry, I decided one thing. I would always be me, but I would incorporate into that concept of self what I felt would make me a good wife. I lived with my father and my brother for five years in the Retreat—after Daddy woke up from the Sleep and awakened Michael and me, so he could teach us how to raise ourselves when he returned to the Sleep, until it was time to awaken Momma and Paul and Natalia. I learned a great deal about men in those five years. Michael went from being a little boy to being essentially the man he is today. And suddenly one day it wasn't Daddy and his little boy, it was John and Michael, two men, competing with each other good-naturedly most of the time. Each time Michael would prove that he was as good as Daddy at something, Daddy would prove he was still a little better. And for a while," Annie said softly, "I thought it was mean of my father, and then I realized that all he was doing was making Michael just get better and better at everything because Michael still had something to try for, someone to beat."

Annie changed position, her right arm getting stiff from holding the M-16 so rigidly. She looked at Maria Leuden again. "I heard my dad telling Michael this once. You arm-wrestle with your father until you realize that the next time you do it you might win. And then you don't do it anymore. Because once you've beaten him, you'll be sorry you did. I guess I looked at it the same way when Paul and I disagreed. If I'd beaten him, I wouldn't have won and neither would he. We would have both lost."

There was movement far off in the distance. A truck or tank. Annie Rubenstein couldn't tell which. She took up the German binoculars and looked through them, pressing the button to automatically adjust the focus.

Maria, beside her, said, "If he sends his men against us, and the gas is used, they will all die. Karamatsov could not be so insane."

Annie still studied the object through the binoculars. It was a truck. And behind it coming over the horizon was an armored personnel carrier. And then another.

She said to Maria Leuden, "What if Karamatsov doesn't send his men—but sends women instead?"

Chapter Forty-seven

The trick of entering the Soviet domes, as he had discovered by accident when he had been first officer of the United States Attack Submarine John Wayne years ago, was to capitalize on the one niche of expediency in the Soviet defense posture. Once he had discovered it and escaped with his life, then given over the data to Mid-Wake scientific intelligence, he had been informed as to why it existed.

The sharks which were utilized as a living defense system against enemy divers and controlled by electronic signals to their brains were also monitored by means of electronic signals. The sonar net which blanketed the lagoon beneath the surface of which the Soviet submarines, both Island Class and Scout, would dive when leaving, and from which they would surface when returning, could not be desensitized to the electronic emissions coming from the sharks, the emissions powered by the electro-chemical energy produced by the creatures' brains and unable to be turned off. The emissions emanated from the sharks at a frequency which would duplicate the sonar shadow of an approaching enemy vessel and consequently activate the Soviet alarms and defensive systems.

For that reason—as Jason Darkwood had learned the hard way—there was a "tunnel" inside the sonar net through which the sharks were moved by their programmers, leading in and out of the lagoon.

Jason Darkwood, Sam Aldridge, and the others of the commando team sent to rescue this five-centuries-old Russian woman from her Russian captors hovered near the mouth of the sonar tunnel.

No radio transmission could be trusted here and they huddled together now in a circle, their helmets touching, wings cocooning about them, the helmets able to sympathetically pick up the vibration of human speech and allowing them to confer, although the hollow sound of human speech heard this way was maddeningly strange, like voices heard while the ears were adjusting to the sound of an explosion and had automatically compensated by reducing volume level.

Jason Darkwood spoke. "The sharks travel through this area to leave the lagoon and to enter it again. The width of the 'tunnel'—which is really just an open space within the Soviet defense grid—is about six feet wide as best we can estimate it. So—if you and a shark bump into one another, use his body position as your reference point and give yourself eighteen inches or less on either side of him as still being sonar-clear. If one of them attacks you, there is no advice I can give. Get out of its way if at all possible. Now this is just a hunch, but I would venture to say that the tight control on them while they travel back and forth through the tunnel is unpleasant for them—maybe gives them a headache." He laughed. "But at any event, they probably want out of there quickly and would be little inclined to giving a fight. When I originally discovered this 'tunnel' I asked the same question you're probably asking yourselves now: how do the Soviet technicians keep the sharks within the parameters of the tunnel? And the answer is simple. When the sharks stray from the tunnel and into the sensor net the sharks are given a painful sensation. When they re-enter the 'tunnel', the pain is turned off and pleasure centers of their brains are stimulated. Any sharks we do encounter will probably be so well-trained by now, the last thing in the world they want is to stray into the sensor net and get the pain turned on. It'll be up to us to stay cool if we bump into them. Any questions?"

Sam Aldridge spoke. "The Captain tells me we're following this tunnel right up to two hundred yards from the Soviet docks, which is a sonar-clear area as best as past intelligence data can tell. We follow Commander Darkwood—no matter what. Any questions?"

There were none.

Without the vision-intensification capabilities of their helmets, seeing at this depth would have required the aid of artificial lighting, which could have betrayed them.

Darkwood tapped Sam Aldridge on the shoulder and spread his wings, starting into the invisible tunnel. His wingspan gave him a safe clearance of only a foot one either side and he kept dead center to the tunnel, the incoming sonar readout on his chest pack giving negative readings. If his wings or his flippers touched into the sensor net, the readout would go off the scale.

As Darkwood moved ahead, he hoped that didn't happen . . . .

Alexeii Serovski stood beside the comrade marshal there at the height of the path leading down to the hydrofoil launch which would take him and the same six Elite Corps personnel he had detailed to accompany the Hero Marshal to the submarine. The Hero Marshal spoke. "Serovski, I am entrusting you with a delicate mission. I will confide to you freely that I am quite interested in a potential alliance with these new comrades. Yet, as a wise commander must, I have my trepidations. You must keep in mind that the ultimate goal of your mission is to bring back my wife, Major Tiemerovna. Ideally, alive. But, should something occur which would preclude this, then I wish her dead despite the fact that her death would forever deprive me of the pleasure I would derive from delivering her to death myself. Is that understood?"

"Yes, comrade marshal."

The Hero Marshal smiled. "Good. Now—I have given the Colonel Feyedorovitch coordinates for what I have called neutral ground. I do not believe he quite understands the capabilities of our helicopter gunships, and that is excellent, all to the better. We will rendezvous . . ." And the Hero Marshal consulted the very fine gold watch that he habitually wore on his left wrist. "We will rendezvous at a small island of some historical significance near the twenty-fifth parallel, Chinmen Tao. Although the level of the sea has risen, a portion of it remains above the water, but the depth surrounding it would likely be such as to preclude their submarines getting very close. Are you a student of history?"

Serovski thought for a second. "Comrade marshal— only insofar as such study may advance the cause of Communism." Serovski wasn't certain how the comrade marshal had taken that, but the comrade marshal continued to speak.

"In the American Presidential campaign of 1960, two small islands became focal points. One of them was named Matsu Tao, which quite literally means 'ugly.' The other is Chinmen Tao—it was then called Quemoy. If the final undoing of the forces of so-called democracy is to be negotiated, this seems like a fitting place. Be there in twenty-four hours. I have become, recently, very distressed with Colonel Antonovitch—his succumbing to the gambit of the Rourke family, his loss of my prisoners and my gas. I would like to be confident that a qualified replacement awaits, captain. Do I make myself clear?"

Serovski drew his shoulders back. "Yes, comrade marshal. I will neither fail you nor the Soviet people!"

The Hero Marshal smiled. "Just see to it that you don't fail me and you will do well, Serovski. Very well." The Hero Marshal turned and walked back up the path.

Serovski looked down toward the sea.

He would not fail the Hero Marshal or the Soviet people—or himself. He called to the six men who stood some distance away. "Follow me!" And he started along the path . . . .

Rectifying the colostomy had been neither as onerous nor as complicated as his own medical experience had caused him to predict. Utilizing a methodology which seemed to combine local anesthesia and accupuncture, he

350

had been awake and felt no pain, yet had been aware of movement and able to follow with his own eyes, as he had requested, what was, to a physician of his training five centuries in the past, wizardry. A small incision, a specialized surgical instrument he had never seen before, and the use of something that looked more like a twentieth-century band-aid.

Remquist had told him, "This is synthetic tissue. Unlike the real thing, it cannot be rejected. There would have been no need for the bag at all if this hadn't been emergency surgery. I appologize for that inconvenience, Doctor Rourke. But the snythetic tissue must be typed to your own and then cultured in a rapid-growth medium. You'll have to see the lab where it's done. I find it rather mundane, of course, but I'm certain you'll find it fascinating. It is self-adhering and will grow together with your own tissue, and they will become as one. Six weeks from now, if I were to open you up again, I wouldn't be able to tell where the artificial had been and the real was without consulting my surgical diagrams and X-ray scans. I'd keep off rough food for a few days—sometimes these operations can cause a bit of, shall we say, over-enthusiastic response in the GI track. And, of course, you should rest for a few more days. Other than that . . ." And Remquist, the unabashed doer of wonders and miracles, had only smiled.

John Rourke sat in the chair from which Ellen, the pretty black nurse, had helped him to stand. The IV was still in his left arm. His Rolex was on the table near his chair beside a glass of fruit juice. He sipped at the fruit juice and looked at his watch. He pushed the call button for the nurse, and after a few moments Ellen came in again. "You work every shift?"

"Sometimes you get a special patient—you know how that is. What can I do for you? Wanna run the mile today?"

"Tell President Fellows that he seemed eager for information. I'm eager for it too and I'd like to see him."

"Oh, sure—I'll just call up the President. You bet!"

And she laughed.

John Rourke didn't laugh. "Get the hospital administrator to do it."

"You're not kidding, are you?"

"No—I'm not."

Ellen dug her hands into her uniform pockets, flaring out the skirt a little as she seemed to balance her decision and her body on the balls of her feet. Then she very quietly said, "You're the doctor," and walked from the room . . . .

Michael Rourke, stripped to his underpants, pushed his head above the surface. It was choppy, the wind that touched his skin like a finger of ice. The Soviet submarine was dead ahead and amidships there was a ladder—he imagined for use with the launch, because the ladder fed into an open berth of approximately the same size as the hydryfoil launch. He saw movement on the foredeck and gulped air, then tucked down.

With his knife, Michael had cut holes into the duffel bag so it would not hold water, then used the uniform belt from his stolen uniform (the rest of which he had buried in the sand near where he had entered the water) to make a drag for the perforated bag. Because of its weight, the bag compensated naturally for its own buoyancy and hung almost dead in the water beneath him, secured cross-body as he swam now, nearing the dark shape of the Soviet submarine's hull, his knife in his right fist clenched tight.

He had found himself thinking of Maria Leuden and of Annie and of his mother and of Paul—that he would never see any of them again. But what recriminations he had felt for the selfish decision to satisfy his own desire for vengeance against the man responsible for the death of his wife and child had vanished once he had seen the submarine and realized that here might be the one clue to his father's and Natalia's whereabouts. His father had risked life and limb often enough for him.

It was time for repayment, although full repayment was

something he could never accomplish and, strangely, would never want to. His father was unique and no one could match him. Once he had realized that and accepted that, Michael knew, he had felt better about both his father and himself.

He was beside the hull. If the skin of the submarine had sensing equipment, he doubted it would be so sensitized as to detect his presence. Otherwise, every good-sized sea creature which came near it would set alarms ringing. He hoped. He broke the surface and looked right and left and then above. There was no sign of anyone.

Michael Rourke moved laterally along the hull toward the berth for the launch and the ladder which serviced it—on closer inspection he was convinced that was the purpose now. He reached the ladder, then tucked down, slitting open the duffel bag at the top, reaching inside and extracting the large poly bag which held his weapons and his clothing. He had the bag now and used his knife to free himself of the harness, the duffel bag sinking away. He smiled as he surfaced his head and took in air. He had packed a rock into the bag so it would sink away. Like his father, he had planned ahead.

He reached out for the ladder now, moving the poly bag against the lower rungs to make sure that it was not electrified. It was not. The copy of the Life Support System I old Jan the swordmaker had crafted for him after the centuries-old pattern was ill-suited to carrying in the teeth—because of its weight, certainly, but more importantly because of the saw teeth that ran along the blade spine. But, carefully, he brought it to his mouth and clenched his teeth to the steel. The bag with his belongings in his left fist, he started up the rungs.

He heard motor noises behind him and looked to his left—around the prow of the vessel he could see the launch coming. He quickened his pace, reaching the deck and sliding his nearly naked body through the access in the deck rail, the knife back in his fist again.

Michael looked to right and left. All that he knew about submarines was from videotape movies and books and the

story Natalia had recounted of her and his father bein
taken aboard a U.S. submarine for what was to have bee
a special mission to the West Coast of the United States
but had turned out to be an attempt to seize control of ai
unfired U.S. nuclear weapon. There was a series a hatche
here on the deck—for missile-launching? He ran towar€
the sail, nearly slipping in his bare feet. As he neared th
massive sail, two uniformed men came from around th
other side.

They saw him, shouted.

Michael's guns were inaccessible to him. He charge€
toward them as they went for pistols in holsters at thei
right hips. If he dove into the water, they'd get him an€
any chance at reaching his father would be gone.

He dove for them, impacting both men at once, th€
knife gouging into the chest of the man nearest his righ
hand, Michael and the two Russians impacting the deck
plates. He rolled clear, wrenching his knife from the ches
of the man he had stabbed, the second man going for hi
pistol, Michael slashing the knife diagonally upwar€
across the man's right forearm and abdomen as the gui
started moving from the holster, the gun—some peculiar
looking automatic—clattering to the deck. The man's eye
opened wide in pain or fear or bewilderment, Michae
wasn't sure which as he brought the knife back an€
across, ripping open the man's throat.

The poly bag with his guns—it was too many steps awa\
and Michael dove for the fallen automatic pistol, findin₃
what he hoped was the safety as more men came fron
around the sail now. Michael stabbed the pistol towar€
them and fired, the pistol making a strange "plop" soun€
each time he fired, men swatting at points of impact, stil
coming for him. What kind of pistol was this? he thought
He emptied it toward the men, then body-blocked into on€
of them near him who was charging for him just as th€
man went for his own gun and Michael simultaneously
realized his peculiar pistol was empty.

They rolled across the deck, the man's hands going fo\
Michael's throat, Michael's right elbow snapping out and

354

back, finding something hard and suddenly yielding as the man shouted words in Russian that were unmistakably a curse. And then Michael was clear of him, to his knees. The men Michael had shot with the odd pistol were starting to stagger and drop. Michael threw himself toward the bag as another of the Russians came at him. Michael had the bag, rolled, slashing outward with the knife, which was now in his left hand, catching the man across the shins, the man screaming. To his knees now, to his feet. Michael started for the rail. It was time to abandon the plan in favor of withdrawal.

As he neared the rail he felt it, in the small of his back, then another and another, like pinpricks across his back and shoulders, and he lurched forward, nausea sweeping over him in a wave, and he reached out toward the rail, the knife falling from his hand and clattering to the deck plates.

He staggered.

His eyes were washed with green, and suddenly the cold of his nakedness was replaced with cold sweat, and he reached for the rail with both hands—where was the bag?—and . . .

Paul Rubenstein froze. As he had finally reached the beach—the Russian guard had climbed back into his truck after defecating in a neat pile beside it—Paul had seen the fight. It was Michael, clearly. And he saw Michael Rourke shot down.

There had been no sounds of gunfire—pistols with integral silencers?

He started into the surf, the Schmeisser in his right fist. And he looked hard at the submarine, its immensity. He looked at the gun in his hand. He dropped to his knees in the water.

"There has to be a way!" he shouted into the wind. And as he looked up, there were more men flooding onto the Soviet submarine's deck, and he could see several men in the uniforms of Karamatsov's KGB Elite Corps and some of the others—not Elite Corpsmen but men of the submarine crew presumably—were carrying Michael's naked-looking body between them like a sack of something.

He could swim out to the craft. He could try to board it. Even if Michael were . . . Maybe his father still lived.

Paul Rubenstein's breath was coming hard. "You damn fool!" Paul shouted into the wind. He knew no one heard him. "God bless you." He prayed someone heard him.

Paul got up from his knees. He ran back into the rocks, stripping off the Schmeisser and the musette bag full of spare magazines for it and the High Power. He pulled the High Power from his waistband. He looked up and down the beach. There would be no better place and the rocky promontory overhead could serve as a marker if he ever came back for them. He stripped away the Soviet uniform jacket and wrapped the Schmeisser into it, stuffed the High Power into the musette bag, and shoved the bag and the submachine gun into a niche in the rocks that he hoped was above the high-tide line.

He pulled off his boots and threw them on top of the guns. All he had was the Gerber MkII knife.

It would have to be enough.

Paul Rubenstein started into the surf. With the confusion on the sub's deck, he told himself, his chances were vastly better for sneaking on board.

He threw himself over a breaker and started swimming, swallowing water, choking on it, spitting it out. He kept going. Should have stuck with the YMCA classes longer, he told himself. He kept going. Once he boarded the submarine, if it didn't start out before he reached it or he didn't drown in the attempt, he had no idea what he would do.

"One thing at a time," he said aloud, swallowing water again and spitting it out. He kept going.

Chapter Forty-eight

Jason Darkwood's helmet broke surface into the mist which perpetually shrouded the lagoon. And immediately, the surface of his helmet began to fog over. He touched a control on his chest pack and the helmet began to defog. He was approximately a hundred yards from the docks, Island Class submarines everywhere, a Scout sub moving low in the water about 200 yards from him. The submarines had to be given exit paths through the sonar net. Otherwise they would produce the same results as errant sharks. He logged the detail away in his mind in case he got out of here alive, which seemed rather doubtful. He felt something tug at his right leg and for an instant panicked—a shark. But it was Aldridge, he realized, tucking down beneath the surface again, letting his wings fan out around him, beating slowly, steadily, so he could hover. Darkwood gave Aldridge the OK sign and Aldridge nodded, then made hand signals to his men.

Now that they had penetrated the lagoon, there was the obvious question of where to go, but hopefully Aldridge could settle that as he had promised. Aldridge signaled to his right and Darkwood understood, letting Aldridge take the lead now that they were out of the tunnel.

The water of the lagoon was quite clear, and the brilliance of the artificial light source above was like sunlight—he had seen sunlight several times. His wings propelled him along, his hands and flippers working too now to speed him on, Aldridge doing the same ahead of him and, as Darkwood glanced back, the Marine commandoes doing the same as well.

He touched his chest pack and the central section of his helmet switched from vision intensification to magnification and he could see in detail ahead of them now. Some drum containers were littered about near the base of the docks. There was even an AKM-96, old and rusted nearly to oblivion. Some Soviet Marine Spetznas had paid for that, he bet himself.

Just barely visible ahead now—the LCD rangefinder which was projected over the image in the front of his helmet read out a distance of twenty-five meters—was a ladder. It was evident that Sam Aldridge was aiming them toward it. The Sea Wings. He brought them to hover, letting the Marines pass him by, then fell in after them. Ahead, Aldridge was ascending the ladder.

Accelerating the vibration of his wings, Darkwood glided toward Aldridge, then hovered, Aldridge half up the ladder, wings cocooned. As Darkwood looked up, Aldridge's helmet broke the surface, then quickly drew back. The Marine captain touched the crown of his helmet to Darkwood's. "We're right between the Scout pens and the lagoon. I say we go for it. Nobody I could see in the immediate vicinity."

"You and I go for it. You first since you've been a guest here."

"I figured you'd say that, Jason." He turned in the water and touched helmets with Tom Stanhope briefly, then turned back to Darkwood. He nodded he was ready, then started for the ladder, unlimbering a stolen Russian PV-26 anti-shark/anti-personnel gun. In this instance, the Russian product was better than the American. Darkwood did the same, following Aldridge onto the ladder.

Aldridge's right foot bumped his helmet and Darkwood dodged back, nearly losing his hold on the ladder, regaining it, continuing up after him. Not a propitious beginning, he thought. He touched his chest pack and switched off magnification and rangefinding.

Darkwood's helmet broke the surface, and already Aldridge was dashing across the dock toward the cover of some parts containers, cylindrically shaped and at least five feet in diameter.

Darkwood pushed himself up onto the dock and ran as well, already starting to feel the loss of oxygen in the atmosphere here, dodging behind the cylindrical containers and to his knees beside Aldridge. Aldridge's helmet was already removed, Darkwood starting to do the same, gasping air as he broke the seal.

Darkwood shook his head to clear it. Breaking Atmosphere, as the Russians called it, was never pleasant after a dive of such long duration. The body got strangely used to breathing one kind of air, and the sudden change gave a momentary feeling of nausea.

Darkwood started to open the hermetically sealed container pouch built into his environment suit, drawing his pistol. He looked at it for a moment—"U.S. Government Model 2418 A2, Cal. 9mm LC"—then worked the magazine release catch to pull the fifteen-round magazine and replaced it with one of the thirty-rounders that stuck out of the butt but afforded double the firepower. As he looked at Aldridge, he saw that the Marine captain had done the same.

"So—we clear, you think, Sam?"

"As clear as you can be here, yeah, Jason."

"Go get the guys and I'll cover you."

"Right."

Darkwood moved toward the edge of the makeshift cover as Aldridge crossed the dock and swung down over the side and disappeared for half a second, then reappeared. Aldridge stayed in a crouch, his 2418 A2 Lancer in both fists. The A2 was a better gun, titanium-framed rather than alloy, the slide-release catch ambidextrous like the safety rather than switchable for left-handed use like the A1.

Tom Stanhope reached the dock, the rest of the Marines swarming over behind him, Aldridge pointing them toward the cylindrical containers where Darkwood already was, Darkwood stepping out and letting them pass, some of them starting to remove their helmets already, all of them armed with the Soviet PV-26s.

Aldridge was the last one to reach cover/concealment, and Darkwood ducked behind the packing materials just after them. They started stripping away their Sea Wings and the environment suits as they talked, two of the Marine raiders on guard, their 2418 A2s drawn. These two had been designated to return to the comparative safety of the lagoon with the underwater gear for the rest of the team.

Darkwood was out of his environment suit, the black penetration suit beneath it. He took the hood from the compartment on his left thigh and pulled it over his head, only the center of his face unrestrained by the hood. He secured the spare magazine from the hermetic pack on his environment suit to the chest pouches of the penetration suit, all except the fifteen-rounder, which he secured in the thigh pocket that would form the holster if he ever got to put the 2418 A2 away. He doubted he would. He took his knife from the right-leg calf-sheath on his environment suit and resheathed it on the right calf of his penetration suit. The issue knife was a good knife, but there were still people who made knives for a hobby or to supplement their incomes, and they found ready customers among the Marines and some of the Navy personnel as well. Darkwood had found the best of the custom-makers and worked with the man to design a fighting knife that would fit his needs.

He secured the safety strap to lock the knife into its sheath. To his left thigh he secured the grenade array, standard high-explosive, sound/light, and smoke.

Darkwood looked at Sam Aldridge, Aldridge identically attired except for the knife. Aldridge's personal knife had been with him when he had been captured and was, he assumed, gone forever. A standard-issue blade rode where it would have been.

"Now where to, Sam?"

"If they've got her, captain, after all the trouble Rourke put 'em to, they'd be bigger assholes than I know they are not to have her just where I said—the detention area beneath the military command post-office complex."

"Deploy your rear guard, Sam—then let's get the hell on with it."

Sam Aldridge turned to the two Marines designated to be left behind. "You heard the man—the word is given."

The two Marines repositioned their helmets, grabbed up the gear from the rest of the force, and Darkwood tapped his wrist chronometer. The senior of the two men nodded his understanding and Darkwood and Aldridge covered them as they made the dash to the edge of the dock, then took the ladder down rather than risking the noise of a splash dive.

"You're the man who knows where he's going, Sam—let's do it."

Aldridge gave a thumbs-up sign and left cover, Darkwood right behind him, looking back once at the packing materials. The Russians were arming with nuclear missiles. He was sure of it.

The 2418 A2 was bunched tight in his right fist, his thumb poised near the safety as he sprinted alongside the Marines, following Sam Aldridge. . . .

Paul Rubenstein had nearly reached the Soviet submarine, the waves higher now, crashing over him as he tried to increase his pace or at least maintain it.

But the submarine had started underway.

Some 200 yards or so remained, and already the submarine was moving away with a rapidity he wouldn't have thought possible.

Paul Rubenstein treaded water.

Paul Rubenstein cried and prayed. . . .

The President of Mid-Wake told John Rourke, "Anything you wish, sir."

"I need to talk to somebody who knows nylon cord or whatever your equivalent is. I need some to rewrap the handle of one of my knives. And I need the knives so I

361

can do it."

"Certainly, Doctor Rourke, but if you would like, simply tell me what you desire and it can be done for you."

"No thank you, Mr. President. I'd prefer to do it myself and know just how it's done. Where are my guns?"

"They're here. Quite safe. They can be returned to you whenever you wish."

John Rourke considered that. "What about the ammunition?"

"I was told it would have spoiled with the exposure to salt water it received."

"Probably so," Rourke said quietly. "Could you duplicate it for me, if that were possible?"

"I, ahh—I can get someone up here to answer that question. Please. Allow me," and Jacob Fellows picked up what apparently passed at Mid-Wake for a telephone, but was in the same general shape as an orange. And this one was even the right color. "Computer. This is the President." Fellows paused, then, "Locate and direct to join me at this exchange and number Director of Ordnance, Mid-Wake Armed Forces. As soon as possible. Instruct that he come prepared with data concerning—please pause." Fellows looked at Rourke. "What type of guns are they, sir?"

"The caliber in question is designated commonly as .45 ACP, or .45 Automatic Colt Pistol. I am specifically concerned with the reproduction of the load I habitually use, or failing that what was commonly known as standard military hardball, a 230-grain Full-Metal-Case bullet ahead of—"

"Please, Doctor Rourke—I'll never remember all of that." He spoke into the orange again. "Computer. Ordnance Director should be equipped with data concerning most commonly encountered loads for caliber designated as following: .45 ACP or . . ." He looked quizzically toward John Rourke.

".45 Automatic Colt Pistol, Mr. President."

"Computer—that was .45 ACP or .45 Automatic Colt Pistol. Thank you, computer." The President set down the orange. "So—is there anything else that I can do to accommodate you, sir?"

"I would appreciate your cooperation, sir, in two matters which concern me greatly. They are of virtually equal importance, each in its own way."

"Certainly."

"I would like to request that my family be contacted on the surface and alerted to my presence here and that I am well."

"That may take some doing, but it can be done, Doctor Rourke. And the second request?"

"Get me the hell out of here and loan me one of your submarines and a few people to run her and some scuba gear, and I'll go after Major Tiemerovna myself."

Jacob Fellows smiled good-naturedly. "Sir, I would venture to say that scuba gear, as you call it, and certainly that term is still used, has changed rather radically since your day."

"No doubt," Rourke whispered.

"Yes—and, ahh—well, the Wayne will be ready to leave port soon enough, but with the Reagan gone—to achieve just the goal you desire—we cannot leave ourselves quite that vulnerable."

"I looked out the window, Mr. President. A place this size and you only have two submarines?"

"No—no—of course not. We have a fleet only slightly smaller than that of our Soviet adversaries. We have the equivalent of their Island Class submarines—"

"Island Class? What are Island Class submarines?"

"Their monster—"

"The big ones. Very impressive."

"Ours are nearly as large and certainly more efficient. We have various other vessels. But the job you speak of requires the best attack class vessel available. And that is either the Reagan or the John Wayne."

"What happens if the Reagan doesn't make it?"

"Well—the skipper of the Reagan, Commander Darkwood, is the best there is. So was his father."

"His father?"

"You have no familiarity with the Darkwood family, of

course. Perhaps you would feel better, rest easier if you understood the competent hands in which your Major Tiemerovna's fate has been placed."

"Perhaps," John Rourke whispered.

But then, without his guns, his knives, and a submarine, there wasn't much else he could do at the moment other than listen.

"Excellent. Let me ask you a question first, Doctor Rourke. As an intelligence agent, which I understand you were—the CIA, was it?"

"Yes."

"Excellent. Were you at all aware of the Mid-Wake Project?"

"In those days, things were on a need-to-know basis, of course. I didn't have the need to know."

"As it should have been, of course, Doctor Rourke."

"Do you have anything like a cigar around here?"

"A what?"

"It's a thing made out of leaves that are rolled up and you put one end of it in your mouth and light the other end of it and you inhale the smoke into your lungs."

"My God, sir! What sort of insidious torture is this?"

"Forget I asked." John Rourke smiled. "Tell me about Mid-Wake—or the Mid-Wake Project."

"Well, I don't have to tell you that in those days the Russians and United States were competing in various areas, not the least of which was defense. But they also competed in space."

"That's how we got to the moon."

"You would have seen that—live?"

"Yes—I saw it live."

"By God, I envy you. I envy them," the man said, a trace of genuine sadness resonant in his FM-announcer voice.

"It was quite a sight," Rourke said, realizing that such an understatement sounded horribly lame considering the circumstances.

"Such heroes, those men." The President inhaled deeply, then continued, picking up the thread of his thought. "At any event, then, you are conversant with the situation. There was considerable effort to build space stations, the Russians having the jump on the United States to a degree, to a degree not. But both nations wanted something truly spectacular and yet wholly functional in the skies, not just what budgetary constrictions would allow. And that's how Mid-Wake was hit upon, Doctor Rourke. All of our personnel were either involved in the space-oriented scientific disciplines or in marine biology, oceanography, and the like."

"I don't know if I follow you."

President Jacob Fellows was apparently enjoying his revelations. "Sir, you are here, now, inside the greatest space station ever conceived."

John Rourke wished he had that cigar.

"By the mid-1980s," Jacob Fellows began, "with the emphasis on relieving the growing national debt, with the Congress spending in support of dying social programs which had the primary purpose of assuring re-election, and with growing environmental problems of which the vast majority of the American people had little knowledge, the practical uses of space had become self-evident to all those who wished to see. And to capitalize on the space program and at the same time keep costs down, it was necessary to build a permanent space station beyond the limited scope of what had been openly proposed. The only terrestrial environment which comes close to duplicating the environment in space is, of course, under the sea.

"And there was another need for Mid-Wake as well," Fellows continued. "The Soviets were talking—with some sincerity it is believed by today's historians—about arms reduction. And while the Soviet officials were talking arms reduction, the KGB and other ultra-conservative groups within the fabric of the Soviet State were making themselves even more ready for war. The trouble with a totalitarian system is that it can be so easily subverted. At any event, the Soviets had a naval super-base in Vietnam at Cam Ranh Bay, and the KGB and others knew very well that if arms talks between the Soviet government and the

United States did proceed into true progress toward reduction, eventually the European missile problems would be ironed out and talk would turn to submarine-based missiles again."

"This was built as some sort of defense against that?" John Rourke asked.

"More as a compensation, Doctor Rourke. I mentioned the Darkwood family. Well, because of our small population base and the necessary population-maintenance level—all voluntary, mind you—family integrity has remained pretty constant. Everyone here can trace his or her ancestry back to the first scientists and technicians who came here and were eventually trapped here when the war came and it was learned that the atmosphere was doomed. The Darkwood family is one of these original families. Nathaniel Darkwood was a scientist of considerable abilities, as well as an Olympic athlete."

"Now I know why that name—Darkwood—has been gnawing at me. Nate Darkwood—that's what he called himself. He won a fistful of gold medals in swimming, and he was one of those rare athletes that was equally good at two sports. Biathalon, I think—yes."

"Skiing and marksmanship combined—I've seen old tapes."

"Cross-country skiing and rifle marksmanship," Rourke said. "He was involved in a number of projects in marine biology and—I read one or two of his papers on sharks—but then, there was some kind of storm and the ship he was on went out of radio contact and there was a long search, I remember."

"He was never lost at sea. Nathaniel Darkwood and a handful of others—many of them the people supposedly lost at sea with him—were formed into a special scientific intelligence unit. It was a result of their efforts that the data was obtained which made Mid-Wake a top-secret national priority."

"Because of the Cam Ranh Bay naval base?" Rourke asked.

"Certain persons of power in the KGB and the Soviet

Navy saw a means of having the ultimate weapon, a weapon their perceived enemy would never know existed. Using Cam Ranh Bay as the operational base, they began constructing beneath the sea the Soviet domes from which you were fortunate enough to escape. The domes served two purposes. The scientific purpose was seen as allowing the Soviets unparalleled research opportunities with geo-thermal energy, marine studies, and—much like Mid-Wake—research that would prove invaluable in the construction of a large-scale, permanent space station. The defensive purpose was their primary interest, however. Once the domes were complete, they would have a strate-gic base beneath the sea where existing submarines could be serviced and new submarines that could not officially be counted in strategic arms talks could be built. When it was learned that the Soviets were doing this, it was realized that an effective counter to this base had to be devised, and since Mid-Wake was already in its early stages, Mid-Wake was selected to be the counter to the Soviet base. The United States government couldn't blow the whistle on the Soviet base without destroying what progress had been made in detente with the U.S.S.R. And, for that matter, without revealing Mid-Wake. Not to mention the sources of the intelligence data which sub-stantiated the existence of the Soviet base. A group of people whose deaths had been faked and were operating only with the knowledge of the President and a few trusted Congressional leaders, but without the authority of law. And the cost for Mid-Wake was in the billions of dollars, yet the research benefits would have paid for the project and actually yielded a profit within twenty years and saved billions in research dollars for the future. So the base was never mentioned."

"And after the Night of the War and the Great Confla-gration, both Mid-Wake and the Soviet base survived. And for you, the war never ended."

"Yes," Jacob Fellows said quietly.

"And?"

Fellows looked at Rourke and smiled. "You're a percep-

367

tive man. All right. This is in strictest confidence, Doctor Rourke."

"All right," Rourke nodded.

"The Soviets used most of their nuclear warheads and lost a number of their submarines during what you call this night of war. We had nuclear capabilities, but very limited, and we were not able to assist our friends and families on the land to any great degree. There was violent submarine warfare and many lives lost, but we could provide no true, direct assistance in terms of resolving the war on the surface. For some time, we played cat-and-mouse games, as the expression goes. But it was discovered we both utilize the same fault in the earth's crust as our source of geothermal power, what keeps us going here. Both of us. If we destroyed the Russians, with nuclear weapons, we might destroy ourselves. And the Russians have the same data. So we kept our war non-nuclear. For almost five centuries, we kept it that way. Occasionally they would have the advantage, and occasionally we would. But now, all of that has changed. They have produced Island Class submarines with missile-launching capabilities, and they have been mining raw materials for producing bomb-grade plutonium from beneath the sea. We have been forced to do the same. It appears that the Russians are involved in a program which has the eventual aim of retaking the earth's surface. Our scientists and strategic planners estimate the Russians will not have full capability in this area for several more decades. And, with the recent confirmation that there is substantial life still on the surface . . ."

"If they started another nuclear war, the surface environment wouldn't only be destroyed, so would the oceans. The atmosphere couldn't bounce back again. It was so weakened. Are you aware at all of the enemy we fight on the surface?" Rourke asked.

"We have been so concerned with survival, aside from a few brief sorties and some unsubstantiated data, we know very little. The Russians outnumber us. Considerably. Mid-Wake is essentially unchanged since its inception.

There is the central Hub and six additional spheres which are reached by means of causeways—people commonly call the causeways and the spheres they service 'tentacles.' We have never been able to divert the resources needed to expand. The Russians had a primarily military facility when World War III began. We had what was primarily a research facility with some military potential. They were already manufacturing submarines. We were building our first, experimentally, and its primary use was to be research. We have held our own, but never caught up."

"On the surface," John Rourke told him, "we have a situation in some ways analogous to your own, in that we contend with a Soviet power which has spent five centuries perfecting its military machine. The Soviets survived in what is referred to as the Underground City. It was built into the Urals as a massive civil-defense project and was wholly self-sufficient, as we understand, prior to the Night of the War. A man came to that city who is a survivor of the pre-War era, like myself. His name is Vlamdir Karamatsov."

"Is?"

"Yes. I should explain how I'm here, I suppose."

"Cryogenic sleep. I know there had been some experiments done concerning its use for deep-space travel."

"Exactly," Rourke told him. "On the Night of the War, the entire United States Space Shuttle Fleet was launched from Kennedy Space Center, which was in Florida. An international astronaut corps was assembled in the years before the Night of the War, ostensibly for training in deep-space flight, but with a secondary purpose in mind as well. That was as a doomsday project. Its name was the Eden Project, but I always thought it would more appropriately have been named as having something to do with Noah's Ark. Because that's basically what it was.

"They would periodically have drills," John Rourke went one, "where the astronauts would be assembled, board the shuttles, and be put into cryogenic sleep. When the Night of the War came, the President had wisely scheduled a drill, as was policy during periods of height-

369

ened international tensions. And then, that night, the shuttles were actually launched, and no one knew why until the crews opened their secret orders and learned that this was a project to save humanity and that they would sleep for almost five centuries while the shuttles followed an elliptical flight path taking them to the edge of the solar system and back. The flight crews were to prepare the ships for long-duration flight and then enter their own cryogenic chambers while the computers operated the ships. It was a gamble and the odds against success were enormous, I'd suppose, but in the event that the nuclear exchange actually destroyed all life, it was a gamble worth taking. There were one hundred and twenty people, of all races, male and female, of course. The computers held the accumulated scientific knowledge and cultural data of mankind. Cryogenically frozen embryos of useful domestic animals, birds, and other life-forms went along as well. But the only way the cryogenic process could work—both the Russians and ourselves had been performing experiments in cryogenic sleep—was by use of a special serum."

"What for?" Fellows asked.

"It was easy to put people into cryogenic sleep—or comparatively so. But the brain would go into such a low level of activity that the subject could not be aroused from the sleep. A sort of living death. So there was considerable interest among the Soviets when the Americans developed a formula which was injected into the sleeper immediately prior to the Sleep. The formula prevented brain activity from dropping below a specified level and, when the sleep chamber's computer program said it was time to wake up, the sleeper could awaken. Without the formula—cryogenic serum, if you will—cryogenic sleep was nothing more than what I said—living death."

"How were you able to utilize cryogenic sleep then?"

John Rourke smiled. "The details form a rather long story. But in essence, Karamatsov's KGB people wanted the serum, we had it, they stole some, and we had no more after the Eden Project was launched. Karamatsov was actually out of the picture then. There had been a fight and I thought I had killed him. My error in judgment was unforgiveable. He lived, was taken to the Soviet Underground City in the Urals, and—with the help of some personnel loyal to him and a small amount of the serum and some cryogenic chambers—was able to survive to be awakened after five centuries."

"But—how about you, Doctor Rourke?"

"Major Tiemerovna's uncle, General Ishmael Varakov, was the commanding general for the army of occupation which invaded the United States and Canada following the Night of the War. Karamatsov was in charge of the KGB for North America. After Karamatsov's apparent death, the man who replaced him set out in earnest to carry out Karamatsov's plans and to assume the position Karamatsov had intended to hold—essentially, ruler of the earth. They were completing a facility built into a Cheyenne Mountain site after the Soviets seized it. That was in Colorado. They called it the Womb. Which was exactly its purpose. Aside from arming themselves with all manner of potentially useful devices and weaponry, including particle-beam devices that were to be used to shoot down the Eden Project when it returned, they had amassed a considerable number of cryogenic chambers. After they stole the serum, which was manufactured in a small town in Kentucky by people who I'm certain had no idea what it was they were making, the KGB Elite Corps—which Karamatsov had started and his replacement now commanded—was set to survive the Great Conflagration when the atmosphere caught fire. Their scientists were able to predict the occurrence within a few days. The man in charge of the KGB Elite Corps was named Rozhdestvenskiy."

"Wasn't that Stalin's real name?"

"No, I believe his real name was Dzhugashvili."

"Then how did you get this serum and the cryogenic chambers?"

Rourke still wished he had the cigar. He didn't. "Natalia's uncle, General Varakov, was a decent man. He was only a patriotic Russian soldier doing his job for his country, not a butcher. He realized that the KGB Elite Corps planned to dominate the earth and planned to destroy the incoming Eden Project shuttles, which Varakov perceived of as a new beginning for mankind. And, frankly, he was obsessed, as any parent would be, with his niece somehow surviving. She wasn't really his niece, you see. She was the daughter of a woman he had loved very dearly and lost. And when this woman and her husband died, Varakov raised Natalia as his niece. I think he not only loved her for herself, but because she so reminded him of the woman he had lost. And he was determined that Natalia should live. But he was also affronted at the fact that the cryogenic chambers and the serum that would be used to keep the KGB Elite Corps alive could have been used to keep alive the best and brightest of Soviet youth instead. All of those factors must have swayed him. Because of him, we survived."

"How?" Fellows asked.

Rourke smiled. "He recruited a group of men from the Spetznas who were loyal to him and were decent men and realized that what Rozhdestvenskiy planned was beneath contempt. They were lead by a very courageous officer named Vladov, a captain. An American officer named Reed, an Army Intelligence guy originally, led the American detachment from U.S. II, the Chambers government."

Fellows nodded. "I'm familiar with that from the Gundersen memoirs."

"Natalia and myself, Vladov and his unit, Reed and his people—we attacked the Womb. We were able to steal cryogenic chambers and serum. Natalia and I got out alive. Vladov and his people died buying us time. Reed and his people did the same, Reed climbing up onto one of the particle-beam towers to place an American flag there. He was killed in the attempt. We got the cryogenic chambers and serum back to my retreat in the Georgia mountains—"

"That was a southeastern coastal state, wasn't it?"

"Yes. A beautiful state. Paradise in many ways. Natalia, my wife Sarah, our young children Annie and Michael, my friend Paul, they were all asleep. The sky was beginning to catch fire with the dawn. Rozhdestvenskiy had followed us, but his forces were being destroyed by the ball lightning, being burned alive. I did a stupid thing but I'd probably do it again. I thought about Reed and I climbed out through an escape hatch and raised the Stars and Stripes. I just made it in as the fires consumed everything around us. Rozhdestvenskiy was gone. I thought everything was maybe gone."

"And so you awakened in five centuries and there was your old nemesis again, this Karamatsov?"

Rourke nodded. "I used the cryogenic chambers, though. I awakened before the others, and then awakened Annie and Michael and worked with them for five years until I felt they could survive on their own with the aid of what I'd taught them. Then I returned to the Sleep and the children didn't. When I awoke again, and this time Sarah and Natalia and Paul awoke with me, the children were adults. My daughter, Annie, eventually married Paul. My son found a survival community that had gone wrong and he saved the life of a girl from there. Her name was Madison. They were married too. In the intervening time, I learned Karamatsov was still alive, the Eden Project shuttles returned and were nearly blown out of the sky by Karamatsov's army, and we made allies with the Republic of New Germany in what was Argentina and the communities of Lydveldid Island, or Iceland. It was during a Soviet suicide raid into the Mt. Hekla community in Iceland that Michael's wife, Madison, and their unborn child were killed."

"Where is this Eden Project now?"

"For a variety of reasons, they landed in Georgia. They are still there, building a permanent base, rather slowly." Rourke smiled. "The Germans are helping them. My wife and daughter were in Iceland, and I presume they still are. There's a German base protecting the Hekla Community. It's safer. Paul and Natalia and Michael and I were involved with pursuing the Soviet army under Karamatsov. You see, he—Karamatsov—attempted to take over his own government by means of a gas that was buried before the Night of the War. We were able to prevent that. So, technically, there are two Russian states. It's possible that the government at the Underground City in the Urals might be brought around to allying with us against Karamatsov. I don't know. But in any event, Natalia and Michael and Paul and I pursued Karamatsov's army to China. He wanted the unused portion of the pre-War Chinese nuclear arsenal, and almost got part of it. Natalia and I were walking along the coast, were separated for a bit, and then I heard sounds of a struggle and went to aid Natalia." Rourke grinned. "It didn't work out quite as planned."

"That's an amazing story, Doctor Rourke. So—you've been fighting this war for five centuries as well."

"But with a little intermission," John Rourke nodded.

"You must tell me—"

There was a knock at the door, interrupting Fellows. The door opened.

A tall man, gray hair, militarily erect, books and computer printouts under his arm, filled the doorway. "Our ordnance expert, Doctor Rourke."

Rourke extended his right hand. "Forgive me for not getting up—I'm John Rourke."

Chapter Forty-nine

Annie Rubenstein's worst fears had been confirmed. The forces sent to recapture or destroy the gas stolen from Karamatsov were female members of the KGB Elite Corps and female troopers from Karamatsov's armies. Females were unaffected by the gas.

She had witnessed the women deploying their forces in the valley below, setting up mortar emplacements and heavy machine guns. The process had seemed unending.

And then she had seen a flag of truce and over a loud-hailing system from the valley below, a strident-sounding voice had called out in English, "I wish to speak with the Rourke family under the white flag of truce. This is Captain Svetlana Grubaszikova acting under the command of the Hero Marshal Karamatsov. I demand an immediate response!"

"Sounds like nice girl, doesn't she?" Annie commented to Maria Leuden.

"Are we going to talk with them?"

"We have to—stall for time. Han might have reached the J-7V with the internees, but he won't have gotten any Germans or the Chinese in to back us up yet. We'll talk. Stay close to Rolvaag and his dog." Annie grinned, moving back from the lip of the rise which overlooked the valley and crawling along until she would be out of sight from the valley floor, then standing, running to find Ma-Lin, and notify her that she—Annie Rubenstein—was officially taking charge and would negotiate with the Russian woman.

375

She found Ma-Lin and had the woman translate for her to the ranking Chinese officer. The man's face betrayed his displeasure, but he agreed that she should stall for time as much as possible and in order to do that had to confer with the commander of the Soviet forces. Annie didn't mention the part about officially taking charge, but from his expression again, it seemed he had detected her sentiments.

She wasn't about to rip the only slip she had with her, and there were no white towels or scarves, so she stepped into Han's command tent, hitched up her skirt, and took off her slip to use as a white flag in its entirety.

When she re-emerged from the tent, Ma-Lin and the ranking Chinese officer were waiting outside. The man spoke, Ma-Lin translating. "Lieutenant Liu wishes that I convey his best wishes for your success, but that I also convey the fact that the ultimate decision here rests on his shoulders."

Annie smiled, realizing she was still holding her underwear. She stuffed her slip into her pocket. "You tell Lieutenant Liu that I am well aware of the fact that he is the ranking man here, but by the same token, if any of those gas trucks get perforated by a stray bullet, no man here will be capable of command. I don't intend to give away the store, just stall for time."

Annie walked away, taking out her "white flag" again and slinging her M-16 forward and trying to figure a way in which she could secure the slip to the flash-hider without ruining it. She finally bunched up the edge of the garment at the waist and pushed enough of it through the sling between the swivel and the buckle that she could tie a loose knot to keep it from pulling out.

There was PA capability on the truck Maria and Michael had used, and Annie climbed into the truck cab and turned the key to power the radio, then hit the PA switch. She spoke into the microphone. "This is Annie Rourke Rubenstein, the daughter of John Rourke. My father has decided that I should represent the Rourke family and other forces gathered here woman to woman in a personal meeting with you under the white flag of truce. My flag will be tied near the muzzle of my rifle. I'm coming down and will meet you halfway between our respective positions."

She cut the PA switch and the power, and started down out of the truck. If she could keep alive the idea that her father was present, it might buy still more time. She doubted that there were many among Karamatsov's forces who wished to tangle with her daddy personally.

She saw Maria, standing next to Rolvaag, smiled at them, and heard Maria's shouted stage whisper, "Good luck, Annie."

She called back, "Cover me, guys." And she started down the footpath into the valley.

The wind was blowing colder all the time and, although her slip hadn't been warm, changing the layering of her clothing had not helped. She kept walking, the M-16's butt against her right hip the way some women would carry a baby, the slip, her white flag, blowing in the breeze near its muzzle.

And she could see this Captain Svetlana Grubaszikova moving up the hillside now, a more traditional white flag in hand. The woman wore black battle-dress utilities and a heavy parka over them and was not visibly armed, although Annie felt the woman most certainly would be armed, visibly or not.

Annie picked her way down some loose rocks and kept walking.

The Russian woman walked with a stride as broad as a man's. Annie increased the length of her stride.

At a point roughly equidistant between the hillside defenders and the valley forces, Annie Rubenstein stopped. She kept the M-16 in her right fist, balanced against her right hip, her underwear blowing in the breeze, her thumb beside the selector to lever it into full-auto mode.

The Russian captain was still coming.

Annie smiled.

The Russian woman stopped about two yards below her.

377

"Your English is very good," Annie told her.

"Thank you, Miss Rourke."

"Mrs. Rubenstein. I married my father's best friend."

"Congratulations."

"Thank you. It was a small ceremony, but I had a lovely dress."

"I am sorry that I was unable to attend."

"Well, the guest list was rather small, really. What can I do for you?"

The Russian woman smiled. Her teeth were very white but very uneven. She could have been pretty if her dark brown hair wasn't cut as short as a man's and the wire-rimmed glasses she wore had highlighted rather than distorted the color of her blue eyes. "I have come to ask for the obvious."

"Our consideration for your people when you surrender? Well, of course we'll abide by all the accepted rules of war. Funny, though, I thought gas had been outlawed."

The Russian captain actually laughed. Not a good sign, Annie thought. "I came to ask for your surrender. I will guarantee nothing except that you will not be immediately executed."

"That's nice of you—gosh. You listen, lady—we have the gas and if the gas gets out, maybe you and your friends down there will be immune but the rest of Karamatsov's army won't be."

"The forces of the Soviet people under the leadership of the Hero Marshal are well out of effective range of the gas."

"Bullshit, captain."

"You are behaving like an irresponsible child, you bitch."

"Better than being a dyke."

"I am not familiar with this word."

"You and your girls down there—have good times every night, do you?"

"I will personally enjoying showing you.

Annie grinned. "I bet you would, too—but I'm happy being a woman and don't have to play games being

378

something else. And as for your surrender terms, why don't you shove 'em up your ass if it isn't too crowded there?"

"You will die."

"That's the best alternative you've offered. But you remember, lady captain, what happens if that gas does leak and a nice big cloud of it drifts over your dumb-ass Hero Marshal's army and they come after you and kill you and your finger friends, huh? Talk over?"

"Talk is over."

"Cheer up—maybe your period will start," and Annie Rourke turned on her heel and walked back up the hill. She was aware of two things. First, she could easily be shot in the back. Second, if her father or mother—or husband—had heard the way she had talked, despite her age they would have washed out her mouth with soap.

There were always risks in war.

Chapter Fifty

Paul Rubenstein, his clothes still wet, his weapons retrieved from the rocks where he had stashed them in the vain hope of boarding the Soviet submarine, scrambled over the rocks and along the high ground near the sea, the submarine long since vanished beneath the waves. All hope had vanished as well, hope of rescuing Michael or John or Natalia.

It was up to him, now. Up to him, and with Annie's help he would continue the fight and someday . . . Paul Rubenstein stared down toward Karamatsov's encampment. "Someday—and real soon," he whispered.

He looked around.

Two Soviet soldiers were climbing up onto the rise, both of them holding hands. Paul swung the Schmeisser forward and the two men released hands and went for their assault rifles. Paul Rubenstein's left hand swept back the German MP-40's bolt and his right first finger touched the trigger. Two perfect three-round bursts, cutting down both men.

He knew he should run, but he stood there for a moment and thought about John Rourke teaching him how to use the Schmeisser, telling him to recite the words "trigger control" each time he fired it.

And then he ran because the sound of gunfire would have traveled down to the camp and in minutes the two dead men would be found and then everyone would be chasing after him.

And as he ran, he thought of the line from the Robert

Frost poem, about 'promises to keep'. . . .

Michael Rourke's head felt as if it would explode and he opened his eyes to try to find out why, and very suddenly he knew why. He was still naked except for his shorts, and his wrists were tied in front of him with some sort of plastic cord. He pulled at the cord and only succeeded in making his wrists hurt.

"Screwed up good this time," he said aloud as he sat up. He was on a bare floor, and there was some sort of blue light in the open doorway of what otherwise seemed like a cell.

He remembered the fight on the deck and he realized what the odd pistols were—dart guns of some type which had put him to sleep. As he tried to stand, he felt a sudden wave of nausea and the headache was no longer a headache but a pain unlike anything he had ever known, and he fell back. . . .

Natalia Anastasia Tiemerovna had been given her own clothes to wear, female guards observing her carefully as she had changed from the Soviet uniform and been ushered to a shower stall. There had been soap and shampoo awaiting her, and she realized that there was no way of utilizing either the shower head or a faucet handle as a weapon and there was nothing from which to hang herself with any efficiency, so she had cleaned her body and cleaned her hair. A brush and comb had been given to her, and she had used them to get her almost black hair into some semblance of order. Then she had removed the robe that had been given her to use and dressed in her own clothes.

Inside herself, as she zipped the black jumpsuit up the front, she knew why. Her husband or his emissary would soon be arriving. She sat on the end of a plastic bench and pulled on her boots, and as she did the fingers of her left hand felt the interior of the left boot's outside seam. The single-edged, German plastic razor blade was still in place. The question now was to get at it and have sufficient time to utilize it to open an artery. A vein would be too slow. . . .

John Rourke had not really felt up to walking, but had decided that he must. The ordnance expert had felt confident that he could duplicate the 185-grain Federal .45 ACP hollow-point load in limited quantity. Conventional priming compound could be formulated quickly enough, and the cases would have to be hand-cut to proper length, and there had been many other problems he had foreseen and some he declared he could not foresee, but he had assured John Rourke that acceptable ammunition would be fabricated by morning. He had not seen the urgency, but when Rourke had insisted, the President of Mid-Wake had insisted as well. The ordnance expert had also pledged that he would provide the nylon cord Rourke needed to rewrap the handle of the Crain knife.

Rourke stood on the balcony of the hospital room and stared out across the yellow sphere at the end of the yellow tentacle. There was nothing on the far side of the hospital but the wall of the sphere, which was really more a dome than a sphere. He had been able to see the sea very faintly. But from here, he could see the hospital grounds, schools, some living space. A young man and a woman walked hand in hand several floors beneath him. It was the end of the day, although the light was unchanged. It was always daylight there in this under-siege world of the future. He methodically rewrapped the handle of his knife.

He thought back to the last exchange with Jacob Fellows. "Just what do you think you could accomplish that my people cannot, Doctor Rourke?"

"No slight intended to your people, and you can't know how sincerely I wish them success in their endeavor. But as you told me a moment ago yourself, if they haven't returned by morning, chances are slim that the mission

382

has gone as planned. Putting it another way, your Russian enemies are going to use Natalia Tiemerovna as a bargaining chip with my Russian enemies. And if an alliance between Karamatsov and your enemies comes to pass, we may not have a world left. For everyone's interests, Natalia has to be gotten out before that alliance can be effected, before she can be handed over to her husband, Karamatsov. You don't know what he would do to her. I do. If your mission doesn't work, I'll go after her. I'm feeling stronger by the hour. By tomorrow, I'll be in decent enough shape to move around reasonably well. By the next day when we'd reach the Russian domes, I'll be fit enough to fight."

"You cannot leave here without a vessel, Doctor Rourke," Fellows had said after a moment. "I'm sorry, but you know that."

"And if you don't help me, you should order your people to kill me now, because I'm going with your blessing or without it. There's no choice for me."

Fellows had left the room, not responding.

John Rourke still worked at rewinding the handle of his knife. Both the Life Support System X and the A.G. Russell Sting IA had been given excellent attention, oiled, their edges untouched, just as he had preferred. Sharpening gear had been provided for him, but he would touch up the edges of the knives after he finished rewinding the handle of the Crain knife.

His guns had not been returned, the ordnance man saying that they had been stripped, cleaned, and reassembled and would be needed in order to test the ammunition for functional reliability. The only other .45s at Mid-Wake were the few in the hands of private arms collectors and a few more in the Museum of American Culture, none of these latter having been fired for centuries.

If the ordnance man blew up his Detonics .45s, admittedly a difficult task, he would throttle the man, good intentions notwithstanding. It was possible the Germans could hand-make duplicates of the guns for him, but not without the originals to work from, and somehow it wouldn't be the same.

After the betrayal in Latin America so long ago that had resulted in his quitting the Company and turning to the private pursuits of teaching and writing about survivalism and weapons training, he had begun carrying the little guns. He had never found anything he liked better. The Beretta 92F military pistols, such as his son habitually carried, the various other guns he respected in the world, like the Browning High Power Paul Rubenstein carried—these had been fine guns, like the Sigs, the Walthers, the Colts, but he had never found semi-automatic pistols more to his liking than these little .45s. The Python was an excellent revolver, despite the fact that its hand-fitted action gave it a delicacy that some eschewed for rugged use in the field. But he had learned to completely gun-smith the revolver and could see to any problems it might have. Natalia's Metalife Custom L-Frame Smith & Wessons—world-class revolvers to be sure. And then there was the excellent hand-crafted Trapper Scorpion .45 Sarah carried. But his little Detonics .45s . . . As soon as he got them back and some ammo to use in them, he would be gone from this place, one way or the other. . . .

Jason Darkwood, Sam Aldridge, and the others had reached the access tunnel leading beneath the military command complex. "If I'd known this tunnel was here, it would have helped Rourke get to her," Aldridge whispered.

They crouched in a nest of pipes and valves at the juncture of two intersecting tunnels, the height a scant three feet, and roughly the same width. To the left, the tunnel went on beneath the People's Institute for Marine Studies, and to the right, beneath the passage which connected the main domes to the smaller dome which was the headquarters of the government and the military high command. "Rourke never would have made it if you had the time of day right. Once we enter this tunnel," Darkwood advised, "the only way out is directly beneath

384

the office complex and we'll wind up right in the detention area. They keep to a diurnal circadian rhythm just like we do, which means we'll be hitting them at about two o'clock in the morning according to their body clocks and the guard shift should be lighter and the guys on guard should be a little less alert. Rourke would have hit them when the shifts were heavier. And there are a dozen of us and there was only one of him. No matter how good he is, he would have bought the farm."

Darkwood looked at the men clustered around him and Aldridge. "We'll be passing right under the heart of their military establishment and we'll come out right in the middle of it. We find the woman and we get her back into the tunnels and we run like hell. If we get separated, rendezvous is dockside at six hundred sharp. We've already synchronized chronometers and each of us has a death capsule. If live capture seems imminent, use the capsule. I don't like advising any man to take his own life under any circumstances, but if they learn that we know about the sensor tunnel into the lagoon, any future strategic value the tunnel could have would be lost. And someday, that could make the difference, the critical difference, for the survival of Mid-Wake. It's our only access. Any questions?"

There were no questions.

Darkwood looked at Aldridge. "We're moving." Aldridge nodded, then gestured to his Marines. Darkwood gave one last glance back, then started into the tunnel, the 9mm Lancer Caseless 2418 A2 tight in his right fist. . . .

Natalia Anastasia Tiemerovna, guards in a semicircle behind her and on both sides, stood before the triumvirate in the great marble hall.

The Chairman spoke. "In a few moments, you will be presented to the delegate of Marshal Karamatsov. You will be pleased to know that we have just received word that the marshal himself, although he could not come, was seemingly quite enthused at the prospects of your reunion, major."

"I am certain that he was," Natalia responded.

"Do you know a Captain Serovski of what is called the . . ." The Chairman seemed to consult notes before him on the three-man desk. "The KGB Elite Corps?"

"I do not know a Captain Serovski. But if he is an officer of the KGB Elite Corps, I know what kind of man he is. Evil. I will say this only once, but if you truly value the interests of the Soviet people here beneath these domes whom you represent, you will not trust Marshal Karamatsov. He has no interest in the welfare or future of the Soviet people or of anyone—other than himself. He is a ruthless, perverted butcher. I am not pleading for my life. I am simply making a statement. Despite what I have revealed concerning my defection from the KGB and my assistance to the American cause, in my soul I will always be a Russian. I left the KGB because I realized that in working to serve their interests I was working to perpetuate war and toward the eventual undoing of all people everywhere, the Soviet people most particularly. I have nothing to gain by telling you this, because you will turn me over to Serovski and he will convey me to my husband and my husband will inflict upon me the most hideous of tortures and eventually, mercifully, I will die. My cares will be over forever. But the Soviet people must not die. The Soviet people must help to rebuild our devastated world, and all people must learn to live together as one people and work for the common good. If you and your fellow members of the troika trust Vladmir Karamatsov, he will lead you only to destruction. John Rourke is dead, and with him went my will to live. John Rourke was a man like no other. But killing John Rourke will not alter the inevitability of right over wrong. There are other men—his and my friend Paul Rubenstein, his son Michael. There are women. His wife, Sarah, and his daughter, Annie. There are thousands like them, comrades. Germans, Icelandics, Americans—Russians too. They will continue to work for a day of freedom, and many who now serve my husband's evil will realize that what they do

386

serves no one but my husband and they will join with the forces that fight him. You stand at a moment in history, one that is critical to your survival. If your decision is based on the personal lust for power, your heirs will revile that decision and curse your folly. It is not too late for you. But once you have sold your souls to Vladmir Karamatsov, it will be. I have said what I wished to say. Thank you for the opportunity."

The eyes of the Chairman were unmoved.

As Natalia had known they would be.

But conscience had forced her to try.

They waited in silence, Natalia standing almost at attention, the men of the triumvirate shuffling through paperwork on their desk, her guards unmoving, the muzzles of their weapons unmoving as well. Her chance would come for death, she knew. But perhaps her death could serve a higher purpose. She had gone weaponless to her husband once in order to buy freedom for the people she loved. He had nearly killed her. This time she would not be weaponless. The razor blade in her boot, sewn in for her by one of the German craftsmen, could slice open the artery in her husband's neck before it cut open her own. Perhaps she would not die totally in vain.

She heard the click of boots in the hallway and turned her eyes toward it. She recognized Boris Feyedorovitch of the Marine Spetznas. He now wore colonel's rank. Perhaps because he was the man whose bullet had ended John Rourke's tenuous hold on life. And walking beside him, as though the senior officer, but wearing captain's rank, was a tall, thin, blonde-haired man in the black dress uniform of the KGB Elite Corps. The uniform had always reminded her of the SS of Hitler, and so had the men who wore it. His knee-high boots shone with polish, as did his pistol belt and the holster, which sagged just slightly by his appendix. His cap was at the perfect angle, uniformly correct yet jaunty. As he neared her now and their eyes met, she could see the blue coldness there.

He walked right past her, came to rigid attention, saluted the troika, and announced, "Captain Alexeii

Serovski, Elite Corps, Committee for State Security of the Soviet Union, comrades. I have the pleasure to bring compliments and greetings from our glorious leader, Hero Marshal Vladmir Karamatsov, to the government and people of this Soviet State."

Since no one in the triumvirate, although all three dressed alike, was in military uniform, he lowered the salute without waiting for it to be returned.

The Chairman responded. "Greetings, Comrade Captain Serovski, and on behalf of the Government of the Soviet People I welcome you and heartily accept the wishes of your military commander, Marshal Karamatsov. And here, comrade captain, is his prize."

It was the most animated she had seen the Chairman as he gestured expansively toward her with a sweep of his left arm.

"Thank you, Comrade Chairman."

Serovski performed a snappy right face and took a pace closer to her. Natalia watched his eyes. "Major Tiemerovna!" He saluted, but had not called her comrade. "The Hero Marshal's compliments, madame. Please kindly consider yourself under arrest on behalf of the People of the Soviet state for your various crimes against the State, among these high treason, espionage, sedition, and murder."

"Do you speak English?"

His eyes sparkled a bit. "Yes, major. I do."

"Good." Natalia smiled. "Go to hell."

Chapter Fifty-one

If the submarine had stopped, Michael Rourke could not be certain of it. He had tested the barrier and found it was electrical energy of some sort, but that it traveled in waves and was not solid. By utilizing a strip of blanket from the meager bedding in the cell, he had found where the energy was concentrated and where it was not. If the plastic cord at his wrists could not be tugged apart, rubbed apart on the frame of the cot or the edge of the toilet seat, it would have to burn apart. Utilizing more strips of the blanket he had constructed small fuses which he would put between the plastic cord and the flesh of his wrists using his teeth.

He knew that at any moment he could be discovered, but there was nothing to lose and everything to gain.

With several of the blanket fuses—which did burn—in place, he dropped to his knees, bent forward, and got his wrists as close as possible to the electrical field, swishing the long, thin fuses of blanket into the edge of the electrical field so they would catch fire. Apparently, disruption of the electrical field triggered no alarm, at least on the small scale which the fuses of blanket produced. Three of the fuses began to burn, getting closer to his wrists.

Gently, he blew on them to make them continue to burn. One went out. The two others continued to burn, one of them already causing the plastic cord which bound his wrists to smolder and smell disgustingly bad. A second fuse went out. The third one still burned, Michael closing his mind to the pain the fire caused his flesh. The odor of the plastic was getting worse and he hoped it wasn't toxic. The plastic cord smoldered and went out. But, as he craned his neck and twisted his wrists to better see, he could tell that a small portion of the plastic cord had actually burned. He turned around, still on his bare knees and began, tearing out more strips of blanket, slightly wider this time so the flames would be higher by the time they reached the cord.

If he could get his hands free, when they came for him and expected him still bound, there might be a chance. To do what, Michael Rourke wasn't certain. . . .

Serovski had ignored her, turned back to face the three leaders. "You may have already have been informed, Comrade Chairman, that just as your excellent undersea vessel was about to get under way, your men and my own had the good fortune of jointly capturing Michael Rourke, the son of the infamous John Rourke, whom the comrade marshal had been informed was killed by Comrade Colonel Feyedorovitch after a protracted gun battle with your late Colonel Kerenin."

"We were so informed, captain. I take it you wish to discuss the fate of this prisoner."

"Yes, Comrade Chairman. He is an infamous war criminal. He is wanted by my government so he can account for his crimes."

"Michael's only crime is holding my husband responsible for the death squad that caused the death of his wife and their unborn baby!"

Serovski didn't even glance at her. The guns leveled at her were pushed closer to her. Natalia remained where she was.

The Chairman spoke. "I was also given to understand

that your Marshal Karamatsov had some doubt as to this John Rourke's death. Will presenting Marshal Karamatsov with this second Rourke assuage his concerns?"

"I cannot, Comrade Chairman, speak in that context on behalf of the comrade marshal. Yet it would certainly serve, I believe, as a further symbol of trust and the desire for harmonious relations between all the Soviet peoples."

"What about the Soviet people in the Underground City in the Urals that Karamatsov tried to use his poison gas on?" She kept her voice calm, low, even. If she started sounding like an hysteric, they would likely remove her.

"I understand," the Chairman said softly, "that there is indeed some debate as to the exact nature of Marshal Karamatsov's leadership function."

"You have been fed insidious lies, Comrade Chairman, by this wretched woman. Whom do you believe? An officer who serves the Soviet Union, or an unfaithful wife who betrayed the trust placed in her so innocently by the Soviet People?"

Natalia licked her lips.

The Chairman said, "You may have the other Rourke as your prisoner. There is refreshment available. I understand that your rendezvous with Marshal Karamatsov on the island of Chinmen Tao in the Formosa Strait is scheduled for some twenty hours from now. That allows you considerable time to refresh yourself before the return trip."

"Thank you," Comrade Chairman. I request that the woman prisoner be transferred immediately to the custody of my KGB Elite Corpsmen and taken aboard the vessel which shall be used for the return trip."

"I understand your interest in her safety. But I assure you, captain, all our interests will best be served if she is allowed to continue her confinement in the detention area below us. At any event, I am afraid you must indulge me."

"I shall report this to the Hero Marshal."

"Then you shall. Please—join us now for a brief refreshment despite the hour."

"It will be my pleasure, Comrade Chairman."

The Chairman, without looking at her, said, "Return the major to her cell."

Chapter Fifty-two

The tunnel narrowed, more so than the swim-by chromatic heat scans had indicated it would, Darkwood moving on knees and elbows now, the temperature from the steam which traveled through the pipes all around them insufferably hot. But there was no choice remaining. It would have been impossible to turn around in the tunnel even had they wanted to, and crawling backwards through the tunnel would have only been more time-consuming, and they would still have faced finding another means of entering the detention area beneath the military office complex.

Aldridge was right behind him, and behind Aldridge the dozen Marine raiders.

But ahead of him now, he saw the tunnel take a bend and, if the chromatic heat scans were accurate, beyond it would lie the entrance into the detention area. Darkwood quickened his pace, reaching the bend in the tunnel, awkwardly moving around it, not envying the Marines behind him. Each man had a Soviet AKM-96 assault rifle and a backpack loaded with ammunition and explosives, and the men had some distance back given up on worming their way through the tunnel with their gear in place and now just pushed it along ahead of them. The AKM-96s were selected for the mission because the Soviet and American assault rifles were, of course, incompatible and, although the American rifle was better, the Soviet rifle was good and would allow possible ammunition resupply from captured weapons in the field.

Darkwood was around the bend now, the low-level lighting in the tunnel making it hard to tell for sure, but he thought he saw a ladder ahead. He quickened his pace as best he could, the knees in his penetration suit, despite the padding, all but gone, as were the elbows. The 2418 A2 was still tight in his right fist.

He could see it now, rubbing sweat from over his eyes with his right sleeve—a ladder. Darkwood kept moving.

The ladder went up through a wide-diameter pipe and he couldn't see as of yet where the ladder finally ended up. He kept moving, taking his flash from the pouch on his left upper arm, setting it to lowest level only, and moving ahead.

He stopped at the base of the ladder. There was a hatchway that looked as though it were taken off a submarine. And it was indeed fortunate that this John Rourke hadn't tried coming this way, or the man would have been trapped. There was no access wheel on this side of the hatch.

Darkwood exhaled so loudly that he realized it sounded like a sigh. This was not a permanent obstacle, only a delay. They had explosives with them which could easily have blown the hatch, but the resultant explosion would not only deafen them in the confined space of the tunnel, but might kill them as well. There was the ancillary benefit that the noise of the explosion would alert every security man and Marine Spetznas in the area.

"This isn't an explosives job," he said aloud to Sam Adlridge behind him. "Which one of your men has the magnetic pick?"

"Harkness—job for you. Up the ladder, corporal."

"Yes, sir."

Darkwood pushed past the access pipe and so did Aldridge, and so did Stanhope.

Harkness—short for a Marine but solidly built—moved forward on knees and elbows and stood up into the pipe. "Could one of you gentlemen please pass up my pack, sirs?"

Darkwood reached for it, but Stanhope already had it.

"Whatchya need, Harkness?"

"The magnetic pick, of course, sir, and the clamps. But I can't get the clamps up here while I'm using the pick."

"Pick coming up," Stanhope grunted. "I'll be standing by with the clamps, corporal—tell me when."

"Yes, sir. Thank you, sir."

Harkness's voice sounded hollow, reverberating out of the pipe. Darkwood hoped it wasn't traveling through into the detention area that should be directly above. "Keep the noise to a minimum, corporal, please."

"Yes, sir."

Darkwood wiped his right sleeve across his forehead again, hearing the scratching sounds of the magnetic pick being positioned. If it worked right and the operating wheel for the hatch had any ferrous metal in it, the wheel could be worked open from this side. If the operating wheel weren't metal at all, it was back to the unpleasant prospect of using explosives on it.

Darkwood shone his light against the face of his chronometer. Unlike most men these days, he still preferred analog readouts rather than digital, but digital was necessary, so he had saved his money and purchased a Steinmetz, the only handmade watch on the market. It had sucked up two months' pay like water through a drinking straw, but he had never regretted the purchase. Aside from dual display, it was the best diving chronometer made.

And the Steinmetz showed Darkwood that he was running out of time. If he didn't get the woman in time to allow sufficient travel time back to the docks, and then swim-out time through the sonar tunnel, if Sebastian followed orders, the Reagan would move from its position near the Pillars of Woe and head for the open sea.

Both the analog and digital displays of the Steinmetz kept ticking away . . . .

Had the situation been as it was when she had been in the detention area before, as soon as she was left alone she would have freed the razor blade from inside her boot top

395

and taken her own life.

But Natalia Anastasia Tiemerovna realized now that, although she might save herself, she would be acting in a cowardly fashion. And there were more important considerations to take into account. She might be able to kill her husband. But more importantly than that, she had to attempt to aid Michael. With his father dead, he would be more vital than ever. And it was what John Rourke would have wanted her to do.

She had been taken from the great marble hall and held in an antechamber for some time, and without a word as to why, she had then been ordered to move on and started down toward the detention area.

She had cooperated.

Escape was impossible and her goal now was not escape, but to reach the submarine aboard which Michael was incarcerated, at best to help Michael to escape, at worst to be taken to her husband and to have the chance to murder him, slaughter him like the animal that he was.

Her six guards completely encircled her as they descended along the moving staircase toward the lowest level of the detention area where the maximum-security and suicide-watch cells were located. She hoped they would not order her to undress again.

At the base of the moving staircase as they started to turn into the corridor, she heard something, and so too apparently did the leader of the guard detail. The leader, one of the three women, signaled a halt to the detail and called out along the corridor—in Russian, of course— inquiring if something were wrong. An answer came back that a chair had been overturned. The woman seemed to consider this, then physically shrugged and ordered detail and prisoner ahead.

Natalia sensed something. She did not know what. She slowly began focusing energy, preparing herself. But who? Had Michael escaped the submarine and come looking for her? Had they told Michael she was here? For a fleeting instant she thought of, and almost said aloud, the name of John Rourke. But he was dead and—

There was movement to her right as they entered the detention cell block and she dodged left, figures in black darting from an unelectrified cell, others from behind a desk, two others dropping from the ceiling.

The leader of the guard detail was the only one armed with an assault rifle instead of one of the dart pistols, and Natalia hurtled herself at the woman, Natalia's left hand grabbing for the rifle as her right hand went for the throat. She hammered the guard-detail leader to the floor. There were thudding sounds, muted cries, all around her, Natalia's left hand pinning the assault rifle to the floor, her right hand releasing the woman's throat for an instant, then balling into a fist and crossing the woman's jaw hard once, then again and again, the woman's body going limp under her.

Natalia started to grab for the rifle. A gloved man's hand reached it simultaneously. "You must be Major Tiemerovna. I mean, you do speak English, right?"

She tracked the voice to the face, her hand and his hand still on the rifle. He stood over her, crouched slightly, in his right hand a pistol that looked vaguely similar to a Beretta 92F but with an impossibly long extension magazine. "I speak English."

"Good. I'm Commander Jason Darkwood, Captain of the United States Attack Submarine Reagan. You're John Rourke's friend."

There was no hesitation when he said the word "friend," as if he were making more of it. "How do you know?"

"Well, Doctor Rourke told us about you for—"

She was to her feet before she realized it, the palms of her hands flat against his chest. His dark brown eyes sparkled with a mixture of amusement and concern, and what she could see of his face beneath the hood which covered his hair and obscured the sides of his face seemed to exude strength. "John is—"

"Alive? You bet he is, ma'am." She turned to the new voice. A black man. About the same height as the white man against whose chest her hands still rested. "I don't know if he got the chance to mention me before he fell off that balcony, but I'm Captain Sam Aldridge, United States Marine Corps. John Rourke was being operated on but the notion was that he'd be fine. Had the best doctor at Mid-Wake. So, unless something went wrong, ma'am . . ."

She turned from the man named Darkwood and threw her arms around the black Marine captain's neck and kissed him full on the lips. "Thank you—bless you." She inhaled, feeling light-headed suddenly as if she were going to faint. She looked at the other man, the first man, went to him, embraced him, and kissed his cheek.

"I like that—the Marine gets a kiss on the lips ands the Navy guy who got him here gets a kiss on the cheek."

"Hey, what can I say, Jason?" She heard the black Marine captain laugh.

She rectified the situation and kissed Darkwood on the lips. And she felt herself going faint and his arms going around her. . . .

Natalia opened her eyes. It hadn't been a dream. The man named Darkwood and the man named Sam something looked down at her. Her head was resting on something, and she realized it was a backpack. Both Darkwood and Sam had removed their hoods. Sam had close-cropped kinky hair and a high forehead. Darkwood's hair looked almost too long for a Naval officer's and was richly dark and rumpled with curls. Darkwood smiled down at her, "I don't usually have that effect on women, Major Tiemerovna."

She felt her cheeks flush with embarrassment. "And I'm not usually the fainting type. It's just that—I thought—"

"I understand you and Doctor Rourke have been close for quite some years, major. If you thought he was dead and now you know he isn't, well, the reaction's purely understandable. You up to travelling? I think we need to get out of here."

Sam nodded. "That's for sure."

"Both of you—all of you." She looked at the two officers and the twelve men, most of them clustered near her, some guarding the entrance to the detention cells. "I can never repay you."

"That kiss was good enough for me." Darkwood smiled. She felt herself blushing again. "How about you, Captain Aldridge?"

"Good enough for me, too, Captain."

She sat up. "Easy, ma'am." Sam—Aldridge, that's what it was—warned her.

"I'm—ahh—fine, really."

"I wasn't sure what kind of person to expect. We don't usually go around rescuing Soviet officers. And if you're five centuries old, well I've just gotten a new insight into older women."

"Please, commander—or should I say captain?"

"My rank's commander, my position is Captain. Call me Jason, major. Makes it easier."

"Jason—Sam. Please. I am Natalia."

"All right, Natalia. I think we have to get going."

He helped her to her feet. Then he handed her a pistol like the one she had seen him holding. She looked at the flat of the slide. "U.S. Government Model 2418 A2, Cal 9mm L.C." It had an ambidextrous safety, an ambidextrous slide release, and balanced well. "How many rounds?"

"Thirty with that extension magazine, plus one in the chamber, 9mm Lancer Caseless. Maximum effective combat range seventy-five yards, if you're good."

"I'm good." She smiled.

"If you're that good, take these." And he handed her a shoulder-slung black bag. It was a magazine case, and as she draped it cross body she could tell by feel there were six magazines in it. "Is there a pocket in that thing you're wearing?"

"Yes."

"Here—the standard magazine. Fifteen rounds." Darkwood handed her a standard-length double-column magazine and she pocketed it.

399

"Are we going to get Michael or is there another team out?"

"Who's Michael?" Aldridge asked her.

Her heart sank for a moment. "He's John Rourke's son. They have him prisoner aboard the submarine which just came in."

She saw a worried look enter Jason Darkwood's pretty eyes. "A little boy, huh?"

"He's thirty years old."

"Then how old is Rourke?" Sam Aldridge asked her. "He looks like he's in his middle to late thirties."

"He is."

"Then how can he have a thirty-year old son?" Darkwood asked.

"Trust me—there's no time to explain."

Darkwood looked at her. "All right, we try for the son. But we still have to get out of here."

"The tunnel, Captain?" Aldridge asked.

Darkwood looked at him. "Gonna have to be." He looked at Natalia. "Were they taking you with Rourke's son?"

"Yes. I was supposed to be a peace offering to my husband. He's the commander of the Soviet forces on the surface. He has a very powerful army and is trying to obtain nuclear capabilities. He's an evil man. If this Soviet state allies with Marshal Karamatsov—"

"Your husband?"

"Yes," she told Aldridge. "If there is an alliance, there will be a nuclear war again. I'm sure of it. And the atmosphere on the surface couldn't take it, and I think it would mean the end of everything this time. For good."

"Our friends under the domes have nuclear capabilities and have strong interests in conquering the surface, it appears—has appeared for some time," Darkwood told her. "You might be right about that alliance." He exhaled loudly. "You're saying that without you as a gift to him—a peace offering—and without Rourke's son, the alliance might go in the dumper for a little bit?"

"It would be impeded—yes." She nodded. "And for

400

God's sake . . ." There was an odd look in Darkwood's eyes. "What did I say?"

"It just sounded odd for a Soviet officer to invoke God."

"If it looks like things are going bad . . ." But she really didn't know what to say.

"I get the idea."

She wondered if he did.

"We're leaving, major—stick close." Darkwood called to Aldridge, who was already starting further back into the detention-cell block. "Sam—have your security stick about two minutes behind us and have 'em pick up any weapons."

"Will do—security team—you have the word?"

"We have the word, sir," a young voice sang back. Darkwood was already moving. Natalia fell in after him.

Chapter Fifty-three

John Rourke looked at the Rolex that was back on his left wrist, mentally making the adjustment to Mid-Wake time. It was five o'clock in the morning. He had risen an hour before, slept out with almost eight hours, restless to begin the day. He had showered, bandages replaced the previous evening, after Jacob Fellows had left, by waterproof spray-on material which protected the wound, yet was flexible enough for greater ease of movement and sufficiently porous to advance healing of the skin beneath. Biodegradable, it would eventually disappear of its own accord.

He felt good.

Ellen had been in the room by the time he had exited the shower, and had chided him as he had returned to the small bathroom to dress. It was too soon for him to be moving around so much. He had no business getting dressed in street clothes (he had asked for and received them the previous night), and where did he think he was going anyway?

As he left the bathroom, Ellen turned around from the window. "Don't you ever sleep?"

"I told you. Some patients are special."

"So are some nurses," Rourke told her honestly. He was starting to pull the black-knit top over his head and when he raised his arms he had a surge of pain.

"What is it?" She was beside him.

He smiled. "Not my operations." The forearm wound was nearly healed, as was the head wound, he had

402

noticed. "Just a muscle. I'm a little stiff from inactivity. And I think I took kind of a beating when I fell off that balcony."

"Got shot off, you mean. Here—you let me do that—nice and easy."

She had adopted him, he decided. But he let her help get the shirt over his head and help him to ease his arms through the sleeves. As he pulled it down, she started buttoning the plaquet front. "All dressed up like some kind of damn commando—where do you think you're going?"

"If by six A.M. your time Mid-Wake hasn't heard that my friend Major Tiemerovna is free, I'm going after her myself."

"They just gonna give you a submarine?"

"Hopefully. Otherwise, I'll have to take one. Relax—I bounce back quick and this twenty-fifth-century medicine is great. I was accessing some stuff off the bedside computer. You work miracles nowadays—I do feel like a witch doctor."

"Well, it's just stuff. I mean, a doctor's a doctor. You'd pick up on it."

He smiled at her. "I'll never be able to repay you."

She turned away from him and walked back toward the windows. "Look—ahh—I know you're married. I heard that. And I know about this Russian lady major." And she turned around from the window very suddenly and came toward him. "But you can always use a friend, can't you?"

John Rourke walked toward her and folded her into his arms and she leaned her head against his chest. "Always, Ellen," he told her. . . .

Michael Rourke's wrists were blistered but, as he tugged at the nearly burned-through plastic cord, the cord finally snapped. He saw no one in the companionway outside the brig, already massaging his wrists despite the blisters to get full feeling back into his fingers, hands, and forearms. The cord could be turned into a garrote and, if he could steal a weapon, even one of those dart guns, he might have a chance. If his father and Natalia were alive, they could be aboard the submarine. If they weren't aboard the submarine, they might be wherever it was headed—if it hadn't gotten there already. There were possibilities.

And anyplace was better than here.

Chapter Fifty-four

Sebastian sat in the command chair of the Reagan. He consulted the digital timepiece inset in the armrest and looked away from it. The timepiece readout was most distressing. Doctor Margaret Barrow stood beside him. "Well? Are you or aren't you, Sebastian?"

"Margaret—I have orders. Not only do I have orders, but the orders are indisputably correct. Allowing for the maximum amount of time for all facets of the Captain's plan, allowing for additional delays that might never be foreseen, a return by six A.M. Mid-Wake time is certainly an appropriate deadline. We cannot rely on our sonar-drag array and the Pillars of Woe themselves masking our presence here forever. Not only is it my responsibility to await the Captain's return, but it is also my responsibility to provide for the safety and the lives of the rest of the crew—yours included. At the appointed time, I will follow orders and head for the open sea, and as soon as conditions of proximity permit, I will communicate with Admiral Rahn in order to request further instructions—if Commander Darkwood and his party have not returned. Some time still remains, may I remind you."

"Barely enough time for them to make the swim."

"Jason is quite resourceful, as is Captain Aldridge and Lieutenant Stanhope. Perhaps they will avail themselves of some other means of transportation."

"Sure," she snapped, he thought a bit sarcastically. "Maybe they'll steal an Island Class Soviet sub!"

He hardly thought so. . . .

"We'll have to steal it."

"An Island Class sub?"

"Sure—it'd look terrific over my mantelpiece anyway." Darkwood smiled.

Aldridge didn't smile. Darkwood shrugged. "Look," and Darkwood studied the Russian woman's eyes a moment—they were very pretty and unbelievably blue—and then he looked back toward the Island Class sub. "If we board that vessel, alarms are going to sound and in general all hell is going to break loose, right? We may have time to get aboard, but we won't be able to get back off and into the water and swim out—without getting ourselves killed. And if there's a general alarm, the sharks might roam free in the lagoon too. We'd never make it out alive. And we have no idea what condition this Michael Rourke is in, and we might also sustain some casualties ourselves. That'd slow us down even more. But if we take command of the sub, we can shoot our way out." He looked at the Steinmetz on his left wrist. "And the most telling argument of all, gentlemen, major, is that we are flat out of time. We could never make the swim-out to the Reagan in time to intercept it before Sebastian follows his orders and heads for the open sea. But even if they send an Island Classer against us, we'll still have a little jump on them and can link up with the Reagan and fight our way home if we have to. Plus, it might be nice to see just what's inside the tubes on that missile deck. Agreed?"

No one said they disagreed.

"Good—Sam, you go take that submarine for me." Darkwood grinned.

Aldridge started to speak, then shook his head, trying to hold back laughter.

"All right—here's what to do," Darkwood said seriously. "Tom—you and the two guys already in the water and two more men swim up to the Island Class and come aboard from her starboard side by the hydrofoil-launch berth. Use the PV-26s unless you feel more force is the only way to achieve the objective. I'd rather we avoid making any more noise than we have to."

Stanhope nodded.

Darkwood weighed his pistol in his fist. "Those people on board should be expecting our charming companion to arrive sometime shortly. So what if she arrives a little early, huh?" And Darkwood smiled. . . .

Colonel Harley Wilkes, the ordnance expert, arrived in uniform this time. By Rourke's Rolex, it was exactly five-thirty A.M. here, meaning that in a half hour the immediate disposition of Natalia's fate would be known—either this Jason Darkwood had succeeded or failed.

"Thank you for coming at such an ungodly hour, colonel."

"It's not bad if you've been up all night, indulging a whim, doctor."

Rourke looked the old Marine in the eye. "I apologize for the inconvenience."

"You should sir—and the apology is accepted. I believe I have your special ammunition, although for the life of me I cannot see why our own pistols wouldn't suffice for your needs."

"As a soldier, colonel, you should know that a man fights better with a familiar weapon."

"Very true." The ordnance man nodded. "True." He opened a small box-like attaché case, took from it a red plastic ammunition box, and handed it to John Rourke. Rourke opened it. There was no headstamp and the brass was a little off color. "There is your ammunition, sir."

"Looks good—how does it shoot?"

"We all but perfectly matched the velocity figures you gave us. There's less powder because our powders are

407

mixed differently and our priming compound is more powerful. Chamber pressures seem to be quite reasonable and recoil is not as pronounced as I would have thought this old caliber should be."

"Can I try them out?"

"There's a rifle and pistol range in the academic complex across the way. I anticipated your request. I'll call for a nurse and a wheelchair."

John Rourke stood up. "That won't be necessary, thank you, colonel." He judged another twenty-five minutes remained until the moment of truth. . . .

The walk actually felt good, Rourke's perception of his overall fitness level pleasantly surprising to him. The air here, despite the fact that it was canned, felt fresh against the skin, and he almost thought that he detected a breeze, although such would have been all but impossible. The black BDU pants and the black knit shirt were comfortably cut, the Mid-Wake-issue combat boots with their deck-style soles made for almost effortless wear, and at his waist he had a brass-buckled web belt, identical for all intents and purposes to the military-issue belts of five centuries ago.

The educational complex was imposing, and as they entered it Rourke began a dialogue with Colonel Wilkes. There were grammar schools and high schools servicing each of the primary living areas (of which there were two separate from this) in addition to the educational complex which they were now entering. In this complex were housed special elementary and secondary schools for the gifted, as well as the university and the Naval Academy. The Naval Academy was the one and only military academy and turned out naval and Marine officers. The closest thing to an Army was the Marine Corps (and there were also security police, for which no degree but considerable specialized training was required). To have had an Army when there was no land on which they could fight would have been as silly as having an Air

408

Force when there was no air through which they could fly, Rourke realized.

Here also were Mid-Wake's specialty schools for doctors of medicine and dentistry, the hospital (Mid-Wake's only medical facility aside from smaller clinics) conveniently located to mesh with the integrated program of the teaching facilities. Nursing was as respected a profession as ever, Wilkes confirmed when Rourke questioned him, the requirements in nurses' training nearly as stringent as those for medical doctors.

Here as well were the research centers which provided much of the scientific base for Mid-Wake's technology.

The range was one of several located throughout Mid-Wake, civilian marksmanship encouraged and each man and woman, in the style of the twentieth-century and pre-twentieth-century Swiss, a citizen soldier and required to qualify biannually. The private ownership of firearms beyond the issue military weapons was encouraged, and most businesses and social organizations had rifle or pistol teams. Crime was almost non-existent, and Rourke was reminded of the often quoted remark of the twentieth-century literary futurist Robert A. Heinlein that an "armed society is a polite society."

The range facility was extraordinary in its completeness and integration of computerization. Targets were controlled by computer and could be used in preprogrammed drills or individually programmed. Hits were immediately posted on a computer screen near the firing positions, as well as velocity at the muzzle and at point of impact. Specialized programs were available to measure reaction time, the effects of perceived recoil, etc.

Rourke and Colonel Wilkes were met by a female captain, Wilkes's chief assistant in the ordnance section. She had his pistols and when she gave them to him, John Rourke immediately field-stripped the twin Detonics .45s and inspected them. They had been indeed well cared for. The skillful combination of subtly different stainless steel alloys used in their production had not only withstood the test of five centuries, but the test of salt water. He was told by the woman, a Captain Harriet Bowles, that there had been a few minor rust spots found on the one of the two pistols inscribed with his name, along the slide top strap, which was slightly matted to reduce glare. These had been quickly removed and, despite their saltwater dousing and their age, the guns looked—she sounded amazed—brand new.

Rourke was not amazed and had expected no less.

With mild trepidation, Rourke loaded four of the six-round magazines and fed them up the wells of the two reassembled pistols. Dry feeding was faultless. He felt encouraged. Harriet Bowles programmed the computer to individual combat.

At a flashing-light cue, the computer-controlled electronic targets rotated into position and Rourke, a Detonics .45 in each hand, engaged the various targets, the program telling him that he had 1.5 seconds to reload. He had one pistol reloaded and firing and reloaded the second as he continued the string.

He looked at the computer screen. All twelve shots from the first strings and eleven out of the subsequent twelve shots had registered in the K-zone. The twelfth shot had registered just beneath the K-zone and, on a human target, would have been a kill.

Functioning had been flawless and perceived recoil had been essentially what he was used to. He worked his way through fifty rounds in addition to the twelve he had already fired, selecting at random from several of the boxes of ammunition provided for him.

At the conclusion, he loaded both pistols and stuffed them into the waistband of his trousers beneath the black knit shirt. "Colonel Wilkes. Captain Bowles. Your work has been extraordinary and you are both to be commended. How many rounds are there available to me?" He had removed muffs and shooting glasses.

"We'd like to keep a small supply for our own experimentation and in the event the load should ever need to be duplicated, for use as a benchmark."

"Certainly, captain. How many rounds are available to

me?"

"A thousand?"

"Precisely or more or less?"

"I'd say precisely." Colonel Wilkes smiled.

"Excellent." Rourke smiled. He was loading his spare magazines as he spoke. "I don't think I'll need that much, really." He glanced at his wristwatch. It was five minutes after six Mid-Wake time.

Rourke reached under his shirt and drew both pistols. He had chamber-loaded them. He thumbed back the hammers, Captain Bowles's pretty green eyes widening. Colonel Wilkes took a hesitant step toward him and stopped.

"What's the—"

"It's a little after six. Let's go wake up your President and see if he's expecting my friend Major Tiemerovna to arrive. And if he isn't, I'm about to introduce a new industry into your economy. It's called 'rent a sub'; and if we can find a way of keeping the rates affordable, who knows? Now—these pistols, cocked and locked, will be under my shirt and easy to get at. I'm sorry if I appear to be abusing the excellent hospitality shown me by everyone here. If my friend Major Tiemerovna hasn't been heard from and if your President doesn't want to loan me a submarine and a crew, I'm taking one. Shall we?" And Rourke inclined his head toward the exit from the range. He thought Captain Bowles was suppressing a laugh. . . .

Natalia Anastasia Tiemerovna walked surrounded by men in Marine Spetznas uniforms, Sty-20 pistols and PV-26 shark guns aimed at her. But her blood surged and she felt a freedom of spirit she had not known since her captivity began. She was not only escaping, or trying to, but striking back. Each of the men who had rescued her had had in his gear a Soviet Marine Spetznas uniform. She thought Jason Darkwood and Sam Aldridge looked particularly charming in theirs.

411

As they approached the gangplank leading up to the Island Class submarine, Jason Darkwood whispered to her in Russian, "The language is one of the qualifications for graduation from the Naval Academy at Mid-Wake. And three times each year there's a proficiency test that has to be passed, and if it isn't you are sent into remedial classes until you can pass. Good thing, huh?"

She couldn't answer him, but she wanted to laugh. And she couldn't do that either.

They were almost at the base of the gangplank, two Marine Spetznas privates on guard there with AKM-96 assault rifles. But both Darkwood and Aldridge wore captain's rank.

The two men on guard snapped to attention as they detected the approach. Natalia forced her expression into one of sadness instead of one of happiness. She stopped when appropriately prodded by a Sty-20.

Darkwood pushed past her almost rudely and addressed the two young privates. "You are not prepared for our arrival! Where is your officer?"

"Comrade captain," the nearer of the two men, sandy-haired and pale-cheeked, began, then stammered, "We—we were—were not alerted to your arrival, comrade captain."

"Consider yourselves alerted now, corporal. Step aside!"

The two privates exchanged worried glances. The one who had spoken before coughed, his voice a little shaky as he spoke. "Excuse me, comrade captain. But we were given specific orders that—that—no one . . . And this other officer?" The young private was staring at Sam Aldridge's black skin.

Darkwood smiled and took a step closer to the young private. "This courageous officer standing beside me was the only man to volunteer out of a group of fifteen handpicked officers for a very dangerous assignment to infiltrate Mid-Wake, the success of which was predicated upon his skin being dyed and his features surgically altered so that he could pose as an American of African extraction. As you can see, the effect is quite convincing. And now as to you, private. You have passed your security inspection well, young comrade." Natalia was having a very hard time not laughing. His impression of a Soviet officer was very, very good. "I take it the majority of the crew is ashore and for this reason your guard is necessary?"

"Yes, comrade captain," the young man enthused, evidently pleased with what seemed to be the current turn of events.

"Your zeal in the execution of your duty has earned you a reward, young comrade." Darkwood said quickly. Both of his hands were cupped together as though holding something, and slowly now he began to spread them slightly apart. The young private who had done all of the talking leaned forward to look. The second private started to lean over to look as well. Darkwood's right fist caught the sandy-haired boy with an upper cut, Aldridge taking a long-strided step forward and executing a neat left hook across the second guard's forward jutting jaw. As Darkwood caught the first guard and his rifle and Aldridge and one of the other Marines caught up the second man, Darkwood looked at Natalia. "It works every time—the old curiosity-killed-the-cat thing."

"Very funny—skin dyed, features surgically altered—shit!"

"What'd you want me to say, Sam—the guy's eyes were just deceiving him?"

There were no other remarks exchanged, Darkwood shouldering one man and Aldridge the second, two of the U.S. Marines taking the AKM-96s of the guards and also taking up their posts as Aldridge and Darkwood started up the gangplank. Natalia looked around them, worried that someone had seen, but the hour was still early and she saw no sign that what had transpired so briefly had been detected. In the company of the rest of the Marines, she started up the gangplank after Darkwood and Aldridge.

The gangplank linked to the hull of the aircraft-carrier-sized submarine between the forward section of the sail and the missile deck. She slowed her pace as she saw two officers and four enlisted men coming from the far side of the sail.

Darkwood and Aldridge stopped in their tracks. Before either of the two Russian Naval officers could speak, Darkwood began, "It is fortunate you men happened along. My comrades and I are on special security detail and we found both of these men unconscious at the base of the gangplank. This officer with me is in disguise for a special mission which will entail his posing as an American officer of African descent in order to actually penetrate Mid-Wake military command. Is everything in order here?"

The two officers—both junior in rank to the rank Darkwood and Aldridge wore—almost fell over themselves to respond, Darkwood lowering his human burden to the deck, then rising to his full height. He cut off both of the young Naval officers before they could speak. "I am sorry, comrades, but I'm afraid that there is only one thing to do."

Aldridge had set down the man he carried as well.

The shorter of the two Naval officers finally got a word out. "Comrade Captain, I do not—"

Darkwood raised his left hand palm outward signaling for a cessation to the conversation, then turned to Aldridge and the Marines. "Comrades, show these officers and their men what I mean, please." Six PV-26 shark guns swept up to assault positions and fired instantly once, then once again, Darkwood standing stock still as the Soviet personnel almost surrounding him took the hits, began to stagger, fall. He looked at Natalia and smiled. "We also take marksmanship training very seriously at Mid-Wake. Good thing too, huh?"

She couldn't help herself. She started to laugh. Aldridge and his men started hauling bodies out of sight toward the sail. . . .

Michael Rourke had wrapped the nylon restraint around his wrists, both ends of it secured to thick strips of the blanket and balled inside his fists. He had been shouting for help for what he subjectively considered six minutes, not wishing to look at his wristwatch, which, curiously, they had left him.

And finally, someone was coming.

It was a solitary guard, his only visible weapon holstered at his right side. Michael was kneeling on the floor, and as the guard approached he bent forward, moaning, shouting for help.

The guard spoke to him in Russian and Michael looked up from his knees, resuming his pleading for help just in case the guard did speak English, insisting that he had been stricken with terrible abdominal pains and could barely straighten up.

The guard turned a key in a panel on the far side of the electrified barrier and there was a brief crackle and the barrier was down. The guard drew his pistol and approached, Michael slumping to his side, breathing loudly and rapidly. The guard bent over him, the pistol pointed at Michael's face.

The guard touched Michael's head. Michael dodged his head right and rolled his body against the man's legs. The guard started to stumble and Michael was up, stepping inside the man's right arm to nullify the potential of the pistol for an instant, his fists wide apart now, the cord twisting around the guard's neck as Michael threw his body weight against the gun arm, pinning it to the cell wall, both fists tugging at the cord as hard as he could, the guard sputtering, choking, his face purpling, Michael's right knee smashing up into the groin. He could hear the pistol falling to the floor from the guard's hand as the body started to go limp.

Michael let go of the cord and let the body slide down along the wall. He hadn't killed the man. The man had come to see what the noise was about, come into the cell. He wouldn't repay the man with death.

He picked up the pistol and quickly searched the body

415

for spare magazines. There were none. Michael aimed the pistol toward the guard, the man's normal color returning, moans coming from him. Michael shot the man in the right thigh, the dart pistol making a soft, thwacking sound as the dart impacted. He watched as the guard started to drift off, the head lolling to the side.

Michael checked the man's breathing as he stripped him of his clothes. . . .

As they had started into the hatchway beside the sail, the second Marine Corps officer and his divers came over the side, weapons brandished. Darkwood smiled at them. "Right on time—secure the deck here. Those are our men at the base of the gangplank, Mr. Stanhope."

"Aye, sir."

Then Darkwood led Natalia and Aldridge and the rest of his Marines into the ship. The scuba gear these men used fascinated her. Wings—called Sea Wings, Darkwood had told her. They were positioned at approximately the balance point of the supine human body and powered by hydrogen extraction from the water, controlled through sensor leads in the diving helmet to respond to the diver's needs in terms of direction and speed. The wings also eliminated the need for any sort of buoyancy compensator. The helmet was fitted with a hemo sponge, extracting oxygen from the water, the gas transfer accomplished by normal respiration with the aid of a carbon-dioxide exhaust valve in the top of the helmet. No tanks were required, and no regulators either. He had told her that the divers could even talk to one another under water. Their suit was two-layered, one layer designed to constantly remain equal to the pressure of the sea around it, the other to duplicate normal atmospheric pressure. Thus there was unlimited air supply, unlimited bottom time without ever a need for decompression, and diving could be accomplished at depths in earlier eras thought impossible. The wings looked beautiful, almost translucent. She wanted to try this technique very badly if she someay could.

Natalia had been given back the military pistol and she
eld it out ahead of her like a wand to ward off death as
ne followed Darkwood and Aldridge down through the
ail and into what she realized had to be the bridge of the
sland Class submarine. Electronic gear was everywhere,
ne bridge itself large enough to be used as a small
ymnasium, seating for at least two dozen technicans,
omputer terminals and communications equipment
verywhere.

Darkwood broke into English. "Sam—leave one man
ith me. Major Tiemerovna will stay here as well to help
ut. We'll keep the bridge secure and get things started
p here. Toss anybody you find into the brig if you don't
ave to kill them. We may need some special expertise.
Corporal Harkness?"

"Aye, sir?"

"You're pretty good at figuring out how to work
nings. Think if we stayed in contact for consultation you
ould fire up the reactors so we could get moving?"

"I'll need a hand, sir—but yes sir, I think so."

"Let me—my Russian is perfect and I had a lot of
echnical training five centuries ago. I learned a lot about
ubmarines and nuclear reactors so that I could sabotage
nem."

Darkwood looked at her. Then he turned to the young
nan he had called Corporal Harkness. "Suit you, Hark-
ess?"

"Yes, sir."

"Major Tiemerovna, Corporal Harkness—welcome to
ne Navy—stick with Captain Aldridge until he's secured
ne engineering spaces where you'll be working." He
ooked at Sam Aldridge. "I can make do with just one
nan up here." And now he spoke as he surveyed the
ridge. "Everybody—stay armed and stay on top of
nings. We're doing this pretty fast and we could miss
omebody. Now move out. And let's find that young
Rourke fellow!"

Natalia stuck beside Harkness as they followed Al-

dridge and his security detail deeper into the Soviet
vessel. . . .

The ship was nearly deserted, which confirmed M
chael Rourke's suspicions that it had indeed come int
port. Moving through the vast, empty vessel from deck t
deck reminded him of when he had set out alone fron
the Retreat, investigating mysterious lights in the ligh
sky which he had thought might be the returning Ede
Project. He had only found an old aircraft, its origin sti
a mystery to him, its secrets dead with its pilot. But th
land he had traversed had been barren and lifeless, a
this place was. But less frightening. He had dressed i
the full uniform of the downed Soviet guard and he kep
his pistol holstered in the event that he would stumbl
onto Soviet personnel, hoping he could fool them lon
enough to get close enough to take them out. These littl
dart guns were too slow to take effect and would make
better bludgeon.

He kept moving, a steady low hum attracting him a
he came amidships. The reactor, he assumed. As h
turned down into another companionway, Michae
Rourke came almost face to face with a squad of men i
Soviet uniforms. And with them—"Natalia!" She wa
surrounded by them. "Natalia—run for it!" He drew hi
pistol, readied to fire it, something that looked like
bigger version of the same kind of pistol being thrus
toward him by the nearest of the Soviet uniformed me
around her.

There was something that wasn't right—a Russia
officer with black skin?

Natalia screamed. "Michael! No! They're Amer
cans!"

Michael froze, the gun on line, his finger inside th
trigger guard almost drawing the trigger back.

The black man spoke. "If you don't look like you
father lookin' at himself in a mirror."

"You are American."

418

Natalia came forward and threw her arms around him. "Where's my dad?" He asked her. "Is he—"

"I think he's fine," Natalia whispered, just holding him tight.

Michael Rourke looked into the black man's eyes. "Far as we know, your dad's on the mend." "Took a hell of a fall and got himself all shot up. But, far as we know—"

"Thank God," and Michael Rourke closed his eyes and held Natalia close to him. . . .

"I understand you are armed, Doctor Rourke."

"That is correct, Mr. President."

"What am I to make of that?"

John Rourke had sat down opposite the President's desk. He was beginning to feel a little tired from all the walking. But his strength was definitely returning. The abdomen hadn't bothered him at all. He answered the President. "Sir—I take it there has been no word that Major Tiemerovna has been freed."

"Doctor Rourke—even if the operation had gone off schedule by just an hour—"

"What were the orders for the Reagan?"

Jacob Fellows looked at him frankly. "I imagine you suspect what they were, Doctor Rourke."

"If contact wasn't made, pull out. If it was, send a coded signal."

"Something like that. And we've had no coded signal. But we should hear from the Reagan within another hour asking for further instructions."

"How's that other ship—the Wayne?"

"Ready to sail, Doctor Rourke. Why?"

"I'm going after Major Tiemerovna myself. If your commandoes could get in there so can I, if you'll lend me the ship and a crew to get me there and some scuba gear."

"And what if I don't?"

"I'll put a gun to your head, Mr. President, and somehow I think that will get me the cooperation I

419

need." Rourke had put his cards on the table. He waited for Jacob Fellows now to do the same.

"It would have to be a crew of volunteers."

"Fine—but I'll go in myself."

"You have a deal. Maybe even if Darkwood's mission was a total failure, you might have a chance. They wouldn't expect the same stunt pulled twice in rapid succession."

"I agree, Mr. President," John Rourke told him. He would have told him almost anything to get the ship, the crew, and the scuba gear for the chance to try to save Natalia. . . .

Paul Rubenstein had begun hearing the gunfire at least a couple of miles back and as he had drawn nearer to it, he'd stopped the vehicle, left it, and proceeded on foot. It was emanating from the Chinese camp or very near to it. There was a succession of ridges and valleys, the Chinese camp located on a hill within two miles of one of the higher ridges, and Paul Rubenstein, the Soviet half-track truck parked at the base of the ridge, scaled the ridge in order to assess what was happening. As he reached the top of the ridge, he uncased the Soviet binoculars that had been in the truck. He liked the German ones better.

As the auto focus of the binoculars took over, he was able to see the Chinese camp clearly. A defensive perimeter had been established, but it appeared that there was little happening. Mortars were being fired into it by two mortar teams located well out of range of conventional small-arms fire. There was no sign of the gas trucks.

He asked himself what Otto Hammerschmidt would have done.

The answer was obvious. Move the camp while they waited for Chinese and German reinforcements to arrive and safely escort the gas out of the range of Soviet influence. But he would have maintained the original Chinese camp for appearances' sake. There seemed to be sporadic machine-gun fire coming from the Chinese camp, aimed uselessly toward the mortar emplacements that were pounding it.

And if he wanted to find out what had become of his wife, Annie, and the others, the most logical if least expeditious means seemed to be helping out the defenders of the Chinese camp below.

Paul Rubenstein started back down the ridge. He could take the long way around the valley and come up behind the mortar emplacements. If he could strike quickly and if the Chinese still defending the camp caught on, there was a chance.

He quickened his pace. . . .

The gunfire from the original campsite was clearly audible, but the Soviet mortars sounded more loudly. As Annie Rubenstein stared down into the valley, she realized she was listening to her own future. The Soviet commander, Captain Grubaszikova, was killing two birds with one stone. First, taking care of the minor annoyance presented by the original camp and its few defenders. Second, sending a signal to Annie and the others here of what lay in store for them once the mortar emplacements at the base of the hill started to open up, once the machine-gun crews started to work.

She turned her head quickly around, hearing running feet behind her. It was Otto Hammerschmidt. "Frau Rubenstein, Fraulein Doctor Leuden—I have been in radio contact with the original camp. They will not be able to hold out much longer."

Maria Leuden, crouched beside her in the rocks looking down over the base of the hill, asked, "Isn't there anything we can do for them, Otto?"

"There is nothing, Maria. And shortly we will be in the exact same predicament. The Chinese commander here has hit on a plan for some of us to exfiltrate the hilltop and work our way behind the forces in the valley below. Some of the Chinese, Liu, Rolvaag, and myself. If we can get in close enough before they detect our pres-

421

ence, we may have a chance. The question is, Annie—can you and Maria and Ma-Lin and the few Chinese soldiers here hold the hilltop while we work our way into position?"

Annie smiled at the German commando. "Do we have a choice?"

Hammerschmidt nodded once. "Good—I will let you know before we leave. So now, if you will excuse me, ladies," and he was up and moving, in a low crouch at first and then to his full height.

There was no reason to suppose his plan would work, Annie realized, but it was better than just sitting here and letting the Russians come and kill them like shooting fish in a barrel. It was an old expression, "shooting fish in a barrel." And she suddenly wondered if anyone had ever really done such a disgusting thing. "Yuch!"

"What?" Maria Leuden asked, staring at her oddly.

"I was just thinking about fish."

"Fish?"

"Never mind." She returned her gaze to the base of the hill and the Russian forces there. The mortars could still be heard in the distance, pounding the first camp.

Chapter Fifty-five

Jason Darkwood sat in the Island Class's command chair. Fourteen other Soviet personnel had been captured and brigged, the missing Mr. Rourke had been reunited with Major Tiemerovna, and Major Tiemerovna, Mr. Rourke, and Corporal Harkness had brought both reactors to full power.

He had appointed Sam Aldridge as acting First Officer, which was silly because the only person who knew anything about running a submarine aboard the vessel was himself—and perhaps Major Tiemerovna, who had said she knew how to sabotage one. Which might come in handy.

"Sam—pull in deck security."

"Aye, Jason."

Darkwood cranked the chair right. "Communications—stand by for any signals from harbor control. Don't answer to them, just listen to them."

"Yes, sir."

"You're supposed to say, "Aye, Captain," corporal. This is a naval vessel, remember?"

"Yes, sir."

"Never mind." He pushed the console button. He hoped it was the right one this time. "Engineering—reactors still stand at full power?"

Natalia Tiemerovna's rather lovely, accent-free English came back to him. "Everything is ready, Commander Darkwood. As far as any of us can tell."

"Gimme an educated guess, major."

"Educated guess—we have full power in both reactors."

"Wonderful—bridge out." He looked down toward where Sam Aldridge stood over the plotting table. "Time for you and me to trade places." Darkwood stood up and started down to the control deck. As Aldridge passed him, Darkwood grinned at him. "Lighten up—and all you've gotta do is exactly what I tell you to do. Right?"

"Right."

Darkwood slid into the helmsman's position. "Sam—order the deck crew to take in all remaining lines fore and aft and to clear the deck and notify me immediately as soon as the main hatch is closed."

"Right, Jase."

"'Right, Jase,'" Darkwood repeated, just shaking his head. He flexed his hands over the controls.

"They got all the lines cast off and the main hatch is secured."

"Marvelous."

He heard Corporal Bacon's voice. "Hey, sir—the Russian harbormaster is throwin' a fit. He's demanding to know what we're doing."

"He is, huh? Tell him to fuck off or the nearest Russian equivalent you can think of. Sam—tell engineering to sustain full power on both reactors and to listen for bells off my console. And for God's sake to remember which bells mean which speeds."

"Gotchya."

Darkwood suddenly panicked that the two men he'd detailed to disconnect from the gangplank had forgotten. "Sam—just say everything I say—to engineering."

"Right, Jase—ready."

"Two-thirds power to portside bow thrusters now!" The dual rudders directly abaft the dual propellers of the Island Class vessels supposedly gave them magnificent low-speed control despite their enormity. But he'd never had one of the Island Classers to practice on before. "Full power on portside bow thrusters immediately and fifteen degrees right rudder, bring up to all ahead one third and hold it there." He was sweating. "Communications—anything new and exciting?"

"Same old shit, sir."

"Right. Sonar—the stuff making sense to you?"

"I think so, sir," Corporal Lang answered. Lang was an experienced underwater cartographer, the closest thing to a sonar man available.

"Wonderful, corporal—tell you what. If anything funny starts happening, tell me, huh?"

"Sure thing, sir—fact of the matter is, there's some funny bumpy sounds against the hull."

Darkwood smiled. "Rest easy, corporal—that's just the Russians shooting at us." He turned his attention back to the plotter. "Sam—tell engineering to kill the bow thrusters and bring the rudder amidships."

"Right."

"Then tell 'em to hold at all ahead one third." He called back to Corporal Lang. "Lang—get me some bottom readings—if we get less than fifteen feet beneath the hull tell me quickly."

"Right, Captain."

Darkwood realized this was insane, but he had realized that earlier, so the revelation wasn't startling to him. Apparently they hadn't hauled the dock with them, which was a plus. "Sam—get the forward video composite up for me now."

"How do I do that?"

"Ask the computer—and hurry."

"Right."

"Sonar—how we doin'?"

"Pretty good, sir, I think—sounds like more bumpy things on the hull, though."

"Just keep an eye on the bottom and let me know if anything unfortunate's about to happen." He looked over his shoulder. "Bacon—anything on communications?"

"They're ordering us to stop, sir."

"Even after that nice thing you told them?"

"Yes, sir."

"Goes to show, huh—hang in there. Sam? Video?"

"I think I got it coming—ha-ha! There it is!"

425

There was full forward scan on the composite video, and what Darkwood saw matched some of the terrain beneath the lagoon that he remembered from the swim-in. He called for ten degrees right rudder and started working the diving planes. "Sam—tell engineering I need negative buoyancy."

"Negative buoyancy comin' up, Jase."

Negative buoyancy was for going down, actually, but he didn't bother confusing the issue. He asked for another fifteen degrees right rudder and as best he could tell he got it, the Island Classer going below, but the response so much more sluggish than the Reagan. He didn't like a vessel that couldn't be directly controlled from the helm either—it made for slow tactical responses. In his mind, in case he got out of this alive, he was logging away the details of how the Island Classer performed. They would come in handy the next time he met one in combat.

He leveled the diving planes, starting the Island Classer into the sonar tunnel, not to avoid sonar detection—she was too big for that—but because he knew the terrain there. "Communications—switch to the Soviet emergency band and start repeating that code phrase just as soon as we're out from under the dome. If the Reagan's out there, Sebastian'll come running."

"Aye, Captain."

Finally, somebody was getting that right at least. . . .

Sebastian had followed orders. "Communications—Lieutenant Mott, please broadcast the code phrase 'bad luck' to Mid-Wake. We should be just within maximum range for interception."

"Aye, Mr. Sebastian."

Margaret Barrow had been haunting the bridge before Sebastian had turned the Reagan for the open sea and since. He looked at her now. "Margaret—be of good faith. It would be hard to imagine a more competent officer than Jason Darkwood or Samuel Aldridge. We

426

may get permission to return to the Pillars—"

"Mr. Sebastian!"

Sebastian rotated the chair. "Yes, Lieutenant Mott?"

"I'm getting a distress signal off a Russian sub. It's very faint and my range and direction finding almost puts it right outside the Russian domes."

"The nature of the signal, Mr. Mott?"

"I can't make out the words, Mr. Sebastian."

"Keep the code phrase going to Mid-Wake on automatic only so you can devote full attention to the Soviet distress signal." He looked at Margaret Barrow. "May I suggest that you return to sick bay, commander? Since I may very shortly be taking the Reagan into combat, it might prove more advisable than waiting here." He ignored her presence. "Warfare—ascertain that all systems are functional. What is torpedo status?"

"Fore and aft, one through four, ready to go, sir."

"Thank you, lieutenant. Navigation—procede by most direct course toward the Russian domes at all ahead two thirds."

"Aye, Mr. Sebastian."

"Engineering—reactor status?"

"Port and starboard reactors full on line, Mr. Sebastian."

"Thank you, Commander Hartnett. Communications? What can you tell me?"

"Sir, I'm getting a lot of jamming—but every once in a while, I'm making out a word."

"Which words are you making out, Mr. Mott?"

"Something about 'Johnny comes marching home,' sir."

"Navigation, increase speed to all ahead full and hold here." He already had full-forward video display and he fixed his eyes on the screen.

Andrew Mott's voice sang out. "Mr. Sebastian. Receiving coded transmission from Mid-Wake."

"Decrypt, Mr. Rodriguez."

"Computer decrypting, sir."

Jason Darkwood had used the final option they had discussed just before Jason's departure. He had stolen a

Russian vessel.

Julie Kelly called to him. "Sir—I'm getting an Island Classer pursued by other Island Classers on long-range sonar."

"Thank you, Lieutenant." He turned the chair to his left. "Warfare—arm all forward torpedoes." He turned the chair another ninety degrees. "Computer?"

"Decryption ready, sir."

He turned the chair facing forward again so he could visually monitor the screen, then summoned ship's computer on the console on the chair. "Computer. This is First Officer Sebastian."

"Confirming voice print." There was a pause which, though he realized it was of standard duration, seemed inordinately long. "Voice print confirmed."

"Text of decrypted message from Mid-Wake, please."

"Processing." There was another pause. Then, "Attack Submarine Wayne en route to your position. Do nothing. Message ends."

"Thank you, computer." He turned toward Andrew Mott. "Mr. Mott, use the scrambler—we don't have time for encryption and decryption. Communicate to Mid-Wake that Commander Darkwood has apparently liberated the subject Major Tiemerovna and is proceeding from the domes in command of a Soviet Island Class submarine, and that he is being pursued. Then attempt direct contact with the Wayne and suggest to Commander Pilgrim that he might care to join us in assisting Commander Darkwood."

"An Island Classer, sir?"

"Just relay the messages—and hurry, lieutenant."

"Aye, sir."

"Sonar—any change in the pattern?"

"No, sir—except the first submarine is moving a little erratically."

"That is unfortunately to be expected, Lieutenant Kelly. The Captain is the only one of the raiding party who knows anything about maneuvering a vessel. Estimated time until rendezvous with the lead vessel, Navigator?"

"Seventeen minutes at present course and speed, Mr. Sebastian."

"Thank you, Lieutenant Bowman." He stood up from the command chair and walked down the three steps and reached to the overhead. "For your information. This is the Bridge. The Captain is apparently commanding a Soviet Island Class submarine which has just left the domes and is being pursued by several Island Class vessels under Soviet command. The situation is under control and I will keep you advised. Move to Battle Stations. I repeat. Battle Stations. This is not a drill." He switched off and hung up the microphone.

Communications called to him. "Mr. Sebastian. The Wayne has already responded. John Rourke is aboard her. Commander Pilgrim sends his compliments and awaits your instructions, sir."

"Convey to the commander my compliments as well. Suggest that if he has not already done so, he should move to Battle Stations—stand by. Sonar—how many pursuit vessels—do you have that now?"

"Aye, sir—four of them."

"Thank you, lieutenant. Communications—convey also to the Captain of the Wayne that the commandeered Island Class submarine is now confirmed as being pursued by four—I repeat, four—additional Island Class vessels. And please also convey my compliments to Doctor Rourke on his restored good health."

He studied the video composite—and he wished, with the Reagan going into battle, that Jason Darkwood were aboard her. . . .

John Rourke stood beside the command chair on the bridge of the Wayne, watching her Captain, Commander Walter Pilgrim, with considerable admiration. The man was very good at running a submarine. The Communications Officer, a pretty red-haired girl named Maureen O'Donnell, was relaying a message. ". . . additional Is-

429

land Class vessels. And please also convey my compliments to Doctor Rourke on his restored good health."

Pilgrim told her, "Signal message received and understood. Wayne out." Pilgrim's chair rotated and he called to his First Officer, Lieutenant Commander Bruno Smith. "First Officer—order Battle Stations," the short, stocky man said.

"Aye, sir. Ordering Battle Stations now."

Pilgrim rotated his chair to face John Rourke. He ran both hands through his balding hair and his blue eyes smiled. "Appears that quick briefing we gave you on our scuba gear, as you call it, won't prove necessary. Which is probably just as well. Just out of the hospital, I wouldn't want to try it for the first time either, even if I were experienced in other diving techniques."

"What happens now?" John Rourke asked.

"We go to Battle Stations and so does the Reagan. We intercept the Island Classers—"

"Those are the big ones, right?"

"Big is an understatement. But both the Reagan and the Wayne are well suited to outmaneuvering them and we're faster, by a considerable margin. Jason Darkwood's as good a skipper as they come. If anybody in our Navy could handle one of those suckers, he can. And, I'd venture to say, he's got your Major Tiemerovna aboard with him. We'll get in there and run interference for Darkwood—"

"I take it that football isn't a lost art at Mid-Wake?"

"No—yeah, we play football—and some of us just used to." Pilgrim laughed. "So—we run interference for Darkwood while he gets himself clear and gets the Island Classer to full speed. As long as we buy him about ten minutes and he's got a straight course, the other Island Classers can never catch up to him."

"You make it sound easier than it is."

"Ohh, it won't be easy, Doctor Rourke. Especially if that Island Classer's got missiles, and knowing Jason, he wouldn't have bothered snatching it if it hadn't. The Soviets won't want us looking at their little missiles.

430

They'll try to blow their own vessel out of the water before that."

John Rourke didn't say anything more. He turned his eyes to the composite videoscreen, as it was called, and watched ahead of them. Natalia, he thought . . .

Alexeii Serovski held his pistol tight in his fist. It was clear to him now that all aboard this submarine was not as it should be. The main hatch had been closed and, at times, he had the definite sensation of motion. Yet there seemed to be almost no one aboard the vessel.

He had heard voices and he had been uncertain of their speech. And as he had approached nearer to the sound, the voices had vanished. Logic dictated that the command center of the submarine would be near the central portion of the ship and probably on one of the upper levels.

He made his way in that direction now, his pistol as ready as he was. . . .

Jason Darkwood set the course on auto and left the navigation station hurriedly, the Island Classer at flank speed now. "Gimme the chair, Sam—hang loose," and he slid into the command chair as quickly as Aldridge vacated it. He needed touch with the rest of the ship and rapidly. If the Reagan had received his distress signal and code phrase, they still wouldn't rendezvous with the Island Classer's present course for several minutes, and the last thing Bacon had gotten off the hailing frequency was that the pursuing four Island Classers were preparing to fire unless he killed all engine power.

"Aft Torpedo Room—anybody down there?"

"I am, sir—this is Hornsbey."

"Private Hornsbey—listen carefully and I'm going to give you a procedure to follow in order to verify that all our torpedo tubes are dry and to ascertain their exact status. Now—do exactly as I tell you and remember, if you open a torpedo tube and the other end is open, we're in deep shit—right?"

"Yes, sir."

"Good—here's what I want—"

"Stop!"

Darkwood turned the chair around 180 degrees. There was a Russian officer with a handgun standing between computer and sonar stations near the periscope array. "Who the hell are you?" Darkwood snapped in English, not thinking that fast.

"I am Captain Alexeii Servoski of the Elite Corps of the Committee for State Security of the Soviet Union, under command of Hero Marshal Vladmir Karamatsov. You are under arrest!"

"Your English is very good. And you are also out of your mind. Shoot me, mister, and this submarine goes to the bottom because I'm the only man on board who can command her. Miss me and put a bullet hole into one of the instrument packages and we might be as good as dead as well. And what the hell kind of uniform is that? And who's this cockamamie Karamatsov character?"

The Soviet officer's face became livid with rage and Darkwood threw himself out of the chair and toward the man. "Sam!" The pistol discharged and Darkwood felt a burning sensation across his rib cage, and heard something electronic pop behind him as his left hand closed over the gunhand wrist and his right fist hammered forward. With pain across his ribcage the roundhouse punch wound up a short right jab. But Aldridge was there the next instant, and the Soviet officer's body was ripped away from him and slammed into the overhead like a rag doll at the mercy of an angry child.

"All right! Don't kill him. We might get something out of him." Darkwood's right hand came away from his left side covered with blood. "Ohh, wonderful! Great." He half walked, half lurched into the command chair. "Hornsbey—you still there?"

"Yes, sir, Captain—what happened?"

"We had a visitor—stand by—get right back to you."

432

e pushed the button for engineering. "Major iemerovna—Natalia. Do you know a Captain Seroski?"

"Servoski?"

"Something like the KGB Elite Corps or some such onsense? And something about a Hero Marshal some-ling—began with a K I think?"

"Serovski!"

"If the reactors are all under control and Mr. Rourke nd Corporal Harkness can handle engineering, why on't you duck up here for a sec and check out this guy. kay?"

"Yes—okay."

"Great—look forward to it. Bridge out." He cut back the aft torpedo room. "Okay, Hornsbey—you ready?"

"You betchya, sir."

"Go ahead—inspire me with confidence." As he started lling Hornsbey the procedure to follow, he realized that he didn't get a torpedo or two ready to go pretty quick, and everyone else aboard was in genuine trouble.

Chapter Fifty-six

Otto Hammerschmidt and the others had gone. Mar~
Leuden was beside her. The mortar bombardment of tl
first camp had stopped more than an hour ago an
Captain Svetlana Grubaszikova's "women" were massir
for attack. And what had happened to her husband an
brother?

She worked the bolt of the M-16 and charged tl
chamber, leaving the selector on safe for the momen
Maria had an M-16 as well. She liked this girl an
Michael loved her, whether he knew it or not yet. And sl
trusted to Maria's good judgment that if Michael didn
know it, he soon would. If any of them survived this thin
alive.

"I think they are going to attack us." Maria con
mented.

Annie smiled at her. "I think you're right."

"I wonder if Michael is all right—and your husban
too, of course."

Annie didn't know what to say.

Grubaszikova's people were definitely getting ready *
move—and not to a different neighborhood. She move
the M-16's selector to auto.

"Where is Otto?"

"Getting into position down there—I hope—be read
Maria."

"What will they do to us if they win?"

"Since you wouldn't want to know, the logical thing
to keep them from winning. Hang in there, Maria."

"I will—yes."

Annie debated if one really decent shot—if she'd had her father's Steyr-Mannlicher SSG sniper rifle it would have been a different story—but if one decent shot could take out Grubaszikova. If only her father could have been behind that rifle. She felt tears welling up into her eyes. He was dead, they all felt. They never really said that he was, but they all felt it. Michael and Paul didn't want to believe it, and maybe it was a sign of their strength that even though inside them somewhere they did believe it they still kept looking for him. But she would have known, somehow, somehow.

Annie moved her selector back to safe.

Battle would come soon enough.

Her father had to be alive.

Chapter Fifty-seven

Natalia Anastasia Tiemerovna had asked Commander
Darkwood for his knife as soon as she had reached the
bridge. He had been sitting at what looked like a naviga
tion station, Sam Aldridge in what would have been the
command chair, his feet resting on Serovski's chest.

She had noticed too that Darkwood was wounded and
against his protests, had knelt beside him at the naviga
tion station, utilized the first-aid kit from the bulkhead
nearby, and seen to his wound, quickly but adequately.

"We should be rendezvousing with the Reagan in a
couple of minutes. Don't worry, major—we'll get out of
this."

"You remind me of John Rourke," she told him. For
her, it was the ultimate compliment she could give any
man besides John Rourke.

"Your eyes remind me of my mother's eyes. They were
blue like that. Doctor Rourke's a very lucky man."

"Everyone misunderstands—he is married."

"We all have problems."

"His wife is a wonderful person and he loves her a great
deal. He was never unfaithful to her with me." Why was
she telling this almost total stranger this?

"Then he must be a man of iron will, your Doctor
Rourke."

She felt her cheeks warming again. "Your wound isn't
deep—but you could use having a doctor take a look at
it."

"Know anybody who's any good?"

436

"Yes. I do."

"I'll keep that in mind. That man under Sam's feet—you know him?"

"He was sent by my husband as his delivery boy." She looked at Serovski, set down the medical kit, and picked up Darkwood's fighting knife.

"Your husband."

"The most evil man on earth, I think."

"He's a marshal? That's an old Russian term for a general, isn't it?"

"He has an army. If an alliance between the Russians you fight and my husband becomes reality, then . . ." She couldn't finish it.

Darkwood seemed to be thinking. "Major—Natalia. Listen. Do you think you could persuade our friend to tell us where he's supposed to meet your husband? I mean, after all—your husband's apparently expecting an Island Class submarine. This very one. Such an important man. I guess I was thinking, if we make it out of this alive, it might be a real nice gesture on our parts if we didn't just leave your husband standing there waiting—for his ship to come in, so to speak." And Jason Darkwood grinned at her.

Natalia stood up, the knife in her fist. "Sam—hold him down for me."

"My pleasure, major," Aldridge responded.

There was fear in Serovski's hard eyes. It was justified, she felt, as she knelt beside his face and touched the knife to his throat.

It was perfectly justified.

"Where are you supposed to bring me, captain?"

"Comrade major—have you no loyalty?"

"I have loyalty—but unlike your loyalty, it is not misplaced. This is a very fine knife, and I imagine it is very sharp. And if you know me by reputation, you know that I am very good with a knife. Either tell me where you are to meet Marshal Karamatsov and when, or we will both find out together just how sharp this very knife happens to be."

"You wouldn't."

437

She shifted the knife to her left hand and her right hand reached down to his crotch and found the zipper at the front of his uniform.

"No!"

She started to reach inside his pants and he screamed like a woman. "Wait! Please! I will tell you!"

"Where and when?" She drew her hand back but brought the knife to his throat.

"The Island of Chinmen Tao in the Formosa Strait—the rendezvous was to be . . ."

"Look at your watch," she ordered.

He raised his left wrist. "About four hours—Chinmen Tao."

Natalia moved the knife. "Quemoy," she said softly. If they could trap Vladmir, then kill him. If . . .

It would have been slow going with the trucks filled with the internees from the death camp, but by now, certainly, Han had reached the J-7V and used its radio to call in help. And by now, help would be coming. Perhaps a large German force, or perhaps only some German aircraft lifting in Chinese troops.

The mortar bombardment would start, softening them up, but they would have to be very careful of the range because, despite Captain Grubaszikova's bravado, Annie knew, the last thing the Russians wanted was to explode the trucks loaded with the deadly gas.

And she had a sudden flash of inspiration. "Maria—you and Ma-Lin. Get the others together and get them to barricade themselves immediately around the gas trucks."

"But if the trucks are hit, Annie—"

"If the trucks are hit, any men in the vicinity will be affected anyway. But the nearer we all are to the trucks, the more careful the Russians will be with their fire. Just do it."

"What about you?" Maria Leuden asked.

Annie looked at the girl and smiled. "I'll be right along." If she could hold to this position long enough,

438

Grubaszikova would lead her female soldiers up the hill. And once Grubaszikova was in range of the M-16 and Annie's abilities . . . "I'll be with you before you know it," Annie told her.

Chapter Fifty-eight

John Rourke sat at the engineering station, the Wayne's Engineering Officer, a pretty Eurasian-looking woman named Su Lin Davis, having left the bridge to personally supervise the monitoring of the Wayne's port-side reactor, a problem she described as "a stuck gauge most likely." It had freed up a chair and John Rourke, determined not to leave the bridge, had needed a place to sit. Common sense and his own medical experience, the miraculous healing techniques of the Doctors at Mid-Wake notwithstanding, dictated that he was doing too much too soon after such a serious operation.

On one level of his consciousness, he monitored the activity of the bridge. The Reagan was ten minutes ahead of the Wayne in terms of reaching the fleeing Island Class submarine commandeered, it seemed, by Captain Jason Darkwood. The Reagan and the Island Classer, as they were generally called, would rendezvous in less than a minute, it appeared from the last communication between the Reagan and the Wayne.

Transmissions being sent by the stolen Island Classer were still being effectively jammed by the pursuing Soviet submarines, and so there was no definitive word as to whether or not Natalia had indeed been freed.

On a second level of consciousness, John Rourke saw to his weapons. The Life Support System X made for him five centuries before by Texan Jack Crain was as perfect as ever. The sheath had suffered in the saltwater bath it had gotten when Rourke had been taken unconscious into the waters of the Soviet lagoon, but it was restorable. The same could be said for the double Alessi shoulder rig for the twin stainless Detonics .45s. The leather was a little dry and stiff, but would be serviceable for the time being and, with careful work, would be restorable to full functional efficiency. The sheath for the little A.G. Russell Sting IA black chrome was somewhat the worse for wear as well, blood and salt water having been a bad mixture as a leather dressing, but the knife was in excellent condition and this sheath as well could be restored. The Milt Sparks Six-Pak was in similar condition.

All told, Rourke thought, smiling ruefully, his equipment was in the same or better shape than himself at the moment, functional but requiring some restoration. . . .

Lang had sufficient presence of mind, despite his lack of skill, to summon Darkwood to the sonar station and for that Darkwood was grateful. "I don't know what the noise is, sir, but it seemed to come from all four of those Island Classers that are doggin' us."

Darkwood took the headset and listened, then checked the visual interpretation displays on Lang's computer consoles. "You may not know shit from shoe polish about sonar, but thank God you thought to ask. Four wire-guides."

Darkwood crossed to the navigation station in three strides and threw himself down behind the console. "Sam—relay these orders to Engineering." There was one chance against four wire-guides in a vessel that couldn't outrun them. "Fifteen degrees right rudder and maintain full flank speed. Stand by for rudder changes." His eyes jumped from the forward video display and the plot. They were alongside the volcanic vent which was the source of geothermal energy for the Soviet domes and for Mid-Wake. And the only chance was to take the Island Classer into the vent. "Rudder amidships and all back one third." He worked the diving planes down. They were nearing the vent now. "Fifteen degrees left rudder and back to all ahead full." There was a pinnacle of rock rising almost directly ahead of them. "Rudder amidships. All stop. Blow auxilliary tanks one, three, two, and four now! Ten degrees right rudder. All ahead full—now, Sam—tell 'em!" What he was doing was like skimming a rock off the water, he hoped. There were many ponds in the living modules of Mid-Wake, and little boys grew up skipping rocks or pennies off their surface, and he'd always been very good at it. But he had never tried it with a submarine. "Ten degrees right rudder." He could hear the hull scraping against the upthrusting rock, feel the drag, and then there was a lurch and the Island Classer was moving up and ahead. "Rudder amidships, back one third." He worked the diving planes again, the vent opening before them. "Fifteen degrees left rudder. All stop. Ten degrees left rudder." The submarine was settling into the vent. The composite video display looked like a laser light show, volcanic sediment rising in showers of spray and bursts of color. "Five degrees right rudder, all ahead two thirds. Tell Engineering to advise me if hull temperatures reach into the danger zone. Rudder amidships and all ahead full. Sonar—what's the story on those four wire-guides?"

"Looks like they're still on our tail, Captain. But my sonar is going nutso. There's noise everywhere."

"Keep your fingers crossed those four wire-guides are having the same difficulty." The Island Classer rocked violently to starboard, a brilliant flash of light from the portside of the ship washing over the composite video display, Darkwood nearly sliding out of his chair. "Sam—tell Engineering to talk to me."

He could hear off the speaker. "This is Natalia—if I'm reading the scanners correctly, we're not taking in water."

He hoped she was reading the damage scanners correctly.

The vent widened and he ordered, "Five degrees right rudder," taking the Island Classer dead center along the vent's course. "Rudder amidships. Sonar—how's the wire-guide situation?"

"Nothing, sir—oh-oh."

"What's 'oh-oh' mean?"

"Four more sounds like the ones before—maybe they
1st launched four more after us, Captain."

If the Russians were insane enough to risk a nuclear
etonation in the vent that supplied both their cities with
eothermal power, it was a drastic measure. And drastic
1easures required drastic countermeasures. "Communi-
ations—anything from the Reagan?"

"Nothing, sir."

"Good—get the hell out of that chair and slide over to
1e weapons station quick. I need direct control of the
luster charges and now, Bacon."

"Aye, sir."

"Sam—alert the aft torpedo room that on my signal I
ant all four aft tubes launched simultaneously. Bacon—
)u at the weapons station?"

"Sure am, sir."

"Get ready to fire the ship's entire compliment of
uster charges on my signal."

"Arming now, sir—I think."

"That's right, fill me with confidence, Bacon. Be
ady. Sam, tell Engineering that I want them monitoring
l damage-control scanners until I say otherwise. So-
ar—what's the story?"

"The remaining three out of the first four wire-guides
e right on our tail, sir—about a hundred yards off the
ern. The other four wireguides are moving faster. About
1other hundred yards back."

"Tell engineering I want rudder amidships, Sam. And
flank speed maintained no matter what. Bacon, how
ose cluster charges coming?"

"Armed and ready, sir."

"Good man—on my command. Fire! Sam! Tell aft
rpedo room to fire tubes one, two, three, and four
)w!"

The Island Classer seemed to vibrate, or maybe it was
s imagination—he didn't know which as he hauled
ick on the diving planes and shouted, "Tell Engineering

I want every ounce of air they've got and right now!'

"Advising Engineering."

The video display was a blur now, the Island Classer rising, the detonating cluster charges causing landslides on all sides now, the vent collapsing around them. "More air!"

"I'm tellin' 'em. Hold on." There was a pause. "You got all the air there is."

"Tell 'em to red-line the turbines—if I can't have more air I gotta have more power!"

"Advising Engineering!"

He watched the depth gauge, the Island Classer's rate of ascent starting to increase drastically, his body being crushed into the back of his chair. "Sonar—can you make out what happened to those wire-guides?"

"I'm goin' deaf, sir—I think—yeah—just like the other noise. There's one. Another one—holy shit!" And Darkwood craned his neck to see Lang falling from his seat, holding his ears. So much for Sonar.

"Bacon—see to Lang if you can!"

"Aye, sir!"

"Sam—tell Engineering to maintain revolutions no matter what the instrument panels say!"

"Right! What the hell are we doin'?"

"Tell 'em—if we do it, I'll clue you in!"

The depth gauge was going wild now, Darkwood's ears popping as he swallowed, his fists white-knuckled on the diving plane controls.

"I'm back on Sonar, sir. I've lost track completely of all wire-guides—I think we got 'em."

"Good man—stay with it. Bacon—get on Communications and hail the Reagan."

"Aye, sir."

"If you get her, tell her we're surfacing."

"Aye, sir."

He could hear Bacon reciting the call litany, and then the litany broke. "I've got the Reagan, Captain. Wait a minute. They say one Island Class submarine apparently damaged. The Reagan had fired wire-guides, sir. Hey

Hey! Another Island Classer damaged. The Wayne is coming up."

"Tell Mr. Sebastian to hold off five hundred yards from our bow as we surface and to disengage with the Island Classers and see if they run home to Momma. Convey my compliments to the Captain of the Wayne and ask Commander Pilgrim if he would kindly take up a position five hundred yards off our stern as we surface, and suggest that he might care to disengage with the Island Classers."

"Aye, sir."

Jason Darkwood called to Sam Aldridge as he began easing the angle on the bow planes. "Tell Engineering back one third." They were almost surfaced.

Chapter Fifty-nine

Natalia Tiemerovna stood on the missile deck of the Island Classer, the wind in her hair feeling good to her. The launch the Island Classer had sent out was returning now, and aboard the launch she could see John Rourke coming from the Wayne.

Michael Rourke stood at her right side. He had told her about the internees Vladmir Karamatsov had brought to his little death camp, about the way in which the gas had been stolen, that likely her husband's forces were trying even now to get it back. There were still so many things unresolved—but John was alive. He was coming to her now.

It was hard to care about anything else, even though she knew that she must.

Jason Darkwood stood at her left side. "I'd always pictured life on the surface as harsh, but peaceful at least. From the way both of you talk, I'm getting the distinct impression we're all fighting the same war."

"We are," Natalia said to him. "Whether the enemy is my husband and his forces or a man like Kerenin, whom John killed, or a man like Feyedorovitch, who's probably just finding out what happened—it does't matter."

"I'm eager to discuss something with Doctor Rourke. Something to our mutual advantage," Darkwood said.

The launch was coming alongside and moving into it

446

berth. And as she looked over the rail, John Rourke waved up at her. She blew him a kiss.

He started up the ladder. She stepped back. "Go ahead, Michael."

Michael looked at her for a moment. "You're a fine woman," he said at last. And as his father stepped through the gap in the rail and onto the deck, Michael walked forward and father and son embraced.

And then John Rourke turned to her. His hair was windblown. The dark shirt he wore—black—made his five o'clock shadow more visible than it usually was. His coloring was pale. But he walked toward her vigorously and swept her into his arms.

"I'll always stay with you—as long as you want me to," she whispered, his lips touching her cheek. And he turned her face up toward his and his hands exuded strength and life and she wanted to cry and just have him hold her. "Always," she said again.

And his mouth came down and touched hers and she let her body go limp in his arms for an instant.

Darkwood's voice. She heard that as she leaned her head against John's chest. "You seem marvelously recovered, sir. I'm Commander Jason Darkwood, Captain of the Reagan. We've met, but I doubt you remember."

John Rourke turned her around and held her close against his left side as he extended his right hand. She kept her face against John's chest, her arms holding John tight against her. John Rourke and Jason Darkwood clasped hands.

"Commander—it's a pleasure to meet again. For saving Natalia and for coming to the aid of my son here," and he drew Michael against him, his right arm folding across his son's shoulders, "I will never be able to repay you."

"Friends don't have to worry about that sort of thing, do they, Doctor Rourke?"

"No—they don't."

"I'm sure you'd appreciate a tour of our captured

447

Russian submarine, but it appears there are a few urgent considerations still remaining. Want to talk below or up here in the fresh air. I'll confess, for me it's a novelty."

"After the last few days," John told him, "it's become a refreshing novelty for me as well." And John looked at Michael. "How are your mother and sister and Paul? And that Maria Leuden?"

"Michael has been filling me in, John—there are some real problems," she said, taking her face away from his chest, shaking her hair in the wind.

"And," Jason Darkwood said, "it appears we also have a chance to nail your Marshal Karamatsov. Major Tiemerovna was supposed to be handed over to him on the Island of Chinmen Tao—it is sometimes called Quemoy—in the Formosa Strait." And he consulted his peculiar-looking watch. "In just about two hours from now. He was expecting an Island Class submarine, which this is, and he was expecting her to be brought to him by men in Marine Spetznas uniforms, which I am wearing. And we even have the commander of the detail aboard with us, a certain Captain Serovski. Not a nice man. Anything interesting suggest itself to you, Doctor Rourke?"

"Quite a few things," John told him. "Do you have an extra uniform in my size?"

Darkwood smiled. "I think that could be arranged, doctor."

John looked down at her. "Now—what about Annie and everybody?"

"Mom's in Iceland—she's safe," Michael told him, standing at the apex of the triangle formed by Jason Darkwood and his father, Natalia still in the crook of John's arm. "Annie, Paul, Maria, and myself, with the help of Han and Otto Hammerschmidt and a really small force of Chinese, all eventually wound up looking for the two of you in the same place. Karamatsov's base camp. We didn't find what we were looking for, of course, but

448

we found out that Karamatsov had picked up several hundred Chinese and was taking them to a sort of death camp and was planning to use his gas on them. Maybe as some kind of a test or something. I'm not sure. So, anyway, we stole it, bluffed our way out with the Chinese prisoners, and I went back one more time to see if there were any sign of the two of you. And that's when I saw his submarine surfacing, and I was watching from up in the rocks overlooking the sea and I kept watching. An officer from this submarine brought Karamatsov a gift— Natalia's guns and her knife. And I figured that these people had you both. I swam out to the submarine and things were going great." He smiled. "Then not so great and I got myself nailed."

"But he also had himself free by the time we took over the ship," Natalia said quickly.

John said nothing for a moment. Then, "Michael— with the gas and the people you freed from the camp— what is your assessment of what would have been the next logical move for Paul and Annie and the others to make?"

"Maria and I talked about it briefly before I switched to one of the trucks we were using to haul out the internees. I didn't think Karamatsov would let us get very far with the gas, but I also thought that the gas would have been his primary concern."

"Could Han or Otto summon help?"

"We had radios, but since we pulled the thing off in the dark, we had a good chance of eluding them temporarily, and if we used the radios, we would have called them in to our position—the Russians. I don't know what they did after that."

John was silent again.

"What are you thinking, doctor?"

John Rourke looked at him—they were the same height, Natalia noticed. Exactly. "Probably, the situation with the rest of my family and the stolen gas has been

449

resolved—but if it hasn't, they could be in deep trouble Could I make a two-fold request?"

"Certainly—and since I'm out of range of Mid-Wake," he said, smiling, "I can't radio them and ask for permission. So I'll have to use my own discretion. Request away."

"Can the Wayne, with my son aboard her, make best speed possible to the coast near Karamatsov's base camp, let off my son and some Marines? Michael can lead them in toward where Annie and the others might still be. Then the Wayne proceeds along the coast and—the Wayne has the capabilities—it can begin a bombardment of Karamatsov's base camp."

Darkwood grinned mischievously. "Doctor Rourke. Aside from the fact that the skipper of the Wayne and myself would be taking it upon ourselves to declare war on a foreign power, I see no fault in the idea at all. And since I am out of radio contact with Mid-Wake, I can't ask their advice. So, if Walter Pilgrim isn't any brighter than I think he is . . ." And he started to laugh.

John Rourke smiled. "The Captain of the Wayne struck me as being quite an intelligent man."

"Yes, but he's as fond of getting into tight places as I am. So—if Walter Pilgrim goes along with it, I believe we can land some Marines and then create quite a diversionary bombardment of Marshal Karamatsov's camp. And the Reagan can hang back while we take this Island Classer—which has a full complement of nuclear missiles, by the way, so we do have to be a little careful not to lose her—while we take this Island Classer right up to Marshal Karamatsov's doorstep."

"He'll recognize you, John—you can't . . ."

John looked at Natalia. "I can stay to the rear of the group. He won't recognize me until it's too late. You're the one who'll have to be careful."

"I need my guns and my knife back anyway." She smiled.

"I got mine—found 'em in an arms locker below," Michael announced, patting the two Beretta pistols stuffed into his belt.

"Then we have a plan, gentlemen—and madam," Darkwood said.

"We have a plan," John Rourke agreed.

The plan frightened Natalia, but there was no other way.

Chapter Sixty

Paul Rubenstein's truck had slipped a tread on the half-track and he abandoned it. There was no possibility of one man repairing it in less than several hours. There had been no survivors in the first camp, but he felt certain that most had escaped rather than been killed because he had only found four bodies. He had followed the trail of the Soviet vehicles through snow that was sparse here, the ground soft enough that a blind man could have followed the tread imprints with his cane.

And now he was upon them, at the furthest rear of their lines, mortars firing every few seconds, explosions erupting at the top of the hill beneath which the Soviet positions were located. There seemed to be no answering fire from the hilltop and this worried him, but he rationalized that Annie or Hammerschmidt or Han would have known that conservation of ammunition was more important at this stage, because the mortar fire had only begun within the last forty-five minutes.

And then he saw movement in the rocks below him and to the north. He saw a shock of blonde hair. "Hammerschmidt," Paul whispered. Hammerschmidt would have done the logical thing for a man with his training, of course. Assembled a small unit and left the camp at the top of the hill, perhaps under cover of darkness, and circled behind the Soviet position.

Paul started working his way obliquely toward where he had momentarily seen the German commando captain, his Schmeisser ready. . . .

Annie Rubenstein had burrowed as deeply into the rocks as she could, and she had pulled her heavy shawl over her head to afford her as much protection against the constant rain of rocks and dirt as possible. The noise of the explosions as the mortar rounds impacted was unnerving her, she knew, and each time one of the mortar rounds fell near her, she could feel her skin go cold and her stomach churn. But waiting here was the only chance if somehow Hammerschmidt's mission failed, if somehow Han had not already gotten help to speed toward them. And she had learned the lesson well from her father. "It pays to plan ahead."

And by staying here hidden in the rocks overlooking the hillside, she was doing just that.

Captain Svetlana Grubaszikova would have to take her forces up the hillside eventually. And when Captain Grubaszikova did, Captain Grubaszikova would be a dead woman. Annie Rourke Rubenstein clutched her M-16 tight against her, protecting the rifle as much as she protected herself, and waited as the rain of debris poured down around her and her ears rang with the cacophony made by the explosions.

Chapter Sixty-one

The girl Michael Rourke ran beside through the surf was so ridiculously pretty, it was hard to imagine she was a Marine lieutenant. He had grown up seeing Marines in videotape movies at the Retreat. And if they weren't John Wayne, they all tried to look like him. But Lieutenant Lillie St. James, Security Officer of the Wayne, didn't look a bit like the man the vessel was named after.

She was gorgeous. Blonde. Blue-eyed. Rosy-cheeked. "Hubba-hubba, Marines!" Lillie St. James rasped as they broke from the surf and made for the rocks, Michael still right beside her.

They took up defensive positions at the height of the beachhead, Michael sliding into a niche of rock beside her.

Her assault rifle in her right fist as though it didn't weigh a thing, she looked at him, and a little smile crossed her pretty lips. "Where to now, Mr. Rourke? I have orders that tell me to take orders from you until we reach the objective. So—where to?"

Michael pulled the compass from his borrowed USMC battle-dress utilities—a better choice of uniform than the Soviet equivalent he had been wearing when he had launched over to the Wayne just before it had gotten underway. She was already spreading out the rough map he had drawn for her, and copied for Commander Pilgrim, the Captain of the Wayne. "As I told you before, lieutenant, I can lead us to the first camp and after that—if, as I suspect, they have abandoned it—we've gotta find them."

"Unless, of course, the Russkies are already hitting them. In that event, we shouldn't have too much difficulty finding them at all, should we? Lead the way, Mr. Rourke."

"Yes, ma'am." He grinned. "May I?"

"What?"

"Follow me?" he said softly.

Lieutenant Lillie St. James laughed and then shouted to her people, "Let's move out, Marines!"

Michael started from the rocks in a dead run, Lieutenant St. James right beside him. He looked back toward the beach, the rubber boats that had brought them already halfway back to the Wayne. . . .

John Rourke stood on the bridge of the Soviet Island Classer, Natalia beside him. He looked at her. Beneath her black jumpsuit she had secreted his Sting IA black chrome, and across her shoulders she wore a shoulder holster for one of the U.S. service pistols. The 2418 A2s looked interesting enough, but he wasn't about to exchange his Detonics .45s for a set of them.

"Mr. Sebastian—our position from Chinmen Tao Island, please."

"Position as follows, Captain. Twenty-three nautical miles north by northeast. Estimated time of arrival to our calculated offshore position, approximately fifteen minutes. The Reagan is three minutes behind us, Captain."

"Very good, Mr. Sebastian." Darkwood rotated his chair to face Rourke and Natalia. Although Darkwood had imported some of his own people from the Reagan, there was still an abundance of vacant seats on the bridge. "I think your later idea is the best course of action—that way, if Karamatsov sees you, so what?"

455

"Exactly." John Rourke nodded. "If he sees me as a supposed prisoner, it may arouse his interest but shouldn't terribly arouse his suspicions." Rourke wished for a cigar. "Who's minding the Reagan—with your First Officer here and the others?"

"My Engineering Officer, Lieutenant Commander Hartnett, has the Con, and we're filling in the best we can otherwise."

Several officers and some enlisted personnel had come over from the Reagan—the tall, black Lieutenant Commander T.J. Sebastian; the Medical Officer, Lieutenant Commander Margaret Barrow (a rather pretty woman, Rourke thought); the sonar operator, Lieutenant Junior Grade Julie Kelly; and a Chinese Machinist First Class named Wilbur Hong. These and the security contingent under the command of Sam Aldridge, assisted by a young man named Tom Stanhope, were filling in at whatever jobs needed to be done aboard the huge craft. In the brig were several Russian prisoners taken when the Island Classer had originally been commandeered. Darkwood had said that they would be debriefed by hypnotherapy and then incarcerated on Mid-Wake until a prisoner exchange needed to be worked out with the Russians, or until the Mid-Wake taxpayers got tired of feeding them and returned them anyway.

Aldridge and Stanhope appeared on the bridge now, a Russian officer between them, his hands bound. The uniform was familiar to John Rourke, the black uniform of the KGB Elite Corps.

Sam Aldridge was dressed in some of his scuba gear—it looked fascinating and Rourke was determined to try it if he could—and Tom Stanhope was outfitted as a Soviet Naval officer.

Darkwood smiled at the Russian. "Ahh, Captain Serovski—so happy you could join us. I had such fun the last time you joined us on the bridge." Darkwood massaged his rib cage where an hour ago Doctor Barrow, the Reagan's Medical Officer, had sterilized and bandaged it.

456

"You will all die."

"Ahh—then Captain Aldridge and Lieutenant Stanhope have been filling you in, I see."

John Rourke studied Serovski for a moment, and Serovski turned his eyes toward him. "You!"

John Rourke smiled. "Captain—you know my fondness for your organization. And you doubtlessly know how I would have felt had you succeeded in turning over Major Tiemerovna to Marshal Karamatsov so he could torture her and execute her. I'd suggest you consider something. The one thing that is keeping you alive is the fact that we need your assistance with our operation. We could get along without you, but with you present it will make things a little more believable. Major Tiemerovna and I will both be posing as prisoners. We will both be heavily armed. Commander Darkwood, Lieutenant Stanhope, and some others from Captain Aldridge's Marines will be posing as officers and men of this vessel, assisting you in delivering us to Karamatsov. Captain Aldridge and the rest of his Marines will come up behind Karamatsov's position after exiting this vessel and swimming in. By the time we surface, they'll be in position. I'm not so naive as to assume that this will all go like clockwork and Karamatsov's fate is already sealed, but I'd say we have a good chance. You do exactly as you're told and you'll get out of this alive—we can send you back to Karamatsov's army or drop you anyplace else. That's immaterial. You cooperate and you have my word on your freedom and good health. Don't cooperate, and I'll personally break your damned neck. Is that clear?"

Serovski nodded. "Yes."

"Then here's how we do it. You will be completely uniformed and have your pistol at your side with a magazine in place. The magazine will be empty, as will the magazines on your belt. We've already taken care of that. You will do as you normally would—take us right up to your Hero Marshal. When Natalia or I shove you aside, hit the dirt and take cover and just worry about

457

staying alive. We'll do the rest. Play it straight and you'll have the same chances of getting out of this alive that we have."

"The Hero Marshal will have many men there—and helicopters. You will not have a chance."

Darkwood said, "But we'll have the Reagan offshore, and our deck guns can hit with pinpoint accuracy. The helicopters won't be a factor—although I confess I'd rather take a ride in one than blow one up. I've only seen pictures of them. Doctor Rourke's word will be binding on us all. If you do your part, no matter how this turns out, you'll be free. We want Karamatsov, not you. No offense."

Aldridge looked at his wristwatch. "I've gotta go— Captain."

"Good luck, Sam," and Aldridge left the bridge.

"Mr. Stanhope—leave our friend Captain Serovski here on the bridge while you coordinate with the rest of our party. Meet you by the main hatch."

"Will he be okay here, sir?"

John Rourke looked at Stanhope, then at Serovski. "Trust me—he'll be just fine."

"Be about your business, Mr. Stanhope."

"Yes, sir," and Stanhope did a neat about face and left the bridge as well.

"Sit down, Captain Serovski. Just make yourself comfortable. Right there by the warfare station. And if you touch anything, Major Tiemerovna has my authorization to cut off your hand. And I'll even loan her the knife."

John Rourke smiled and reached to his side where the Crain Life Support System X was sheathed. He unsheathed it and handed the knife to Natalia. "She can use mine," he said. . . .

Paul Rubenstein had linked up with Otto Hammerschmidt and the others without considerable difficulty, quickly learned that Han had taken the trucks loaded

458

with the freed internees of the camp and gone for help but hadn't heard from since, then continued on with Hammerschmidt toward a position in some high rocks seventy-five yards to the rear of the Soviet lines.

Paul had been amazed that Karamatsov had sent an entirely female force against the hilltop, amazed and also sobered. It meant that Karamatsov was willing to explode the gas if he had to in order to prevent anyone else from having it, ready to risk his entire army if the wind were blowing in the wrong direction.

Hammerschmidt, beside him, gave the order. "Open fire!"

Paul Rubenstein brought the metal stock of the MP-40 to his right shoulder, concentrating the submachine gun's firepower toward the nearest mortar emplacement. One of the Chinese, Lieutenant Liu, was operating a multi-barreled grenade launcher with devastating effectiveness.

Hammerschmidt shouted, "That machine-gun emplacement—attack!" And he was up, running, Paul clambering over the rocks, running beside him. The Soviet forces were starting to respond, small-arms fire blowing into the rocks and ground and sparse snow around them as Paul Rubenstein and Hammerschmidt ran, Hammerschmidt grabbing a grenade from his belt, hurtling it toward the machine-gun emplacement.

"I thought you wanted the gun!" Paul shouted to him over the noise of the gunfire."

"I do—I never pulled the pin on the grenade! Look!"

The machine-gun crew was running from the entrenched position, Paul opening up with the Schmeisser, Hammerschmidt's assault rifle thundering beside him.

Paul reached the machine-gun emplacement first, Hammerschmidt snatching up the grenade as he dove in beside him. Hammerschmidt pulled the pin and hurled the grenade toward the fleeing machine-gun crew.

"I know." Paul Rubenstein laughed as he swung the gun on its mounts. "Waste not, want not!" He averted his eyes as the grenade blew, dirt raining down near them. And then he touched his finger to the trigger of the machine gun and opened fire. . . .

They had heard the noise roughly thirty minutes after overpowering the two-man team with the Soviet half-track truck and subsequently stealing it. Michael Rourke drove, Lieutenant St. James beside him in the cab, some of her Marines clinging to the truck cab on each side riding the running boards, the rest in the truck bed, the tarp pulled away for clear fields of fire when they reached the sounds of the battle.

The ground rose and fell sharply all around them as he drove, high ridges, shallow, dish-shaped valleys, steeply rising hills splotched here and there with snow. He kept to the low ground for the sake of the vehicle, pushing it, the half-track bouncing and jostling over the ground, vibrating maddeningly with each pothole or large rock. But the battle sounds were getting louder. His sister. Paul. Maria. They needed him. . . .

Annie Rourke credited the Soviet commander, Svetlana Grubaszikova, with tremendous courage or abysmal insanity. With Otto's small force behind her, she had ordered a charge up the hill. She was coming, running at the head of her troops, the bullets from their assault rifles like a swarm of insects in the air as Annie crouched in her position, waiting her chance, the M-16 tight in her fists.

She looked back once—Maria Leuden was shouting to her but Annie couldn't hear her. She waved back to Maria, then tucked down again, waiting.

There was a crack between the rocks behind which she crouched, and she could see Grubaszikova intermittently through it as the Russian woman led her troops. "Come on, lady—just a little more," Annie cooed to her. "Come on—you can do it. Another fifty yards. Come on!"

Annie lost sight of Grubaszikova. But then ...
"Twenty-five more yards, lady—come on!"

Grubaszikova was running at the head of a dozen females in Elite Corps battle-dress utilities, the army troopers behind them. She looked to be turning around, saying something to one of them as she ran. And now six of them broke off at a tangent to the right, Grubaszikova leading the other six left.

"Close enough," Annie whispered.

She moved the safety tumbler to semi and pushed up to her knees, just as she had rehearsed it, resting the rifle, its front handguard wrapped in a section of blanket to make for a more effective contact against the hard surface of the rocks. She cheeked the rifle, seeing Grubaszikova over her sights, then seeing her across them.

"Good-bye," Annie Rourke whispered, exhaling, holding the rest of her breath, starting the trigger squeeze, Grubaszikova coming right for her at an angle. The M-16 rocked, the tinny sound of its springs audible to her right ear, Grubaszikova's run swerving, her legs starting to buckle, her right arm snapping out and her rifle sailing from her hands, staggering now, twisting once, and falling backward.

Annie Rubenstein tucked down, gunfire hammering into the rocks around her.

Grubaszikova was dead, and now was the time if ever there would be a time. "Maria! Let's go!" She looked back, Maria waving back at her, up, running, a half-dozen Chinese soldiers formed around her. And as they neared the rocks, Annie was up, running beside them, her M-16 set to full auto as they started down the hillside, Rolvaag and his dog bringing up the rear, her two huge warriors bounding gracefully over the rocks.

Paul Rubenstein had taken the machine gun from its mounts. He'd seen guys do it plenty of times in movies five centuries ago and it didn't look that tough then.

"This is a heavy sucker!" he shouted to Hammer-schmidt, beside the German commando captain, closing now with the forces still at the base of the hill, the enemy mortar emplacements useless against this attack from their rear, but the enemy numbers still too high.

They threw themselves down behind one of the Russian trucks, Paul rolling from behind it and balancing the machine gun enough that he could fire from beneath the undercarriage.

The pattern of the gunfire changed and he shouted to Hammerschmidt over the din. "To the left there—what's—"

"A single Russian truck—but there are people firing from the truck bed. I don't recognize their uniforms, but they are firing at the Russian forces, it looks like."

Paul Rubenstein had to see.

He rolled back from beneath the undercarriage, his bare flesh brushing lightly against the barrel of the machine gun, scorching from its heat. To his knees now. He hauled the Russian binoculars to his eyes.

He recognized the uniforms. But he didn't believe his yes. "They're—either I'm crazy and blind too or—shit—they're U.S. Marines!" He grabbed up the machine gun, Hammerschmidt beside him, and started running up the hill. . . .

Michael Rourke geared down, taking the truck past the left flank of the Russian force along the steeply inclined hillside, gunfire from the truck bed behind him almost deafening him, Lieutenant Lillie St. James beside him firing through the open window into the Russians. And they were all women, he realized. "The gas," he snarled, stomping the accelerator pedal even harder. . . .

Annie Rubenstein closed with one of the Elite Corps women, both their rifles out, the woman inverting her

462

rifle like a club and charging for her. Annie stepped back and let the M-16 fall to her side on its sling, drawing the Scoremaster from her right hip. She had holstered it cocked and locked, and she thumbed down the safety and fired as the weapon came on line, the .45 bucking in her fist as the Russian woman's body impacted her, both of them falling, rolling, Annie on top, stabbing the .45 upward as the woman's hands went for her throat. Annie fired, the muzzle inches away from the Russian woman's attractive face. And Annie averted her eyes and felt the wet stickiness as the bullet did its work.

She fell back, her hand shaking, covered with blood and gore. And as she looked up, she saw the truck coming. To her knees, both fists on the butt of the Scoremaster, the muzzle aimed for the truck cab.

As she started to fire, she caught a momentary flash of the driver's face. "Michael?" It couldn't be Michael. She licked her lips. The men from the truck bed were vaulting off now, closing with the Soviet forces hand to hand, the truck stopping. If it were Michael—

Overhead—she heard the sounds of gunships and her heart sank. Coming from the coast. Karamatsov was finally committing gunships.

She got to her feet and looked back toward the truck.

Michael was clambering across its hood and diving into a half dozen of the female troopers. Annie ran toward him, shouting, "Michael! Michael!" As she ran, she saw the uniforms of the men from the truck—and two of them weren't even men. The uniforms were camouflage fatigues and emblazoned in olive drab on their chests were—"Marines," she gasped.

Michael was to his feet, a rifle butt smashing upward in his hands and impacting the jaw of one of the Russian women. And he was swinging the rifle now like some sort of club, beating the Russians down. There was a Marine beside him—and as the Marine dodged, the helmet fell off and blonde hair cascaded out of it. A woman.

Annie was beside them in the next instant, a pistol in

463

each hand, firing point blank into the Russians.

The gunships—she heard them again. She looked up—they were coming in low now, and she knew what they would do. "Michael! Soviet gunships!"

Michael butt-stroked one of the Russians and in a single stride was beside her. "You all right?" He pushed her back toward the truck.

"Yeah—what the—who are these people."

"The Marines have landed, Annie."

"The Soviet gunships are coming—look!"

Michael looked where she pointed and swore. "Shit!" He looked to right and left, then shouted, "Lieutenant St. James! Soviet gunships coming off the horizon!"

Annie was ramming a fresh magazine into her M-16.

"Where's Paul?"

"He went after you."

"No—damnit!"

"You swear too much," she advised good-naturedly, not telling him about her conversation with the female Soviet officer earlier.

"He can't have come after me! Where's Maria?"

"Out there—fighting."

Michael's hands were on her waist and he was picking her up and she was being stuffed into the truck cab. She shrugged and slid across the seat and rested the M-16 against the frame of the open driver's side window and took aim on the lead gunship. . . .

It was Maria Leuden, locked in hand-to-hand combat with a Soviet soldier, and Paul Rubenstein changed direction and ran for her. The machine gun was long since emptied and he had switched back to his Schmeisser, the submachine gun in his right fist, the battered Browning High Power in his left.

As the Russian woman was driving down with her fighting knife, Paul thrust the submachine gun toward her and fired, Maria Leuden screaming, falling to her

nees. He safed the Browning and stuffed it into his belt.
Otto! Over here!"

"Paul," she shouted up at him.

With his left hand, Paul Rubenstein hauled her up
om her knees and pulled her against him. "You all
ght?"

"Yes—where's Michael?"

"A long story—not a good one. Where's Annie?"

"She was heading toward that truck."

"We are too—come on—"

"My rifle—"

"Leave it," he ordered, half-dragging her now as he
n.

She was screaming at him as Hammerschmidt closed
ith them. "Where's Michael? Answer me!"

He started to tell her and he stopped, almost losing his
alance. He felt his face seaming with a smile. "Right
ere! I don't know how. But—come on!" And he ran
w, Maria and Otto running beside him, toward the
uck.

"Paul! Thank God you're alive!"

As Paul Rubenstein looked past Michael Rouke, he
most said, "Not for long." Soviet gunships. He heard a
oman's voice, in English, shouting orders and it wasn't
s wife. He looked to the sound. A blonde-haired girl,
etty—she was forming up the Marines.

Paul reached the truck. "Where's Annie?"

"In the cab—there—"

And Paul released Maria Leuden's hand, a blur of her
shing into Michael's arms as Paul clambered up into
e truck cab, Annie wheeling toward him, crouched on
e seat on her knees, then turning around, coming into
s arms. "Paul!" she screeched, hugging him tight
ound the neck.

"Gunships coming in—look out," he told her, pushing
er down, machine-gun fire ripping across the hood of
e truck, the windshield shattering under the impacts,
s body covering hers as the glass or whatever the

465

Soviets used these days sprayed over them. He let go of her and stabbed the Schmeisser through the shot-out window, firing the submachine gun toward the nearest of the gunships.

"Down here!"

It was Michael's voice, and Paul grabbed Annie by the hand and dragged her across the seat and out of the cab, then pulled her under the truck with him, Michael, Maria Leuden, Otto, and the woman Marine and some of her troopers already there.

"They got us good—shit," Paul snarled.

"Wait a minute," Annie said. "Hold on a second."

He looked at his wife. "What?"

"I hear something."

"You hear the enemy, lady," the woman Marine officer said.

"No—wait—"

"I hear it too," Hammerschmidt shouted.

"They wouldn't start the bombardment for another five minutes at least," the blonde-haired Marine lieutenant said.

"What bombardment?" Annie snapped.

"They're timing a Naval bombardment of Marshal Karamatsov's base camp with Doctor Rourke's and Major Tiemerovna's attempt to capture the marshal—"

"Doctor Rourke? My father!" Annie hugged Paul tight.

Michael said it. "Dad and Natalia too—they're alive, well, and they're going after Karamatsov on an island in the Formosa Strait called Quemoy."

The Nixon-Kennedy debates, Paul Rubenstein thought. "But they're alive. They're really alive? Where the hell did these Marines come from?" And he looked at the woman officer.

"Mid-Wake, sir. And there are lots more of us where we came from."

"Don't ask," Michael told them.

"Wait—those sounds—" It was Hammerschmidt.

466

"Those are German!" And Hammerschmidt was crawling out from under the truck, Paul letting go of Annie and going out after him.

In the northwestern sky, like a swarm of insects, black.

Paul Rubenstein started laughing. Annie was beside him now and he heard her shouting. "Han got through. He got through and got us help! Ha-ha!"

Paul Rubenstein realized that the reason he was laughing was because he had just been rescued all in one day by the United States Marines and the German Air Cavalry. And he hugged his wife tight against him, the Soviet gunships veering back toward the sea.

Chapter Sixty-two

According to the black-faced Rolex on his left wrist
the Naval bombardment of Karamatsov's base camp
would begin in precisely two minutes. John Rourke
wound the nylon cord back around his wrists, looking a
Natalia. She smiled, but her almost surreal blue eyes
showed the fear that he already knew was there.

The Island Classer's launch rolled over a breaker on it
cushion of air and settled into the sand.

They had agreed not to speak out of character les
Karamatsov had them monitored from the high ground
where the helicopters were landed by some type of para
bolic microphone, or even something as simple as a lip
reader.

Darkwood elbowed Rourke as he stood, saying in
Russian, "Do not make any heroic attempts, Docto
Rourke."

Rourke almost smiled. Darkwood was enjoying hi
playacting.

Rourke stood and Natalia stood beside him, Darkwood
and Stanhope climbing down out of the launch, some o
their disguised Marines assisting them and keeping th
launch steady, then Serovski, who also looked as thoug
he was playing it to the hilt, climbing down as well.

As John Rourke stepped from the launch, Natali
beside him, her hands, like his, "bound" in front of he

he looked up into the black rocks. And if blood could turn cold, he felt his do it.

Vladmir Karamatsov was walking down out of the rocks, surrounded by a dozen men in the black uniforms of the KGB Elite Corps, assault rifles slung at patrol positions beneath their right arms.

Karamatsov's hair had grayed slightly but was still full. His posture was erect, his jaw firm, his eyes dark pinpoints of light as he drew closer. He wore black BDU pants and black jackboots and a gray long-sleeved shirt, a sleeveless padded vest over it, the vest black, part of the harness of his shoulder holster showing from beneath vest's armholes.

Darkwood and Stanhope flanked John Rourke and Natalia Tiemerovna, Serovski just ahead of them, the rest of the Marines—three of them—behind them.

Rourke didn't like it that Karamatsov had brought so many men down with him. It might make Serovski confident enough to try something stupid.

The sun was very bright and John Rourke squinted against it.

Karamatsov, still a hundred yards away, stopped and shouted across the sand over the roar of the surf. "He was not dead, Serovski?"

Rourke looked at Serovski's back, Darkwood and Stanhope moving up a little to flank the Elite Corps officer. "Comrade marshal. A submarine of the American attack class was intercepted and Doctor Rourke was aboard it, restored to his full health. It required considerable negotiation, but I was able to convince our Comrades that Doctor Rourke should be brought to you as well."

"Good work, Serovski. My wife and her lover." And Karamatsov took a few paces further forward. "So, Doctor Rourke—after all this time. We at last meet on my own terms."

"Fuck you," John Rourke said in English, because it was in character for him to say it as the sacrificial victim

469

and just because it felt good to say.

"I had not realized your tastes had so changed, doctor." Karamatsov laughed, enjoying his own humor, it seemed.

Serovski walked forward, John Rourke and Natalia behind him slightly and Darkwood and Stanhope flanking him, the three U.S. Marines in Soviet drag still behind them.

"Where is the rest of the detail, Servoski?"

Serovski had a rehearsed answer again and Rourke waited until the Elite Corps officer started to give it. "Comrade marshal—there were only so many who could fit into the launch."

Karamatsov stopped, his vest wide open, thumbs hooked into his belt. John Rourke could see Natalia's pistols stuffed in the waistband of the BDU pants beneath the belt. "Surely, one or two of our men could have accompanied you."

John Rourke licked his lips.

Vladmir Karamatsov took a half step back and moved his hands from his pockets.

Serovski shouted, "My Hero Marshal—it is a trap!"

John Rourke released the cord that he held about his wrists and with his left hand drew the Crain Life Support System X knife and rammed it forward, his right hand going for one of the twin stainless Detonics .45s beneath the borrowed winter coat, the point of the knife gouging into Servoski's back as the Russian started to move severing the spinal column, the body flopping to the sand at John Rourke's feet, his hand letting go of the knife as his right fist stabbed forward with the little Detonics and he fired.

But Vladmir Karamatsov was already moving, dodging left, Rourke's bullet striking one of the KGB Elite Corpsmen who had been surrounding him, Natalia's pistols in Karamatsov's fists now, spitting fire, John Rourke stepping forward, Natalia about to fire and also

470

to be hit, he knew, the left side of Rourke's body shouldering Natalia away. Darkwood fired and so did Stanhope, two more of the Elite Corpsmen down. John Rourke felt a tongue of fire kiss across his left bicep and he dropped to his knees and fired again, a double tap, chunks of rock near where Karamatsov's head had been exploding.

And Karamatsov was running up into the rocks.

John Rourke had the second little Detonics out now and fired, Karamatsov's left leg buckling under him, Karamatsov falling, lurching forward and out of sight into the rocks. Sand spurted up into Rourke's face. Natalia was firing now. Rourke's right sleeve wiped across his eyes and he blinked. He was up, running, Darkwood and Stanhope at his right, Natalia at his left. He looked back once—the three Marines had fanned out to right and left into the rocks by the lapping surf, their Soviet assault rifles firing, Elite Corpsmen going down. Rourke emptied both pistols into his adversaries.

He reached the rocks, pistol-whipping one of the Russians aside as he started up the path in a dead run, the abdominal surgery hurting him now, running.

"John!" It was Natalia's voice, behind him. He shoved one of the little Detonics pistols into his belt and buttoned out the magazine from the other one, pocketing the empty, grabbing a fresh one from the Sparks Six-Pak on his belt beneath the coat, ramming it up the well, his right thumb working down the stop, the slide slamming forward. There was no time to reload the second one. There was gunfire still behind him.

Ahead of him—He raised the little Detonics in both fists and fired, Karamatsov lurching forward, stumbling, then running on. Rourke fired again and missed. He kept running, Natalia almost passing him, real pain in his abdomen now from the surgery, his breath coming hard. He kept running, shouldering past Natalia, shouting, "I want you—Karamatsov!"

471

"I want him more, John!"

Natalia was even with him again, and in her right fist she held the American pistol, in her left the blood-dripping knife he had used to kill Serovski.

The helicopters—their rotors were turning, Karamatsov running toward the nearest of them, Rourke stabbing the little Detonics toward him, firing it out. Karamatsov's body lurched once again and he stumbled to his knees, was up, ran on. John Rourke's body screamed at him to stop. He kept running, Karamatsov just twenty yards ahead, limping badly.

Karamatsov wheeled, Natalia's pistols in his fists, firing them out, Natalia screaming, Rourke lurching forward as one of the .357 Magnum rounds ripped his left leg from under him. He looked at Natalia, her right arm limp at her side, her body thrown back against the rocks, her left fist still clutching the knife. "Get him!"

Rourke drew himself to his feet, throwing himself into the run, his left leg dragging. Karamatsov kept using the pistols, but they were empty now and he flung the one in his right hand, then the one in his left, Rourke dodging the guns as they sailed toward him, Karamatsov running toward the nearest chopper.

The distance was less than ten yards, Rourke's abdomen on fire with pain, his left leg numbing. Karamatsov stumbled, fell, spilled into the dirt and snow, pushed himself up. John Rourke hurtled himself toward Karamatsov, his hands grasping for the shoulders, Karamatsov lurching forward, Rourke tearing the vest from Karamatsov's back, Karamatsov crawling across the ground, Rourke throwing his body against the man. Rourke had him, his hands closing over Karamatsov's neck. Karamatsov's left fist hammered up and Rourke sagged away. To his knees now, Karamatsov to his feet.

Gunfire ripped into the ground beside him from the open helicopter door. Rourke pushed himself up and ran. More gunfire, but from along the path in the black rocks.

Rourke seeing the body of the Elite Corpsman in the open fuselage door stitched across the chest in red.

Karamatsov threw himself into the fuselage doorway, reaching for the fallen Elite Corpsman's assault rifle. John Rourke's hands closed on Karamatsov's waist and he threw his weight back, tearing Karamatsov away from the helicopter, the gunship going airborne, the Reagan's deck guns opening up in the distance, shells landing around them everywhere as they rolled across the ground, Karamatsov's fist hammering at Rourke's face and neck and head.

Dirt and rocks rained around them, John Rourke's left elbow snapping back into Karamatsov's jaw, the Russian's mouth suddenly washed with red, Rourke's right fist impacting Karamatsov's left temple.

Karamatsov fell back.

Rourke was to his knees. Karamatsov threw his body toward Rourke and Rourke fell back. Karamatsov's right fist crossed Rourke's jaw.

Karamatsov was up, running, Rourke lurched forward, to his knees, to his feet.

More shells were falling from the Reagan's deck guns, helicopters exploding in the air and on the ground, their fiery skeletons falling from the sky. As Rourke ran, he dodged chunks of burning debris.

"Karamatsov!" The Hero Marshal was running for the last of his helicopters, the machine already hovering three feet from the ground, two Elite Corpsmen in the open fuselage doorway, firing, Rourke throwing himself to the ground behind the still-burning tail section of one of the downed Soviet choppers. From over the rise behind the last chopper, he could see Aldridge and his Marines, their assault rifles blazing. Aldridge fired a grenade from the tube beneath the barrel of his rifle. The last Soviet helicopter seemed to hesitate in midair, and then there was a burst of flame and a fireball of black and yellow and orange belched skyward.

473

"Karamatsov!" Rourke had a fresh magazine up the butt of one of his pistols as he pushed to his feet, running forward. "Karamatsov!"

And Rourke stopped. He saw him. Karamatsov had reached the edge of the promontory on which the choppers had landed. He stood there. Rourke ran toward him.

Karamatsov's right hand moved to his shoulder holster and John Rourke dodged left and fired. Karamatsov fired, Rourke fired, Karamatsov fired. Rourke fired again, throwing himself to the ground, rolling, Karamatsov's pistol discharging still, the slugs furrowing the ground, Rourke firing blindly, emptying the little Detonics toward him.

Karamatsov's gun was empty and Rourke pushed to his feet as the Hero Marshal started to ram a fresh magazine up the butt of his Model 59. Rourke had no time to reload. He launched his body toward Karamatsov and impacted, Karamatsov's pistol flying from his hand over the edge of the precipice and gone, Rourke's hands going for Karamatsov's throat as they fell, Rourke's body taking the impact, Karamatsov's right fist slamming into Rourke's left cheek, Rourke's right knee smashing upward into Karamatsov's groin.

Karamatsov fell back.

Rourke was up as Karamatsov stood. They charged at each other, John Rourke's left snapping out, catching Karamatsov across the chin, the Russian's head snapping back, Rourke's right impacting Karamatsov's left ear, Rourke's left hammering Karamatsov's nose to pulp.

Karamatsov's body wheeled left, his right foot snapping up and out, John Rourke's body feeling as if it were exploding as the Hero Marshal's jackbooted foot struck into his abdomen. Rourke staggered. Karamatsov closed, fists flying, Rourke's hands and arms going up to protect his face.

Rourke was falling back, the pain in his abdomen washing over him, consciousness starting to go.

Rourke wheeled half right and lashed back with his left elbow, striking bone, Rourke's right fist hammering forward, Karamatsov's head snapping back hard, his body rocking back.

John Rourke's hands gripped at his abdomen and he sagged forward to his knees, coughing blood.

Karamatsov was on his knees, his right hammering forward, John Rourke lurching against him, Rourke's own right impacting the center of the Hero Marshal's face.

Karamatsov's body weaved, fell. John Rourke tried to stand.

Vladmir Karamatsov was crawling away from him. Rourke got to his feet, lurched after him.

Karamatsov crawled to his feet, staggered back, by the edge of the precipice over the sea.

Karamatsov's right hand shot forward and in his fist was the little snub-nosed Smith & Wesson revolver he had carried five centuries ago. "You are dead, John Rourke!"

John Rourke stood there, hands clutched to his abdomen, about to throw himself against Karamatsov and hurtle them both over the edge and into the sea on the rocks below.

And then he heard Natalia's voice. "No, Vladmir!" And she rose up beside Karamatsov and Karamatsov turned to look at her and in both her tiny fists she held the short-sword-sized Life Support System X and the steel moved in her hands over her head and around in an arc to her right and then—

The Crain knife stopped moving.

Karamatsov's body swayed.

The little revolver fell from his limp right hand.

His head separated from his neck and sailed outward into the void.

Blood sprayed geyser-like into the air around Karamatsov like a corona of light.

The headless torso of her husband rocked backwards

475

and was gone over the edge.

Natalia screamed.

John Rourke closed his eyes.

This time, death was forever.